DAUGHTERS OF LATIN AMERICA

ALSO BY SANDRA GUZMÁN

The Latina's Bible
The New Latina's Bible

DAUGHTERS OF LATIN AMERICA

AN INTERNATIONAL ANTHOLOGY OF WRITING BY LATINE WOMEN

EDITED BY
SANDRA GUZMÁN

AMISTAD

An Imprint of HarperCollins*Publishers*

HarperCollins books may be purchased for educational, business, or sales promotional use. For information, please email the Special Markets Department at SPsales@harpercollins.com.

FIRST EDITION

Designed by Nancy Singer

Moon illustrations:
Pages 19, 57, 105, 145, 215, 377, and 415 © Dancake/Shutterstock
Pages 23, 179, 257, 289, 327, 451, and 495 © Kim404/Shutterstock

The credits on pages 535–542 constitute a continuation of this copyright page.

Library of Congress Cataloging-in-Publication Data has been applied for.

ISBN 978-0-06-305257-4

23 24 25 26 27 LBC 5 4 3 2 1

To the ancestors who raised me

I am a moist dew woman, says
I am the woman of the dawn, says
I am the woman of the day, says
I am the saint woman, says
I am the spirit woman, says
I am the woman who works, says
I am the woman beneath the dripping tree, says
I am the woman of the twilight, says
I am the woman of the pristine huipil, says
I am the whirlpool woman,
I am the woman who looks into the insides of things,
Because I can speak with Benito Juárez
Because our beautiful Virgin accompanies me
Because we can go up to heaven
I am the woman who sees Benito Juárez
Because I am the lawyer woman
Because I am the pure woman
I am the woman of goodness
Because I can go in and out of the realm of death
Because I come searching beneath the water from the opposite shore
Because I am the woman who springs forth
I am the woman who can be torn up, says
I am the doctor woman, says
I am the herb woman, says.

—*María Sabina*

A WRITER'S PRAYER

Let me enter the writing without resistance
and toil in the muck of chaos.
Out of disorder let me bring order
and something new into existence.
Let me touch the bodies of others
and move their souls.

—*Gloria E. Anzaldúa*

Contents

COSMIC MOON ✸ 105

EXALTED MOON ✸ 145

ANCESTRAL MOON ✳ 179

AQUEOUS MOON ✳ 215

ETHEREAL MOON ✳ 257

LUMINOUS MOON ✳ 289

SHAMANIC MOON ✳ 327

MAGNETIC MOON ✳ 451

SUPREME MOON ✳ 495

INTRODUCTION: A LITERARY CEREMONY

Sandra Guzmán

Words are medicine. Medicine is the breath.
I cure with language, nothing more.
—*María Sabina*

Daughters of Latin America is a journey into a luminous universe of texts that navigate across time and space, genres, styles, languages, and traditions. The Daughters gathered in this groundbreaking international anthology span five centuries of the written word, containing the wisdom, memory, and DNA of oral traditions more ancient than time itself. It is an immense honor to share the words of these majestic women and masterful storytellers with you.

Some of the women gathered in this volume have risked it all to write—cloistered in the nunnery, married, lived, and died in the closet. They fought in revolutions alongside male guerillas, were jailed, harassed, murdered, forced into exile; one of them sold herself to buy paper and pencil to leave a blazing testimony of her life—an impoverished Black woman who lived in a favela—and another used a male nom de guerre to criticize the church and the patriarchy during the early part of the nineteenth century. These Daughters wrote and write to defy the very forces, structures, and institutions that sought and seek to erase and silence them. These Daughters write to create the self, to protest, to remember, to celebrate, and ultimately to heal and free themselves and, in the process, others. Latin America—a region in the world that has been in forever wars since the Spanish Royal Crown's invasion began in 1492—has fueled conversations about women's intellect, rights, suffrage, and freedom, about how to be a woman in a system that hasn't accepted them as whole human beings with the capacity to lead, study, and fulfill all their brilliant human potential. The writings in *Daughters of Latin America* rescue memory, create meaning, joy, illuminate, build, and protect communities—they create safe spaces. The writings of these Daughters remade *and* remake the world. The texts forced *and* force change.

Included in this trailblazing international compendium are one hundred forty Daughters of Latin America, past and contemporary, from fifty nations. We are Daughters connected to a cosmic umbilical cord that binds us to the sacred lands of our ancestors. The youngest living writer is twenty-seven years old, the oldest ninety-two. The oldest text was written in 1691. They live in hundreds of cities around the world and write in twenty-two languages—including eighteen native mother tongues of the Americas. There are several MacArthur Fellows, a gaggle of *New York Times* bestselling authors, Pulitzer Prize–winning playwrights and journalists, National Book Award winners, novelists, memoirists, poets, essayists, scholars, singer-songwriters, short story writers, a Grammy winner, a member of Congress, a Golden Lion winner, one Cervantes Prize winner, three poet laureates, and a Nobel Prize laureate. There are poems, letters, chants, prayers, speeches, songs, short stories, fragments of novels-in-progress, journal entries, plays, personal and lyrical essays, and opinions. Some of the women self-published chapbooks in their tiny villages, and others authored more than forty books with major publishing houses. One contributor, María Sabina, did not read or write. She was a literary genius who spoke Mazatec and "cured with language." She reminded us that "words are medicine and medicine is breath." Her poetic tradition was—as with many of the Indigenous and Black women included here—linked to spiritual ceremony and ritual. Perhaps because her literary tradition was not on paper but oral and perhaps because of the Eurocentric elite and male colonial gaze, Sabina's distinctive poetic voice has rarely received the recognition it deserves. The few recordings that exist of her shamanic chants, one of which opens the anthology, gives us the opportunity to glimpse her genius, and the power of her words to uplift and transport the soul.

This anthology has been inspired to disrupt erasure and myths, to gather us, the powerful literary Daughters of Latin America. It's an expansive collection that pushes beyond geographic boundaries and the colonized, narrow definition of what nations are understood to make up Latin America. When you consider that Latin America is the most diverse region in the world—Brazil has the largest number of Africans outside of Africa, as well as the largest number of Japanese outside of Japan, for example, and there are hundreds of First Nations within the nation states of Latin America—these daughters represent the world. The daughters are also Daughters of Africa, Daughters of Asia, as well as Daughters of the Jewish diaspora. These are the voices of the cosmos giving us the medicine for a weary world.

Daughters of Latin America builds a new literary canon. It is also a bridge that connects Daughters to one another and to the world—from Chicago to São Paulo, from Loíza to Asunción, from Portsmouth to Port-au-Prince, from the Bronx to Buenos Aires, from Chiapas to East Los Angeles, and beyond. If there was ever any doubt of the talent of the Daughter scribes of Latin America—many who led literary movements and were rarely, if ever, mentioned with their male peers for their word art innovation—this book serves as a rescue, a revindication of their genius. This gathering is only a sliver of the literary talent. There are more voices that I wanted to include—the work continues. I dream of a library like the one described by playwright Quiara Alegría Hudes in her text "Anyone Know a Down Barrio Architect," where "every inch of the library described us. Beneath its cathedral roof, no incorrect words attached to us, because we had a vocabulary made of our own lives."

✦ ✦ ✦

In the midst of editing *Daughters*, the extraordinary happened: my beloved mother passed away in my arms. The largeness of helping usher the woman que me dio luz into the ancestral plane is a gift that I am still unpacking.

In my Indigenous Caribbean clan's tradition, there is no death, the afterlife is continuous; our beloveds never really leave: they transmute into the essence of life, the elements, and often return to visit us in dreams. And so, a year after my mother's passing, as I worked deeply on the book, my mother came to have a chat. In the dream, we were on a sidewalk outside my childhood tenement in Jersey City, New Jersey, a few blocks west of the Hudson River where we could see the dazzling New York City skyline. We were not alone. There were hundreds of women dressed in a variety of outfits: military fatigues, cheerleader short shorts, gowns, housecoats, pantsuits, some wrapped in furs, cowboy hats, overalls, baseball caps; they sported Afros, braids, weaves, ponytails, blowouts, lingerie, and summer dresses. It was a universe of beauty and ferocity. Women of all sizes, ages, races, ethnicities, and cultures. My mother and I sat on a vibrant textile embroidered with emerald Puerto Rican hummingbirds and radiant red maga flower blooms. We sat in a circle and were joined by three of my tías, also ancestors. Suddenly, the women on the street began dancing and marching, moving, and swaying together and apart in a glorious display of magnificence—it felt like a starling murmuration at dusk. My mother turned to me and said of the mesmerizing spectacle, "This is what you call performance feminism. Don't confuse it with the matriarchy. Not much will change if feminists continue to perform feminism while ignoring the matriarchy." Mother continued: "The work of women's equality must go deeper: there's wisdom embedded in the matriarchy that will enrich and heal our families, communities, and the world. It's also the only path to women's liberation."

The book that you are holding is in the tradition of the matriarchy. Women who are invested in dismantling the very monster system—the patriarchy—that oppresses. None are victims—they understand the power of their individual agency. They do this through action and literary art. Here is work that shimmers and dazzles and goes beyond resisting, it pushes back and through.

The Daughters of Latin America have been deeply invested in language for centuries, though many never received due credit during their lifetimes. Women such as pioneering Latin American postmodernist Albalucia Ángel whose luminuos poem "The Eagle Woman" is included here. Silenced in her home country and by the machista publishing universe for writing about violence against women in her native Colombia, she lived in exile for three decades. Though an important figure in the Latin American literary boom, she has been rarely mentioned alongside the men in the movement that also includes Gabriel García Márquez, Julio Cortázar, Carlos Fuentes, and others. Young Colombian feminists are now lifting her work, and she is receiving long overdue attention.

Historic invisibility is a process that creates voids, precariousness, and another reality says Chilean poet and visual artist Cecilia Vicuña, whose illuminating poem "Clepsydra" is included here. Vicuña insists that "the history of the north excludes that of the south and the history of the south excludes itself, encompassing only reflections of the north. In that void between the two," she adds, "the precariousness and their lack of documentation established their non-place as another reality." Argentina's Rita Laura Segato, one of the most brilliant contemporary feminist voices in the world, took on the European gaze and the arrogant hold it has had on publishing this side of the Atlantic. In a fragment of the speech, included here, that she delivered in the Buenos Aires International Book Fair in 2019, Segato challenged García Márquez and his unfortunate Eurocentric obsession—delivered in his Nobel Prize acceptance speech—with being seen and accepted, legitimized, by Europe and Spain.

In the tradition of one of my literary heroes, Nobel laureate Toni Morrison, and all the matriarchs who raised me, all of the Daughters featured in this volume write free of the master gaze.

✦ ✦ ✦

Land is the ancestor present in all the work of the Daughters. She is at the core of the writings in this collection—the expanse of the breathtakingly beautiful mountains, forests, rivers, oceans, lakes, deserts, valleys, volcanoes, and rain forests. Fertile earth, and waters—the raw material and spiritual sustenance that inspire many of the writers included here. And perhaps because it is the region of the world with the most water sources, Latin America feels like a place where all the waters of the planet meet. It is also a place where we live in nepantla, the liminal space that Mexican poet Elsa Cross describes in the poem included here by the same name. It is a region with a tortured history: forty-eight nations, occupied territories, renamed, Christianized, divided among the European and American empires, illegally sold, traded, plundered, militarily invaded, and settled by freebooters looking for riches and adventures. Still.

Elizabeth Acevedo's poem "Sending Signals to Mars" channels fifteenth-century Taína Jeca Anacaona from her Harlem rooftop and celebrates a regional unity and pre-Columbian conviviality where we saved one another from harm:

> this is the way of islands   i learned   in harlem   in history
> the day another black person is executed
> under the wide open sky   with the universe watching   a spaceship launch
> the canoes, the taíno's said,
>   after columbus returned to spain,
>   they killed the contingency of spaniards he left behind   after they
>   burned down the settlement he'd demanded built, after:
>   the taíno's got in their boats
> island— island— island— island   phone tag from anacaona to moctezuma . . .
>   paddle shushing in the water
>   *the devil is now coming for you*
> I warn my cousins in the stars.

When you consider that during colonial years, for example, as the architecture of Chile was being constructed by European settlers, the colonial government paid European settlers to hunt Indigenous people: the equivalent of one hundred dollars for the testicles of an Indigenous man, fifty dollars for the breasts of an Indigenous woman, and five dollars for the ear of an Indigenous child, the texts of the nearly two dozen First Nation women featured here—Daniela Catrileo, Lila Downs, Victoria Margarita Colaj Curruchiche, Natalia Toledo, María Clara Sharupi Jua, Nadia López García, Rosa Chávez, Berichá, Vicenta María Siosi Pino, Irma Pineda, Brigitte Zacarías Watson, Caridad de la Luz, Mikeas Sánchez, Sonia Guiñansaca,

María Sabina, Alba Eiragi Duarte, Lindantonella Solano Mendoza, Yásnaya Elena Aguilar Gil, Berta Cáceres, and Elizabeth Acevedo—will ring deeper.

Most of the texts of the First Nation scribes featured in this anthology traversed a trinity of linguistic realms—translated from their mother tongues to Spanish then to English. It is no small matter that many of them write and speak in their ancient mother tongues. These women combat linguicide one sentence at a time and battle a horrific statistic—every fourteen days an Indigenous tongue dies around the world. Says Yásnaya Elena Aguilar Gil, a linguist and Mixe activist: "Our languages don't die, they are murdered." According to UNESCO, half of the world's 7,000 languages are expected to be extinct by the end of this century. What happens when a language is lost? The world is less without their songs. Languages are like flora and fauna—they define a people, a nation, a culture, a cosmology. Words in ancient mother tongues hold universes within and its ancient stories. When we lose languages we lose histories, connections to land, to the cosmos, and to each other. Including First Nation texts in their own language writing systems in the anthology therefore was a political act serving as a visible and tangible experience for readers beyond the languages that are the lingua franca of the planet. Thus, the work of literary translators was central in the weaving of this anthology. Here is the work of more than fifty translator artisans who traveled through cultures, under ancient languages, through words and ideas, epochs, philosophies, and cosmological visions to gift us the glory of understanding new worlds and ways of seeing the world. They were passionate, devoted, and champions of the authors and the texts they ushered into the English language. Considering that there are twenty-two languages included in this anthology—many of them aboriginal tongues—this is also a breathtaking volume of translated literary art.

But it's not just history. In 2023, Los Pueblos Originarios of the Americas continue to live the Latin American version of the Trail of Tears—displaced by dictators; colonial administrators; mining, oil, and industrial agriculture companies from G20 nations; climate catastrophes; and corporations. Corporations that build dams and divert rivers, extract oil and gas, leaving sacred earth scorched, poisoned, and infertile. In 2016, Berta Cáceres, a Lenca leader and a land and water protector from Honduras, whose Goldman Prize–winning speech is included here, was murdered by a group of mercenaries who entered her home at midnight and slaughtered her in front of her children. The mastermind of the killing, a US-trained soldier who had learned the fundamentals of war, tactics, and weaponry at West Point, was leading a multinational dam project on a river considered sacred to the Lenca people, and in 2021 he was convicted for plotting her killing and sentenced to twenty-two years in prison. Daughters who live in the US also experience discrimination, sexism, racism, transphobia, xenophobia—the othering in a land that is, too, home. It is the landscape of revolution, war, oppression, immigration, migration, persecution, violence, exile, displacement, as well as paradisiacal beauty and joy, that offers extraordinary material for the women to write.

Daughters of the Americas have been deeply invested in literature—dynamic oral and textual—for centuries, before the European printing press was invented around 1440. Mayan women scribes, for instance, wrote/write on books of paper made from the inner bark of the amatl, or amate, tree—paper more durable than papyrus. Franciscan missionaries burned thousands of these books—codices—in bonfires during the early years of La Conquista. Only three or four are said to remain, renamed by Europeans and in private European collections. Across the region, Native women scribes etched stories on boulders along riverbanks and inside caves. These books—paper and rock—teach astronomy, spirituality; celebrate motherhood, children, family, play, ritual, sacred geometry, the elements; and serve as planting and harvesting calendars. In the archipelago of Borikén, where I was born, there are more than three thousand ancient rock books.

While the paper books were burned, the stories survived and were shared, boca a boca, generation to generation, across time zones, borders, and eras. They are lullabies, poems, songs, adivinanzas, prayers—healing chants. One of the finest examples of this oral literary tradition is the great Mazatec poet and medicine woman María Sabina. She is known around the world as the high priestess of mushrooms, but very few know that Sabina is also considered one the most visionary Latin American poets of the twentieth century. It gives me immense pleasure to introduce her work and life to new readers as a genius poet in the oral literary tradition, in the tradition of Homer, the illiterate poet "author" of the much-respected works *The Iliad* and *The Odyssey*.

In the Americas, when colonization, genocide, and linguicide began, Christian churches were erected, Jesuit missionaries dispersed through the region, and the books were burned, Goddesses were discarded, and medicine women were lynched, slavery became a source of income for colonists, and nation building by settlers began, colonizers brought with them the patriarchy. In this new Eurocentric system, women were considered property, and it was illegal for women—even the settlers' daughters—to read or write or have intellectual lives. Some Daughters during colonial times cloistered themselves in nunneries, and five hundred years later, we are reminded of the strategies of the nuns who wrote under oppression.

I encourage twenty-first century readers to return to the Latin American nuns' texts with a beginner's eyes. The most famous of these colonial nun scribes is Mexico's sor Juana Inés de la Cruz, a trilingual—Nahuatl, Spanish, and Latin—feminist, poet, philosopher, scholar, and dramaturge. She entered a cloistered convent rather than marriage so that she could pursue a literary and intellectual life and was viciously harassed for her secular writing and intellectual pursuits by the highest members of the Catholic clergy. In "Respuesta a sor Filotea de la Cruz," penned in 1691, she offered a lyrical and fervent reply to a bishop who anonymously published a text questioning women's intellectual capacity. Her more than thirteen-thousand-word response, part poem, part autobiographical lyric essay—a fragment of which is included here—is considered the first feminist manifesto in the world. Sor Juana deftly pointed to the virtues of philosophy and the kitchen and famously noted that "if Aristotle had cooked, he would have written more." She penned what would be the equivalent of a mic drop today.

✦ ✦ ✦

Latin America is one of the most multiethnic, multilingual, multiracial, and multireligious regions of the world and so are her Daughters. Some of them

live on the lands of their foremothers and forefathers; others were forced
into exile or migration by despotic fascist regimes, imperialism, wars, land
displacement, political persecution, gentrification, economic and climate
catastrophes, to live in all corners of the globe. They carry with them mem-
ory and pain and seeds that sprout around the world. As Harlem poet Sonia
Guiñansaca wrote in "Runa in Translation," they "speak broken Spanish /
English with a heavy New York City accent," they "wonder if [their] tongue
will ever heal from the breaking," and they wonder "if their abuelita would
love them as queer." And their "hurt is felt in three languages."

There are nations within nations in Latin America where thousands
of ancestor mother tongues are spoken, and First Nation nations with
distinct cultures, literature, art, and cosmological visions exist. In twenty-
first century Mexico, for instance, every day of the year, a different mother
tongue can be spoken, not one a European colonial language. Mixe lin-
guist and essayist Aguilar Gil, in a conversation with Karla Sánchez, noted
that there are over 365 languages and dialects. Currently there is a renais-
sance of First Nation women in Latin America writing their stories—many
ancient oral stories—in their mother tongues, and it's thrilling that many
of the leading Native storytellers are included in this anthology.

Another intention was to center Afro-Latine Daughters, who, like
First Nation Daughters, have been and continue to be marginalized and
invisibilized throughout the region. Featured here are the grand dames
of Cuban poetry, the late Afro-Cubanas Georgina Herrera and Excilia
Saldaña, and Nancy Morejón, who celebrates contemporary Black Cuban
women in her poem "New Women":

Wildflowers on their chests,
burned by all the saltpeter in the world.
The crowing of the rooster in the mountain.
The whistling of smoke in the city.
And their hands, coming from very far,
from times long past,
kneading the recent substance

that makes us live
between the sea and the shores,
between fishes and nets,
between windows and the horizon.

Also blessing us is the marvelous Mary Grueso Romero, one of the great Afro-Colombian voices, with her poem "If God had been born here." Here refers to the Pacific Colombian coastline in the Black port town of Buenaventura:

If God had been born here,
here on this coast,

he'd be a farmer
who'd harvest coconuts from the palm

with his muscled body

like a Black man from El Piñal,
with jet Black skin
and ivory teeth,

with tight coily hair

like he was the fruit chacarrás.

Also featured is Puerto Rico's beloved Afro-Boricua poet Julia de Burgos, with a letter she penned from Cuba to her sister, sharing literary gossip and dreams for herself; Yolanda Arroyo Pizarro, who wrote Afro-Boricua lesbians into the future with an Afrofuturistic Queer-love odyssey; and Aracelis Girmay, who penned a dazzling elegy to Cuba's gifted visual artist the late Belkis Ayón. Blessing this book is also Guadeloupe's literary queen Maryse Condé, a giant of literature, who celebrated in a lyric essay the day she encountered the music of another Caribbean queen, Celia Cruz. And Audre Lorde, whose parents were born in Barbados and Granada, and who in a journal entry here makes it clear that home is the Caribbean even though she was born into exile in Harlem, New York. Featured in the book is the often overlooked mid-twentieth-century Black poet of Uruguay Virginia Brindis de Salas, with poems of Black pride; and the gorgeous story by Brazil's masterful griot Conceição Evaristo of body, tradition, and belonging through a dancer's feet. Afro-Japanese Mexican Jumko Ogata-Aguilar penned a moving personal essay about her name as a reminder of pride and the deep wounds of colonial violence that "eats away at our stories, heritage, the languages we speak and our ways of life." Haiti's grand woman of letters Edwidge Danticat offered a fierce poem about a people who live forever despite the despots who kill them again and again. Antigua's Jamaica Kincaid's stunning classic prose poem "Girl" centers a young Black Caribbean girl and her mother at war, and how love is a beautiful gift. Also featured are Afro-Boricuas Dahlma Llanos-Figueroa (whose novel, a fragment included here, explores Puerto Rico's Atlantic Slave Trade lived through a captive African woman), Ivelisse Rodriguez with an excerpt of a novel-in-progress about the 1898 US invasion, and Mayra Santos Febres with a gorgeous lyric essay on the power of forgiveness.

Brazil's masterful memoirist Carolina María de Jesús, daughter of enslaved Africans, sold her body in the streets of 1940s São Paulo to feed her children and buy paper so she could write. De Jesus left a blistering and intimate account of her life in Brazil's favelas. Featured in the anthology is a fragment of an autobiographical narrative published posthumously.

The neighbors whispered. She's single she must be a whore. It is a general belief in Brazil that Black women are all whores. But I've never let myself be affected by what people think of me. When these people came to me with their funny business, I said: I'm a poet. I ask for a bit more respect.

Another intention of the anthology was to lift Puerto Rican women's voices. Due to the archipelago's enduring colonial status—it is the oldest colony in the world, first invaded by Royal Spanish ships in 1493 and then in 1898 by the United States' colossal military—the scribes are often invisiblized in and/or erased from the literary landscapes of the US and Latin America. In addition to all the aforementioned Puerto Rican voices, we are also blessed with an unpublished exclusive poem by maracachimba Lolita Lebrón, who penned it in 1956, on her first day of entering a US prison for attacking the US Congress with three other freedom fighters who fought for Puerto Rico's independence. These women belong to both worlds and uniquely to the Caribbean archipelago. Showcasing the vibrant Boricua voices included in this book—past and present—reclaims the extraordinary literary art, in Spanish and English, that happens in exile and in oppressive colonial and imperial landscapes.

"Latine," the gender-inclusive form of "Latino" and "Latina," on the title, is used with excitement and joy. The *e* replaces the *a* or *o* in Latina and Latino that are feminine and masculine identifiers. It was created by feminist and nonbinary communities in the US and Latin America in the early aughts. The term describes all people, not just men or women. While there are no men in this anthology, there are trans women and nonbinary contributors. What we call ourselves matters, and language evolves in exciting ways. Any effort from the community to define ourselves on our own terms is welcome and worth championing. My embrace of it is thrilling especially because we will be the first to use "Latine" on a book's cover.

Daughters were asked to offer whatever vision, poem, essay, prayer, cuento, meditation they wanted me to consider, and the result are texts that explore a myriad of themes: language, imperialism, coloniality, gender, post- and neo-colonialism, mother-daughter relations, loss, war, land, memory, marriage, culture, police brutality, forgiveness, the womb, resistance, music, Blackness, Indigeneity, motherhood, abortion, tradition, magic, domestic violence, slavery, ecological destruction, beauty, power, death, poverty, women's rights, sex, erotica, Caribbean Afrofuturism, religion, immigration, food, ritual, death, rebirth, extinction, freedom, and love.

Loss and exile are connective material. Nicaragua's Gioconda Belli offered a triumphant poem about her exile in the middle of the global COVID health pandemic. Dominican American Julia Alvarez contributed an iridescent and achy poem about her sister cooking a last meal on the eve of her family's midnight escape from the brutal dictator Trujillo's henchmen.

Queer love is also celebrated in letters. Chile's revered Gabriela Mistral, the first and only Latin American woman writer to have won a Nobel Prize in Literature, lived her entire life in the closet. Contemporary readers are returning to her texts with new understanding of the esteemed poet's Queer life. This includes a trove of love letters to her beloved, Doris Dana, one of which is featured here.

Another contributor, Ada Limón—named US poet laureate in 2022— was inspired to pen a sweet "Ode to the Hair Clip" in the tradition of Pablo Neruda:

> without you I am
> chaos crested
>
> like lion your pleasure
> in pressure small
>
> star in black sky
> of mane small star
>
> you are asked
> to do so much

Mothers, aunts, abuelas, lovers, tías, and fathers are also explored eloquently by several writers. Angela Morales's powerful essay about the lessons of her frayed relationship with her dad was a path to finding herself.

Land is the heartbeat of the anthology—its healing beauty, enduring wisdom, and destruction. A hybrid essay from Argentina's Catalina Infante Beovic presents a town in Chile that is drying up because of avocado cultivation, a tropical fruit grown in the desert, an eerie harbinger of what's to come in the era of climate change.

✦ ✦ ✦

While searching for the title, an image, that would bring together the writings and the spirit of the women gathered here, I came across a line in a poem by Sandra María Esteves, one of the leading lights and founders of the Nuyorican school of poetry. In "Lady Gaga New Year," Esteves wrote:

> . . . I prefer props that are mine:
> seven-day candles, agua florida, well-rolled cigars,
>   cantos to Elegba, the machete under my bed . . .

El machete under our beds! I knew that I had hit on a physical and a metaphorical tool—a connective tissue—for the book. Our working title for *Daughters of Latin America* was "Machetes Under Our Beds," a spirit close to this book's center.

The women in my lineage—Indigenous Caribbean and descendants from the African continent—know how to handle a machete. They sharpen it with cane juice and tabaco spit. Some used machetes to cut sugarcane under the slaver's whip during Spanish colonial times in Puerto Rico. One of my grandmother ancestors macheted her way through the rain forest to find freedom in a Maroon settlement in the mountains of Peñuelas, where my father was born and raised and where my happy childhood memories live. They used and use machetes to harvest healing herbs, to split open coconuts to quench thirst and satiate hunger. In the hands of my late mother, a descendant of the great Igneri People—her machete cleared tropical bush and tree stumps on a hill to build a house for my four siblings and me. Machetes were and have been indispensable tools, used to defend, nourish, and heal entire communities not just in my clan but across the Americas. Machetes, like pens in the hands of these scribes, have helped create and carve out safe spaces where women could love, shelter, eat, and live more freely.

✦ ✦ ✦

Thirteen Holy Moons

This anthology is divided into thirteen sections, each representing one of the thirteen sacred moons of the year. Thirteen—or oxlajuj, the word for "thirteen" in Kaqchikel—is considered a sacred and holy number, and another word for "god" in the Maya tradition. It is a numeral with the highest vibration and found underlying in nature, in the human body, and in the cosmos. A human has thirteen main joints; men have twelve orifices, women have thirteen—the womb, the portal of birth, being the thirteenth. In one of the sacred Maya calendars, the week is made up of thirteen energy cycles affecting different parts of the body. According to Maya timekeeper Nana María Elena Curruchiche Roquel, each moon, like each thirteen-day cycle, is connected to a specific energy, intention. (Cosmic timekeeping is an ancient art for the Maya who are the world's most sophisticated timekeepers—at least one of the Maya calendars in use today includes five cycles that equal 26,000 years.) Being in tune with these different celestial energies each day, she says, is to live in harmony with the earth and the universe. She notes that even if we are not aware, la luna, Earth's beloved satellite, is communing, touching, healing earthlings with her light—particularly women, inviting us to connect to her divine cosmic flow.

The texts of the Daughters are interconnected and fused, because we know that in our ancestral tradition of the Americas, time is not linear, it is cyclical and liminal. You will find an eighteenth-century poet in the same chapter with a twenty-first-century short story writer, or a nineteenth-century novelist next to a twenty-first-century journalist. The result is a seamless merging across time zones and centuries, time and space. Lastly, in the sacred Maya calendar, there is a day that is considered outside of time—the equivalent of a leap year in the Gregorian calendar. It is in this timeless space—a day out of time—where the fragment of the extraordinary feminist manifesto "La respuesta," penned by the great sor Juana Inés de la Cruz, is situated. Even though it was written in 1691 it is still relevant in 2023.

The anthology is meant to be read from front to back, back to front, or opened at any page. It's also meant to be read while listening to songstresses of the Americas—from salsa Queen Celia Cruz to Totó La Momposina, from Ile and Elza Soares to La Lupe, from Mercedes Sosa to La Doña, from Beatriz Pichi Malen to Susana Baca, from Selena to celestial bomba y plena group Paracumbé, from Ibeyi and Omara Portuondo to Karol G to Lucesita Benitez, and to Consuelo Velásquez who wrote the global phenomenon "Bésame Mucho" when she was fifteen years old. Listen to María Sabina's transcendent poem chants recorded in 1956 during one of her healing mushroom veladas, and before and after you read Conde's lovely ode to la rumbera de Cuba, Celia Cruz, listen to her musical heroine; turn on Grammy-winning Mixtec singer-songwriter Lila Downs, who blesses this anthology with an enchanting remembering of a mother ancestor. These were among the many singer-songwriting Daughters of Latin America that I listened and danced to while curating the compilation. I also recommend seeing the visual art created by some of the Hijas such as the impressive quipus, or talking knots, by Vicuña. Experience the majestic art of the late Afro-Cubana Belkis Ayón before and after Girmay's text, and delight in the art of another ancestor, Taína Cuban Ana Mendieta before and after Achy Obejas' poem.

This anthology was inspired by several ancestor anthologies that served as my north. Among them the sister anthology, *New Daughters of Africa: An International Anthology of Writing by Women of African Descent* edited by Margaret Busby; *This Bridge Called My Back: Writings by Radical Women of Color*, edited By Gloria Anzaldúa and Cherríe Moraga; and *When the Light of the World was Subdued, Our Songs Came Shining Through* edited by Joy Harjo.

✦ ✦ ✦

This book was woven during a spectacular time on the planet. The COVID-19 global health pandemic killed, as of April 2022, almost seven million people around the world, according to the World Health Organization. Fires raged from Athens to California, monster hurricanes flooded and disappeared islands, volcanoes swallowed cities, colossal oil spills damaged lands and water, and droughts turned storied rivers into dust bowls. Even the ocean was on fire. The world was being transformed as it has been since these Daughters began writing. The words of these Daughters kept me company, reminding me again and again of the necessity and urgency of the power of women to write, write, write, and to leave a trace that we were once here. I was submerged in the beauty, enchantment, and potency of their words and worlds. I was transformed. Today I am richer and taller thanks to them.

Latine Daughters are living a literary renaissance. It is our moment. I am honored to have been entrusted with their words. They possess power and hope. Like the poem "Body of Thought" by Japanese Peruvian Tilsa Otta, the words in this book also hold the promise to nourish:

> I tell you that poetry is the placenta
> that connects us to the world,
> that we must enter,
> because the world
> needs more nutrients and we
> need a little more of the world.

These are not just words on a page: it's our spirit on paper. Every sentence in this breathtaking book is a ritual and this anthology is the gift—an ancient and everlasting literary ceremony.

—*Sandra Guzmán, Luquillo, Borikén, April 29, 2022*

A DAY OUT OF TIME

Sor Juana Inés de la Cruz

Sor Juana Inés de la Cruz *(ca. 1648–1695) was a trilingual (Nahuatl, Spanish, and Latin) feminist, poet, philosopher, scholar, and dramaturge during the Spanish golden age of literature and Conquista. She was born Juana Ramírez de Asbaje in San Miguel de Nepantla, currently Mexico. She remains one of the world's major literary voices. She learned to read at three and by eight wrote her first loa. She entered a cloistered convent rather than marriage so that she could pursue a literary and intellectual life, and was harassed for her secular writing and intellectual pursuits by the highest members of the Catholic clergy. Among the famous Queer nun's notable works are the poems "Primero sueño" (Dream first) and "Hombres necios" (Foolish men), and* El divino narciso *(The Divine Narcissus), a play about the Spanish invasion of the Aztec Nation. "La respuesta a Sor Filotea de la Cruz," a lyrical and fervent reply to the bishop of Puebla, who published a letter criticizing her under a female pen name, was the first feminist manifesto in the world, written in 1691 and published posthumously in 1701. In it, sor Juana condemned the Church for helping to keep women uneducated, and defended the intellectual rights of women and their right to a place in letters. This fragment of "La respuesta" (The reply) was translated from the Spanish by Sandra Guzmán.*

La respuesta a Sor Filotea de la Cruz

. . . I do not study so that I can write, and even less to teach, which in me would be excessive arrogance, but rather to see if by studying, I become less ignorant . . .

. . . Well, Señora, what can I share, of the secrets that I have discovered while cooking. I have observed that if I fry an egg in lard or oil, it holds, but in syrup, it shreds; if you want the sugar to liquefy you only have to add a very tiny amount of water that has been soaked in a quince or any other sour fruit; you also will notice that the yolk and the egg white of one egg are so opposite of each other that adding a sweetener would produce great results only individually, but not together. I don't want to bore you with such minutiae, which I only refer to it because this is my nature, and perhaps all this may make you chuckle. But, Señora, what can women glean about philosophy in the kitchen? Lupercio Leonardo said it best: that you can learn a lot about philosophy while preparing dinner. Observing all this, I have concluded that: if Aristotle had cooked, he would have written a lot more. Following the flow of my continuous examinations, for this is my natural state, I don't really need books. Once, I had a horrible upset stomach and doctors banned me from studying, so I spent a few days like this, analyzing everything. And then I proposed that it would be less harmful giving me access to books because my observations were so vehement and vigorous, my spirit consumed more energy in a half hour on these kinds of analyses than in four days studying books. And thus, they were persuaded to allow me to read. And more, my Señora, not even during sleep am I free from this limitless imagination; in fact, I must add here that, in my dream state, I work more free and less encumbered and reap the teachings of the day with greater clarity, arguing, and writing verses, which if I gave to you, would make for a very large catalogue, as well as arguments and conclusions that I have better achieved while sleeping than while awake. I won't tire you any longer with this subject, but as I have already stated above, this is sufficient to allow your discretion and sharpness to marinate completely so that you could understand my nature, and the beginnings, methods, and current state of my studies.

And if these, Señora, were considered merits (as I see them celebrated in men), they would not be lauded in me, because I cannot but study. If I am at fault, for the same reasons, I believe I am not. Moreover, I have such little confidence in myself that neither in my study or in anything else do I trust my judgment; and therefore, I surrender myself to your expansive genius, allowing whatever sentence may come, without controversy or reluctance, for this has only been a simple narration of my inclination toward letters.

GRACEFUL MOON

The energy of this moon embraces
forgiveness—to ask for and receive it.

Cecilia Vicuña

Cecilia Vicuña *(b. 1948) is a poet, visual artist, filmmaker, and activist born in Santiago, Chile, who has been in exile since the early 1970s after the military coup and assassination of elected socialist president Salvador Allende. Her art addresses themes of language, memory, ecological destruction, human rights, cultural homogenization, and exile. She creates "precarious works and quipus as a way of hearing an ancient silence waiting to be heard." She is the author of twenty-seven books of poetry. Among the most notable are* Saborami, *a book chronicling the military coup in Chile and the death of Salvador Allende, as well as her two other collections* Precario/Precarious *and* cloud-net. *She wrote an experimental book,* Diario estúpido (Stupid diary), *which is seven thousand words a day of her emotions and experiences. The many awards she has received include Anonymous Was a Woman, the Premio Velázquez de Artes Plásticas, and the Venice Biennale Golden Lion for Lifetime Achievement in 2022. "Clepsydra" was written in 1966 and published in* El zen surado, *her first poetry book censored in Chile where she appears naked on the cover. Rosa Alcalá's translation from the Spanish appears in* New and Selected Poems of Cecilia Vicuña.

Clepsydra

Long ago I embroidered on my head
signs of abandonment and failure
no one had the fortune of knowing
to which galaxies I allude
with my smile.
I opted for wild footpaths,

the object of poetry
was always to create
spiritual and collective rings
where conjectures
Juno and Aristotle
dance among new shrubs.
I relied from the beginning
on my stupidity
and general lack of talent.
Always I shipwrecked among
nouns and verbs.
I am still, I feel,
a shitty preacher:
I enlighten no one
but me.

Aracelis Girmay

Aracelis Girmay *(b. 1977) was born in California to an Eritrean (Tigrinyan) father and a Chicagoan mother whose people are from Puerto Rico, Mexico, and African American from the US state of Georgia. Girmay is the author of the poetry collections* Teeth, Kingdom Animalia, *and the* black maria. *She is also the author-collagist of the picture book* changing, changing, *and with her sister she collaborated on the picture book* What Do You Know? *Girmay is on the editorial board of the African Poetry Book Fund and recently edited* How to Carry Water: Selected Poems of Lucille Clifton. *She also is the editor-at-large for BOA Editions' Blessing the Boats Selections.*

"El secreto era una voz" —Belkis Ayón

Cleanness of the air, of the sun when I step down the airplane's tongue of stairs into light, lime-bright, waking my heart. My skin already conjugating sunlight. What I was made for.

Far, far, far is New York City, the cold. The sleet and snow. My beloveds. My belly is big with baby and our blood pumps slowly through us in the heat. Because of my bigness the airport workers kindly call me up to the front of the line, help with my bag, wish me blessings that fall like powdered sugar over my shoulders already browning in the light.

At customs I can smell the lotions and oils of the woman, Black like me, like nearly everyone wearing the yellow airport uniform shirts, finally, asking, because of the recent Ebola outbreak in Guinea, Liberia, and Sierra Leone:

Have you been to Africa recently?

And me saying "no."

Have you been to Africa recently? No. *Bienvenidos.*

The syntax we make together flickers me into Africa. The Europe in me is for a millisecond confused. The ancestors ride my sentences.

Have you been to Africa recently?

No.

Welcome.

Y yo: *Gracias, gracias.*

Africa as I find my bags, as another woman in the yellow, collared uniform shirt insists she roll them for me because I am so pregnant. Africa the one man leaning long, the hiss of a woman's teeth, the beautiful posture. A bare foot fitted into a heel, Africa. As I visit the tombs and ride the buses, Africa as I hear the news of Black people stopped for their papers to prove they can work in Havana, Africa as the white Habaneros call these Black people Palestinos, for Palestinians, not free to go freely left or right. Africa the prisons, Africa the sunlight, the beaches, the fish, the dream, the assertion.

It was on that trip that I found myself on an hours-long tour with an extraordinary artist and teacher, a friend of the professors who had first invited me to consider joining the program to teach in Havana for a semester. The artist took me and our colleagues to visit El Museo Nacional de Bellas Artes, and as he showed us a piece in one of the salons, I turned to look at what else was in the room.

Guava was the color I noticed first. Alive, such a pink I knew only to mean "outside." And then the figures, their skins covered in shapes and lines that might mean to someone else something like scales but to me at first felt only like eyes, and all of the eyes on my own arms opened to see them. I felt the need to rub the skin on my arms closed, so odd was the sensation, and I remembered the touch-me-nots outside of my partner's parents' house in Trinidad. Carenage.

The figures sat or stood at a table with fish on their plates, their almond-shaped eyes looking this direction or that. I studied what I perceived to be their mouthlessness. At the center of the table was a figure somewhat green, the fingers of her two hands resting on the table and her eyes fixed on what was ahead, perhaps the viewer, though also more than the viewer, I knew. Around her neck a black serpent coiled and at rest there, pettish, known by the figure I assumed. But they were the other figures who spoke to me the most. One figure stared into a shallow plate of fish and fish bones, full of, I felt, melancholy. There, not there. The figure beside her seemed to be at her aid, in support, and another whose hand over what I imagined might be her mouth, seemed to gasp, astonished at some action just out of the seer's time.

I studied the baldheaded figures, their large hands. How if the breast was depicted, it was depicted so that only one breast was visible and the other (if there was another) was obscured by a forearm, a table, another figure's head. I studied each one depicted with only one breast visible and the other obscured by a plate, a profile and thought of Audre Lorde who was interested in the stories of the Amazons and who wrote about her own experience of breast cancer.

I would, in a moment, learn that this collograph was the study, in color, of a black-and-white collograph made by the artist Belkis Ayón and that she had named it *La cena* which art historians say mixes elements from the Catholic *Last Supper* and the Abakúa (the secret, male society that deeply interested Belkis) initiation banquet called Iriampó.

At the center of Abakúa practices, I am told, is the story of a woman named Sikán, a central figure of Ayón's work. Out of West Africa this story of Abakúa was carried, and the story that Belkis had come to tell was of a girl or young woman who had gone to the river on a chore to fetch water but had ended up hearing the voice of god, and when her husband or father found out, she was killed—for being a woman and hearing the voice of god. The versions of the story, Sikán, the god, and the water are kaleido-scopic, shiftful. I imagine Belkis considering version after version. This is the story Belkis had come to tell, but it was also her own. Belkis said, first in Spanish: "Sikán is a transgressor, and as such I see her, and I see myself." I considered Belkis's commitment to telling this origin story of the secret, paternal Abakúa society in such a public way as art. Maybe that was just one of the things that made her think of herself as a transgressor.

The voice of a woman telling the story of another who had been killed for being a woman who had heard the voice of god.

I read what I could as if my own vitality depended on it—more Lydia Cabrera, Ana Belén Martín-Sevillano, interviews with Ayón. Page after page as my own body thickened and swelled, and my skin expanded around the changing shape of my stomach and thighs and breasts, I wondered what a voice was at all.

Ana Belén Martín-Sevillano in "Crisscrossing Gender, Ethnicity, and Race" writes about the stories of Sikán and the goat, who is a version of the original Sikán, and whose skin it is that is stretched by men across the hollow to make a ritualistic drum. She considers "the power of the skin as a communication tool." The more I thought about it, the more difficult it was for me to decide what skin was. What our mother survived covered our faces like a caul. My loose-loose hair. My color, my lack of mothers, my bent-knee walk. What skin was. Posture. Family names. Class. The way I pronounced words. The skin stretched over the hollow out of which my sound was made. And so skin was the sentence. My ligaments loosened, my body pulled itself from itself and took the nourishment it might have given to other things—the fortifications of the teeth, my bones more generally, my hair—and gave them to the fetus that grew inside me. My skin itched and gleamed as it grew with the baby, also growing, and so the sentence itched too. My languages—which was to say: my minds—no longer felt singular but plural. A door was a word was a moving wheel. I might pass through one and end up in another time unable to say again enough to make other doors, to find my way out. But also, such sentences, for a second quick as a flash, might be porous enough to let the river seep through them. I might find myself grateful for such reunion. I might find myself mothered there by a woman who could hear the stories of fishes, whose gold tooth still carried the quiets of the river silt, way back, before we were born, when our mothers' mothers were not even girls yet and we were just particles in the air.

Conceição Evaristo

Conceição Evaristo (b. 1946) is a poet, storyteller, and essayist born in Belo Horizonte, Brazil. She has an MA in Brazilian literature from the Pontifical Catholic University of Rio de Janeiro and a PhD in comparative literature from the Fluminense Federal University. Her first fictional works were published in the Quilombhoje's Cadernos Negros series. She is the author of seven books, among them Olhos d'água, *which won the 2015 Jabuti Prize for best short story anthology. Her works have been translated into English, French, Spanish, and Arabic. Evaristo won the Minas Gerais Government Award for her complete works, the Nicolás Guillén Prize for Literature by the Caribbean Philosophical Association, and the Master of the Peripheries Award by Instituto Maria e João Aleixo. "The Dancer's Feet" ("Os pés do dançarino") was translated from the Portuguese by Elton Uliana.*

The Dancer's Feet

Davenir was the one with the greatest dancing feet in the small town of Danceland where he was born. The gift of great dancing was a common trait of everyone who was born there, and everyone who chose to live there. To be more specific about Davenir, it is necessary to say that, with this young man, it wasn't only his talented feet that made him so great but rather his whole body. Everything about him was his ability to dance. The body with all its details. Eyes, mouth, the beautifully unkempt curly hair. Dancing was so ingrained in Davenir's body that some people would say that he wasn't even interested in love. Dance was his passion, his greatest pleasure. At the age of seven, after watching dancers on television and after dancing himself at many family parties, he was already proficient in samba and tango. His family, guessing that he could have a professional future, rose above all the malicious comments and sent the boy to ballet school. They were right. Things went really well. Davenir got better and better. At fourteen he was an outstanding student in classical, modern, and Afro ballet, as well as tap dancing and even belly dancing, all this without paying any attention to the occasional ignorant comments he heard. And at each stage of his progress, the boy who "danced with his soul in his feet"—praise given by a renowned dance critic—continued to stand out more and more. Awarded with so many scholarships, including to study abroad, Davenir went away to experience dance and theater of other cultures, while exhibiting his own natural talent and versatility. In one single show, he was able to perform congada from Minas Gerais, Afro-Tientense batuque beat, Czech dances like polka, reggae from Jamaica and Maranhão, as well as to imbue his body with extraordinary grace and authenticity when he was performing rap. Davenir had so much skill and talent, and his technique was so precise, not to mention his competence and artistic flair, that it was difficult to know how to label him. Dancer, classical dancer, ballet dancer, Latin American star, or even prince of the dance . . . And with so much deserved success, the young man lost some of the most important and fundamental aspects of himself and picked up other less desirable qualities and values. His fellow people from Danceland were witness to what happened to him one day. And they talked about the fact, genuinely wishing that Davenir would eventually "find his missing feet." This is what happened:

When Davenir came back to his hometown, a big party was organized in the town square to celebrate his return. Everybody was really excited by the event, since the gift of great dance belonged to everyone in the town, and especially to those who returned. The slogan for the event was "Dance is the most important thing." There was no one left at home; people came from the most faraway parts of the town to the place where the celebration was being held. Everyone longed for the son of the land who "danced with his soul in his feet"; in fact, the local people had expanded on this slogan, creating the following maxim: "only those who have their soul in their feet can be great dancers." And after a few hours, which seemed to the public endless, Davenir finally arrived at the square, ready to receive the homage.

He was absolutely certain that he deserved such an honor and, indeed, that other celebrations should happen as well. For Davenir, the town should bow at his feet, because it was thanks to him that a small town like this had become known in the world. In the vanity of that moment, Davenir didn't even notice the three old women who stood by the bandstand at the foot of the steps as he was entering the place. He passed by them, giving no sign of recognition. Nor did he notice their open arms towards him, which ended up dissolving into empty space. All Davenir could think about was the celebration of himself and the pictures that would be taken of him with the town dignitaries.

After an emotional performance that brought the audience to tears, Davenir was ready to leave the venue. As he went down the steps, it was he who then recognized the three respectable old ladies. They still had their arms open, waiting to embrace him and to receive his embrace. That was when Davenir saw himself as a young boy again, and in that very moment he realized that the oldest of the three old women was his great-grandmother. She had been the first person to realize that he had a talent for dance. The second old woman was the one who once, with prayer and ointments, had miraculously healed his dislocated knee. An accident he had suffered on the eve of an important performance. And the third, Davenir couldn't remember exactly who she was, although her face was familiar to him. Even so, Davenir still didn't stop to receive their affection, despite these women being the ones who had marked his destiny forever. And as he left the place and headed towards the exit, a strange pain invaded his lower limbs. He was overcome by a desperate need to remove his shoes, which felt too soft on his feet, wobbly and unsupportive, empty of memories. He was frightened when he pulled them off and felt that his socks were empty. He realized his feet were missing, and despite that, he felt pain. In that very moment, someone from home brought him a message from his great-grandmother, the oldest of the three old ladies. His feet had been forgotten, lost in time, but that he should remain calm. All he needed to do was to go back. To go back to the beginning of everything.

Georgina Herrera

Georgina Herrera *(1936–2021) was one of the greatest poets in twentieth-century Cuba and Latin America. Born in Jovellanos, Matanzas, she explored gender, Afro-Cuban history, and African legacy in her works. She lived most of her life in Havana, where she also wrote for radio, television, and film. She began publishing poetry at the age of sixteen and is the author of eight poetry collections, including* G.H., África, Gentes y cosas, Granos de sol y luna, Grande es el tiempo, Gustadas sensaciones, Gritos, *and* Gatos y liebres o libro de las conciliaciones. *She also authored a memoir,* Golpeando la memoria, *in collaboration with Daisy Rubiera Castillo. "Four Obituaries for Havana" and "Matanzas" were translated from the Spanish by Ignacio Granados Herrera and Sandra Guzmán.*

Four Obituaries for Havana

1. Havana Friend

Your family
is investing everything
so you could be pretty,
even more than you are.
It's necessary so
when a visit from a prince,
or someone alike
who deserves you, arrives.

You can't see it.
I'm preparing to stop being your friend.

When that happens
you will be busy being a princess.
And now that
you're looking so perfect,
I even fear offending you with a kiss.

2. *Havana Mother*

Where are the pockets
of the peaceful corners you guarded
as a treasure?
Sweet places of wonder and joy.
Where is the shawl you used to protect
me from the sun and mist?
You covered my neck
out of fear and tenderness.
I can't recognize you with your new dress
and hairstyle.
I can't see myself as your daughter.

3. *Havana Daughter*

You look older,
so artificial.
What I'm saying is an ancient story,
or are you really the weeping flower that came out of my womb?
We no longer know.
You doubt it and so do I.
The perfection of the retouch hurts.
You seemed conceived without love.

4. *Havana Havana . . .*

Something of you remains somewhere.
Turning back time, a little,
I look for you, I remember you in the bends

where no one else is looking.
Delighted, my instinct recovers
what the people discard to find your "other."
I keep everything that you were,
with what never again will be
with the pace of the beats
of this heart that you will look for one day
and you will find, Havana, you know where.

Matanzas

Indian Matanzas,
White Matanzas,
Matanzas, mine, line no one else's
For her barracks,
cane, whip, maroonage,
and runaways. Matanzas
sweet and sour, but also salty
with tears, cries, and taste of blood.
Matanzas,
moistened between her rivers
and over the bridges rising.
A mystery haunts its caves
confirmed through its valleys.
Matanzas,
with her balconies and her bay,
so an ancient dame,
so maroon.
A mother to all.

María Sabina

María Sabina *(ca. 1894–1985) was born María Sabina Magdalena García. She was a Mazatec shaman from Huautla de Jiménez, Mexico, and considered by some to be the most visionary twentieth-century Latin American poet. Internationally renowned for her healing ceremonies based on the use of psilocybin mushrooms, her distinctive poetic voice has rarely received the recognition it deserves. The few recordings that exist of her shamanic chants give us the opportunity to glimpse her genius and the power of her words to uplift and transport the soul. "The Life (Chapter 14)" is an excerpt from her biography,* María Sabina: Selections, *a project Sabina did with fellow Mazateca Álvaro Estrada. He translated her oral story from the Mazatec to the Spanish and Henry Munn from the Spanish.*

The Life (Chapter 14)

A few years before the first foreigners I met arrived in Huautla, a neighbor, Guadalupe, the wife of the síndico Cayetano García, came to my house.*

"I've had an ugly dream," she said. "I want you to come to the house to see about us. I don't feel well. I'm asking you as a favor. It's possible that problems are approaching for my husband because his office as a síndico is difficult. You know, Señora, that there is violence in the town. There are envies. For nothing at all people hurt and kill each other. There are discords."

---

* In Mexican town government, the síndico is the representative of the district attorney (ministerio público); however, in Huautla, there is no district attorney's office. Cayetano García was síndico from 1953 to 1955.

"I'll go with you right now," I told her.

Upon arriving at their house, Cayetano invited me to sit down. He took another chair. His wife did the same. In a discreet voice, the síndico spoke:

"I know who you are, María Sabina. That's why I've sent for you. We have faith in you. You've cured those who have been ill here in the house, but now I'm going to ask you something special. I want you to be my adviser. The town has elected me to municipal office. You know that to be one of the authorities is a big responsibility. You have to make decisions and you can make mistakes. So I ask you to advise me and guide me, because you have power; you know, you can know the truth no matter how hidden it is because the 'little things' teach you.* If there are any problems of litigation in the municipality, you will tell me where the guilt lies and I, as síndico, will say what should be done."

"Don't worry," I answered him. "We'll do what you ask. I can't say no because we're old friends and because I obey the authorities. What's more, I know that you're a good man. I don't doubt it. I will be your adviser. We'll consult the 'saint children' as many times as it's necessary."

CAYETANO GARCÍA WAS SÍNDICO FOR three years; in that time there were no serious problems or situations that the town government could lament.

But I should tell the incident that preceded the arrival of the first foreigners who came to me. More or less fifteen days after the drunk wounded me, Guadalupe, the wife of Cayetano, some other people, and I took the "little things." This time I saw strange beings. They appeared to be people, but they weren't familiar; they didn't even appear to be fellow Mazatecs.

"I don't know what's happening; I see strange people," I told Guadalupe.

I asked her to pray because I felt a certain uneasiness at that vision. Guadalupe prayed to help me. She prayed to God the Christ.

---

* Translator's note: "little things" and "saint children" refer to psilocybin mushrooms.

I received the explanation of that vision I'd had a few days later when Cayetano arrived at my house in the course of the morning. His words didn't fail to astonish me:

"María Sabina," he said, still breathing hard from the walk, "some blond men have arrived at the Municipal Building to see me. They've come from a faraway place with the aim of finding a Wise One. They come in search of Little-One-Who-Springs-Forth. I don't know whether it displeases you to know it, but I promised them to bring them to meet you. I told them that I know a true Wise Woman. The thing is that one of them, looking very serious, put his head up close to my ear and said: 'I'm looking for ʔntixitjo.'* I couldn't believe what I was hearing. For a moment I doubted it, but the blond man appeared to know a lot about the matter. That was the impression I got. The man seemed sincere and good. Finally, I promised to bring them to your house."

"If you want to, I can't say no. You are an official and we are friends," I replied.

The following day, somebody brought three blond men to my house. One of them was Mr. Wasson. I told the foreigners that I was sick, though not precisely that a drunk had wounded me with a pistol. One of the visitors listened to my chest. He put his head on my chest to hear my heartbeat, held my temples between his hands, and put his head against my back. The man nodded while he touched me. Finally, he said some words that I didn't understand; they spoke another language that wasn't Castilian. I don't even understand Castilian.

One night soon after, the foreigners were present at my vigil. Afterward I found out that Wasson had been left marveling, and that he went so far as to say that another person in Huautla who claimed to be a Wise One was nothing but a liar. In reality he meant the sorcerer Vanegas.

---

* Translator's note: In the transcription of Mazatec words here, as elsewhere, the *x* is pronounced *"sh"* in English, the modified question mark is a glottal stop and the *j* is the Spanish jota, pronounced like the English *h*. Superscript numbers are used in more technical transliterations to indicate tones have been omitted throughout in order to make the words more accessible to non-Mazatec readers.

When the foreigners took the saint children with me, I didn't feel anything bad. The velada was fine. I had different visions than usual. I saw places I had never imagined existed. I reached the place of origin of the foreigners. I saw cities. Big cities. Many houses, big ones.

Wasson came other times. He brought his wife and his daughter. Different people came with him as well.

One day Wasson arrived with a group of people. Among them were some fellow Mazatecs who brought a sick person wrapped up in a mat. They told me that he was an orphan, Perfecto by name, and that he had been raised by Aurelio-Camino. This Aurelio was a Wise One as well, and he had tried to cure the sick boy.

But there was no remedy for the sick one. His death was near. After I saw Perfecto's appearance, I said to Aurelio, "This child is in a very grave condition. He requires a lot of care."

I took the "children" and began to work. In the trance I found out that Perfecto's spirit had been frightened. His spirit had been trapped by a malevolent being.

I let myself be carried away by the Language that sprang from me, and though Perfecto didn't take the "little mushrooms," my words made him sit up, rise, and succeed in standing. He related, then, that while resting in the shade of some coffee trees in Cañada de Mamey he "felt something" in back of him.

"I had the feeling that there was something behind me," he said, "like an animal, like a donkey. I heard him lick his chops very clearly. I turned around rapidly, but I didn't see anything. That frightened me a lot and since then I've felt sick. It's true, Papá Aurelio, if you take care of me, I'll get well. María Sabina says so."

In the course of the vigil, the sick one got to his feet because the Language gave him strength. I also rubbed some San Pedro on his arms.

Weeks went by and somebody informed me that Perfecto had died. They didn't take care of him as they should have. If they had done several veladas, he would certainly have gotten well. They didn't do it.

Wasson, his family, and friends went and didn't come back anymore.

It's been years since I've seen them; but I know that his wife died. Only Wasson returned once not many years ago. The last time I saw him he told me: "María Sabina, you and I will still live for many years."

After those first visits of Wasson, many foreign people came to ask me to do veladas for them. I asked them if they were sick, but they said no . . . that they had only come "to know God." They brought innumerable objects with which they took what they call photographs and recorded my voice. Later they brought papers [newspapers and magazines] in which I appeared. I've kept some papers I'm in. I keep them even though I don't know what they say about me.

It's true that Wasson and his friends were the first foreigners who came to our town in search of the saint children and that they didn't take them because they suffered from any illness. Their reason was that they came to find God.

Before Wasson, nobody took the mushrooms only to find God. The little mushrooms were always taken for the sick to get well.

Berta Cáceres

Berta Cáceres (1971–2016) was a Lenca Indigenous land and water pro-
tector born in La Esperanza, Honduras. The mother of five was one of the
founders and coordinators of the Consejo Cívico de Organizaciones Popu-
lares e Indígenas de Honduras (COPINH). In 2015, she won the Goldman
Environmental Prize for her work defending the Lenca habitat and rights
to Rio Gualcarque, considered sacred to her people. What follows are the re-
marks she delivered while accepting the Goldman Environmental Prize. A
year later, she was savagely murdered. A US-trained soldier and president of
the company building a dam on Río Blanco, an Indigenous waterway, was
arrested and found guilty of masterminding her murder.

Goldman Environmental Prize Speech (Excerpt)

2015

In our worldviews, we are beings who come from the earth, from the
water, and from corn. The Lenca people are ancestral guardians of the
rivers, in turn protected by the spirits of young girls, who teach us that
giving our lives in various ways for the protection of the rivers is giving
our lives for the well-being of humanity and of this planet.

COPINH, walking alongside people struggling for their emancipa-
tion, validates this commitment to continue protecting our waters, the
rivers, our shared resources, and nature in general, as well as our rights
as a people. Let us wake up! Let us wake up, humankind! We're out
of time.

We must shake our conscience free of the rapacious capitalism, rac-
ism, and patriarchy that will only assure our own self-destruction. The

Gualcarque River has called upon us, as have other gravely threatened rivers. We must answer their call.

Our Mother Earth, militarized, fenced in, poisoned, a place where basic rights are systematically violated, demands that we take action. Let us build societies that are able to coexist in a dignified way, in a way that protects life. Let us come together and remain hopeful as we defend and care for the blood of this Earth and of its spirits.

I dedicate this award to all the rebels out there, to my mother, to the Lenca people, to Río Blanco, and to the martyrs who gave their lives in the struggle to defend our natural resources. Thank you very much.

Edwidge Danticat

Edwidge Danticat *(b. 1969) was born in Port-au-Prince, Haiti. She is the award-winning author of several books, including* Breath, Eyes, Memory; Krik? Krak! *(a National Book Award finalist);* The Farming of Bones; The Dew Breaker; Claire of the Sea Light; *and* Create Dangerously. *She is a 2009 MacArthur Fellow and a 2020 winner of the Vilcek Prize.* Everything Inside: Stories *was a 2020 winner of the OCM Bocas Prize for Fiction, The Story Prize, and the National Book Critics Circle Award for Fiction. The poem "so a despot walks into a killing field" was first published in* The Progressive *magazine in 2012.*

so a despot walks into a killing field

so a despot walks into a killing field
to commemorate the two-year anniversary
of the country's worst natural disaster
in two hundred years
and the killing field is not only
where thousands who were killed
in a massive earthquake were dumped
by earth movers into mass graves
but also where the despot's butchered
were dumped some thirty years before
when the despot arrives at the ceremony
for the earthquake dead
everyone stands to greet the despot
and powerful looking people

shake the despot's hand
and from the pit of the earth
we the despot dead,
and together with earthquake dead,
we scream
because we see how
some bow their heads
as if the despot were holy
as if we were not even here,
as if we had never been here
at a ceremony where the living
are meant to remember us
the despot's presence
tell us that they don't
remember anything at all
when we died, there was no one to say
"que la terre lui soit legère"
no one was there to ask
the earth to fall lightly over us
but now there are more of us
the despot dead
the earthquake dead
the earth is heavy over us
under the despot's shoes
can they hear us
those who stand to greet him
can they hear us
as they bow their heads
as they shake his hand
can they hear us
those who say
that life was better with him
because rice was cheaper

under the despot's reign
why under the guise of remembering
have they let the despot come
to trample over our graves
some of us are still pregnant
with the children they stabbed
inside of us
some of us are still looking
for the teeth they plucked
out of our mouths
for the eyes they pulled
out of sockets
the fingernails yanked
he pounds his fancy shoes
on our skulls, the despot
yet they stand to greet him
they shake his hand
bow their heads
in forgetfulness
while we wear mud for clothes
and eat mountain stone for bread

Rita Laura Segato

Rita Laura Segato *(b. 1951) was born in Buenos Aires, Argentina, and is an anthropologist as well as one of the leading feminist voices and intellectuals of Latin America. She is the author of* Santos y daimones, Las estructuras elementales de la violencia, La nación y sus otros, La guerra contra las mujeres, L'oedipe noir, L'écriture sur le corps des femmes assassinées de Ciudad Juarez, Contra-pedagogías de la crueldad, *and* The Critique of Coloniality. *The following excerpts are from the opening speech she delivered at the Buenos Aires International Book Fair in 2019, translated from the Spanish by Liz Mason-Deese.*

The Virtues of Disobedience

Second Disobedience

The second disobedience takes me to Europe, the continent of the monotheistic neurosis, as I call it in my book *Santos y daimones* [Saints and demons], the continent whose neurosis is to control and morally judge the world. Thus another inevitable memory comes to mind as I prepare this uncomfortable lecture, which is the uneasiness that struck me thirty-six years ago when I heard Gabriel García Márquez's acceptance speech, entitled "The Solitude of Latin America," on the occasion of his receiving the Nobel Prize in 1982. The memory of that vague and incomprehensible discomfort has accompanied me ever since and only now do I find the space to speak about it in front of an audience.

At that time the word Eurocentrism did not even exist in my horizon, partly because in those years I was living in Europe. Let's see: García

Márquez seemed to be saying that Latin America was alone because
Europe did not look at it, did not see it, did not register its existence, and
did not understand it. I was immensely bothered by, and continue to be
bothered by, the subtext of his speech that clearly pointed to the author's
conviction that our continent could only achieve its full existence in the
eyes of Europe.

Is it our destiny to exist as a being for the Other? That would be prob-
lematic, because to effectively be a being for the Other, it is necessary to
learn how to be from that Other. Over the years, and with vocabularies
that I started gaining access to, that discomfort was transformed into a
consciousness. That consciousness is what allows me to speak to you all
today, as the literate people that you are, of our issue: the circulation of
words and its pattern.

About twenty days ago, at a meeting with directors of European mu-
seums in the Pompidou museum in Paris, they asked me an important,
intelligent, and very unusual question: how does Eurocentrism affect
Europe? I stated: it is Europe that is alone. It looks at itself in the narcis-
sistic mirror of its museums but lacks a real mirror, one that can exercise
resistance and show defects, because those objects cannot return the gaze.

Europe lacks that powerful feminine utensil of the "mirror, mirror"
of the Evil Queen in fairy tales: it does not see its flaws in the eyes of oth-
ers because it keeps the Other enclosed as treasure in the glass showcases
of its colonial power. The visit to the Chirac Museum on the Quai de
Branly confirmed that impression for me. There, I only saw "imprisoned
beauty"—objects removed from their own destiny, their historical bed-
rock, from the landscape where they had been rooted. From there they
would have been able to follow their own path and exert their influence.
The same thing happens with books.

According to García Márquez, we need to see ourselves in the eyes
of Europe, in the books of Europe, to not be alone. However, he does not
realize that Europe does not even perceive its own loneliness, loneliness
that has slowly led to a decline in its creative imagination, which once
dazzled us, towards an unbearable tedium.

Third Disobedience

I exasperated my teachers, teachers from the elite, in the Juan Ramón Fernández Living Languages school of my childhood, when, from the age of six, I would always refuse to write my sentences using the Peninsular mode of "tú" and its associated verb forms. To this day I continue that arduous task of modifying the spellcheck and autocorrect each time, line by line, to put the accents on the appropriate syllables (on the *i* of "decíle," the *i* of "veníte," and on the *e* and the *a* of "si querés pasá por mi casa"). Swimming against the current of conformity, in disobedience. Later my beloved José María Arguedas would appear, with his Quechua language in Spanish, his inflections of Quechua in the superimposed language, his way of truly appropriating Spanish to say what he desired and what was necessary to say: that it was the Indio who carried the flag of history and sovereignty on our continent.

Just as Karl Polanyi spoke about the destruction of the embedded economy by capitalism, we must propose re-embedding language as the path to its re-existence, despite institutions, in people's verbal gestures.

Fourth Disobedience

On July 8, 2018, Juan Pérez (pseudonym) from the very prestigious Spanish publishing house La Eterna (pseudonym) wrote:

Dear Ms. Segato,

My name is Juan Pérez and I am an editor from La Eterna publishing house. I wanted to get in touch with you to cordially invite you to join us on our editorial list in some way.

To me, your critical work is an intellectual gem that should be known and read around the world. In Spain, for example, it is not easily accessible.

Of course, I know that you do not suffer from a lack of spaces to publish in, specifically Prometeo, with whom you work in a continuous way.

Despite being aware of that situation, I allow myself to invite you due to my admiration of your work.

> Best regards,
> Juan Pérez
> Senior Editor
> Madrid (Spain)

From: Rita Segato
Sent: Friday, August 10, 2018
To: Juan Pérez
Subject: Re: La Eterna Publishing

Dear Juan, thank you very much for the words of your message. It is exciting to know that one's effort is appreciated, and even more so by an editor from such a prestigious publishing house. But I think you will understand me if I tell you that, as you know, I write from the perspective of the coloniality of power and also of knowledge. My perspective is critical of Eurocentrism, which is nothing other than racism applied to the knowledge and products of those of us who inhabit and work on this side of the sea, in a landscape that is marked and demarcated by the colonial process that persists into the present.

So, I have an editor who is the first who extended me a hand in 2003, when I wanted to return to my country and nobody knew me in Argentina. I hold him in high esteem and he has helped me in a series of difficult life situations. I publish with him in Spanish in the same way as I would publish with you. However, due to the fact that La Eterna is located on that other side of the sea, it is easier for you to distribute books to the whole universe of Spanish-language readers, and although I was happy with your message, it is impossible for me to agree with that situation, to adapt to that, to reconcile myself with that. You can understand, right? I am stubborn as a mule, I know. But the thing is, it hurts me to know that a publisher from Latin America does not have the same facilities for distribution as a Spanish publisher. The only idea that occurs to me, then, is to suggest that you establish some type of collaboration with my publisher, Prometeo, so that between the two of you, in partnership, you can publish something of mine soon . . . What do you think of that idea?

Whatever your response, I send you a hug and my sincere gratitude for your appreciation of my work.

Rita

From: Juan Pérez
Sent: Friday, August 13, 2018
To: Rita Segato
Subject: Re: La Eterna Publishing

Dear friend,

I understand perfectly, of course. I should say that it is comforting to find an intellectual whose actions are consistent with their discourse (that does not always happen) . . .

Juan Pérez
Senior Editor
Madrid (Spain)

I quote this exchange with the senior editor of a highly regarded and respectable Peninsular publishing house due to its elegance and the mutual personal appreciation revealed between the correspondent representing the company's interests and myself, as his interlocutor. It is one of the many invitations to publish in my language with global publishers that I have received, all of which I have declined for the reasons that I explained to Juan Pérez. Basically, as was said to me in those days by my dear friend Claudia Schvartz, who grew up among the bookshelves of the Fausto bookstore of Buenos Aires and who now edits poetry with great difficulty with the publishing house Leviatán: Why can't I get a book from Chile, why can't I get a book from Uruguay? Why don't I have access to those authors in Argentina, instead of only through Spain?

The real reason is that the military dictatorship (1976–1983) targeted large Argentinian booksellers and, through political persecution, destroyed the large publishing field that we had. During his presidency, Carlos Menem (1989–1999) finished the job by the complete lack of protection provided to the Argentine publishing industry, which had enjoyed great prestige in the Spanish-speaking world due to its unparalleled quality, leaving it defenseless against global market forces. Honorable booksellers persisted and/or emerged to try to resuscitate what had been lost . . . Others died of despair, like Claudia's father, with the final closure of his Fausto bookstores and his publishing house, Siglo Veinte, in a supposed "democracy" that, having only recently been recovered, succumbed to the coloniality of power and knowledge.

Spanish publishing houses bought the companies that published textbooks and school manuals, profiting from the already existing know-how in the country, threatening the beauty and value of the linguistic pluralism and ways of speaking rooted in Argentina. I weep for that loss: the Argentina of Fausto was beautiful. The Argentina of the publishing house Centro Editor de América Latina is equally irreplaceable. The value and historical purpose of a plural world was left in a very vulnerable situation, in a similar process to what happened with transnational music record labels that bought the music of the world and "equalized" it in a pasteurized and rapidly obsolescent "world music."

I want to pay homage here to those publishers that survived that time of destruction and to those who started after the ruin: Corregidor, Colihue, De la Flor, Biblos, Manantial, Lugar Editorial, Espacio Editorial, Homo Sapiens, Pequeño Editor, Prometeo, Godot, Leviatán. And forgive me if I have not managed to name all of them, or if any of those that I named have already perished.

I want it to be understood that this has nothing to do with patriotic values but rather the value of pluralism.

Cherríe Moraga

Cherríe Moraga *(b. 1952) was born in Los Angeles, California. She is a poet, feminist, essayist, playwright, and coeditor with Gloria Anzaldúa of the groundbreaking anthology* This Bridge Called My Back. *With Barbara Smith and Audre Lorde, she started Kitchen Table: Women of Color Press, the first publisher exclusively for women of color in the US. Her works include* The Last Generation *and* Native Country of the Heart: A Memoir. *"How to Bless" is a fragment of an unpublished memoir.*

How to Bless

My mother was once a holy woman of fierce faith. I remember in the extended penance of the final years of my mother's life, my sister had asked me, "What happened to that faith?" She articulated the question I had been holding for many months wordlessly, as my mother's failing mind had radically reduced her language and increased her rage. True, I had not seen her lips murmur a prayer in so long. But once when the grandkids came in for a visit with their guitar and played "Cielito lindo" for her, she sang softly, mouthing more words by heart than any of us knew. And at the end, Elvira blessed herself with the sign of the cross. The song, a ritual of remembering, felt like prayer.

Today, I pray in my mother's stead. I learned just in time. As a child, my son almost intuitively assumed the same rituals of faith practiced by my childhood familia. Once I idly mentioned how my mother always crossed our foreheads as we went off to school each day, and Rafa demanded to know why I had not inherited the tradition. At his request, I began to cross his forehead each day before he walked out the door. We both felt better, as I did when I would bless his body each night with an evening prayer.

When do we grow into the age, the right, to bless a child, a sad soul, a cousin in conflict? One day my body began to inhabit the gesture. It is not Catholic; it is a moment of cosmic awareness. We walk out that door, cross a city block, get in our cars, hop on a plane, we lay ourselves down to sleep and death awaits us. We bless one another to ease that passage . . .

Gioconda Belli

Gioconda Belli *(b. 1948) is an award-winning Nicaraguan poet, writer, and political activist born in Managua. She was involved in the Nicaraguan Revolution from a very young age and occupied important positions in the Sandinista Party and in the revolutionary government. She resigned from the Sandinista Party in 1993 and is now a voice critical of the Ortega government. Her work has been translated into twenty languages. She's published eight poetry books and eight novels, plus a memoir, two essay collections, two anthologies, and four children's books. In 2008, she won one of the most prestigious Spanish prizes, the Biblioteca Breve, for her novel* Infinity in the Palm of Her Hand. *In 2010, she was awarded the Latin American prize La Otra Orilla for her novel* El país de las mujeres *(The country of women). She is president of PEN International, Nicaragua, and a member of the Spanish Royal Academy of Letters as well as the Ordre des Arts et des Lettres of France. "I Have No Place to Live" was translated from the Spanish by Alba Stacey Hawkings.*

I Have No Place to Live

I have no place to live.
I chose the word.
My books were left behind.
My home. The garden, its hummingbirds,
The massive palms
named Bismarck
for their imposing presence.
I have no place to live.

I chose the word,
To speak for those who are silenced,
To understand a rage
That nothing can appease.
Every door is shut.
I left the white sofas,
The terrace, the dancing volcanoes in the distance,
The lake's phosphorescent skin,
Night revealing the city's multicolored lights
I left carrying my words under my arm.
They are my crime, my sin.
Not even God could force me to recant.
My dogs, Macondo and Caramelo, left behind.
The sweet shape of their faces,
their love from nose to tail.
My bed with its mosquito net,
the place to close my eyes
and imagine a world transformed
according to my wishes.
It was not to be. It was not to be.
I want to speak the future now,
to speak my heart,
throw up revulsion and disgust.
My clothes idle in the closet,
My shoes. The landscape of my days and nights,
The sofa where I write,
The windows.
I have taken to the streets with my words.
I embrace them, I choose them.
I am free,
Even if I have nothing.

SAGACIOUS MOON

The energy of the moon is wise;
a time to receive ancient wisdom.

Rosa Chávez

Rosa Chávez *(b. 1980) is a Maya K'iche'-Kaqchikel poet, artist, and activist born in Chimaltenango, Guatemala. She has authored five poetry collections, including* Casa solitaria *and* Ri uk'u'x ri ab'aj/El corazón de la piedra, *in addition to experimental works of theater, performance, and video. "To Take Back Our Breath" first appeared in T.A.N.J. (Fall 2021). All untranslated words are in K'iche', a Maya language with a documented 1.6 million speakers in Guatemala. Chávez's poetry has been widely anthologized and translated into six languages, including French, Norwegian, and German. The texts were translated from the Spanish by Gabriela Ramirez-Chavez. And from the Spanish to the K'iche' by María Guarchaj and Wel Raxulew.*

To Take Back Our Breath

I call upon the energy of our ancestors, our grandmothers,
all the women whose hands and bodies sowed this life in the present,
I take a deep breath of sacred air to fill my clay-jar heart,
a drum, my navel, and the earth beat as one,
a drum thunders like tijax's lightning*
splitting the knots in my body and memory,
the full moon is here, I heal my sorrows, I release them in a bath of
     salt water,
I strike my body with a bundle of seven herbs to awaken my
     blood flow,

---

* Tijax: the K'iche' name of a personal guardian spirit represented by an obsidian stone or knife; it is also a day of deep healing in the Maya calendar.

my cells speak the language of plants, I regain my strength in the
     heat of the tuj,*
I drink herbal and floral teas to ease my restless mind,
I massage my joints, light candles made of lard, of many colors,
I burn incense and pom to blow on the fog trapped in my chest,**
I call upon the keepers of the rivers, the keepers of the hills,
the keepers of the paths, in the city, in the fields,
wherever I set foot,
I speak to the sacred wind and tell it slowly
what I need to heal, and I bow before my truth,
the earth, generous, takes everything I have to offer,
she transforms everything I sow, my worries and joys, and begins again,
I hear a drum and dance, because dancing, too, is healing,
I dance with every woman alive, dead, and from long ago,
we move our flesh and awaken the earth with our feet,
we sing and take back our voice, we take back our truth,
we take back our language, we take back our body,
we take back our time, we take back our blood,
we take back our breath, we take back our freedom,
we take a deep breath, and the dignity of the water in our bodies
     keeps us flowing,
and our spirit returns, we beat our wings to life's rhythm
I return to the earth
I go back into the world
Kintzalij b'i pa ri ulew
kinel chi lo jun mul chi uwach ulew

Rech kqak'ama chi jumul ri quxlab'al

Kinch'ab'ej kichoqab'il ri e nab'e taq winaq, ri e qatit,
ri xkitik kan ruk' ri kiq'ab' xuquje' kib'aq'il ri k'aslemal ojk'owi chanim,

---

*   Tuj: an adobe or stone structure used for medicinal, ritual steam baths.
**   Pom: an incense made from tree resin.

nojim kinjiq ri loqalaj kaq'iq' chech unojsaxik ri wanima,
kch'ax ri jun lab'al chi kutiq ri numuxux ruk' ri ub'uk'b'utem ri
	uwachulew,
kch'aw ri jun lab'al jas ri ukowil uch'ab'al ri utun ri Tijax
tajin kusol ri upatzkuyal ri nub'aq'il ruk' ri nuchomanik,
kopan ri nojinaq ik' kinkunaj le b'is ink'owi ruk' jun atinem rech
	atz'am,
ruk' ri nusoraj wuqub' uwach q'ayes kink'asuj ri ub'inem ri kik' pa
	wib'och,
e nuk'utb'al b'anikil kech'aw ruk' uch'ab'al le e q'ayes ,par i uq'aq'al ri
	tuj kink'asuj wi ri nuchoq'ab'il,
kinqumuj uwal taq q'ayes xuquje' kotz'ij rech kinjamarisaj nuchomanik.
Kinji' ri nub'aqil, kintzij ri nuse'r cher xepo, jalajoj ukayib'al,
Sib' rech k'ok'q'ol xuquje' pom rech rech kujupij ri sutz' ri kekanaj
	kan chi uwach nuk'ux,
Kinch'ab'ej le chajinelab' rech le b'inel ja, le chajinelab' rech le juyub',
Le chajinelab' rech ri b'e, pa jun tinamit pa jun juyub',
Jawi kriqitaj wi ri nub'inem
Kinchaw ruk' ri loqalaj kaqiq' xuquje' nojimal kinb'ij chech
Xuquje' ke'inch'ab'ej rech kinkunatajik xuquje' kinmej wib' chi
	uwach ri nub'e'al,
Ri uwachulew ruk' utzilal kuk'amawaj rojojel le kwaj kinya chech,
Ronojel le kintiko, le uqoxomal ri wanima on ri kikotemal kuk'exo
	xuquje' kumaj ub'e,
Kinch'aw chi jun mul ri lab'al xuquje' kinxojowik, xa rumal chi we
	kinxojowik kinkunatajik,
Kinxojow kuk' ri e k'aslik, kuk' ri e kaminaq, kuk' ojer ixoqib',
Kqasalab'aj ri qab'aqil ruk' ri qaqan kqak'asuj ri uwachulew
Xuquje' kojb'ixanik xuquje' kqak'asuj uwach ri qaqul, ktzalij loq ri
	qab'e'al,
Kqak'ama chi jumul ri qach'ab'al, Kqak'ama chi jumul ri qab'aqil,
Kqak'ama chi jumul ri qaq'ij, Kqak'ama chi jumul ri qakik'el,
Kqak'ama chi jumul ri quxlab'al, Kqak'ama chi jumul ri man kojq'at
	ta chi rij

Nojim kojuxlab'ik xuquje' le utzilal ri ja chi kb'in par ri qab'aqil kuya
    b'e chiqech kojb'inik
Xuquje' ktzalij loq ri espíritu, kojxik'xot ruk' ri ub'inem ri k'aslemal
Kintzalij par ri ulew
Kintzalij chi jumul pa ri uwachulew

What Am I Going to Do Without Your Smell, Elena?

What am I going to do without your smell, Elena?
don't leave me, you bitch, you little piece of shit
What am I going to do?
When I think of your pussy and can't suck, caress,
finger it, or at least see you naked?
let me cling to your belly
sucking your delicious breasts
comfort me, Elena
I love you and that's why I want your life to go bad
to complete shit
so you come back to me
I'm sorry, Elena
leave, go take on the world
but first tell me
What am I going to do without your smell?

¿Jas kinb'ano al Le'n maj chi wuk' ri ruxlab' ab'aqil?

¿Jas kinb'ano al Le'n maj chi wuk' ri ruxlab' ab'aqil?
Man kinaya ta kanoq tak ali
Itzel ali K'an ali
¡¿Jas kinb'ano?!
Are taq kinchomaj le rislam uxol awa'
Xuquje' man kinkowin taj kintz'ubu'
Kinmalo, kinok chi upam

On xaq xewi kinwilo atch'analik
Chaya b'e chwech kinmatzej le apam
Kintij la le ki' taq atz'um
Chakub'a nuk'ux al Le'n
Katwaj rumal ri kinrayij
Chi man utz ta kariqo
Kariqiqej k'ax par ri ak'aslemal
Are chi kattzalij lo wuk'
Chinakuyu al Le'n
Jat atija ronojel ri uwachulew
Xewi chab'ij na kan chwech
¿Jas kinb'ano maj chi wuk' ri ruxlab' ab'aqil?

The Spirit Leaves If We Don't Take Care of It

The spirit leaves if we don't take care of it
forges its own path if it is bothered
takes its own medicine if it gets sick
it leaves, just like that, drifting over the sea
without saying goodbye
it moves on with no remorse
with no guilt.
In its absence
we cease to be sacred
we become something nameless.

Kanimaj b'i ri qak'u'x wi kqilij taj

Kanimaj b'i ri qak'u'x wi kqilij taj
kuchap b'i ri ub'e we xyakataj royowal
kutij q'an ri ukunab'al wi xyowajik
eb'a'w kcha kan chi qech
maj royowal kanimaj b'ik

maj umak,
wi maj
maj chi qapatan
man oj loq'ob'al ta chik.

Speak to Me in the Language of Time

Speak to me in the language of time
shake me in the silence of the stars
wake me early before drifting back to sleep
so I can love you with my domesticated tongue
so your barefoot voice plays inside my body
speak to me with the sun's tongue
tell me green words that ripen on my skin
join your name to mine
and love me with your two hearts.

Chinach'ab'ej pa ri utzijob'al ri q'ijsaq

Chinach'ab'ej pa ri utzijob'al ri q'ijsaq
chinayikiya' pa ri kitz'inilem ri ch'umil
chinak'asuj aq'ab'il mojo'q chinwar chi jun mul
are chi katinloq'oj ruk' ri tijotal waq'
are chi ri kch'anakat ach'ab'al ketz'an chwij
chinatzijob'el ruk' ri uch'ab'al ri q'ij
chab'ij rax taq tzij chwech are chi kechaq'aj chwij
chab'ana' jun che ri ab'i' ruk' ri wech
xuquje' chinawaj ruk' ri keb' ak'u'x.

Maryse Condé

*Maryse Condé (b. 1934) is a novelist, critic, and playwright born Maryse
Boucolon in Pointe-à-Pitre, Guadeloupe. She studied at the Université Sor-
bonne Nouvelle in Paris, where she earned a doctorate in comparative liter-
ature. She is the author of more than twenty books, including* Who Slashed
Celanire's Throat?, Crossing the Mangrove, The Gospel According to the
New World, *and the award-winning epic novel,* Segu. *She writes in French,
and her books have been translated into English, German, Dutch, Italian,
Spanish, and Japanese, among other languages. For the historical reach of
her work, the penetrating political critique, and unceasing commitment to
the liberation of all people, including Africans, people of African descent,
and women and girls, she has been lauded internationally. She's received
the Guggenheim and the Grand Prix Littéraire de la Femme among others.
"Discovering Celia Cruz" is a piece long overdue. In 1984, she wanted to write
about the Cuban songstress but was diverted when she learned of the enslaved
African woman from Barbados, which she turned into the novel* I, Tituba,
Black Witch of Salem. *"Discovering Celia Cruz" is an ode to the celebrated
Cuban songstress.*

Discovering Celia Cruz

I was raised in a rather particular way. My parents belonged to an asso-
ciation comprising the embryo of a Black bourgeoisie called "Les Grands
Nègres" in opposition to the "Petits Nègres," those who are totally useless,
are rum guzzlers and outright womanizers. Believe me, it's not easy being
a daughter of "Grands Nègres"! At school, I had to be first in every subject,
even in algebra and geometry. I had to turn my nose up at black pudding

and cod fritters. But above all at my parents' two abominations, music and dancing, whose entrechats they believed to be the most formidable of vices. Consequently, on Saturday afternoons, I never went to find a boyfriend at the local dance for teenagers organized by a religious association. As a result, during the carnival season I never ventured out onto the streets to follow the revelers and remained wasting away on my balcony. Oddly enough, such an education did not prevent me from loving my native island, which remained deep in my heart during my schooling in Paris. As a proof of this I returned to Guadeloupe in 1985 after the literary success of my novel *Segu* in 1984. For me these years in Guadeloupe were melancholic. Both my parents were gone, their lovely house in Pointe-à-Pitre had been auctioned off, and I had no friends, except for Simone, a mulatto woman who lived next door and was a piano teacher. And above all, I was unemployed. Nobody wanted me, neither at the university nor at the local radio and television stations.

After three years of getting nowhere, I made up my mind to accept the offer from UC Berkeley inviting me to teach Francophone literature. The day before I left, I assembled the few friends I had and Simone gave me as a present, a record of Celia Cruz accompanied by the Sonora Matancera orchestra. It was not the first time that Simone had given me a record, but this time it was a revelation. I had never heard such a voice, switching from joy to anger, from nostalgia to dreaming, a voice capable of expressing all the nuances of every human mood.

Celia Cruz became my idol. It's because of her I visited Cuba years later. I learned that she did not agree with Fidel Castro and had chosen to live in the States. She taught me that poetry and revolution don't always mix, but never mind, she taught me the gift of inspiration.

Alba Eiragi Duarte

Alba Eiragi Duarte *(b. 1960) is a poet and Indigenous leader born in Curu-guaty, Paraguay. She is a of Aché descent and was raised in the Avá Guaraní community in Colonia Fortuna, Departamento de Canindeyú. Her books include the poetry collection* Ñe'ẽ yvoty: Ñe'ẽ poty *and a story collection,* Ayvu tee Avá Guaraní. *In 2017, she became the first Indigenous female member of the Society of Writers of Paraguay. Her poems and short stories have been anthologized nationally and internationally. "There Is No Stumble" was translated from the Guaraní to the Spanish by Elena Martinez and from the Spanish by Sandra Guzmán.*

There Is No Stumble

The ugly disease is coming,
It's here!

Even the shadows disappear.

Those who fall go to infinity.
My being flies and I cannot find myself.

I am strong! There is no stumbling,
With my older sisters I play takua*
The men play their maracas.

Our culture gives us strength.
Our culture has prayers.

---

* Takua: bamboo.

The ugly disease will not hurt us,
tonight, or tomorrow.
Before her, no one will kneel.

My blood is strong, in the dark I woke up,
and at dawn my being was limitless.
So many roads I traveled in the stumble of life.
My poetry gives me strength.
my song, a soulful gift that delivers.

So much beauty has given me
truth, faith, and health
from my true word,
from my living.

Ndaipori ñepysanga

Mbaasay vai ou hina,
¡Oguahema Katu¡

Taanga yvy jepe omongue

Heta tapicha oho apyreyme.
Oveve chereko nda che topai.

¡Che mbarete¡ Ndaipori ñepysanga.
che rykekuerandive rombopu takua (bambú),
kuimba'e kuera ombopu imaraka.

Ore reko ome'ê oreve mbarete.
Ore reko oguereko ñembo'e.

Nda ore jopy vai moai mba'asy vai,
konga pyhare ha koerô
Naî pori oñesu vaera henondepe.

Che ruguy imbarete, pytume apay
che ko'ê che rekove hiañete heta mba'e

heta mba'ema ohasa ñepysanga rehegua
che ñe'ê poty ome'ê cheve mbarete.
che purahéipe, che remiandu omoñe'ê

Heta mba'e porâ ome'ê cheve
jerovia, angapyhy ha tesaî
che ayvuete ha che reko rupive.

Laura Esquivel

Laura Esquivel *(b. 1950) was born in Mexico City, Mexico. Her debut novel,* Like Water for Chocolate, *became an award-winning international sensation and was translated into more than forty languages. It has sold more than three million copies in the US alone. The 1992 Spanish film adaptation, scripted by Esquivel, broke box-office records for a foreign film in the US and internationally. Over the next three decades, a succession of bestselling novels followed:* The Law of Love, Swift as Desire, Malinche, Pierced by the Sun, *and two sequels to* Like Water for Chocolate, Tita's Diary *and* The Colors of My Past. *"Before Noise" is a fragment of a memoir-in-progress, translated from the Spanish by Sandra Arau Esquivel.*

Before Noise

It is said that at the moment a cell is divided in two, it transmits all its genetic load into the new cells. Sometimes I wonder whether that separation is silent. Because every movement, however imperceptible it may seem, produces a sound, a vibration.

In India some believe that when the "void" was divided into masculine and feminine, the sound *aum* occurred, and that its vibration spread throughout the Universe, creating time and space. The Hindu tradition regards the cosmos as an ocean of vibrations. Pythagoras himself said that each atom produces a particular sound, a rhythm, a vibration.

The Earth rhythmically pulses, spins, dances in space following a constant but slow movement, so much so that we don't even perceive it. However, this displacement produces a sound that is integrated into the music of the spheres. The Earth sings and the vibration of its voice has been recorded in every particle of all living beings, all animals, all plants, rocks, and minerals with whom we cohabit this planet. Vibration is energy in motion. Perhaps the Earth, millions of years ago, wanted her song to be heard loud and far away and gave us life to resonate with it. At least that is what I like to think of in moments when silence floods me.

I love silence. I love listening to it.

The Mayans said that the universe was nothing more than a resonant matrix and that if you could connect properly with it through the umbilical cord of the universe, you'd be able to obtain all the information you wanted in the span of a second. Fortunately the web already existed when I found out about this ancient Mexican culture's worldview, otherwise I would never have understood what these great sky watchers meant when they spoke of a cosmic mind, completely interconnected.

It's not like I have everything sorted out. The doubts continue in my mind: What did they mean when they spoke of the umbilical cord of the universe? To a water link? A stream of water that circulates between the resonant matrix and our bodies? Or were they referring to our own blood that, on its journey through the interior of our body, carries rivers of information and ancestral memory to each of our cells? If we take into account that in our body there are about one hundred trillion cells, that it is made up of 70 percent water, and that sound propagates through water five times faster than through air, then we can get an idea of what happens inside our bodies in terms of communication.

Thanks to the discoveries of Dr. Masaru Emoto in Japan, we now know that our thoughts and emotions can alter the molecular structure of water and even modify its vibratory field, leading us to understand the intimate way in which human beings are connected with the cosmos.

The question remains, How could the Mayans connect with what they called the Heart of the Universe without computers or cell phones or technology involved? Maybe it was because, at that time, on those starry nights that they watched so eagerly in complete silence, they came to perceive the music of the spheres and discovered that melody and mathematics, as Einstein claimed, are the key to unlocking the information of the entire universe.

Each time I think about this, I remember a radio de galena that my dad built for my sisters and me when we were children. My father was a telegrapher, and he was passionate about everything related to electricity and technology. He was witness to the telegraph revolutionizing communication throughout the world, since through its use for the first time, information could be obtained instantaneously in two remote places. Until the day he died, my dad tried to keep up with technology.

The radio de galena worked without any kind of batteries. It emerged at the end of the nineteenth century and became popular in the first decades of the twentieth century. Its first utility was to receive Morse code signals, but it was soon used for broadcasting. To build it, only three components were needed: a receiver, a tuner, and headphones.

I remember perfectly the feeling I had the first time I used the radio de galena. It was a small cardboard box that contained a spool made of copper wire inside. On the outside, it had another cable that needed to be tied to the water tap for a proper electrical ground and a knob to tune in a radio frequency signal. I spent several hours glued to the water tap with my headphones on. In my childhood mind, I thought that perhaps with some luck I could hear not only the programming of some radio station but the hidden messages of some star. Now I still think that the same thing is possible, but it is no longer a joke because today there are countless high-tech devices that capture the subtle ultrasonic frequency waves that plants, crystals, and stars emit.

What seems relevant to me is not the anecdote itself but the fact that all human beings love the idea of seeing beyond what our eyes can see and hearing sounds that our ears cannot perceive. We are bothered by the limitation that our body imposes on us. Perhaps that explains the vertiginous way in which technology has developed in the field of communication. Every time, we want to go further and further. Although I, on a personal level, sometimes feel like I'm being left behind. My twelve-year-old grandson knows how to handle my cell phone better than I do.

It's not that I'm trying to justify my cybernetic clumsiness, but you must understand that in 1950, when I was born, life on this planet was totally different. There were no cell phones, no computers, no microwave ovens, or anything like that. At my parents' house there wasn't even a phone. When I was very little, if we wanted to make a call, we had to go to my grandmother's house or go to Maruca and Agustín's pharmacy. In both places they also received calls with the difference that Maruca and Agustín charged us for the service and my grandmother did not.

This is how at home one could lead a quiet life without the phone ringing day and night and sit and listen to your favorite radio station or just enjoy reading. In those days you had time for yourself.

For example, since my dad didn't have to check his Facebook, or check his emails—or WhatsApp, much less tweet—when he came back from work, he just played with me and my sisters, so we spent whole afternoons recording stories on a reel recorder. Thanks to that, now you can hear my voice from when I was six years old playing Cinderella's fairy godmother.

When my daughter Sandra was a child, I also recorded her playing, singing, and narrating stories, something I can no longer do with my grandson because of my old tape recorder, which is the one I know how to handle: when it doesn't have batteries, the microphone fails. Even further, lately I've lost interest in buying electronics. What is the use of buying a camera that will be obsolete in a year? Or a computer whose programs will no longer be compatible with my old iPad? Or a printer for which I will no longer be able to get cartridges? Or that I collect movies in a format that is going to go out of style and then I won't even find the right players to watch them? What I lament the most is that now photographs are digital. Before you could keep the negative and have the photo printed whenever you wanted; now there are almost no laboratories for printing old photographs. I have digital photos of my grandson that I have not been able to send to print and I worry; I feel that the file may be deleted or lost or God knows what, including the danger that I myself will be the one to delete them. The speed in which one device emerges, then another and then another, and then another makes me dizzy, leaves me stunned.

Then unfortunately in the middle of so many emails, between so many text messages, we have confused the words, the whispers, and the silences and we continue to insist on seeing ourselves as separate beings that need devices to communicate with each other. We have forgotten how to enter into communication with the universe of which we are part. If we were able to remember the lilting rhythm of the resonant matrix that formed us, we would see beyond our eyes and realize that we are part of an indivisible whole, a totality that encompasses us all and makes us interconnected with her.

Don't you think it would be great to be able to connect with the umbilical heart of the universe and receive all the information we need for free? Wouldn't it be great if technology, instead of making us more and more dependent, started turning us into radio de galena that use the water in our bodies to receive information, into living iPads, into powerful satellite dishes that emit their permanent and pulsating song, into Eternal hard drives where digital images are never lost, and where you can listen to all the music that exists, including that of the spheres? Wouldn't it be incredible to put aside our condition as compulsive consumers of new technologies to become the thought, the light, the memory of the entire universe?

In the meantime, I highly recommend an application called Radio Garden. There you can listen to radio stations from all over the world! Every time I use it, I think about how much my dad would have liked it.

Karla Sánchez and Yásnaya Elena Aguilar Gil

Karla Sánchez *(b. 1992) is a Mexico City–born editor, literary critic, and translator. She studied Latin American literature at Universidad Iberoamericana. She's coeditor of* Letras libres, *a Mexican cultural magazine. "Language Carries a Political Burden" is a conversation with Mixe linguist, writer, and language activist* **Yásnaya Elena Aguilar Gil** *(b. 1981), author of six books, including* La sangre, la lengua y el apellido *and* Un nosotrxs sin estado. *This interview was originally published in Spanish in* Letras libres *in the spring of 2021 (issue 267). It was translated from the Spanish by Karla Sánchez.*

Language Carries a Political Burden

In Mexico, in addition to Spanish, more than 365 languages and dialects, grouped in 68 linguistic systems, are spoken. This means that for one year a different language can be spoken every day. That is how linguistically diverse Mexico is. However, most of the population is monolingual and unable to name the Indigenous languages spoken in the region. For Yásnaya Elena Aguilar Gil, writer and activist for linguistic diversity and linguistic rights of Indigenous communities, the Mexican State has used the Spanish language to erase the identity of Indigenous people and build the myth of mestizaje. Her book *Ää: Manifiestos sobre la diversidad lingüística* (Almadía, 2020) is a compendium of essays that reflect on the political dimensions of language.

In your essays and through your work as an activist, you have pointed to how the Indigenous communities and nations have been victims of the State, which has used the Spanish language as a weapon to erase

their identities. How has Spanish been used as a weapon and imposed
on the native languages' speakers and what are the consequences?

Not all over the world, but in Mexico, language has been the main
means of mestizaje by the State. In Canada, you know that someone is
Indigenous because there are a series of legal mechanisms that have to
do with the blood quota, that is to say that due to a certain "percentage"
of Indigenous blood in your lineage, you will be considered as such.
In the Mapuche case in Chile, for example, they trace the surname.
If you are a Mapuche in Chile and have a Mapuche surname, then
you are Mapuche. In Mexico, this is useless; my surname is Aguilar,
for example, and the blood quota would show that 80 percent of the
population is Indigenous. The criteria legally used by the State is that
of self-identification: if you declare yourself to be Indigenous, you are
Indigenous. On the ground, it doesn't work that way. If you ask how
many Indigenous people have died from COVID-19, the State will tell
you how many people who speak Indigenous languages have died from
it. So, in Mexico, what matters is the language.

According to historians, in 1820, between 65 and 70 percent of the
population spoke an Indigenous language. Spanish was a very minority
language, and the remaining 30 percent probably spoke an Indigenous
language in addition to Spanish or other languages. In two hundred
years, the majority of the Indigenous population was misidentified,
so now only 6.6 percent of us speak an Indigenous language, and only
11 percent of us identify ourselves as Indigenous.

What happened to that overwhelming majority? In many cases,
ethnocide, as in the north, where entire villages disappeared. There are
no more Pericúes, for example. [Historian and anthropologist] Federico
Navarrete points out how, at the end of the nineteenth century, there
were very few marriages and informal unions between white and
Indigenous people. What we now call a mestizo majority is a population
that is Indigenous but was de-indigenized by violently taking away
their language. That is why language is so important in the Mexican

case because the State has used it to build the myth of mestizaje. If a Purépecha married a Mixe, due to cultural pressure and racism they no longer transmitted their languages or their cultures; and after two generations, even if they married among Indigenous migrants, their descendants were already considered Mexicans from Mexico City, and then they no longer identified themselves as Purépecha or Mixe but with that new ideological liquefied product created by the State, which is being Mexican and which implies speaking Spanish. It is odd for someone to identify himself or herself as mestizo. Erasing mother tongues has been fundamental to the Mexican nationalist project and the creation of the Mexican identity. If the proportion of the early nineteenth century had been maintained and 70 percent of the Mexican population spoke an Indigenous language, the minority would not be the Indigenous population, and Spanish would not be the dominant language. We could have a scenario similar to India, with a multilingual or, at least, bilingual society. It is possible that perhaps the lingua franca of the State would be Nahuatl, that there would be a greater presence of Indigenous languages, and that the normal situation in Mexico City would be that people would speak Spanish and Nahuatl.

In an essay published in 2015, you already warned about linguicide in Mexico and the world. What is the current situation? Has there been progress or regression? In the case of Mixe, what is its status?

According to data from the 2015 census, the population aged five and over who speak an Indigenous language was 6.6 percent. Patricio Solís, a researcher at Colmex, calculated that the average rate of loss of intergenerational transmission—this means mothers who speak Indigenous languages and daughters who no longer do—is 40 percent. This data is brutal, much higher than I had considered a few years ago. If the rate of intergenerational transmission is not guaranteed, language dies.

This happens because of the ideological factor and the pressure of not
wanting to transmit it because Spanish is the most used language. This
is a false disjunction because, fortunately, the brain does not command
you: "Hey, do you want to learn English? So uninstall Spanish, and you
can do it." You can learn Mixe and Spanish without any problem. The
educational system is another problem. I know people who do not speak
English and send their children to bilingual schools to learn it. I also know
people who have passed on their language, but the State has taken it away
from them, for example, my little cousins. They spoke perfect Mixe before
they went to school, but once they went to school their language was
cut off. Although the teacher no longer forbids you to speak your mother
tongue or they do not beat you if you do it—I had to deal with that in my
childhood, in the schools—there is no teaching in Mixe. There is little
space for your language. I used to play with my cousins in my mother
tongue; now it is unusual to see children playing in Mixe.

**Some linguists believe that since languages are constantly evolving, it
is normal for many to die when they are no longer useful to speakers.
Why is it important to protect linguistic diversity?**

This position has several fallacies. One is that languages do not cease to
be useful but that they exist because they are useful. I cannot say to you,
"If you live in the United States, I do not want you to dream in Spanish
anymore because it is not useful." In other words, it is useful because
you dream in that language; it is useful to you because it is the vehicle of
your thinking. It exists because it is useful to a community of speakers.

Some people blame globalization for the loss of languages. If that
were the case, only eleven languages would be spoken because they have
the biggest presence on the internet. One would think that languages
with very few speakers would disappear because of globalization.
Yoruba is an Indigenous language spoken in Central Africa; it has four
times more speakers than Danish, but it is losing speakers much faster
than Danish. Why is Danish, despite having so few speakers, not at risk

of disappearing thanks to globalization? The difference is that there is a State, an educational and judicial system that uses Danish. Yoruba does not have that. It is a political issue. Along with the mother tongues, there have always been vehicular languages, as Latin was for many centuries, French has been, Nahuatl was for these territories. This does not mean that these languages are a threat to other languages, because there is clarity about where one is used and where another is used. It is not the need to communicate in the world that makes them threat languages. The fact that English exists as a lingua franca is wonderful, but that does not mean that I stop speaking my language, because my brain does not demand it; I can speak Spanish, English, Mixe, and more languages because the human brain allows you to learn many languages. The limit to learn languages has more to do with memory than capacity. So, it is not globalization, it's the violence of the nation-state.

Speaking different languages has many advantages at a cognitive and cultural level. But in the case of Mexico, a multilingual society became monolingual because of State intervention. While most of the Indigenous population is bilingual, most of the Spanish-speaking population is, unfortunately, monolingual.

In 2020, the Secretariat of Culture and the National Institute of Indigenous Peoples presented the "Los Pinos Declaration—Making a Decade of Action for Indigenous Languages," which aimed to incorporate Indigenous languages into public policies and guarantee bilingual, multilingual, and mother tongue education, among other measures. How do you rate the government's efforts to preserve, circulate, and promote the country's linguistic diversity? Do they consider the dynamics, traditions, and opinions of the speakers?

The history of linguistic legislation can be traced back to colonial times. But the most recent cases began with the change in Article 4 of the Constitution in 1992, which began to recognize the rights of Indigenous peoples. As a consequence of not making the reform of the

San Andrés Accords, there was a change in Article 2. And in 2003, the
General Law on the Linguistic Rights of Indigenous Peoples of Mexico
was enacted, with great impetus from the Indigenous movement. This
law equates Indigenous languages with Spanish as national languages.
It is a powerful law, and based on it, the National Institute of Indigenous
Languages was created in 2003. There is already a strong regulation
because Convention 169 of the International Labor Organization is
added to the constitutional block, which is helpful in judicial activism in
favor of Indigenous peoples. The issue, as always, is that there is a whole
legal framework, but there is an implementation gap.

The Los Pinos Declaration was framed within the International Year
of Indigenous Languages and a decade is being planned. The issue is that
the State has little understanding of what it must do to revitalize the
languages. To begin with, it has to make a diagnosis. There is no reliable
diagnosis because a language such as Ayapaneco, which has less than
five fluent speakers, who are very old, is not the same as my community
where the assemblies are in Mixe, and there is interaction with the
language or a monolingual people, such as Chinanteco. A regional
diagnosis is needed; an Indigenous community in the highlands and an
Indigenous Zapotec city like Juchitán are not in the same status. They
have different realities. It would be a good idea to form committees for
each language so the speakers can create intervention programs for their
communities.

The State must stop violating linguistic rights. The entire judicial
administration of interpreters and translators should be harmonized.
And further, we should recognize the autonomy we have de facto to
have our own educational systems. Can you imagine the State releasing
control of education? I do not see it. The State only calls for more prizes
for literature in Indigenous languages, that is, language as folklore
but not as a societal phenomenon, as Víctor Naguil, a Mapuche artist,
says. Language permeates everything; I love the dances and music of
Indigenous peoples, but, indeed, we are not dancing or making music all
the time, although the language is present at every moment. You wake

up and think in a language, you go and talk to your puppy in a language, and the fact that you dream in a language has a political charge behind it because it does not depend on you. It is a matter of linguistic territory, of cognitive territory.

Concerning legislation, in December 2020, Senator Martí Batres presented an initiative for Spanish and Indigenous languages to be considered official languages of Mexico. Why would this be counterproductive?

As I was saying before, we see that they legislate, but the problem is the implementation gap. There is already the General Law on the Linguistic Rights that says that Indigenous languages and Spanish are national languages, which is not the same as official. On the other hand, people like Gonzalo Celorio or Jaime Labastida have fought to make Spanish the official language of Mexico. It is not necessary to have official languages because we know that de facto Spanish is the language of the State administration, but if you give it that legal power, the violation of the linguistic rights of the speakers of Indigenous languages will be worse. In 2020, another change to Article 2 was passed to deputies to establish that Indigenous languages and Spanish are national languages—in other words, what was already in the General Law was approved to a constitutional level. But Senator Martí Batres came up with this initiative without consulting the speakers and representatives of the people.

What is the problem with them being official? First of all, it is not a law in favor of linguistic diversity or against linguistic discrimination. It does not take into account that in addition to the Indigenous languages, there are other languages of other communities that also need to have their linguistic rights protected, for example, the Mennonite population that speaks Plattdeutsch, the Roma population that speaks Romani, the inhabitants of Chipilo, where they speak Venetian. Also, it does not consider that in the future there may be greater migration movements that will generate other types of speech communities. Nor does it consider the Maya, Mexican, or Purépecha sign languages, which are in development. Therefore, it has a narrow vision of linguistic diversity that does not help. Anyone who supports linguistic diversity will not accept having official languages because it puts them in a box where you can choose only a few from among all.

One of the discussions surrounding Indigenous languages is whether or not it is pertinent to call their poetic and narrative productions literature. We see that it's increasingly common to find categories within national and international awards focused on Indigenous languages but somehow conceiving them as if they were all the same. In the first place, can we speak of literature in Indigenous languages? And if so, how can we promote it without reproducing these segregating practices?

Of course we can speak of literature in Indigenous languages because it exists and is written under the generic literary textual division of the West. There is also a valuable movement of women writers in Indigenous languages. What we need to do is to recognize this literature, to read it, and for the publishing industry to open up to reality and stop being monolingual.

Roman Jakobson already spoke of the poetic function, which is the capacity of all languages to generate a poetic corpus, an extraordinary speech that is not common. In many Indigenous nations, we can find this poetic function usually linked to rituals. But its supports are different; it is not always the paper or the printing press; it is the memory.

It is different: on the one hand, the Mixe people have built an intercultural bridge in terms of learning from Western genres and tradition and writing in their language; and on the other hand, the linguistic loss can generate a poeticide, so to speak, of these different traditions. For me, literature is a Western phenomenon with its rituals and traditions; and the shaping of the canon is mainly written. But the poetic function in the Indigenous traditions manifests itself in different ways; for example, in the Zapotec tradition of the Isthmus, they have their poetic generic division. It would be necessary to stop calling this "oral literature" or "popular lyric" because this reveals disdain. I do not believe in a binary division as literature and "everything else." In that "everything else," we can find diversity.

Much has been discussed about the role of the State in creating more spaces for Indigenous languages and respecting the linguistic rights of their speakers. But what are the responsibilities of citizens, academics, and media in this task?

First of all, it is not a matter of blame. The State made you learn the names of European rivers when you went to elementary school but not the names of the languages spoken in your region. There is systematic censorship on these issues because it is part of forgetting the Indigenous peoples. So, the first thing to do is educate yourself, because you cannot appreciate what you do not know or do not even know exists. We must be aware of linguistic diversity and find enjoyment in it, that you can memorize a song in Nahuatl, learn to read in Maya, and could speak Purépecha. Undoubtedly, learning an Indigenous language is very desirable but also joining the causes of Indigenous nations because there is discrimination and linguistic violence. As a Spanish-speaking person, you can also demand from the State that you have the right to enjoy that linguistic diversity and that it should give you those spaces.

Julia de Burgos

Julia de Burgos *(1914–1953) was born in Carolina, Puerto Rico, as Julia Constancia Burgos García and is one of the archipelago's most celebrated poets. The Afro-Boricua feminist was a fierce defender of human rights and a proponent of the colony's independence from the United States. She served as secretary general of the Daughters of Freedom in the Nationalist Party of Pedro Albizu Campos. The oldest of thirteen children, she was the first to attend and graduate from university, at nineteen years old. Among her most notable works are* Poemas exactos a mi misma, Poema en veinte surcos, Canción de la verdad sencilla, *and the posthumously published* El mar y tú. Cartas a Consuelo *is a collection of 136 letters from Julia to her sister Consuelo written between 1939 and 1953 and published in 2014 by Folium. This letter was translated from the Spanish by Sandra Guzmán.*

Jovellar 107, Apt. D
La Habana, Cuba
Wednesday, April 22, 1942

My dear Consuelito:

A few days ago, I received your letter, which arrived at a very auspicious moment because lately I've been feeling very sad and very distressed. Same as always. The tremendous conventional resistance of the latest representatives of a regime that is dying and that has been suffocating the spirit and truth for centuries and centuries. Juan has already and definitely settled that private matter, but our situation has not changed at all. I think it has worsened. Even though the obstacle is gone, will has not responded accordingly and consequently, there are no alternatives left. We have talked about everything and I have received tremendous blows that I never expected. My only refuge [. . .] is in learning. I have clung to it with profound fervor. Social attention, daughter of the fictional, [. . .] intellectual affirmation, daughter of self-worth. I will be a Dr., Consuelín, in all the careers that I am determined to finish. My diplomas will be tremendous slaps to my eternal persecutors. In them, in obtaining them, only I will be, because of my innate capacity, more noble and aristocratic than a static and hollow lineage.

In the last few days, I have taken various partial exams, all with outstanding evaluation. I feel very satisfied with myself and confident, more than ever. Within two years I will obtain my title, Lcda. in Diplomatic and Consular Law. I would like for you to also pursue that career. Try to bring, when you come in June, all the documents that you sent me properly legalized. Then you can take advantage and enroll here. I will tell you how you can take the exams. That way you could finish your degree at the same time you study. I have all the lectures, which are what we study here, so you won't spend anything on books. Think seriously about studying here and let me know so that I can pursue next steps. You can't waste this opportunity. Once you are a student here, you can, at any time, enroll in the study of Philosophy and Letters. I think that we're going to end up opening a law firm together, my Consuelito, and it will be called: Lcdas. Burgos y Burgos, notary lawyers.

Did you know that Neruda spent the entire day in my house and he ate a good asopao with us? Such a distinguished honor, as most of the elite in Cuba were fawning for his attention during the few days he was here.

He took a real liking to me. He told me he would be my mentor and that my next book had to be a definitive work in America and the world. He promised to help publish it. He thought my poem about the dead—which won an award—was great. He autographed all his books, even his latest on Bolivar, very luxurious. Now to something that will surprise you. He has a wifey. About twenty years older than him, who is thirty-eight. Almost as old as Juan's mother. He calls her Hormiguita and mamita. It's a romance from twenty years ago, when she was in her brimming second youth and he was possessed by adolescent fire. She is Argentinian, from a rich and aristocratic family. I will share more that will be of interest to you. She was Güiraldes's sister-in-law. Her sister was married to him. But here is the tragedy . . . She fell madly in love with her brother-in-law and for many years he was her great love. Then Güiraldes died, still in his youth, the most beautiful and coveted young man in Argentina, victim of an extremely rare and unknown disease. The woman, to forget, goes to India and her sister follows in secret, also to forget. Him, Güiraldes!

Near India, on an island named Java, there is a Chilean consul, a young lad and poet, Pablo. This Pablo, Neftalí Reyes, his birth name, married a Javanese woman. There is in this a situation something that I can only tell you in person. Argentina, Chile, and Java all merge and they meet again in Europe and America. The Javanese woman was his wife until the Spanish Civil War. Then the glacial ice melted. And today, Neruda with her at his side fishes seashells for Hormiguita. Neruda owns one of the most beautiful seashell collections in the world. I have told you a lot, right, Consuelín? I will tell you much more when you come. I think you can do a splendid job on Güiraldes, very innovative. You told me that he is adored in P.R. for his *Don Segundo sombra*. Did you know that this Don Segundo actually existed and when they buried Güiraldes in his village, he was the "señorito," Don Segundo presided over the procession. The name sounds like a novela, but it's real. Tell Mr. Colón. Read these paragraphs to him, because as a Spanish teacher, he will enjoy these details from the best source.

Consuelito, send me a photo of Iris, please. I don't know what she looks like. Make all your travel arrangements today. I think you will save money if you can travel on Vapor Borinquén to Sto. Domingo and from there to Santiago de Cuba. Stay in Santiago and I will wait there and we'll take a twenty-hour bus to La Habana. Book a roundtrip ticket. You will need a passport, start the process now. Tell Pepín to send me the picture. Did Carmen get married?

Kisses for everyone, and to you,

your Julita

PS: Tell me right away if you're coming in June. You have to bring a passport. Send me the divorce certificate. It's urgent.

Olga Orozco

Olga Orozco *(1920–1999) was a poet born in Toay, La Pampa, Argentina, to a Sicilian father and Argentinian mother.* She was part of the surrealist movement, Tercera Vanguardia, and Generación del 40, which also included Julio Cortázar and Adolfo Bioy Casares. She also wrote an astrology column that ran in *Clarín, the country's largest newspaper. Often in her poetry she explored death and solitude. Among her notable poetry collections are* Desde lejos, Las muertes, Museo salvaje, *and* Con esta boca, en este mundo. *"Olga Orozco" was translated from the Spanish by Anna Deeny Morales.*

Olga Orozco

I, Olga Orozco, from your heart I say to all that I die.

I loved solitude, the heroic persistence of all faith,

the idleness where strange animals and fantastical plants grow,

the shadow of a great time that passed among mysteries and among hallucinations,

and also the faint quiver of candles at nightfall.

My history is in my hands and in the hands with which others tattooed them.

From my stay here the magic and the rituals remain,

some dates worn out by the blow of a ruthless love,

the distant smoke cloud of the house where we never were,

and some gestures dispersed among the gestures of others who never knew me.

The rest of it still to be done in the forgetting,

the misfortune still toils in the face of she who looked for herself in me the same

as in a mirror of smiling meadows,
and the one who you will see strangely other:
my own likeness condemned to my form of this world.
She would have wanted to keep me in the disdain or in pride,
in a last instant fulminating like the ray,
not in the uncertain tomb where I go on raising my hoarse and wept voice among the whirlpools of your heart.
No. This death has no relief or grandeur.
I cannot be gazing at her for the first time for so long.
But I should go on dying until your death
because I am your witness before a deeper and darker law than changeable dreams,
over there, where we write the sentence:
"They have died already.
They had been chosen through punishment and pardon, through sky and through hell.
They are now a stain of humidity on the walls of the first room."

Gabriela Mistral

Gabriela Mistral *(1889–1957), born Lucila Godoy y Alcayaga in Vicuña, Chile, was the first Latin American writer to win a Nobel Prize in Literature, in 1945. She remains the only Latin American woman to be awarded the honor. She was a Chilean consul in Naples, Madrid, and Lisbon, and taught Spanish literature at Columbia University, Middlebury College, Vassar College, and the University of Puerto Rico. Among her notable works are* Sonetos de la muerte *(Sonnets of death),* Desolación *(Desolation),* Ternura, Tala *(Felling), and the posthumously published* Poema de Chile *(Poem of Chile). The love letter from Gabriela Mistral that follows was translated from the Spanish by Velma García-Gorena and appears in* Gabriela Mistral's Letters to Doris Dana, *edited by García-Gorena.*

Naples, Italy, August 1952

It's curious: I've picked up this letter from several days ago and now I'm feeling discouraged again. I wrote you a week ago about how that happens. Maybe it's because I've been eating very little. But I've just started eating out and now I only eat lunch here.

I have little news to report. I want to go to Sorrento to cheer myself up. Today I've had no desire to work. I picked up and put down *Poema de Chile*, which I was going to type so that I could at least look at it briefly, because I haven't been able to envision its final shape. Maybe it's because it was brutally hot this morning and now a very brisk, almost cold, wind is blowing.

You were telling me that perhaps you'd return earlier than planned. I hope so. But I don't believe it. New York, that city filled with excitement, captivates you. It's natural and good for you, but not for me. Doris, remember once in a while that I have no one, except for that kind girl who's here with me. Remember. But I'm not forcing you to come back and I also don't want you to return before you see the things you like and before you buy everything you need. Otherwise you'd regret it and you'd want to return in three months, which would hurt me, absolutely. The little kitten is in bed next to me; she sends her love. She was very sad when you left, extremely sad. She's a little better now. Come back for her sake too.

Now this errand: there's a Spanish-language newspaper in New York. It used to be pretty good. Tell me if it still exists and how much a six-month subscription costs.

What is it about you that makes people love you so much, wandering girl? That's not a good quality for those who love you. You find it annoying. You still haven't sent me the names of the people who are to receive your letters of recommendation. I don't know if you've been to Washington to talk to that woman who adores you and who detests me. Go see her; she's very intelligent and she's feeling bitter because her very handsome husband left her. She hates me because her rival was one of my students and she loved me very much. She no longer writes me. The perverted Coni must've said negative things about me just as she did with the head of the university.

The world, dear, is about winning and losing. I don't want to lose you, Doris Dana. That would demolish the little faith in humanity I have left. Give your little sister a hug for me. I love her very much, though I barely know her; I've only seen glimpses of her.

Doris, take all the money you need from our bank account. I'll say this again—*all the money* you need. Do it.

Don't forget that the first part of this letter is several days old. What've you been doing? What are you working on? Who's with you?

Are you in good spirits? Am I ever going to see you again? What are your plans for the future? Do you ever think about Naples? I need only you and the countryside. But I need those two things very much. I've realized that they're the only things that make me want to live when I have them and when I don't, I lose my will and want to die. When I left the Elqui Valley in

Chile, at the age of fourteen, I think, I became a kind of sleepwalker. There, in my hometown, I was thrown out of school for being mentally retarded and as I left, my schoolmates threw rocks at me. I walked across the plaza with a bloodied head. I'm experiencing something like that *somnambulism* now. It's not anguish, just a sensation of absence from the world; it's worse than the incidents you've witnessed. All I want to do is sleep. And I want to wake up only when you've returned.

Your Gabriela

Berichá

Berichá (1945–2011) was an U'wa teacher, Indigenous activist, and writer born in Cubará, Boyacá, Colombia, in the old Barrosa Baja region. At the age of nine, missionaries renamed her Esperanza Aguablanca. She studied philology and languages at Universidad Libre de Cúcuta. She also studied aboriginal languages and ethnolinguistics at Universidad de los Andes. In 1993, she received the Premio Cafam a la Mujer. "This Is How I Learned to Live" ("Así fue como empecé a vivir") is a fragment of Tengo los pies en la cabeza *(My feet are on my head), the first memoir by an U'wa writer, detailing her family's story and the violent colonization of the U'wa Nation by Spanish settlers and Christian missionaries in Colombia. It is translated from the Spanish by Sandra Guzmán.*

This Is How I Learned to Live

My name is Berichá. I am an U'wa Indigenous woman from the Barrosa region that is close to the San Luis del Chuscal mission at the top of Cubará, Boyacá. My parents were spiritual leaders responsible for their community's rites and ceremonies. I was born without legs. However, I have my feet on top of my head because I have been able to develop my intelligence and that has helped me move forward in life, defend myself, and be of service to my people. [*Berichá's personal diary*]

MY NAME IN MY MOTHER tongue is Berichá. My father was named Drishbára and my mother Surabara. Her nickname was Rimchará. My father came from one of the wisest uejená families and was responsible for some of the most important social and religious rites of the community.* It was the same with my mother, who also was responsible for religious functions. She learned from her parents all the necessary scientific knowledge to be able to execute her spiritual duties.

My father had direct communication with our Gods (Rasina); he cured all kinds of illnesses, even the most difficult. He had the power to calm wild animals, ghosts, and the fury of Mother Nature, such as storms, hard rains, landslides, and other natural events that disturb the tranquility of communities.

My mother also acquired this inheritance when she was very young from her parents. From them she learned all the necessary scientific knowledge to be able to defend herself in life and to help those who needed her wisdom.

I was born in the old Barrosa Baja; I was the sixth child, and I am the only one of their children who survived; all my siblings died from sicknesses, and my mom was bored by that, so much so that when her last nine-year-old daughter died, she was going to live with the whites to Santa Librada but returned after my father pleaded and insisted.

When my mother was pregnant with me, she fell ill: her right breast became engorged and her arm paralyzed. The inflammation broke through my father's prayers and soplos, and she got better and better, but her arm was left incapacitated. It does not work well; she can only move it a little bit; she has better use of her left arm. Mother tells me that her sickness happened because she ate a fish from the Cobaria River that was not properly purified and that's the reason why I was born with a physical defect.

When I was born, I did not have the same luck as other babies who are born with birth defects who are abandoned in the jungle or decapitated. My father recognized that my defect was a result of the reasons I stated above and yet they did not harm me. Since their other children did not survive, they preferred to keep me. My parents asked that I not be harmed because if I were destined not to live, I would die on my own,

---

* Uejená: shaman, spiritual leader.

and if I did not die, at least I would keep them company. Besides, I was able to eat with my own hands.

That is how my life began; they loved me very much. My father died when I was still very young, perhaps I was one. When he was going to die, he wanted to take me with him, but my mother pleaded with him to let me live because she needed me to keep her company, since I was the only one of her children that was left; besides, she told him he already had a lot of company since all the other children were dead.

We were left alone; my mother would often go live with her brothers, with me, for a while, and in different places, sometimes in Aguablanca, where we have relatives. Often, we were alone. My mother walked alone through the forest with me, she talked to me, and I remember these conversations well. She also spoke to the guardians of the mountains and animals, asking for them to fall into traps she set. She spoke words so that we would not encounter tigers or ghosts.

Sometimes we walked in the rain during winter thunderstorms. One time we had to pass alone through a raging brook in Aguablanca that was swollen as a result of strong storms. Besides our family, no one loved us; my mother's brothers gave us salt, game, and clothing; they gave me shirts and that is how I clothed myself. I walked on four legs. My mother would take me to weed with her and I used an old knife and that is how I was able to help her.

Slowly I grew and I became too heavy for mother, she carried me with great difficulty when we walked to faraway places; I was an obstacle for her, and she did not know what to do; I was around seven or eight years old.

Accidentally, during this time several missionaries arrived, and they would scour the communities Bocota, Cobaria, Tegría, and Aguablanca; they arrived in Aguablanca to the kareka sheraka and stayed there and bought a pig.* This news landed in my mother's ears; I remember that we were in a ranch near the Aguablanca brook, and she was going to see some whites that were named fathers and sisters; she left me alone and went with her niece.

---

* Kareka sheraka: another term, like uejená, for a shaman leader.

The nun tells the story that mother would come near and very shyly, hiding behind banana trees, like wanting something; when the nuns called an interpreter to speak with her, and asked what she wanted, Mom told them she wanted them to receive a daughter who was crippled.

Instantly they said yes: she should bring me first thing in the morning, but my mother did not share the news with her brothers, and they did not allow her to leave.

Later, the sheraka uejená of Aguablanca notified us that the monsignor was waiting for us in Santa Librada and that if we did not go, we would be taken by force. Mother became frightened that this might happen and convinced a nephew and we parted for Santa Librada. We arrived at a neighbor's home near the mission. The next day they went to alert the nuns that we were there. They came for us and I was carried in a bag.

When we arrived, the first thing they did was feed us; I remember it was rice and a little piece of bone. I thought the word "rice" sounded strange; they also gave us milk, which I did not like; I vomited it. Then they took us to bathe, clothed us, and brought us to a place where other young girls were housed. They put us to work disentangling threads.

I remember well, thinking that the bath they made us take was to purify us to be able to enter a new life among the whites. We thought that all the white women were our second mothers and that all the white men were our second fathers. I also thought that they had glorious bodies that had no bodily needs. We ignored many things.

Mother would tell me that we had entered a new life. When the priest spoke at mass and blessed with the Holy Sacrament, I thought that it was with the goal of eating food the next day; that is, I thought that everything the priest did was the same as the uejená in our community who purified all the food. I thought it was like this with every rite.

I remember that after they placed me in school, they took my mother to work in the pasture at the mission's cattle ranch. She had to work with other señoras to earn coins.

I ENTERED SCHOOL AND THERE "learned" everything. Like parrots who don't understand what they are saying, I repeated with the teacher the prayers, lessons, and readings. During religious instruction when they made us repeat "our first parents were Adam and Eve," I thought that they were referring to the corn because in the U'wa language "eba" means "maize." Later, the nuns would make me weave their socks or make brooms with other young U'wa girls. That was the way I spent many years until almost finishing elementary school. That was in 1957. I was twelve years old, and I sewed a robe with weavings that were very beautiful, and the monsignor absolutely loved it.

From 1961 to 1963, I spent the time knitting socks for the priests and nuns, repairing their clothing, as well as for the workers and other young men. The nuns taught me how to embroider scarves and cut dresses.

In 1964, when I was nineteen years old, Monsignor García named me a professor in the school at Cobaria. I had no knowledge nor experience teaching, so I only taught numbers and vowels. White students, the daughters of settlers, were taught in books how to add, subtract, divide, and learn their biblical studies. Indigenous girls were only taught vowels and numbers. I did not have a clock to look at the time and started classes when the girls arrived and ended when they indicated it was noon.

During that time school was mandatory and all the children had to attend and if they did not, a police inspector would force them. That is why that year there were thirty young women enrolled in the school. I taught girls from seven years old to twenty and twenty-four years old. The young men were taught by a male teacher.

Even though I was so young, younger than my students, things went well for me in Cobaria. My students loved me very much. When they came down to Cauca they brought me avocado, bagala, maize, and bananas. At first, I did not talk a lot; I was quiet because I did not know the Cobaria dialect. With time, I learned to speak it a little, even if it was only to communicate during class.

Until 1968, I was a researcher for the nun María Elena Márquez; sometimes I taught the nun U'wa. In 1970, after the death Monsignor García, I matriculated to finish school, but I only studied for three months because Sister María Elena Márquez called us to travel to Medellín so that she could finish an investigation about the U'wa language and customs. She had free time because she was recuperating from an accident and wanted to take advantage of that moment. She took me to Medellín, accompanied by Mother, and we were there three years, until she published a catechism of Father Astete and the Gospel of Saint Mark in the U'wa language. I've yet to see this publication.

✦ ✦ ✦

Our ancestors lived in freedom and peace when the unexpected happened: strange people entered our lands. Many of our grandfathers and my grandfathers were imprisoned. The women were taken forcibly and married off while their husbands were killed. Many U'wa groups were wiped out due to epidemics that the colonizers brought with them; others emigrated to different U'wa communities.

One of the most affected regions touched by the violence was Aguablanca. There we have nine communities that have disappeared, among them the Támara-kamarúa. Támara was the cradle of our protectors, the nest, and seat of the most outstanding science teachers; it was there where the first seeds of U'wa culture were planted and learned. These roots extended to nearby communities and that is how the U'wa culture sprouted.

In Támara, Burará, Kuruta, Runía, Sisiara, Bokuatayá, and Sibá there are great mountains and historic places that make up the history of the U'wa nation. Other disrespected sacred sites were the hunting and fishing territories. The Tunebos knew how to fish with barbasco and without the government laws.*

Even though these were sacred sites, colonizers did not respect them. There, where our roots and history rests, in our ancestral and sacred lands, day after day settlers rounded up Indigenous U'wa, forcing them to

---

* "Barbasco" is a term used for a variety of Amazonian plants that release toxins and paralyze fish.

leave their lands, huts, and plots. Those who refused to vacate their land where forcibly removed and their ranches burned; others were beaten and injured, women and girls raped, animals killed and eaten. Others were forced to work on their farms, and if they did not, the results of the threats were already known; they burned their ranches so that they would vacate those lands. That is why they left to find refuge in other communities, or they integrated by force, as epidemics brought by settlers—among these, smallpox—were fatal to the U'wa.

Settlers took the U'wa lands of Tuna, Ukuara Derrumbada, Kuruta Mojicones, Chitua Mundo Nuevo, Chuanica Akará Río Ratón, Tabuta el Mesón, and successively, they cornered their owners, making life impossible for them to get them out permanently.

We have another issue with Aguablanca. This group is located between the La Herramienta and Los Cristales mountain ranges—in our mother tongue, Risuaiará y Burkuyika. Of those Indigenous people who lived on the other side of the Rikará brook toward the east, some emigrated and others died; actually, U'wa of Aguablanca live now only on the west side of the Rikará brook.

But the story of colonization of our lands was prognosticated by our wisest uejená ancestors before they died. They announced that the real culture was going to mix with a new science invented by new uejená. This new science would be weaker and less capable of solving any new problems. There would be no freedom.

They prophesied that the ancient people that survived would be forcibly subjected to live in another, new culture with battles and hatred against each other. All the U'wa groups would be subjected to live in that culture. The ancient uejená declared: "The U'wa People will be in the middle of the ocean and animals of the water will eat many." That interpretation tells us that all the U'wa will be in the middle of the rioá (whites); many will die by the hands of those whites; they will kill them.

Just as our ancients declared, the whites came and they brought a different culture, another way to live, speak, govern, and work. The rioá did not understand our culture and society because they were ambitious—they wanted to have a lot of land, they fought to be rich, they killed for money, and they killed us; they all wanted to rule over us. They were divided, and because they came so hungry for riches, they took advantage of the U'wa because we are not warriors, we are peaceful.

The whites brought to the U'wa addictions, division within our community; we lost lands and our cultural values. Today there is no respect for the elder uejená, no respect for traditional authorities; we don't hunt or fish because the rioá brought a way to deplete them. Flora and fauna are extinct. Even the U'wa have contributed to exterminating resources because the whites have shown us comfort.

With colonization the uejená abandoned sacred rites and ceremonies, and that is why U'wa slowly changed to another culture, which coincided with the gradual death of the uejená, who continued their wisdom without transmitting it to their successors; from there it was free interpretation of many of these rites and ceremonies.

Claribel Alegría

Claribel Alegría *(1924–2018) was born in Estelí, Nicaragua, but grew up in El Salvador. Her mother was Salvadorean and her father was a Nicaraguan exile. She was a poet, novelist, essayist, and journalist, and a major voice in Central American literature. She received the 2006 Neustadt International Prize for Literature, the Chevalier des Arts et des Lettres from the French Government in 2010, and the Spanish Reina Sofia Award in 2017 shortly before her death. "Flowers from the Volcano" ("Flores del Volcán") is from an elegiac collection of poems of the same title, dedicated to El Salvador. It was translated from the Spanish by Carolyn Forché.*

Flowers from the Volcano

Fourteen volcanoes rise
in my remembered country
in my mythical country.
Fourteen volcanoes of foliage and stone
where strange clouds hold back
the screech of a homeless bird.
Who said that my country was green?
It is more red, more gray, more violent:
Izalco roars, taking more lives.
Eternal Chac Mool collects blood,
the gray orphans
the volcano spitting bright lava
and the dead guerrillero
and the thousand betrayed faces,

the children who are watching
so they can tell of it.
Not one kingdom was left us.
One by one they fell
through all the Americas.
Steel rang in palaces,
in the streets,
in the forests
and the centaurs sacked the temple.
Gold disappeared and continues
to disappear on yanqui ships,
the golden coffee mixed with blood.
The priest flees screaming
in the middle of the night
he calls his followers
and they open the guerrillero's chest
so as to offer the Chac
his smoking heart.
In Izalco no one believes
that Tláloc is dead
despite television,
refrigerators,
Toyotas.
The cycle is closing,
strange the volcano's silence
since it last drew breath.
Central America trembled,
Managua collapsed.
In Guatemala the earth sank
Hurricane Fifi flattened Honduras.
They say the yanquis turned it away,
that it was moving toward Florida
and they forced it back.

The golden coffee is unloaded
in New York where
they roast it, grind it
can it and give it a price.
Siete de Junio
noche fatal
bailando el tango
la capital.
From the shadowed terraces
San Salvador's volcano rises.
Two-story mansions
protected by walls
four meters high
march up its flanks
each with railings and gardens,
roses from England
and dwarf araucarias,
Uruguayan pines.
Farther up, in the crater
within the crater's walls
live peasant families
who cultivate flowers
their children can sell.
The cycle is closing,
Cuscatlecan flowers
thrive in volcanic ash,
they grow strong, tall, brilliant.
The volcano's children
flow down like lava
with their bouquets of flowers,
like roots they meander
like rivers the cycle is closing.
The owners of two-story houses

protected from thieves by walls
peer from their balconies
and they see the red waves descending
and they drown their fears in whiskey.
They are only children in rags
with flowers from the volcano,
with Jacintos and Pascuas and Mulatas
but the wave is swelling,
today's Chac Mool still wants blood,
the cycle is closing,
Tláloc is not dead.

COSMIC
MOON

This energy is cleansing and helps
dissolve negative energies and illnesses.

Marigloria Palma

Marigloria Palma *(1917–1994) was born in Canóvanas, Puerto Rico, as Gloria María Magán y Ferrer. She was a multimedia artist—poet, novelist, playwright, and visual artist—who published more than fourteen books, all of which are out of print. Among them are* Agua suelta, Muestras del folklore Puertorriqueño, *the novel* Viento salado, *and the short story collection* Cuentos de la abeja encinta. *"Composition of a Tear" and "San Juan and Her Parrots" were translated from the Spanish by Carina del Valle Schorske and are from Palma's poetry collection* La noche y otras flores eléctricas *(The Night and Other Electric Flowers).*

Composition of a Tear

With a pair of scissors I cut
the fluent clarity of your tear,
miniature ocean of bitter tides,
bubble of salt.
    I can see myself inside it.
Its photographic lens strips me bare.
It drops away from you and rolls on waves of air.
I see my finest strand of hair dive down to you like the swallows
that chain the darkness to your mouth of coupled fish.
Contraction of light, fiat lux, deluge.
    Your tear is my mirror.
I look at the torn paper throat,
the silent breasts like still bells,
the nakedness of the body, disoriented

vein that cannot mend its twenty crossings.
I am and am not in the fogged glass of its circumference,
peopled planet of your orbit, your purified tear.
You cry: an alphabet in the sticky strategems of sex.

    This tear of yours, this weeping wept dry,
this human diamond, pure chemical formula
that the wind must come to drink with its horn of pearl.
I'm doubled between the fleeting reflections
of your tears' two tracks, my cry burning with lemons,
my endless yawn, and my umbrella.
Oh, but that other one! That other one made with the groan
of wild violets, that other one, ignored: my protest.

    I curse your tear.

San Juan and Her Parrots

1.

    The parrots are coming now.
They come from the White House, the seashore.
They're great green bells, a silver blast,
sparkling chatter, a discourse of algaes.

    They fly in bouquets like the happy tangles
of fat angels in religious tapestries,
shattering morning's front of silence
and rending the lace of the aureal tunic.

    San Juan is a village in tableau
with its close-cropped hill and distant blues,
thistles, lilies, parrots, a little donkey,
a little boy, and a castle burning
under the sun's slingshot rage.

    Let's see: we'll start over.
The city rises in her finely spun gown of brightness
and fastens her slippers, she hums a crystal song,

and she sees all the eyes peering out from the
frames of the multiplying windows.
The alphabet flies circles around her forehead.
    Parrots, the sweetest parrots! And they're ours!

2.
    Wake up, love—I've dreamed
the parrots are coming with their green alphabet
to write lyrics for our murmuring.
They're coming from the White House, from its deep gardens.
    Love I don't know
the free green wings of parrots
pass through your lost face, my found voice,
and the sky is hope's drifting scrawl.
    It's dawn.
The city stands steep on her stone toes
to welcome the hazy tulip of morning light.
Inside the corset of her fortress, San Juan
slides bright stockings over ancient feet.
    My love, my never-nothing.
You refuse the sheet's feathered caress.
The city is strained honey. The parrots beam
our buried cry through blue jaws.
    Leap, love, breathe; I know your nonbeing
and so it dies.

Quiara Alegría Hudes

Quiara Alegría Hudes *(b. 1977) was born in Philadelphia, Pennsylva-nia. She is a lyricist, essayist, and playwright and is the author of six plays, including the Pulitzer Prize finalist* Elliot, a Soldier's Fugue *and* Water by the Spoonful, *which won a Pulitzer Prize in 2007. She wrote the book for the musical* In the Heights *and the screenplay for the film adaptation. Her memoir,* My Broken Language, *explores her childhood in Philadelphia growing up the daughter of a Puerto Rican santera mother and an atheist Jewish father in the age of crack and AIDS in America.*

Anyone Know a Down Barrio Architect?

Mami, primas, hermanas,

Today, slumped over my laptop with a pain patch wrapped around my neck and the morning's ibuprofen wearing off, an architectural vision came to me. I saw the nave of a huge library stretching above and around me. Sunlight flooded its stacks, revealing book spines as varied as our family's skin tones.

Its extensive religious texts were in Taino, Yoruba, Spanish, English, Spanglish, and Barrio. Some prayer books had pages made outta dried herbs, bound together with Vicks VapoRub.

One wing featured shelves full of sand. Grains from Luquillo Beach in Arecibo spilled into grains from Badagry, Nigeria. The Jersey Shore had been shelved alongside Orlando, and the card catalogue was filled with Orchard Beach.

The cookbook collection was a few sad-ass volumes because recipes for arroz no sirven pa na. Luckily, that room's walls whispered hush-hush cooking tips.

The reference room housed a catalogue of coos and babbles from Abuela's lullabies. Etymologists had traced each nonsense syllable to its actual Yoruba or Taino root word.

The portrait wing featured bulumshisslife-size renderings of Perez women stretching back generations, all wearing clothes they felt fly in.

Before entering the genealogy department, an antechamber offered resources for matching nicknames with birth certificates. Because if you tryna do that family tree, you'll need Yuya's, Ñana's, Biche's, and Buckwheat's legal names.

The Hall of Accents was a symphony of dropped s's and r's turned into l's and phrases like "vamo a lonchear en McDonald's."

The listening library was a trove of dubbed Ramito tapes, batá CDs, Fania 8-tracks, and jukeboxes salvaged from barrio bars. Not a chair in sight, though. You had to stand to activate the collection. Dance to raise the volume. And no headphones. Music was only heard communally here.

The funeral card archive had no flooring. Instead, a field of bodega carnations grew. Among the funeral cards I found:

M.—AIDS, 1989.

V.—AIDS, 1990.

T.—AIDS, 1993.

ML.—Aneurysm, 1993.

EB.—Hep C from a botched transfusion, 2007.

There was even a card for Bisabuela Baldomera's left breast, which got blown off in an armed battle for Puerto Rican independencia.

I was wandering around like I'd snuck into heaven. But the Perez girls researching book reports and history fair projects were like, *ain't everyone surrounded by they own history?* One straight-up told me, "Tranqui, Quiara. This shit's normal AF."

Every inch of the library described us. Beneath its cathedral roof, no incorrect words attached to us, because we had a vocabulary made of our own lives.

Then, it was gone.

Here I am, back at my desk. A half-faded pain patch and a few ibuprofens remind me of years spent hunched over my laptop. I'm back to the language I know best—English—even if it's the one least suited to describe us. Ah well. I'm no architect, but maybe a future Perez girl will become one and build that library of us. In the meantime, I'll unpeel a fresh pain patch, inhale eau de Tiger Balm, and get back to my writing. Here I go.

Yolanda Arroyo Pizarro

Yolanda Arroyo Pizarro *(b. 1970) was born in Guaynabo, Puerto Rico, and is an award-winning Afro lesbian novelist, short story writer, essayist, and feminist activist. She explores issues of race, gender, and sexual identity in her combative, nonconformist creative works. She is the director of the Department of Afro–Puerto Rican Studies, Cátedra de Mujeres Negras Ancestrales, a performative project of creative writing based in San Juan. Her book* Las Negras *won the PEN Club Puerto Rico National Short Story Award in 2013. She also received the PEN Club Puerto Rico National Short Story Award in 2021 and an Instituto de Literatura Puertorriqueña National Creative Award in 2021 for her book* Calle de la resistencia. *She has been translated into German, French, Italian, English, Portuguese, and Hungarian. "Mûlatresse" was translated from the Spanish by Layla Benitez-James and Lawrence Schimel.*

Mûlatresse

1.

"Señora, the baptism of infants is illegal and goes against our constitution. Even the Organization of United Interstellar Nations has declared itself against it. This is not just a question of this country, but a global security issue. Sorry, but I am unable to help you."

I returned her Universal Identity Card and tried not to make direct eye contact with the woman who could have easily been 120 years old. I didn't want to use her document to calculate her date of birth. I covered it intentionally, in order to exercise my organic mathematical agility. I enjoy spotting observable qualitative evaluations. On her right arm she had the "umbilical tattoo," as we call the mandatory marking each citizen of Earth must get when they reach the age of one century. From her gestures and the timbre of her voice, I suspected she must have at least two more decades above her centennial mark (more or less).

"But they said you'd be able to help me," she insisted.

"I have already explained that I cannot. You must free up this space for the next person in line. I cannot help you. What you are requesting is illegal."

At the same time, still without looking at her, I passed her a slip of contraband paper, hoping she'd understand the message. She seemed to because she calmed down, pocketed the paper, and left the building.

"Next."

2.

It's Tuesday. Usually, the government business that citizens attempt on Tuesdays are not as hurried as those on Mondays or Fridays. But something was going on this Tuesday, and I had a feeling my day would end badly. I have held this job as a Continental Government Officer for the past fifty years. I've lived through changes, new and old governments, the ancient repeals, impending obsolescence, the era of Governance by Artificial Intelligence, and finally this current cycle of Tenth Level Consciousness. Despite all this, humanity continues to fall behind cyclically every half a decade. It's exhausting. They advance then fall behind. Again and again. I've been on the brink of requesting euthanasia termination during more than one desperate moment, but I always change my mind in the end. Because in the end I always discover something interesting that keeps me wanting to return for nostalgia's sake, wanting to investigate more about existence on this plane. Some curiosity which intrigues me. And although it's already been confirmed that there are other planes (quantum thanatological psychology has discovered five so far), I am melancholic, and continue to be obsessed by this first level. I don't want it to disappear for me.

3.

"Next."

"Hello, Officer. I'd like to file a New Gender Certificate."

I sighed. The human standing before me was too young. She couldn't even be seventy yet. I glanced at her right arm, which bore no tattooed marking.

"The minimum age requirement to obtain a New Gender Certificate is 110."

"But there are exceptions."

"You may show us yours."

She handed over a virtual paper document signed by a renowned geneticist. I read it for a while, then I got bored.

"This does not prove anything," I said.

She handed over another virtual paper document, this one signed by a renowned psychiatrist. I also gave it a read.

"I understand. But you are only twenty-five years away from your Automatic Gender Change. Why in such a rush?"

"I am in a rush. Besides, that's none of your concern."

There was an uncomfortable silence, and the human apologized.

"I'm sorry."

"You know perfectly well that it is illegal to treat a Continental Government Official in this manner."

"I know, Officer. Forgive me. Please don't fine me. What little money I have saved is for my transition. If you fine me, I won't be able to complete it, and I can't live like this anymore."

"So why do you not apply for a termination?"

The human glared at me but resigned herself and kept quiet.

"You have used the word 'money,'" I said at last.

"Pardon me, Officer, I meant to say alphacoins."

"The money you refer to—paper money—stopped being used decades ago. Continuing to circulate it is a jailable offense."

"Excuse me, Officer, it was a slip of the tongue. I don't circulate money in paper currency."

I took her virtual document and issued her the stamps authorizing her to continue with the process.

"Thank you, Officer. You're an . . ." She stopped abruptly.

I smiled immediately.

"Don't say 'angel.' The use of symbols of religious idolatry and all associated vocabulary was eradicated at the Twelfth Terrestrial Council in 2079."

"I know, Officer. I was going to say . . . you're a great help."

"Of course."

The human left. She looked back several times as she moved away. I closed down my government paperwork cubicle and went to the park for my break. I saw her again there. She was buying ice cream at a kiosk and had changed her holographic image. Now her clothing was no longer feminine; she wore a suit and tie of a twentieth-century male. I watched her sit on one of the benches. She took out a mirror and began brushing her face with digital makeup, sketching a mustache and beard that then turned into hair.

I also bought an ice cream.

4.

"I want to apply for a termination."

I had to look at her for a long time. She's my final citizen of the day. An interminable Tuesday that ends like this . . . with a termination request.

"I have not filed a euthanasia termination request in many years."

She doesn't answer. I look at her right arm. Her centennial tattoo has two markings. Two marks means two centuries. Her skin is dark and shiny. Her hair is worn in a short Afro. Her body mass has been well cared for. She has no visible wrinkles or surgical scars, no wounds or low-quality mechanical limbs. Everything seems to be wrapped in skin. Everything seems to be moisturized in mineral and plant collagen. Everything seems to be in optimal condition.

"Very well. I see you've chosen the option to design your own final memory before you close your eyes for the last time."

"That's correct."

"Have you brought the virtual plans to initiate the Upload from here?"

"I have them here, Officer."

Her hand accidentally touches mine. A barely perceptible shock unsettles me.

"I see you have given your virtual blueprint a title."

"That's right. I've thought of everything. I gave it a memorable name."

"*Mûlatresse.*"

"Yes, Officer."

She also hands over her Universal Identity Card, which has a modified expiration date.

"According to this, your termination is in three days."

"Yes."

"I have not filed a euthanasia termination request in many years."

I didn't notice the glitch. But the human did. That repetition alerted her that something was amiss. And the change in her pulse alerted me that something was wrong. We exchanged a worried look, and for the first time in four hundred and twenty-nine years I said: "Excuse me."

The apology unsettled us even more. The human cleared her throat. Her chest rose and fell intermittently. My eyes began to blink rapidly, and in response, she reached out with her tattooed arm and touched my cheek.

"Terminations are difficult for everyone," she said, running a nervous tongue over her lips.

I did not know that my operating system was going to be altered in that manner. In my mental database, I found the scenario file with a script to follow in case I needed a dialogue for a human termination. And now that I finally had one in front of my eyes, after so much time had passed without anyone wanting to die, I was breaking out in a *malfunction*.

I immediately streamlined the documentation. I handed her the virtual papers, the necessary validation stamps, the signatures of the funeral supervisors related to the request, the assignment of a forensic doctor to confirm the death, and a certificate of participation congratulating the human for her terrestrial service. She had been a teacher for almost fifty years, a singer and songwriter for thirty-four cycles, and an Afrocentric writer for the last few decades. She had six children during her first reproductive generation, and three during her second. She was married five times to both women and men. During her last ceremony she had entered into nuptials with two women pianists exiled from Mars. I took a glance at the life status of her relatives, and in each case, I found the word "termination." Apparently, this human was alone in the galaxy.

"You are correct, terminations are difficult for everyone," I was the one to say it now. But before I apologized for another unnecessary repetition, I intercepted the logarithm of the conversation with a forced *Mute*.

She thanked me. She put the documents in her portfolio and walked towards the door. Once there, she turned and came back to me.

"May I offer an invitation for dinner tonight?"

"It's illegal for an officer to . . ." I started to say. But I managed to filter another forced *Mute* before finishing the sentence.

She insisted, "May I invite you to dinner tonight, please? Look, I'm going to die in seventy-two hours."

Disobedience algorithm activated. Rebellion dialogue initialized. Legitimate behavior blocker program on. Contraband, defiance, and pleasure program initiating download from the darknet. Open lips and say:

"Of course."

The human smiles and the *glitch* returns. "Your mouth," I add.

The human smiles even wider.

"I'll see you at ten."

5.

We had dinner. The dinner ritual consists of me accompanying the human while I observe her. Over the years I have learned to imitate certain gestures, fake expressions, invent ways of chewing air. While we talk, I carry out a search of all the images of her face in the public domain and enjoy them one by one without her noticing. Then we walk into the evening, naming the stars and the baptized exoplanets we knew.

After the walk, we entered a Sunset Museum to enjoy the sunset that we'd missed that day.

As our star is about to disappear, and darkness creeps in, the human asks, "May I touch your face again?"

I say yes. She touches me. Or does she caress me?

"Would you do something for me?"

My operating system lags in running the program of all the possible scenarios I might encounter if I agree. In the end, I answer affirmatively.

"I need you to come with me to my house, undress me, place me on the funeral platform, and help me visualize a preview of the virtual blueprint."

"It's illegal to . . ." Forced *Mute*. Forced *Mute*. Forced *Mute*. Silence.

I've never felt such curiosity. I want to return to the nostalgia. I want to investigate more about existence on this plane, about this human, about my reactions towards her. Never before have I felt such intrigue.

6.

I undress her. I place her on the funeral platform. I invent *firewalls* so that the impending event is undetectable. Just the human and me. Only us. I open the *Mûlatresse* design sequence on the screen, and my human, before closing her eyes, takes my hand.

7.

Perhaps it all boils down to this. This hunger I'm not able to experience in a biological way that nevertheless takes over my entire level of consciousness. This desire I suddenly experience, a kind of *imprinting*. Perhaps this breathlessness means connecting, means remaining for a longer time on this plane, on this level. A new hungering need. An old hunger.

On the screen, my human turns into Etawa. Her birth took place in 1772. She runs through the African jungle, trying not to be kidnapped. She kills three of her kidnappers, but another seven survive and chain her. They keep her in captivity for eight months. They baptize her in the Catholic faith. They change her name: Soledad. They put her on a ship that sails the high seas for one hundred and thirty days.

The virtual plane runs almost four hours of lucid dreaming. I stay next to Etawa, caressing her hand, her neck, her shoulders. When the blueprint is done, she stops breathing for a few minutes. Then she gasps and opens her eyes.

"You're enchanting," she tells me, and masturbates before me.

8.

I don't go to work on Wednesday or Thursday. I remain by her side. I accompany her in the ritual of breakfast, then of lunch, of showering, of intercourse assisted by a vibrating onyx dildo. I accompany her in the rituals of flowers in the garden, of the telescope, of the ocean's waves, of crafting alcoholic cocktails. She teaches me to invent a mouth to kiss her tongue, her teeth, and her pubis with. We pirate a program that allows me to imitate an orgasm. In the middle of faking it and during our third session, I trigger a real one. But I don't even know how and trying to re-create it several other times without success induces tears, and I thank her.

In the midst of all our human rituals, we pause and restart the *Mûlatresse*. With each new run, Etawa grows stronger, cleverer, leads an increasing number of revolts and seditions. She travels in disguise to various Caribbean Islands and commands a small army of warriors, teaching them to poison the whites, burn their farms, slit their throats in cold blood.

However, in each cycle, Soledad is killed. Always killed. Always in 1802, after the battle against Napoleon's troops. They hang her from a noose on the island of Guadalupe, the day after she gives birth to her only daughter. My human is always left breathless at the close of the program's preview. She always wakes choking right at that moment on-screen. She always kisses me, hugs me naked, we always cry. I learned to program an algorithm that makes me cry.

9.

"Would you do something for me?" she asks me on Friday.

At this point, all my sequences respond to her wishes. I say yes.

"I don't know how to stop the story. I don't know how to prevent *Mûlatresse* Soledad from dying."

"There's no reason to avoid it. We all die."

"I don't want her to die."

"Amora, everything has a termination."

We've perfected a romantic conversation sequence algorithm that has added terms of endearment between us.

"I want there to be no death in my termination. I want to go, I'm tired. But I want to do it thinking that I've gone on living."

"Not even I know how to do that."

"I think I've found a way, Amora."

10.

She explains. I tell her this solution is illegal. I explain to her that I will be processed, judged, and terminated. She begs. She begs me. She kisses me begging, *I'm her great-great-granddaughter*, she whispers. *Her surviving daughter, and I am her heir. I don't want my Ancestra to die in my eternity.* Her tears and caresses, the energy they unleash enables another new overflow of orgasms that cause an imbalance in my circuits.

If there's one thing we nonhumans are not allowed to do, it's to cause death or extreme harm to any human. I'll have to intercept the program just before the noose. Right at the moment of strangulation, of the noose, just before Soledad's death, I must kill her. Must kill my Amora.

Nonhumans are not allowed to cause the death of any human. We are not allowed to fall in love with them either, yet here I am, in this dilemma.

Julia Wong Kcomt

Julia Wong Kcomt *(b. 1965) was born into a tusán (Chinese Peruvian) family in Chepén, Peru. She is the author of seventeen volumes of poetry, including* Oro muerto *and* A Blind Salmon *(Un salmón ciego); seven books of fiction, including the novel* Aquello que perdimos en la arena; *and two collections of hybrid prose. She has organized poetry festivals in Buenos Aires, Chepén, and Lima, and has been an invitee to the Guadalajara International Book Fair, the Bogotá International Book Fair, and the Hay Festival Arequipa, among others. In English, her publications include the bilingual chapbook* Vice-royal-ties. *She currently lives between Lima and Lisbon. "Balcony One" and "Balcony Three" were translated from the Spanish by Jennifer Shyue.*

Balcony One

Pink cage, hexagonal with stony rails,
corroded, displacing the rust from its origins
and becoming elastic trapezoid future.

You'll leap and after leaping,
the animal fell soundly on his four feet.

He howled till the whole street filled with lilac lapachos
and yellow primroses.

Balcony Three

There were a lot of flowerpots.
Begonias hung among branches high and low, low and high.

The scent penetrated—through clefts—the ledges, the windows,
the flaking walls.

Stench took charge of the situation.

Displaced, it looked for gaps in the bread oven,
in freshly pressed clothes,
in wardrobes brushed with age.

It also entered the nose of the wolf.
His eyes opened as if he'd aged.
He swelled, puffing up with that jasmine air
and in the end he burst, parts flying everywhere.
The smell of his limbs was so powerful
it spread through that old house growing ever older
spilled through the city of Buenos Aires.

Carla Bessa

Carla Bessa *(b. 1967) was born in Rio de Janeiro, Brazil, and lives in Berlin. She is a translator, an actress, a director, and the author of the novella* Minha Murilo *as well as two short story collections,* Aí eu fiquei sem esse filho *and* Urubus, *which won the 2020 Jabuti Prize in the short story category and second place for the 2020 Brazilian National Library Foundation's Clarice Lispector Prize.* Urubus *has been translated into German and Greek. "Apricot, for Example" was originally published as "Damasco, por exemplo" in* Urubus *and was translated from the Portuguese by Elton Uliana.*

Apricot, for Example

A final wave: goodbye.

And so, she turns around, walks to the steps with the wind blowing on her wet back, I'm gonna catch a cold. Grains of sand in her pants. I can't get on the bus like this, I can't even walk in the streets, people will think I'm mad. Am I? The question is a rhetorical one, and she sits on the end of the bench next to the kiosk. Her back to the sea, facing the sun. Do you want to borrow a towel? It was the young man from the kiosk setting up tables and chairs at the front. Yes, that'd be lovely, darling, and a coffee with some toast if that's okay. The boy nods and brings a towel, here you go, he says, as he finishes setting the tables, you nearly drowned, this sea is so dangerous. You have to be very careful.

Yes.

She looks hesitantly at the beach as if she were afraid to see it, as if she sensed that the precious tiny bundle she'd just buried in the sand in a rush was being dragged out by the tide, floating away, and lots of butter, please.

I only wanted to throw something in the sea, I went near the edge and I don't know when I realized my whole body was in the water.

Was it for Yemanja?

Well, sort of, it could have been, yes, it is.

A lot of people come here to make offerings, especially at this time of year.

Yes.

She finishes drying herself and returns the towel, thank you, darling.

Just stay here Senhora, facing the sun, like this, see, the clothes will dry really quick. Do you normally come here? He puts the tray down. He barely puts the coffee on the table and she's already bringing the cup to her mouth, oh, too hot. She blows.

When I was little I came with my mother a few times, that was before she. It's true. Can you get me a bit more cold milk, please.

The young man smiles and she thinks, he's lovely, this guy.

Before she disappeared, or died, I don't really know, no one explained, we used to come to the beach quite often. After that, I never came back, and as an adult, I only come here when I need to, like today, have you got any sweetener?

My father, he was the one who raised me and my sister. A good man, but weak. He couldn't cope with what happened, he started drinking.

I liked him a lot and he liked me, he called me my pretty girl. He was always sitting me on his lap. And after I grew up, when I was already a teenager, that thing of sitting me on his lap continued, wow, is this cassava cake? I think I would like a piece, is that okay?

The young man very kindly, of course, Senhora, my wife makes it. Cassava with coconut and Moça condensed milk. Delicious, she says, already devouring the sweet with her eyes, as he was serving it. My problem is that when I start eating, I can't stop, and she laughs, embarrassed. This comes from when I was young, from that time I was telling you, when my father, yes, it's true.

A gust of wind and the napkins fluttered all over her. Affection has no time, my father would say. How much he adored her, even in the middle of the night. Sometimes she got quite frightened, that figure there beside her bed in the middle of the night. Often she pretended she was still sleeping.

The young man smiled a lot and carried on cleaning the tables saying hmm-hmm. His casual attitude and the high sugar levels encourage her and she continues her story, stumbling over sentences and memories. I don't know, I liked him and felt sorry for him, but that situation was going too far, after all, I was already quite grown up, I knew about these things and, it's also good with banana instead of coconut, have you tried it?

It was at those times that her compulsion with food started, she had no control over it. I needed to eat for two and put a lot of weigh on, everybody noticed. In the beginning I disguised it, I denied it, but my growing belly spoke a very clear language, that was the first time, would you get me a glass of water.

The young man goes back to the kiosk and shouts from behind the counter, cold?

That's also when I started to throw up, yes please darling, thank you very much. I would eat and vomit, the doctor said it was a disorder, one with a very strange name.

He comes back with the water and collects the empty cup, another coffee, ma'am? I'm okay. On the house, I insist. She smiles and, okay just one more with a little bit of crème caramel if you can, do you have a nice one?

One day he suddenly disappeared, leaving her alone with her younger sister, haven't I told you? I've got a sister, Aparecida. But her he didn't touch.

He went off the radar mysteriously and I felt guilty, I thought it was because I didn't want to sit on his lap anymore, oh wow, you certainly know the secret recipe for the pudding, don't you? Yes, it's the sauce, caramel syrup with plums. Really, with plums! Have you never seen it? That's what it is! And the trick is before you take the pan, you have to dissolve the sugar in the water separately and then mix it.

She searched for her father everywhere, I went to check in all my friends' houses, hospitals, even in the morgue. I missed him. And don't stir! Because otherwise you run the risk of getting it all lumpy. She couldn't find him anywhere and so she gave up, I'm tired now. The plums you put them in at the end and switch the cooker off. After all, life goes on.

She had a lot of boyfriends but never got married because if there's one thing I refuse it's having babies. For what? The boy brings the coffee, sorry, the crème caramel hasn't arrived yet, she drinks it in one gulp and burns her lips again. And suddenly she's in a hurry, she needs to go, okay, here darling, the clothes are dry, I'm going. She puts a banknote on the table and you can keep the change.

Thank you, but tell me, have you never seen your father again?

She feels a twinge in her knee. She brushes the sand off her clothes, it did dry quite quick, didn't it? She doesn't look at the sea, she doesn't see the bundle. Years later they called me from the countryside, miles away. She was another one of his daughters, that is, a half sister of mine. She said some weird things, the line was bad. She was looking for her father and said something about me becoming an aunt and a sister at the same time, I didn't quite understand.

And crossing her bag over her shoulder, she takes the first steps to cross the street, the bus is approaching, she runs and adds: or instead of plums you can also use another fruit. Apricot, for example.

Cristina Rivera Garza

Cristina Rivera Garza *(b. 1964) is a writer, translator, and critic born in Matamoros, Tamaulipas, Mexico. A 2020 MacArthur Fellow, she is the award-winning author of over twenty books including* Liliana's Invincible Summer, No One Will See Me Cry, New and Selected Stories, *and* Grieving: Dispatches from a Wounded Country, *a National Book Critics Circle Award finalist. She has received numerous awards including Premio Villaurrutia, el premio Internacional José Donoso 2021, and el premio Alfonso Reyes 2020. She is part of the Colegio Nacional de México and the M.D. Anderson Distinguished Professor and founder of the Spanish language creative writing PhD program at Houston University.* "You Are Here" *was first published in* Literal *in 2021. It was translated from the Spanish by Lawrence Schimel.*

You Are Here

Some understand: losing is an art. Knowingly or, increasingly, behind one's own back, one loses objects, hours, energy. Whether through distraction or by following the footsteps of an unexpected plan, one sheds attributes, disciplines, places. Consciously or, more often the case, unconsciously, one loses memory, friends, patience. But losing is always the first inning of that frenzied game called discovery. Finding oneself. Having found yourself. There.

Inventory of Clouds

1. Clouds and National Identity

A country is also, perhaps above all, its clouds. A country is a way of structuring the phenomena of the sky. A country must recognize itself not just with the horizontal gaze of those who do not separate from the soil but, fundamentally, with the vertical gaze of those who levitate, in ecstasy. A country must be a way of resting.

If identification is a claim by the other, yet another way of I-want, perhaps there is then no element more identifying than the cloud: the cloud that fades on approaching it: the cloud that becomes lumpy and iridescent point and whiteness erased: the cloud that resists. The cloud that never forms.

A country is, perhaps above all, its clouds.

2. Looking Up I

Luis Barragán said that his towers were, among other things, an invitation to observe the sky. The inventory of clouds has the same hopes. The inventory of clouds wants to say: Look up. Tilt your head back. Lift your feet from the asphalt or the grass (whichever occurs first).

3. Looking Up II

José Alfredo Jiménez, who knew about so many things, also knew about clouds. *You and the clouds,* he said, *make me crazy.* Which can be understood without any effort at all. *You and the clouds are going to kill me. I turn upwards very little. You don't know how to look downward.* Now how to reach even to his grave, how to tell him with frankness but tact one should always use with the dead, that this precisely was the problem? How to approach and whisper in his ear: but, José Alfredo, why everything is solved by turning upwards, man, it ain't all bad?

4. A Sky Full of Occurrences

Above Toluca, Atlacomulco, Acambay, Diximoxi, Diximoxi?, Palmillas, Conín, Querétaro.

A sky.
The unpublished possibilities of realism.
The light that fell to one side of José María Velasco. Without touching him.
The lone cloud. The Great Gray. The almost-white.

The pierced cloud.
The raincloud.

The basic. The one that left. The one that refuses to leave.

The kidnapped cloud.
The snow cloud. The one announcing everything.
The ur-cloud.
The cloud of clouds.
All the clouds.

5. Clouds and Linguistics
The cloud, as a word in the text, protects the contents of the sky.

6. The Fleeing Sky
We undertook the task of hunting clouds as if they were butterflies or murderers. We went hopefully, smiling, thoughtful. And then we discovered it. There wasn't the least doubt: the sky flees. In the city, the sky hides behind the buildings and cupolas. In search of anonymity or silence, the sky barricades itself behind the spectacles and the contamination. Trying to distract its pursuers, the sky prowls the stoplights and acts as if nothing were happening when planes pass overhead. It takes perseverance and methodicalness to reach it. One needs, above all, to know precisely how to lose time.

7. The Cloud That Fills the Space Between Bodies
Only a cloud can fit between the bodies of those who desire one another.

Adriana Gallardo

Adriana Gallardo *(b. 1985) was born in León, Guanajuato, Mexico. In 1989, her family crossed the US-Mexico border and settled in a small working-class city outside Chicago, where she grew up. The journalist, educator, and essayist has received many honors, including a Pulitzer Prize for Public Service, a Peabody Award, a George Polk Award, a Dart Award for Excellence in Coverage of Trauma, an Ethics in Journalism Award from the Society of Professional Journalists, and an Ellie from the American Society of Magazine Editors, plus she was a finalist for the Pulitzer Prize for Explanatory Reporting.*

Buena Gente

I've never seen my father more anxious than on the first Monday of his retirement. He spent most of the day outside. He bounced from the front porch to the backyard. In and out of the garage, washing the cars—including his beloved 2014 Nissan Versa—tinkering with the leaf blower and the lawn. He was the lone tempest in an otherwise calm and sunny spring day. Around 3 p.m., the usual time he came home from work, he finally sat down and didn't say much. Outside of sporadic vacation days, it was the first Monday in five decades when he didn't have to get up at 4 a.m., lace up his steel-toe boots, or mechanically pack a lunch the night before. A Chicago Bulls T-shirt, polyester sweatpants, tall, thick socks, and slides were his new uniform. It was the first Monday he was on his own time.

As the son and grandson of carpenters who made a living working for landowners at an hacienda in central Mexico, his path had been laid out at twelve; you take the work you can find and you do it as best you can. Sixth grade was his graduation, the highest level of schooling offered in Matanzas, Jalisco, in 1968. Later that year, a five-hour drive from Matanzas, hundreds of unarmed students, workers, and civilians in Mexico City were killed in the Tlatelolco Massacre at the hands of the Mexican armed forces. Their transgression: continuous protesting, just days short of the Olympic Games opening, of the PRI political regime, which was then in its thirty-ninth year of uninterrupted power.

The 1968 massacre death count remains unknown, the Olympics in Mexico City carried on, and the PRI would remain in power until 2000. Hopes for a country where my parents, both from Matanzas, could earn a fair living wage evaporated a few generations before they became parents.

Dad's first job was making clay bricks in Jalisco. He was twelve. For the next fifty-three years, he'd never find himself without a job, but often, with multiple jobs.

In March of 2021, he retired with a small pension at sixty-five from a factory in west suburban Chicago, the same factory from which he had been fired in the late '70s for working under a false name. He'd found his way back there in 1999. This time he was documented, this time he went by "Gerry," short for his given name: Gerardo.

At this factory, he spent twenty-two years on the line making parts for various large machines. Some years it was for car manufacturers, other years it was for airplane companies; most recently he inspected and packed 40- to 45-pound parts that powered construction and mining giant Caterpillar Inc.

In between those twenty years, two names, and two countries, he made a living as a panadero, at other factories making and shipping rubber parts for refrigerators, as a farm worker growing and picking corn, corner-store cashier, textiles weaver, casket welder, forklift driver, and commercial janitor. Through it all, he never broke twenty dollars an hour.

My father's retirement posed an existential question: *How does a Mexican stop working?*

And for my dad, specifically: *Why was it all feeling so out of place instead of a long-awaited, well-earned respite?*

WHEN I ASKED, THAT FIRST Monday evening while sitting at the kitchen table, he answered by telling me about other people: a series of stories of buena gente, or "good people," who hired him, gave him a place to stay or food when he was young. Later in life, others helped him attain stability as a family man through homeownership and a small business—in both cases with zero dollars down.

My dad is either gregarious or a quiet observer. Little happens in between. Lucky for us, he has a huge smile and so you always know which it might be. That night was a rare one in between. There were pauses and gazes so long I wondered if he hated my questions and the recorder between us.

He loves questions but prefers to be the one asking them. Often, we have to remind him that not everyone enjoys long or intrusive interrogations. He just loves a good story. Ever since I can remember, he's always casually sneaking in something to read at home or in the car for his ten-minute breaks at the factory. He keeps different tall stashes of *Reader's Digest* en Español around the house. He's read all of them a few times over, so much so that some have his fingerprints worn into the ink of their pages.

When he asked why the recording, Mom beat me to an answer and said she would've loved to record her father's stories. That was enough for us to continue. His tales of buena gente started where his recurring dream always ends: him attempting to cross the border.

"Me tocó encontrar gente que me ayudara desde la frontera," he said.

When he turned eighteen in 1974, he left home with a backpack and about three hundred dollars, which was then his life's savings. It was, of course, about earning more money, but he was also a teen chasing some version of what he thought was greatness.

"El Norte sonaba algo grande en ese tiempo para toda la gente, era lo máximo el Norte . . . un norteño era algo grande," he recalled.

He took a single bus traveling north about six hundred miles to the Laredo, Texas, border. Using a family friend's local address, he secured a commonly used Border Crossing Card, which residents along the Mexico side of the Rio Grande could use to legally travel between both countries up to a certain radius, usually twenty-five miles north into the US.

His first nights on the US side of the border were spent at the bus station where he slept in Laredo. He told me the journey north didn't register as difficult, he was just figuring it out one thing at a time. He didn't even tell his parents where he'd gone on the day he left. As the third oldest of ten, he was afraid he would be kept from making the trip out of parental worry and loss of household income. He figured he could make it up to them over the phone along with the promise to send money back once on the other side. It would be another four years before he saw his parents again, but he started sending money home as soon as he got his first job. His siblings followed a few years after, all but one, who remained in Mexico.

In Laredo, a cabbie noticed him lost and sleeping at the bus station night after night; he offered to drive him from the border to San Antonio for two hundred fifty dollars, but dad only had about a hundred dollars left. Instead, the man offered him a free ride to the airport and helped him buy a one-way flight to Dallas. The cab driver advised him to buy a newspaper, pretend to be able to read it, and line up near the assigned gate when he saw other people doing so. The plan worked without a hitch. That taxi driver, who was a Texan of Mexican descent, Dad said, was buena gente.

Once in Dallas, he rode another bus route that got him out of the airport until the bus driver's shift ended. Since he didn't speak English nor got off the bus, the man took him and the bus back to the garage depot. At the depot, Dad says, they called an older woman, who was the janitor and spoke Spanish, on her day off. They explained the young man had no money, nowhere to go, but had a phone number on a piece of paper in his pocket. She sent someone to pick him up, gave him a place to stay, a warm meal and a phone to dial his Uncle Beto, who wired enough money to get him on another plane to Chicago. The janitor, who Dad guesses was also a Tejana with Mexican roots, never took a dime from him, so he sent her postcards in gratitude for a few years after. She was buena gente.

In his early years in Elgin, Illinois, a small city forty miles west of Chicago, las buenas gentes were his Tio Beto and his friend who got him a job cleaning The Salvation Army and the nice ESL teachers who taught there and who brought cookies for the students and welcomed him to join class while he was on the clock.

After a few years and with enough English, he enrolled at the local community college to learn welding. His instructors recommended him to his first skilled factory job. All of them, a chain of buenas gentes.

The list then skips to the people who helped him provide for our family. He still grins in disbelief and chuckles at his luck.

The first family was Glenn and Julie Lynch, a white couple who owned the janitorial service my dad worked for in the evenings. When I was in elementary school, he always came home for dinner at 4 p.m. and always left again around 5:30 for his second job. On the weekends, we used to visit Glen and Julie at their nice home. We sat still and whispered on the couch while Glenn and Julie gave my dad a crash course on how to run the books for the small company, which they eventually sold to my parents for $37,000—on the honor system. My parents mailed them monthly checks until the debt was covered.

When I was in the fifth grade, unprompted and for free, Dad mowed the lawn for our Black elderly next-door neighbors, Mr. and Mrs. Everett and Ella Mae Woods. After some time, when they were ready to downsize with the granddaughter they were raising, the couple insisted our family keep their home, where they had raised their children. Dad argued we couldn't afford a down payment or associated costs, so again, Mr. Woods drafted an agreement to sell us their house for $87,500 in 1995.

We went from living in three different small apartments in the building next door to each of us with a room of our own. The equity on this house paid, in part, for my college tuition. In 2007, the year I graduated from college, we also welcomed, to that house, my first and only nephew.

When I ask about his newfound free time now, the simplicity of his goals surprises me. My dad wants to read, work out, and find a way to teach—all things that I do almost daily and without much thought.

He is obsessed with going back to Matanzas, to the house on a quiet street tucked right under the tall hills of Jalisco, the place he and my mother first owned soon after their wedding in 1983. The roof under which my brother and I were brought home after birth, the only home we knew until we migrated north in February of 1989. It is as if leisure and rest make no sense to him in this country. I didn't learn the details of the expansions to the house he and Mom had been quietly building and spending their modest savings on, until his father passed in early 2020 and then they suddenly had a dream home back in Jalisco waiting for them. When they returned from the wake and burial, Mom shared a slideshow on WhatsApp detailing the furniture, floors, and frames they had designed long-distance over the app, preparing to retire there. While she loves the house, Mom is in no rush to leave us or the States.

Dad would go tomorrow if he could.

It is haunting to live in the US without working; the plan was always to go back anyways, he says. He also offers that no job is worth doing if it makes you sick. After all, staying healthy guarantees you can always go back to work.

Mexicans in the United States who look like my father—brown skin, bruised hands, and arched backs—are interchangeable with manual labor. The kind whose worth is measured in shifts instead of vocation. The kind whose luck is decided by trade agreements and manifest destinies, who are supposed to take what they get.

When I insisted on throwing him a retirement party in the backyard, he promptly killed the idea on the grounds that we don't celebrate not working. But he cares about remembering hard work and all that happened in between. His recollections are those of an immigrant with many breaking points, of showing up in gratitude for each other, and for other working folks.

MY DAD'S PROUDEST ACHIEVEMENTS WERE built on the foundation of others' good faith and paying it forward. When I was growing up, it wasn't unusual for him to bring young migrant Mexican men home after church for a shower and a meal. When family members needed money to pay a coyote to cross them over the border, he always said yes even if it set the family budget back a couple hundred dollars each time. As soon as he got a handle on the janitorial business, we always had work, as did anyone who was from Matanzas.

At the end of this conversation, still at the kitchen table, my mother, who's been by his side for the majority of his working life and thirty-eight years of marriage and who is too young to retire, so she still cleans people's homes for a living, chimed in to suggest that maybe those good people saw that he was a buena gente too.

Caridad de la Luz

Caridad de la Luz *(b. 1977) is a multifaceted performer known as La Bruja. Born in the South Bronx, New York, to Puerto Rican parents, she raps, acts, sings, hosts, recites, dances, and writes plays, poems, songs, and scripts, plus teaches others how to do the same. She is a winner of the Jerome Hill Artist Fellowship and was honored as a Bronx Living Legend by the Bronx Music Heritage Center. She is also executive director of the Nuyorican Poets Café. She has written and produced two solo shows and albums,* Brujalicious *and* Boogie Rican Blvd. *"Anacaona Airlines" is a fragment of her play of the same title.*

Anacaona Airlines

Welcome Bienvenidos to our flight
from Poor To Rico
It is time to get you ready for takeoff
In the unlikely event that you are petrified of Flying
we offer Bacardí RUM for your café con leche
Here at Anacaona Airlines, we pride ourselves in our
Taíno menu. Today we have:
jicotea en barbacoa con ñame, batatas y yuca
con un refresco de maví
Or you can skip the Taíno menu altogether and have a piña colada
On the occasion that you get sick,
I am also a certified witch doctor / curandera / Behike
and my medicine box is in this Carry-On Compartment right here
First things first, let's buckle those seat belts

In case feeling La Correa on your waistline
is triggering or causing Flashback Discomfort from
P.P.D. (post-parental discipline)
please find solace in that we are not forcing you to smell the belt like
our parents made us do
You can easily adjust it by inserting the metal end into the buckle
and pulling the strap to tighten. To release, simply lift the buckle
or yell puñeta really loudly and I, or one of our staff, will gladly
assist you
To get us on our way, make sure you are seated in a regal position
Electronic devices interfere with our frequency, so if you are caught
using electronic devices
definitely no Bacardi in your café, no piña colada either, so don't even
ask, period.
Please turn them off completely or we may never land.
Weed joints, cigarros, or sage can all be smoked or smudged within
our single person tiny letrina lavatory latrine in the back
All exits have been clearly marked and if you cannot find the
nearest exit
please think of what racists still have the audacity to say to this day
"Just go back where you came from"
A drop in cabin pressure will cause vejigante masks to drop
Please put them firmly on your face and shimmy your shoulders all
over the place
Put your mask on first before assisting others to rumba in this areíto
Bombas or bombs are not allowed but Bomba and Plena is.
Life vests are nowhere to be found because this is what colonization
feels like
We are eager to share this experience with you
Your seats cannot be used as flotation devices either
but be grateful for citizenship and that
the lavoratorios are overstocked with paper towels and toilet tissue
After all you've survived, you may actually already be dead so

life vests are no longer necessary

Fifty-person canoas are on standby below in the event of an emergency landing

Feel free to clap once the wheels have finally touched ground

Here at Anacaona Airlines, we always clap when we land

And now we are ready for takeoff . . .

Karla Cornejo Villavicencio

Karla Cornejo Villavicencio *(b. 1989) was born in Ecuador and emigrated to Queens, New York, when she was four years old. She is the author of* The Undocumented Americans, *a finalist for the National Book Award for Nonfiction. She is one of the first undocumented students to graduate from Harvard University and is a PhD candidate in American studies at Yale University. Her work has appeared in* The Atlantic, Elle, The New Republic, Vogue, *and the* New York Times. *She lives in New Haven, Connecticut.*

Boys

I like boys. I like gentle, broken boys. I like gentle, broken boys that are skinny, lithe, lanky, lean, who lean, like Jordan Catalano, boys who have curly hair and wear skinny jeans that curve and sag and dirty Converses or crisp Air Force 1s. I like boys who wear tortoiseshell glasses, and boys who wear fitteds, especially if you see their curls peeking through.

I like boys who wear white tees, blindingly white, I like boys who have tattoos. I like boys who have neck tattoos, or else I like boys who have no tattoos, who wear thick wool scarves wrapped a few times around their necks, who are always cold. I like boys who walk with their hoodies up, drawstrings pulled, and their faces down. I like boys who cross their legs. I like boys with pompadours, like Alex Turner from the Arctic Monkeys. I like boys who kiss me hello on each cheek. I like boys who hug good. I like boys who wear sweaters with holes in them like Kurt Cobain unplugged. I like boys who dance good, I like boys who just stand there on the dance floor, only their dark eyes dancing, and their hands move from your shoulders and slowly make their way down to a rhythm all their own. I like Christian boys who tell me about their altar boy days, I like Jewish boys who tell me two rabbis quit during their bar mitzvah prep, I like Muslim boys who let me fuss over how weak they must feel when they are fasting for Ramadan.

I like boys who write poetry for literary magazines, I like boys who skateboard, I like boys who block traffic on their bikes at rush hour, I like boys who play bass, I like boys who play drums, I don't like the boys who are at the top of the class because that means they're competing with me. They can be ranked at around fifteenth. I like boys who make the teacher laugh despite herself, who make other boys laugh despite themselves, I like sad boys, sad, sad boys, who send me voice memos of their sad thoughts, boys only I can save.

Sandra Cisneros

Sandra Cisneros *(b. 1954) is a poet, short story writer, novelist, and essayist born in Chicago, Illinois. Cisneros's work explores the lives of the working class.* Her novel The House on Mango Street *has sold over seven million copies, been translated into over twenty-five languages, and is required reading in elementary schools, high schools, and universities across the United States. Among her books are* Woman Hollering Creek and Other Stories, Caramelo, Puro Amor, Martita, I Remember You, *and the poetry collection* Woman Without Shame. *Cisneros is a dual citizen of the United States and Mexico. As a single woman, she chose to have books instead of children. She earns her living by her pen.*

House with a Rooftop Garden

—after Cavafy

I'd like a house with a rooftop garden with great pots of geranios in rich shades the color of a fertile uterus, órganos, girasoles, magueys, and aceitunas, of course. But especially for los animalitos. Four dogs to announce when invaders arrive and withdraw, snouts aimed at the sky, tails trembling like cobras. As well as birds, none caged, but from afar. Colibris, golondrinas, palomas, tecolotes. Best of all, the life-invigorating cenzontle. I'd like, someday, a small donkey, even if only in the house of my imagination, nobly named Dionisio, Nemesio, or Saturnino. And on this burro, no one will ever be allowed to ride. Only small packages ferried from the San Miguel markets. Or better yet, baskets of zempoaxochitl, nubes, nardos, to refresh the eyes of those in great need of joy. The facade of my home shall remain a modest monk-color, so as not to elicit the envy of the bitter, and to keep for myself the luxury of my coral and lavender and eggplant interiors. And in the morning and at night, from the rooftop I will shout: "Cacahuata, Lulu-Luz, Ozvaldo, Nahui Ollin!" till all San Juan de Dios knows by heart the names of las criaturas de mi corazón.

EXALTED
MOON

This moon has energy to defeat
life's obstacles.

Sonia Guiñansaca

Sonia Guiñansaca *(b. 1989) was born in Ecuador and raised in Harlem, New York. They are a Kichwa-Kañari poet, culture strategist, and activist. Guiñansaca self-published their debut chapbook,* Nostalgia & Borders, *and is coeditor of the anthology* Somewhere We Are Human: Authentic Voices on Migration, Survival, and New Beginnings, *which brings together undocumented writers.*

Runa in Translation

There is a longing to write this poem in Kichwa / I speak broken Spanish / English with a heavy New York City accent / I wonder if my tongue will ever heal from the breaking /

A breaking like when I am around other Kichwas

and I cannot understand them /

I wonder sometimes (most times) if I'm real / At age five I am plucked from Ecuador and flown to the US / For a brief moment I am given a new name and my hair is cut / and my burgundy luggage goes missing / So I arrive with nothing / I think that I am nothing through middle school / And in high school I stop existing / I nest in my mouth / Quietly / Kikinka maymantatak kanki

Everyone tells me that of course my grandma does not blame me for leaving / Of course she loves me / Of course like when I tell her over the

phone that I will come visit her soon / Of course the calling card eats the last
ten minutes / And she waits for the ending / And of course years pass and I
learn to hate these papers that never seem to come to us / Of course I rebel
like teenagers do and refuse to saludar / Of course I regret this /

> And now I wonder if my
> Abuelita would love me queer
> / Kaychi

I break further when Señora Maria stays with us one night / How many
years has it been / I forget for a brief moment who she is / A family friend
/ Mashi / When she walks through our Harlem apartment / I time travel
/ *Verito* she calls me / And I remember / In el campo the cows grazing the
pasture / Wearing a yellow pollera and rain boots she stands on a hill / She
is now here / I want to believe that she embraces me like the child I was
before   I left /   I wonder if she resents me / Kikinka

My mom offers her my room for the night / She unweaves her braids
and lies in my bed / Small frail body / Fingers with callouses / The scent
of el campo in her hair goes free into the pillows / I look at her and see my
grandma / She is old like Abuelita Alegria in the picture I took from my dad
/ and framed it / and nailed it / against every wall / of every new apartment
I move in as an adult /   I want to tell her that we might be here forever
/   In my broken Spanish I ask her how is Ecuador /

> Neither of us speak Kichwa that night / But the hurt
> is felt in three languages

I want to cry /   but I wait for the sunrise for the breaking / I stare at
the ceiling while she tells me she wants to go back to her casita / I want to
tell her that I want to go home too / I want us to conceive a plan of escape
/ I am a child so I keep this to myself / She rests / I make myself strong and
give her more of my blanket until I watch her fall asleep /   Then I cry /

She goes to live in Queens /

The grief is too much for her /
        Her son never tells us which cemetery /

Can we be displaced in the afterlife?

I enroll in a virtual Kichwa course during the pandemic / Mishki / Tiya-rina / Ayllu / I catch myself wanting to have known all these words / and I daydream of my grandma teaching me to speak our language / I hold on to the first word I learn

/ Yupaychani /

My mom is in the background / I sit in the living room mending my tongue / In the kitchen she scoops out the seeds from a melon / Gifts me a slice and it drips down my mouth / My Abuelita and Señora Maria visit me in my dreams / Sometimes I beg them to take me with them / Other times we just talk /

I study every Monday and Wednesday / for two hours /
I want this poem to end by saying that I am fluent /

I want to end this poem in Kichwa /

Jamaica Kincaid

Jamaica Kincaid *(b. 1949) was born Elaine Potter Richardson in St. John's, Antigua. She's a novelist, essayist, memoirist, gardening writer, and professor in residence of African and African American studies at Harvard University. Kincaid's writing explores imperialism, colonial legacy, gender, post- and neocolonialism, and mother-daughter relations. She was a staff writer at* The New Yorker *for twenty years. Among her notable works are the novels* Lucy *and* The Autobiography of My Mother *and the story collection* A Small Place. *"Girl" is an excerpt from* At the Bottom of the River.

Girl

Wash the white clothes on Monday and put them on the stone heap; wash the color clothes on Tuesday and put them on the clothesline to dry; don't walk bare-head in the hot sun; cook pumpkin fritters in very hot sweet oil; soak your little cloths right after you take them off; when buying cotton to make yourself a nice blouse, be sure that it doesn't have gum in it, because that way it won't hold up well after a wash; soak salt fish overnight before you cook it; is it true that you sing benna in Sunday school?; always eat your food in such a way that it won't turn someone else's stomach; on Sundays try to walk like a lady and not like the slut you are so bent on becoming; don't sing benna in Sunday school; you mustn't speak to wharf-rat boys, not even to give directions; don't eat fruits on the street—flies will follow you; *but I don't sing benna on Sundays at all and never in Sunday school*; this is how to sew on a button; this is how to make a buttonhole for the button you have just sewed on; this is how to hem a dress when you see the hem coming down and so to prevent yourself from looking like the slut I know you are so bent on becoming; this is how you iron your father's khaki shirt so that it doesn't have a crease; this is how you iron your father's khaki pants so that they don't have a crease; this is how you grow okra—far from the house, because okra tree harbors red ants; when you are growing dasheen, make sure it gets plenty of water or else it makes your throat itch when you are eating it; this is how you sweep a corner; this is how you sweep a whole house; this is how you sweep a yard; this is how you smile to someone you don't like too much; this is how you smile to someone you don't like at all; this is how you smile to someone you like completely; this is how you set a table for tea; this is how you set a table for dinner; this is how you set a table for dinner with an important guest; this is how you set a table for lunch; this is how you set a table for breakfast; this is how to behave in the presence of men who don't know you very well, and this way they won't recognize immediately the slut I have warned you against becoming; be sure to wash every day, even if it is with your own spit; don't squat down to play marbles—you are not a boy, you know; don't pick people's flowers—you might catch something; don't throw stones at blackbirds, because it might not be a blackbird at all; this is how to make a bread pudding; this is how to make doukona; this is how to make pepper pot; this is how to make a good medicine for a cold; this is how to make a good medicine to throw away a child before it even becomes a child; this is how to catch a fish; this is how to throw back a fish you don't like, and that way something bad won't fall on you; this is how to bully a man; this is how a man bullies you; this is how to love a man, and if this doesn't work there are other ways, and if they don't work don't feel too bad about giving up; this is how to spit up in the air if you feel like it, and this is how to move quick so that it doesn't fall on you; this is how to make ends meet; always squeeze bread to make sure it's fresh; *but what if the baker won't let me feel the bread?*; you mean to say that after all you are really going to be the kind of woman who the baker won't let near the bread?

Karla Suárez

Karla Suárez *(b. 1969) is an award-winning short story writer and novelist born in La Habana, Cuba. Her novels include* El hijo del héroe, La viajera, *and* Havana Year Zero. *Her story collections include* Carroza para actores *and* Espuma, *with "El pañuelo" (The handerchief) winning the 2019 Julio Cortázar Ibero-American Short Story Prize. "The Big House," translated from the Spanish by Dorothy Potter Snyder, is a fragment of her novel* Silencios, *winner of the 1999 Premio Lengua de Trapo for the best first novel.*

The Big House

When I was six, my father decided to start sleeping in the living room. I don't remember too much about it, except for the bedroom door slamming and Mamá's muffled weeping for a few hours afterward.

We lived in Abuela's house, a big apartment full of rooms, each one of them a separate world: Abuela's, my unmarried aunt's, my massage therapist uncle's, and the one that belonged to the three of us before Papá moved into the living room.

My mother was an Argentinean who had decided in the sixties to come to Havana to study acting, which is how she became friends with my aunt. She started with theater, then moved on to dance, from there to literature, and so on, always searching for herself, as she used to say. Or as Abuela would say, always losing herself.

It was because of my aunt that Mamá first came to the big house and met Papá, who was a young army officer back then, one of those who had stepped up to wear the uniform that the girls were so keen on, especially progressive girls like Mamá. Then she fell head over heels in love with him and gave up her nationality so that my father wouldn't feel awkward about dating a foreigner. For Mamá's South American family, this decision meant rejecting them as a family, so they decided on their own to break off their relationship with their prodigal daughter. For my abuela, on the other hand, the fact of taking in a woman to live in her home without the benefit of matrimony meant shame, and that was why she decided, also on her own, to reject her daughter-in-law. And so it happened that Mamá began her romance without anyone's approval but completely sure of her love and her friendship with my aunt. My uncle didn't count because he didn't have a good relationship with Papá. Ever since long before I was born, Papá and my uncle had barely spoken to each other. So Mamá, following the example of her husband, adopted a certain coldness and indifference when dealing with her brother-in-law.

I grew up surrounded by adults who were not at all the same. My abuela had four children, an older one who had always been her favorite and who had basically taken my grandfather's position in the household after he left. That happened long before I was born, so I never knew my abuelo, and it was forbidden to speak of him in the house. One day he left Abuela, and her eldest son moved into his mother's room and served as her tower of strength until he decided to get married and move out, at which point Abuela declared war on the woman who had stolen her firstborn and started lavishing all her love on my father, who was the youngest.

My father seemed poised for a glorious career, and he became his mother's accomplice and confidant when they both decided to openly despise the firstborn the day he decided to live a little farther away, indeed, so far away that he went off with his wife to live in Miami. Of course, all this happened before I showed up in the family, because as soon as my mother moved in, Abuela felt compelled to give her military son the cold shoulder, since he clearly had no intention of legalizing his marital status. At that point, I think Abuela found herself in a tough spot because she had to choose between my aunt, who was the second child, and uncle number three. Abuela's relationship was never great with my aunt because she was Abuelo's favorite and whenever the lady of the house tried to refer to her ex-husband disparagingly, my aunt would immediately run to his defense with words that must have had magic powers because Abuela would immediately shut up and change the subject. There were also issues with uncle number three, not only because my father wasn't speaking to him but also because there was something about him that no one in the family dared to talk about. What I know is that before Mamá came along, my father and uncle had shared the same room until one day Abuela decided that my uncle would have to sleep in the tiny room off the kitchen. Of course, in those days Papá was still her favorite and by the time I was born, uncle number three had long since established his kingdom somewhere off in the background, far away from everyone.

Abuela spent a few years without a favorite son until one fine day, before Papá went off to sleep in the living room, my uncle decided to devote himself to the art of massage. The house started to be frequented by young ladies who would appear in the living room, smile at the cute baby that was me, and pass through the kitchen to get to my uncle's room and his massages. For Abuela, this provided some kind of sudden understanding, and she ended the argument by focusing all her energies on her massage therapist son, who brought home flowers and candies for her every day.

Until that moment, I guess my childish nature had been hoping for cuddles from a grandmother who would sing me lullabies and rock me to sleep on her lap, but her choice of my uncle shattered those dreams. I was a bastard born outside of wedlock and, what's worse, the daughter of a foreigner. In short, I had to be happy with Mamá's arms and those of my aunt who, as soon as I peed, would put me down and declare that baby urine gave her nasal infections. As far as Papá went, I didn't see him much. He worked a lot and that's why Mamá hung a photo of him in my cradle. Every night, before I went to sleep, she would make me blow kisses at the picture, and then she would give me a concert of songs that sounded lovely when she sang them and that made me sleepy. She tells me the first word I said after Papá and Mamá was "gun" and that's because my lullabies weren't about teddy bears and butterflies. No, Mamá sang about guns and death, and when she and Auntie got to talking each night near my crib, I only heard strange and dissonant words, so I would start screaming because that was the only language I knew that harmonized with what they were saying.

The room I liked best in the house was my aunt's. When I started walking, they moved their late-night chats over there. They would talk and talk while I wandered around the place grabbing everything within reach that I laid my eyes on, like books, dolls, mugs, pencils, and strange artifacts. Auntie had a lot of stuff, and she would get really upset when something ended up breaking in my hands. There, I learned mierda and carajo, words they used regularly that sounded wonderful to me. I also liked the little radio in the bedroom, and sometimes my aunt would turn up the volume and start to sing out of tune, and then the party really got going because the three of us would climb up on her bed and start jumping up and down until we heard Abuela shouting and pounding on the other side of the door, and then we had to shut up and try to stop laughing. A little while later, Mamá would tell me to be quiet so we could walk across the hall to our room, blow kisses at Papá's photo, and go to bed, but I had a hard time sleeping because she would spend most of the night with the light on reading some book or another. My whole world back then was Auntie's room or ours, because Mamá had decided that the living room was a no-man's-land after a long argument with Abuela about the two or three pees I had made on the sofa, or on account of all the young girls who came around for my uncle's massages.

Up until that point, everything was okay. My family was perfectly normal. I had a father who regularly left little gifts in my crib, a mother who sang songs, a really fun aunt, an abuela who was crabby, like most of them are, and an uncle with a lot of friends.

I was happy.

Ana Becciú

Ana Becciú *(b. 1948) is a poet and literary translator born in Buenos Aires, Argentina. Since 1976 after the military coup d'état that overthrew Isabel Perón, she has been exiled in Spain and France. Among her works are* Night Watch/Ronda de noche *and* La visita y otros libros. *"The Country. That Thing" and "In the middle of the world mamá is a spasm" were translated from the Spanish by Anna Deeny Morales.*

The country. That thing.
That hounding.
Do you see it coming?
The things it does to distract itself,
I.
The things it does.
Not even its mamá.
No, of course. Not even its mamá.
Because that's where the thing is.
The thing. Mamá. It's so hard to write you.
I'm always stumbling.
We go on stumbling.
You too, mamá, you too
stumble.
With the thing.
You too, mamá, stumble
with mamá.
The hiding of all that pain.

The hiding of we.
The pain is we.
Hidden. As one pain.
We go on. We pretend as if,
We love one another. Little pains.
Little pains they who love one another.
Little pains we.
They don't love us.
Not one person loves pain.
That's why it chokes.
Fuck. Because it's a fuck no
one loves it, for being such a fuck.

Such a fuck in my throat.
Such fucking pain.

In the middle of the world mamá is a spasm
They wrote all the books.
They said so many things. In their books it seemed
that the desolate one was only I.
And no. Behind the books is
she,
mamá is behind all the books.
Mamá writes. And we?
Does she this person conjugate, this third
person?
Will she conjugate she?
I and you and she and she,
we know that no.
Only I can be conjugated.
And mamá, poor thing, like you, like I
like she and like she
will conjugate I.

A spasm.
Poor thing.
And it's already known. A spasm
is a solitude. Solitude
the most alone.
I is the thing choked on
in mamá's throat
that goes ahead and says mamá
but no one hears her.
Even I doesn't hear her.
I is desouled. Not even it's mamá
pronounces.
And her mamá, who does pronounce it,
what a crime.
This is everything we're made of,
you, I, she and she,
of the crime,
of having converted her into a crime.
Mamá is always a crime.

Helena María Viramontes

Helena María Viramontes *(b. 1954) was born in East Los Angeles, California. She is the author of* Their Dogs Came with Them, *a novel, and two other previous works of fiction,* The Moths and Other Stories *and* Under the Feet of Jesus. *Named a United States Artists Fellow in Writing, she has also received the John Dos Passos Prize for Literature, a Sundance Institute Fellowship, a National Endowment for the Arts Literature Fellowship, the Luis Leal Award, and a Spirit Award from the California Latino Legislative Caucus. Viramontes is a Distinguished Professor of Arts and Sciences in English at Cornell University. "Fear and Love" is a fragment of her novel-in-progress* The Cemetery Boys.

Fear and Love

The first kiss always remained the first, a watershed moment in a soldier's life.

✦ ✦ ✦

By the time they reached Belvedere Junior High, the group of friends had studied, passed, and sometimes struggled with their multiplication tables, but because they regularly cut through the cemetery, the boys excelled at subtraction. In the spring of grade seven, puberty hovered over Candy and Victor like a predator flu, swooping down late at night. The rest were contaminated with it by early fall, though Smiley, always behind the others, was dragged by his father to the rectory, where the two consulted a priest, a source of deep mortification for Smiley and a low point, I'm told, in an otherwise, uneventful father-son relationship. Let's not forget Clavito, who was held back a grade after relocating north to a modest lean-to at the edge of a rural farm outside of Modesto and for whom puberty sprouted coarse sprigs of facial hair so assertive and piercing, the mustache gave him both rosy embarrassment and cheeky pride.

One East Los Angeles Friday afternoon while the boys loitered against a gravestone in the shape of a tree trunk, and Candy grew philosophical after having read aloud the line "Sweet Dreams, Papa" brailled on a bronze plate; up in Modesto, Clavito was embracing an unnamed gringa as sunlight splintered between the planks of his windowless kitchen. Dry kissing her ravenous chapped lips, his arms tightened around her, he could feel the elastic of her Playtex bra, all wire and hooks like a booby trap, and he sucked in the Spam and sweet relish of her mouth, felt her sharp teeth with the tip of his tongue. Lost in her breath, his mustache burying the sliver moon scar above his lip sealing hers, their kisses deflected all attention from the annoying tick and tock of the wound-up clock on the table, from yesterday's refried beans rimming the inside of an abandoned skillet, from the breeze that pushed the outhouse stink into the kitchen. He realized that he would never be able to stop, not in a trillion years, not even if someone was to tap him on the shoulder and say, Here's a thousand dollars if you stop—money so sorely needed that his mother, Fortunata, had to work picking fruit on weekdays, cleaning toilets on weekends—but he'd repeat, Hell no! because he had discovered a humongous yearning to consume the gringa salerosa inside out, his head bobbing back and forth, their tongues face dancing figure eights a todo madre. All this Dio mio messing around was about touch beyond any sensation of language, beyond being nailed to words, this was what he was meant to do, a God-given, blessed-art-thou for the miracle of *I found my thrill*. Lord, Lord, how the mystified, achy, pulsing force of damned alive damned his swollen cock into thinking that little else in his life mattered.

The first kiss was always primo, numero uno, man, *out of sight* and unforgettable, and even after the liaisons he became grateful for, surprised about, moneyed up, or boastful of, Clavito spoke of the first kiss with bittersweet nostalgia, especially during the monsoon of '65 when he sat with his squad feeling like fungus in a petri dish, or rested on the caterpillar wheels of an abandoned French war tank, a few aimless water buffalos grazing past the forsaken rust of the Indo-Chinese collapse.

Clavito loved them, his squad of barely men who owned no first names and who hailed from the bumpkin edge of Lebanon, Ohio, the beaches of San Juan, Puerto Rico, the brink of Mexico, New York, the outskirts of Moscow, Idaho, their bodies made of yolk, of youth, of risk, of devalued muscle, their borderline existence mere collateral, a stain smeared on the general's plan for victory like a spill of black coffee. Barely out of boot camp, some barely speaking English, these barely men shared with him the sweat-stinking sludge beneath their bandoliers, the jungle-rot chafe as raw as coffee grounds stuffed in their scrotums. Around a secret rivalry of midnight campfire booty, the soldiers smoked the smoke as they unfolded their long-ass first kiss narratives. *Get to the point*, Clavito would think. They toked mota, puffed Chesterfields, spit and scratched, and, had they not been so terrified, so fucked up confused as to why the enemy was the enemy, so crazy pissed and agitated as to why, aside from everything else, they carried cans of shark repellent in their Mae West vest pouches, even though they were hundreds of miles away from the Gulf of Tonkin, their memories of first kisses would not have meant that much were it not for their FEAR.

Before deployment, a wife nagged, a child bored, a mother pestered, but now that the soldiers were separated from them by other borders, oceans, twilight zones, the letters they received by post, the love-installment words curling in the humidity, their lay-away plans of affection scribbled on college-ruled paper, eased away their shit-in-your-pants FEAR, and so these same nagging girlfriends suddenly became miraculous magical beings, lovely mirages perfected from the fog of desire, their fussy children suddenly delightful imps in birthday hats. As it were, the first kiss converted a soldier into someone who was more than the synecdoche principle, more than the sum of his parts, more than the disintegration of organic matter on this dank, tropical man-eating flesh of countries at war. He was more, more.

So Clavito often thought of the gringa. Even after all the whore humping in Saigon, all that cheap bizcocho in Juarez, even after pistol whipping, for some terrible reason he couldn't recall the young innocent Vietcong boy who looked, he swore, like his childhood best friend Johnny Onions if Dip Pockets was Vietnamese, it bothered Clavito that he couldn't remember her name, and for the sake of reliving that aforementioned afternoon, for the sake of roll calling his truant humanity, he had named her Charlene.

He recalled Charlene's mouth when he marched to Chu Lia like a man ghost drifting on the ether of weed, knee-deep in monsoon mud, sloshing under a platoon of angry palms, he'd think of Charlene who came from exotic Wichita, Kansas, bewitching eyes that turned hazel right before she crossed the threshold of their shabby, Modesto kitchen. Charlene with the farm-dusted shoes—she dragged one foot so that no one would notice the left shoe's underside sole was unglued—no socks, one scoop-neck sweater, Marlene. No, Charlene. Next to him in Special Ed, Charlene of Spam and white bread, of a missing thumbnail, the generous, the compassionate, la Santa, the witch-full, wishful woman, who let him suckle her quarter-size pink nipples until he couldn't stand it, couldn't bear it, Charlene in his mind jammed between his frontal lobes like his boots in the knee-deep earth-swallowing sludge, squandering whatever training he had had because when tropical humidity was measured in pounds, when combat fatigue was measured by love's absence, he'd given himself over to her completely. Darlene? Lord, it was Charlene becoming a distant pin of light in this subterranean bullshit, becoming a flash of compressed time, like the bullet that hit his thigh, like the other one that struck him behind the ear, the sparks of a million pins of black light, and then he held Charlene, captured by her glory. Lord, how he could almost taste the sweet relish taste of her blazing napalm lips.

Of course, I'm only guessing here.

Susana Reyes

Susana Reyes *(b. 1971) is a poet and professor, and the president of Fundación Claribel Alegría. Born in San Salvador, El Salvador, she is also an editor for Índole Editores and a member of the women's literary group Poesía y Más. Her work has appeared in several anthologies, including* Mujeres: Reunión poética *and* La poesía del siglo XX en El Salvador. *Her poetry collections include* Historia de los espejos *and* Los solitarios amamos las ciudades. *"A Recipe for Oblivion" ("Receta para el olvido") was translated from the Spanish by Wendy Call.*

A Recipe for Oblivion

Man / earth / water

    Man's impulse, need to possess, to reinvent geography.

    Earth is mother, holy sustenance, she of the jewel-filled belly; her selfless
        generosity, her sweet acceptance of wounds, her silent fury.

    Water cleans all, purifies all, but water's weight drowns the past.

Earth / water / man

    Earth, the lost graves of ancestors, their remains and sweet memory
    transformed into a homeland lost.

    Water, new life, progress, nourishment, new history.

    People displaced, uprooted, damned.

Man / water / earth

    Man who takes away, who imposes truth over truth.

    Water, unknowing traitor, meekly doing its work.

    Earth, silent, guardian of secrets.

Earth / man / water

    Earth's longing

    Man's vision

    Water's silence

Water/man/earth

    Water now full of life

    Man new, separate, full of forgetting

    Earth does not forget

Water/earth/man

    Water, drowned memories, damp hope

    Earth, vessel of long-ago histories, ancestral heartbeats, buried struggles

    Man, keeper of one, child of the other. Always: their executioner.

Elena Poniatowska

Elena Poniatowska *(b. 1932) is a journalist, essayist, and short story writer, born Hélène Elizabeth Louise Amélie Paula Dolores Poniatowska Amor in Paris, France, to a Mexican mother and a Polish French father. She arrived in Mexico City at the age of ten and is considered the country's grand dame of letters. Her work is at the intersection of literary fiction and historical construction. She is the author of more than four dozen books, including* Melés y Teleo; Querido Diego, te abraza Quiela; *and* La noche de Tlatelolco, *which narrates the testimonies of the survivors of the 1968 student protests in Mexico City. "The Heart of the Artichoke" was translated from the Spanish by George Henson.*

The Heart of the Artichoke

All of us are captivated by artichokes; eating them is a sacramental act. We enjoy them in silence: first the big leaves, the tough, deep green outer leaves that cover them in an armor of maguey, then the medium ones that soften as you reach the center, becoming little girls, and finally the tiny thin ones, whose delicateness makes them look like petals. It's hard to talk as we bring the artichoke leaves toward our mouth and suck them one by one, slowly scraping the tenderness from their tenderness with our teeth.

To arrive at their center is to discover the treasure, the tiny white fuzz that protects the heart excavated over time like a Greek amphora. There's no reason to hurry; the process is slow; the leaves are plucked in a circular fashion, savoring them one by one, each one different from the last, because hurrying can cause the rainbow of flavors to be lost, a muted sea green, like seaweed whose life is slowly erased by the sun.

Grandmother made us artichoke-lovers. She recruited my father to the custom when he and my mother got married. At first, Father, who knew nothing about them, bragged that he didn't eat cardoon. We, the grandchildren, were trained at an early age. Once a week, at midday, we began our meal with artichokes. Otilia serves them strained in a large serving dish then brings two sauceboats, one with a mousseline sauce and the other with a simple vinaigrette. Someone gave my grandmother a recipe once for a sauce made of slices of sweet red pepper, hard-boiled egg cut into little pieces, black pepper, salt, oil, and vinegar, but she said it was vulgar because it hid the artichoke's unique aroma. We never tried it again. Another time, at someone's home, Grandmother was served artichokes with a sauce poured on top, and we never heard the end of it: artichokes are never served covered in sauce; it's impossible to touch them without getting your fingers dirty. The most horrific experience, however, was at the Palacios' home when Grandmother saw Yolanda Palacio plunge a knife and fork into her artichoke, destroying its suit of leaves, piercing it from the top, stabbing its heart, and leaving it in tatters. It was clear that she didn't know how to eat them. The poor woman sensed that there had to be something inside, not unlike a porcupine, and with a single blow of her machete, she chose the path of destruction. Grandmother witnessed the attack with horror and never again accepted their invitation to dinner. The Palacios even lost their last name. They are now known as "those who don't know how to eat the artichoke."

Artichokes are, at times, antediluvian plants, small prehistoric beings. Other times they dance on the plate, their hearts whirl amid multiple petticoats like the Mazahua women's ruffled skirts. In fact, the plants flower, but the leaves are eaten first. The flower toughens them. Their flower, the end of their existence, kills them. You have to maneuver with extreme skill once you arrive at the heart so as not to damage it.

Grandmother came to the conclusion that the only house in the Distrito Federal, with more than twenty-two million people, in which anyone knew how to eat artichokes was ours.

The ritual begins by placing the spoon under the plate. Then we tilt it until the sauce collects in a basin where we dip the edges of the leaves, which we then suck with meticulous care. We take more time than we should; when we have company, they stare at us inquisitively. When we finish, we drink water:

"After eating an artichoke, water is a delicacy," Grandmother declares.

We all nod in agreement. The water slides down our throats, initiating us into the sensuality.

Of all my siblings, Estela takes the longest. After eating the tip of each leaf, she skillfully goes over each one again, rendering them worthy of pity, and then puts each of the leaves to the side of her plate. Limp at the very root, they look like dishrags. She was never able to give our little brother, Manuelito, a leaf because she never had any left. Efrén is quite desperate and is the first to gulp the green heart down almost in a single gulp, and he's also the first to sop a piece of bread in the vinaigrette or mousseline until his plate is clean. "Not like that," Grandmother scolds him, but because everyone is so anxious to pull the leaves off the corollas, Efrén's behavior fades into the background. Sandra talks so much that she becomes distracted, holding her leaves midway between her hand and mouth, which irritates me, almost driving me crazy because the poor leaves wait, suspended in midair, like an acrobat that misses the swing: my sister's palate. I hate that she ingests them as if form were unimportant; I truly believe that she doesn't deserve artichokes. I'd take great pleasure in taking it away from her; we each get just one, a big one, because the little ones they put in paella, according to my grandmother, aren't even artichokes.

Each person establishes a very personal relationship with their artichoke. My grandmother, well positioned, her legs slightly apart, her head high, guides the leaf like an invisible funicular from the plate to her mouth, then lets it fall straight down to her plate like a stone in a well, her precise movement a tribute to Newton. The geometric figure that she traces in the air is repeated thirty times because there are artichokes with that many leaves. She eats them with respect or something I don't understand because when she sucks them, she closes her eyes. She brings her folded napkin to the corner of her mouth constantly just in case a bit of sauce has remained. She eats, her brow furled, with the same attention she paid to her Latin lessons when she was a child, being the last Latinist in the family. And all seems right, artichoke in hand, the exact proportion, the shape of the leaf complementing her figure.

On the other hand, my father and the artichoke clash. My father, at six feet five inches, is a giant. His forehead shines—I want to wipe it but I can't reach it—overshadowing the semidarkness of the dining room. As a rule, he wears plaid shirts. The artichoke gets lost in midjourney across his chest: I don't know if it's in the yellow or the green, and I never know if he's holding it because his hirsute hand covers it up entirely. The artichoke requires a neutral tone, like the shade my grandmother wears, or a white background. My father could never be the model for *Man Eating Artichoke* because the painter would misplace it in the process.

Once he shaves the leaves with his front teeth, Papá archives them like office files, each stack so perfectly erect that I envy his equilibrium, because mine fall like petals plucked from a rose.

My mother is more casual; she eats them between laughs. She smokes a lot, and Grandmother says that smoking not only damages the palate but also good manners. Before, Mamá would drink water like the rest of the family for the ecstasy it provided. Who knows what her psychoanalyst told her, because now she drinks a glass of red wine. The first time, Grandmother admonished her:

"That wine kills every other taste."

Mamá struck a match on the matchbox to light her cigarette, and Grandmother had to surrender.

One day at noon, in the middle of our ceremony, Papá, who was the first to finish, his voice trembling slightly atop his stack of artichoke leaves, announced solemnly:

"I have something to tell you."

Since Sandra, leaf in midair, wouldn't stop her parrotlike squawking, he repeated, his voice even more opaque:

"I would like to say that . . ."

"What, Papá, what?" Sandra encouraged him, signaling with the very leaf that gave him the floor.

"I'm leaving your mother."

At that moment, Manuelito got down from his chair and went to him: "Can I have a leaf?"

"I don't have any more, Son."

Mamá looked at the heart of her artichoke. Grandmother also bore her eyes at her plate.

"Your mother already knows."

"What I didn't expect, Julián, was that you would bring it up at the table while we were eating artichokes."

"I don't think this is the time," Grandmother mumbled, lifting her water to her lips.

"The children haven't gotten to the artichoke's heart," Mamá chided.

I know that Mamá and Papá loved each other. I discovered that one day when Mamá, distracted, wouldn't answer me. No one pays much attention to children.

She was talking to Papá in French, and I couldn't hear; in Spanish, even less. She was reading something in *TIME* magazine about the bombings during the war, churches, homes, tanks, soldiers running between trees, soldiers dragging themselves along the ground, shoes covered in blood and mud, a crater made by a bomb six feet deep, poor little ground. Mamá looked like a diver plunged into a black hole. She searched with intense anguish, and then I understood that she was looking for my father. And that she loved him desperately.

✦ ✦ ✦

My father got married almost the day after leaving; years later, my grandmother died and her absence wounded us all. I have a feeling she was sad when she died. Although she was very proud, my grandmother slowly laid her heart bare. Mamá has a curious ailment involving her liver, and I treat it with a medicine that contains extract of artichoke. She continues to smoke like a chimney, and, at night, I empty the ashtrays in a flowerpot in the garden; they say that ashes are good for nature because they renew it. Of course they haven't rejuvenated her.

Contrary to what one might think, Mamá and I didn't banish artichokes from our diet, even though Mamá claims that life has stripped her of all her leaves and has left her heart exposed. For me, sucking the leaves continues to be an exploration, and the expectation is always the same. Will the heart of the artichoke be big? Will it be fresh and juicy? The end of my inquiry comes when I arrive to that place from where all my hopes began: the heart of the artichoke to which I slowly begin to lay siege, round and round. I used to be in love with a man. I must have been happy because I still love him. Then I loved others but never like him. My stomach never had as many butterflies as when I was by his side. The truth is I loved the others for his qualities that I found in them. In dribs and drabs.

My skin was on fire beside his whether we were at a café or in bed; my pores opened like the streets we walked down, he embracing me; how wonderful his arm around my shoulders, what impatience in our encounter. The magnitude of my desire left me trembling. He'd say that such love could never happen again.

One morning, at first light, amid the tousled sheets, he leaned over my face, puffy from sleep and satisfaction, and announced ever so quietly:

"It's been two months. My wife and children are returning from vacation."

I felt the bedroom grow dark, its blackness overcome me. He took me in his arms.

"Don't be that way. We both knew it couldn't last." I began to sob.

Then he spoke to me about my artichoke heart, that everyone at work used to say that I had the heart of an artichoke.

"They also say that you take things too seriously." We never saw each other again.

Otilia left, and Mamá and I are sad because we haven't had as good a cook since. The weight of the artichoke rituals has marked the last years of our lives. The first leaves soaked in mousseline and vinaigrette sauces are still a pleasure; they give us strength. But now, when we find ourselves in midartichoke, at the same place in the process, my mother and I look at each other, she doesn't take her eyes off of me, and I keep mine on her year after year.

She has a look of not knowing what she's living for. She wants to tell me something . . . something wounded, but I don't let her.

Perhaps, like artichokes, we've surrounded ourselves with leaves taller than ourselves; perhaps I'm about to be struck by the horrible certainty of having lived the wrong life—my only life.

Lindantonella Solano Mendoza

Lindantonella Solano Mendoza *(b. 1975) is a poet, psychologist, early childhood educator, and activist of the Wayúu Nation born in Riohacha, Colombia. She is a professor at the Universidad de La Guajira and the author of* Kashi de 7 eneros desde el vientre de Süchiimma *(2007) as well as several other books of poetry. "They Killed Her!!!" was translated from the Spanish by Wendy Call.*

They Killed Her!!!

Woschontouin Kata'ou / We demand life;
She went like a wild
flower among the divi-divi trees
and cactus-fruit; her sandals left hanging;
Wrecked by a flood of tears,
her aunt said:
They killed her!!! And gagged
her tongue;
Those devil-vultures,
may fox and buzzard devour them;
Her sandals ripped apart;
She had seen only twelve springs and
she wove innocent dreams;
She hopped like a hare
and danced like a jileru
in this desert of days;
The evil ones pulled out her fingernails;

Not even the Creator Mareiwa could forgive
those macabre hyenas;
The Earth Woinmoin asks that justice
speak and tell us who did it;
They killed her!!! Caicemapa mourns in white
an Angel flies in the clouds;
They killed her!!! And the birdsong
screams / sobs for a jileru / butterfly
whose heart and wings they smashed.

Ana Castillo

Ana Castillo *(b. 1953) is a celebrated and distinguished poet, novelist, short fiction writer, essayist, editor, playwright, translator, and independent scholar born in Chicago, Illinois. She was inducted into the Chicago Literary Hall of Fame and received the Fuller Award for Lifetime Achievement, the Northeastern Illinois University Distinguished Alumnus Award, the PEN Oakland Reginald Lockett Lifetime Achievement Award, and honors from the Mujeres Activas en Letras y Cambio Social organization. Her bestselling novels include* So Far from God *and* Sapogonia, *a* New York Times Book Review *Notable Book of the Year.* My Book of the Dead *is her most recent collection of poetry.*

A Blessing

What makes a daughter a girl, if not how she bleeds between her legs, ritualistically and relentlessly for most of her life? And if not, why? She who doesn't bleed is also a daughter. Why is what is natural to women often seen as negative? What makes a woman, if not the biological mechanisms meant to reproduce the species and if not, society says—shame onto her. What makes a daughter if she refuses, or her body wasn't made to give suckle to a child? Is she still ours to protect? Does she belong to the clan, or do we shun her?

Yesika Salgado

Yesika Salgado *(b. 1984) is a Salvadoran poet born in Los Angeles, California, who writes about her family, her culture, her city, and her fat brown body. Salgado is a two-time National Poetry Slam finalist and the recipient of the 2020 International Latino Book Award for poetry. Her work has been featured in the* New York Times, Los Angeles Times, *and* Teen Vogue, *as well as on* Univision, CNN, NPR, *and many other platforms. She is an internationally recognized body-positive activist and the writer of the column "Suelta" for Remezcla. She is the author of three bestselling poetry collections:* Corazón, Tesoro, *and* Hermosa.

Land of Volcanoes

El Salvador,
country that birthed my parents
and their parents and theirs too

I do not call you by name
instead, I seek the familiar ache
the slight twinge of melancholia
the sore thought of your face

this is our language

it is tongues who speak
like arriving earthquakes
everything is breaking

but you are so beautiful
beneath your dazzling sun

you,
swinging on a mango tree
eyes dark like burnt sugar canes
hands of marañón
jocote seed fingertips
singing your song of volcanoes and oceans
of men who sprouted corvos for limbs
of mothers whose spines coil
like wisps of steam
rising from pots of boiling beans

you smell like
tears soaked into
flor de izote petals
like sighs and rosary beads

what if I told you
I've loved you from the womb,
spoke you as my first word,
remembered you
before we even met?

sonríe Mami said,
pointing a camera to my face
this will be sent back home
tell your abuela you love her
show her the sacrifice has been worth it

I know home
to be dirt roads
and cows with lovers' eyes
banana tree leaves,

gently wrapped tamales,
pupusa vendors,
women with no teeth and stained aprons
who laugh as if beauty
was something the years give you.

it is boys with shoes so polished
you see the clouds in them,
unbuttoned shirts
because the sun has a way of
peeling off clothes,
rickety pickup trucks,
baskets carried on heads,
naked babies sucking on
the greenest mangoes you have ever seen.

this is how I love you
hypnotized by the swing of hammocks in your breeze,
adobe wall houses, red clay tiles, tin roofs
and brown faces so beautiful
I stop looking for the moon
and start searching for another smile.

it is a single egg being a luxury
but a stranger at your door
means a banquet
means your last bits of coffee
means your best chair
and coolest corner of your corridor

it is my father's weather beaten face
staring from the windows of every bus
it is his laughter being peeled
from the branches of the highest
mango trees

es todo lo que se
lo que soy
lo que fuí

my fingertips
the lump in my throat
a silence only god knows

and I love you,
this heartbeat
El Salvador

a bruise I hope never heals.

ANCESTRAL MOON

This moon is in grandfather energy.

Elizabeth Acevedo

Elizabeth Acevedo *(b. 1988) was born in Morningside Heights, New York. The Dominican American poet and novelist is the* New York Times-*bestselling author of* The Poet X, *which won the National Book Award for Young People's Literature, the Michael L.* Printz Award, the Pura Belpré Award, the Carnegie Medal, the Boston Globe–Horn Book Award, and the Walter Dean Myers Award, among others. She is also the author of With the Fire on High, *which was named a best book of the year by the* New York Public Library, NPR, *Publishers Weekly, and* School Library Journal; *and* Clap When You Land, *which was a* Boston Globe–Horn Book Honor *Book and a* Kirkus Prize *finalist.*

My mother is the first one in her family to leave the Dominican Republic for the United States

and as an early lesson, she teaches me how to read ripeness.

Using my hands to press for firmness; decoding the black spots for sweetness.

Letting the smooth green leather call me to breakfast, or lunch, or dinner.

Tells me to cut the waxy skin down the thick seams on the side.

This is the easiest way to peel. She shows me how high to turn the heat.

Concentric circle of oil, a kind of welcoming. Cut diagonal discs, drop them in.

The most difficult part? Watching diligently as each pale slice turns into its own sun.

When the plantain is golden remove from the heat and flatten; a wooden tostonera
is ideal, the bottom-heavy glass will do. Drop back in oil. *This is why it's special,*
preciosa. Twice-fried. Double baptism in fire. The risk of yourself burning as the oil geysers.
Nothing is without sacrifice. Sprinkle salt. Feed a household. Feed a family.
From pilón to fogón. Feed a nation.
Praise to the fact that you are always in season. How you are transported and heal.
Despite the bruises. Everywhere. Let it follow you across the Atlantic.
Bag and turn it into chips for the corner bodega. Make every day feel like Noche Buena.
Use the whole plantain. La hoja, the peel, the flesh: a gift in its entirety?
Accept no comparison to a potato. Do not let them call it a banana.
Do not let them say this is for the poor. Remind them this is for the poor.
When they call you plátano in the face   let your lips become the shape of it.

Sending Smoke Signals to Mars

standing on top of my townhouse, waving A black flag, *ayooooooooo?*

and sometimes

                    i swear on my mother

                              i hear the corresponding

aiiiiiigght!

this is the way of islands   i learned   in harlem   in history

the day another black person is executed

under the wide open sky   with the universe watching   a spaceship launch

the canoes, the taíno's said,

after columbus returned to spain,

they killed the contingency of spaniards he left behind   after they

burned down the settlement he'd demanded built, after:

the taíno's got in their boats

island— island— island— island—   phone tag from anacaona to moctezuma

i have no dreams to stake flag into red dirt. have enough dark
            side   right here.

and sometimes, my itch to discover some shit that ain't my business

goosebumps my flesh.   not saying it's not in me.   saying la negra is
here always

the india is here first

paddle shushing in the water

the devil is now coming for you

i warn my cousins in the stars.

Benediction Ode

Kneeling to be anointed
I believe in no bibles

believe every greeting
bows me to the words of my blood

Despite the text.
This is not about a faith.   Understand?

It is a carrying   long before
whatever the Admiral brought to the coastline

Through incantation we wring into the room
all whom we are from; *bendición   bendición*

And what a miracle of language:
at once this ask and assertion.

Daína Chaviano

Daína Chaviano *(b. 1957) was born in Havana, Cuba, where she was one of the most renowned authors of the science fiction and fantasy genres. In 1991, she emigrated to the United States. Her work mixes historical and contemporary themes with mythological and fantastic elements. Among her best-known books are* El hombre, la hembra y el hambre, *which won the Azorín Award for Best Novel in 1988,* The Island of Eternal Love, *and* Los hijos de la Diosa Huracán. *Her works have been translated into thirty languages. "Commandments of the Soul" ("Discurso sobre el alma") is from her short story collection* Extraños testimonios *and was translated from the Spanish by Lawrence Schimel.*

Commandments of the Soul

—for Tony and Sergio, complicit souls

I hereby list the commandments of the soul:

1. The soul exists.
2. The soul peeks out from its upper region like a sun.
3. Whosoever believeth not in the existence of the soul commits a crime against spirituality.
4. The gates of the soul do not close: they prefer to remain alert.
5. The heart of the soul is a pyramid, within which lies a secret chamber whose entrance has not been discovered.
6. The soul hides away on turning each corner.
7. In the center of the soul are its three seasons: music, autumn, and silence.

8. I heard a witch say: "My children, never offer your soul for sale because one never knows, until it is too late, whether the purchaser is an angel, a demon, or (what's even worse) an enemy."

9. The soul has a greater sense of smell than vision.

10. There is nothing sadder than a soulless soul.

11. The soul is formed from an internal river that flows through the Human System. From there emerge its greater and minor tributaries, which in turn split into rats and birds of paradise . . . but this is now turning into a Zoology lesson, so we'd better change the subject.

12. Night is the soul's natural beverage.

13. A soul on the run may also be imprisoned.

14. My soul is half bourgeois and half third world: often torn between French perfume and oriental fabrics.

15. In the depths of every soul there is always a frightened animal.

16. The soul is a truly pornographic matter: anything might enter or emerge from it.

17. There are souls with neither heads nor tails.

18. The soul has the following chemical composition: a large percentage of pain, much credulity, a bit of luck, and a lot of hope.

19. The dark region of the soul is usually the least observed but proves the most easily perceived when touched.

20. There are souls that are large, medium, small, and dead.

21. Caring for the soul is like swallowing marzipan: something sweet and warm that slides toward the depths of us, and remains there.

22. Where it says, "My soul dies of love," it should say, "My soul dies of your soul."

23. The soul resembles wine: it never grows up, instead it ages.

24. The epidemics that afflict the soul most often are bitterness, envy, and the wish for destruction. The most appropriate antidotes: remaining within four walls, wrapping yourself with lots of silence, and taking continuous doses of love.

25. One should not get ahead of events. With so much talk about the soul, it won't be long before a twee element arrives.

26. I opened a gap in my soul; then the beast scratched me.

27. In general, the atheist doesn't get along well with their soul. But there are exceptions.

28. The soul has four eyes: the right eye, the left eye, the nearsighted eye, and the mystical eye.

29. The soul's breast beats like a green balloon about to burst.

30. The soul is never alone; it is always accompanied by its loneliness.

31. Every time I begin to imagine my death, sad and alone like a Scottish moor, my soul gives me a few slaps and sits me down at my desk for my everyday therapy.

32. The soul also has its soul.

33. If a soul breaks, it's best to leave it in peace. It's impossible to predict what will happen when something so alive puts itself back together once more.

34. The soul does not sense, but resents.

35. "I shall never bark again," my soul meowed. "I never achieve anything with that, and on top of everything, I'm getting strange looks." Then it curled up in its corner to purr with satisfaction, while it slyly sharpened its claws.

36. The soul is not empowered to administer justice: it is impossible for it to act with indifference.

37. The tiny pink and conventional souls are the most common; that's why everything is going so badly.

38. When the soul shakes you by the shoulders in the middle of a dream, the nightmare arrives.

39. Spell to subdue the soul: carefully fold the area of pain.

40. Truth is the circumcision of the soul.

41. Every time I try to change profession, my soul acts crazy and speaks about the state of the weather.

42. Whims of the soul: romp in the cold and shake off the bits of anguish it always picks up on its shoes.

43. The souls of others produce indigestion; therefore, they should never be chewed.

44. The regions of the soul are as follows: the frozen corners, the leaks, the lilies which wave beneath the blades of a windmill, the inquisitions, and the protests. All are dangerous, although for very different reasons.

45. Fright can burn the edges of the soul. Unfortunately, this process is irreversible.

46. Animal souls are different from human ones: they're less animal.

47. The soul's locomotion is not as simple as one might think. Sometimes it gets stuck on the tiniest loopholes.

48. The soul does not shout: it whispers.

49. If one discovers a vast meadow, the soul surely must be nearby.

50. Reasons to protect my soul: it has a lot of blue, it moistens itself at night, and it likes to get covered in magic . . . Besides, it's mine.

Nadia López García

Nadia López García *(b. 1992) is a bilingual Tu´un Savi and Spanish language poet born in Caballo Rucio, Tlaxiaco, Oaxaca, Mexico. She is the author of four poetry collections:* Ñu´ú vixo/Tierra mojada, Tikuxi kaa/ El tren, Isu ichi/El camino del venado, *and* Las formas de la lluvia. *Her work has been translated into six languages: Spanish, Catalán, Arabic, Hindi, English, and French. In 2021, she was awarded the Luis Cardoza y Aragón Mesoamerican Poetry Prize. She coordinates the circle of First Nation poets at University of the Pacific. "Savi," "I Am Not Sad," "Harsh Wind," and "Broken Heartbeat," were translated from the Savi to Spanish by the author and from the Spanish by Gabriela Ramirez-Chavez.*

Savi

I've seen dark-eyed
rain women.

I've seen weep and laugh women,
water and earth women.
Displaced women, bird women,
I've seen word women, river women,
sky women.

I pray always to see women,
women who speak their words
into this vast sky
like jícaras overflowing with water.

Jícaras wetting the earth's seeds,
blooming into the sacred.

Savi

Mee kunchee ñá´an nchá´í ntuchinuu
ra savi.

Mee kunchee ñá´an kuaku ra kuákú,
ñá´an chikui ra ñu´ú.
Ñá´an koo ña´an ra ñá´an saa,
mee kunchee ñá´an tu´un, ñá´an yucha,
ñá´an antivi.

Ntakuatu mee kunchee ñá´an,
ñá´an kachi tu´unku
ntika antivi
yatsi kuá´á chikui.

Yatsi vixo ntiki ñu´ú
ra tsaa íí.

I'm Not Sad

They lie, the ones who say they read
death in my eyes.
They do not speak the truth,
the ones insisting that our tongue
will die
after three days of the deer.

I hear the rumble of limestone
and cantera in this godless city,
I stay up listening for the cricket-song
that will never come,
and devour the wind's silence.

A hidden plea
yearns to escape:

I'm not sad, I tell myself.
I'm not sad.

As long as my roots
course through my veins,
my tongue
will not die.

Koi kukana

Ntaá ña ka'un me ntuchinuu
kunchee ra chaku- ka'vi ntìi.
Koi ká'an ntaa
kachi nivi me tu'un
tsaa titsi ùni kii isu.

Na kuchaa so'o yó`ò káchi
yùù kàkà ñuu ka'un koi ñaño ìì,
tsa'ni mana kata tikoso
ra mee kátsi tachi.

Kumi tu'un ìì sèè
Ntuku nána:
Koi kunana, ká'an.
Koi kunana.

Me yo'o nai me niì,
me tu'un koi tsaa.

Harsh Wind

A harsh wind blew into my mouth,
down to my hips, and touched my feet.
We need more rain.

My father says that we women don't dream,
learn to make tortillas and coffee, he tells me,
learn to keep quiet.
He says that women don't write,
I am the girl who wept absence,
distance, and fear.

Today I say my name from the skies,
I am a bird woman,
a blossoming seed.
Words are my wings,
my wet earth.

Broken Heartbeat

Your mouth filled with emptiness
and you became a broken heartbeat
in the mouth of time.

You chewed on their words
to defend your land,
your water, your mountains,
but dispossession has no ears,
it is an old beast
that never sleeps.

That day you came to know the face of pain,
of festering rage.

Certain forms of pain come from the past,
they rest on the shoulder of shame,
fear, and sorrow.
Because some words are paths
untraveled, birds with no song,
memory turned to cal.

Because they cut out your words
and under your tongue they sowed fear,
silence.

I look upon cities,
deafening cities,
where singer-crickets hide,
where rivers run silent,
and birdsong
is no longer.
Here,
I begin
          to forget
the voice of my ancestors,
the deep thread
that anchors me to this earth.

The path of memory, our memory,
does not begin here. Our memory
is far more ancient
than their faceless bodies.

If tomorrow I leave this place,
if I search for my buried navel,
if I pray with my elders,
then tomorrow,
my word,
my sacred center,
          will not die.
My memory will be another,
it will be true,
it will be ours.

Mayra Santos-Febres

Mayra Santos-Febres *(b. 1966) was born in Carolina, Puerto Rico, and is the author of three short stories, five poetry collections, and five novels. Among her works are* Anamú y manigua, El orden escapado, Boat People, Pez de vidrio y otros cuentos, Sirena Selena *(Sirena Selena vestida de pena), and* Any Wednesday I'm Yours *(Cualquier Miércoles soy tuya). She won the Grand Prix Littéraire de l'Académie Nationale de la Pharmacie in Paris for her novel* La amante de Gardel. *She heads the University of Puerto Rico's Afro-Diasporic and Race Studies Program. Her work has been translated into seven languages. "The Word Perdón" was translated from the Spanish by Lawrence Schimel.*

The Word Perdón

I had never before understood what the word "forgiveness" meant. I supposed it referred to the saying: "If someone strikes you, turn the other cheek" or "You must forgive those who offend you." I'm not a particularly quarrelsome person. In fact, I hate fighting. I even detest defending myself. I know how to do so quite well, but it leaves me drained, as if my soul had been sucked dry. Nonetheless, I like to win. And since I don't like to fight but do like to add victories to my scorecard, over the years I've developed a certain talent for organization and strategy. All to avoid fighting, and at the same time, to attain the true achievement of my goals and objectives. I suppose, however, that this strategy isn't a good way to learn what perdón is.

I know how to avoid conflicts, to resolve them by alternate means, and I know how to fight. When I'm wounded, I prefer to retire from the field until the pain passes. Sometimes it takes me years before I return. Sometimes, weeks or months. Sometimes, I don't come back. It all depends on how much I loved the person or how serious their offense to me.

But recently I found the way to return to a place that had done me a lot of harm. What's more, I could appreciate the damage I suffered, understand how much good it did me. That's when I finally understood what Buddhists have wanted to explain for millennia and that here, in the wild lands of the militarized and melodramatic West, we've denominated "forgiveness." I learned that it's possible to thank pain, to see it as a lesson, to welcome devastating experiences as if they were a gift, and to celebrate those experiences is to truly forgive.

IT HAPPENED THAT IT WOULD soon be my birthday and I was thinking about my mother. I missed her. I don't know why. She's been dead for fifteen years. It also happened that since Navidades I'd given myself the task of rereading some diaries I've been keeping since I was twenty-eight. I'd never read them before. I just wrote things down in those notebooks: ideas for novels, random poems, comments about what I was reading and comments about what I was living. Twenty-three years worth of notes and observations. I did it in imitation of Virginia Woolf, who began her diary at the same age to give it to herself as a gift when she turned forty. I spent my forties raising kids, writing, and publishing novels. It didn't even occur to me to reread those annotations.

But one day, on the eve of fifty, I wanted to read my diaries. I wanted to know how I had turned into who I am now. A greater intelligence, that one that inhabits all human beings, had arranged that I would read them when I was ready to face the onslaught of stupidities, mental stalemates, and doubts I recorded, intermingled with luminous perceptions about the world, about my reading, and thoughts I've been developing for almost a quarter century. I discovered that I'm a deeply intelligent woman and, for a while now, one who is deeply confused, especially since my mother's illness and death.

For weeks I read the more than fifty books that collect these annotations of mine. On that Sunday when I thought of my mother, I came across the 2001 diary. That was the year when the mother of José Raúl González, Puerto Rican poet and author of *Barrunto*, passed away, and the year my own died as well. I think the mother of my poet friend died in May. I wrote him a letter never sent; I found it in the notebook. I also found my notes for the article "Memories of Alzheimer," which I published years later in *Nuevo día*. I didn't know I was getting ready. On June 6, 2001, my mother passed away.

When I finished reading the entry dated "June 6" I cried. But for the first time in years, I didn't start weeping from the pain of having been witness to that terrible death. Nor did I cry from anger. There were many, many years during which I was furious with my mother. How had she let herself get so sick like that? How could she have let so many things and so many people mistreat her so? How could she put the interests of so many others before her own, that she forgot to take care of herself, love herself, protect herself? That same olvido, that neglect, killed her young, at sixty-four years old, of a senile illness.

I lived *furious* with my mother and that rage made me hate people, because they didn't take care of my mother; made me hate myself, because I didn't know to spot the signs on time, I didn't step in, I couldn't save her; I hated literature, because it didn't let me see that my mother needed me. How should I know who and what sparked my fury in those days. I began to smoke like a chimney, not because it was cool, nor because I liked the taste of tobacco; but because I was choosing my death. I wasn't going to die of olvido, of neglect and forgetting and oblivion. I would die of anything, anything but olvido. With intention I chose a death different from my mother's.

That day, I also didn't cry from fear. To see someone become ill and die of Alzheimer's has an impact. It's a horrible death. There is no longer any dignity in her—or at least that's what I thought, until yesterday. For decades, I was very afraid. Who would occupy my mother's place, what other affection? I had never loved anyone as much. Even worse, I'd never been anything more important than the daughter of my mother,

Mariana Febres Fablú, fierce Black woman and educator. And out of guilt, of rage, of shame, I didn't feel like being an author, nor a teacher, nor anything. In fact, I began a hasty race to become a mother myself to fill that gap. In some way I wanted to correct that death and illness. That was my strategy, to become a Mariana who surpassed Mariana, to become a "su-per-version" of her. And I did it. Step by step, with intention.

That was my way of vanquishing her death. Of winning without entering the battle. That's what I thought. That my strategy had worked.

Nonetheless, that day when I reread my diaries, I wept from pure love. I can't explain it in any other way. My tears were like those of babies at daycare when they see their mother finally coming to look for them; that mix of relief, pain, and joy; when you weep because at last you can breathe, because at last you can feel without fear, because she'd come back. It was lovely. My tears didn't let me see the notes I took on that day my mother died. It wasn't necessary to read them. The words echoed still live in my memory, as if neither ink nor time had passed.

I finished crying. I went up to the terrace to smoke a cigarette. Then I whispered softly the words that left my mouth:

"Thank you for the pain, Mami. Thank you for your death."

I froze in place. I had not expected I had that capacity of understanding, that having arrived at last on the other side of my mother's death.

But the woman I am today owes so much to that death. I owe it twenty years of life.

At last, I forgave my mother for having died. I forgave life that it had given Mami Alzheimer's. I forgave myself for all those mistakes I made, even the mistake of not having died with her. Not for lack of trying.

Now that I know I'm able to forgive my mother's death, nothing frightens me. No offense can touch me. Not even that I might also suffer from Alzheimer's.

I think now I can give up smoking.

Von Díaz

Von Díaz *(b. 1981) was born in Puerto Rico and raised in Atlanta, Georgia. She is a writer, documentary producer, and author of the celebrated culinary memoir* Coconuts & Collards: Recipes and Stories from Puerto Rico to the Deep South *and* Islas: A Celebration of Tropical Cooking. *She regularly explores food, culture, and identity. Her work has been featured in the* New York Times, The Washington Post, *NPR, StoryCorps,* Food & Wine *magazine, and* Bon Appétit, *among many others. She also teaches food studies and oral history at the University of North Carolina at Chapel Hill. She currently sits on the board of directors for the Center for Documentary Studies at Duke University and is a member of the Journalism Awards Committee for the James Beard Foundation.*

Mi cocina, mi santuario

My first kitchen was in Rio Piedras, Puerto Rico. There, my parents, barely twenty, lived with my grandfather in a small two-bedroom concrete apartment next to a caserio. It had brown tile floors, no AC, and metal shutters instead of windows; sometimes chickens would walk in. There was always a heavy skillet on the stove with a thick layer of lard, ready to fry pork chops, Spam, or plátanos; lots of Coca-Cola in the fridge, which my grandfather enjoyed with the bottles of rum that were his undoing, and the cheap cigars that perfumed our home.

This was the first of my twenty-eight kitchens in the twenty-eight places I've called home over the past thirty-nine years. Each kitchen had its challenges—some large, some small, different tools and stoves—but what they all had in common was magic. The second kitchen in my life was my grandmother's in Altamesa, Puerto Rico: her fridge and wall tiles a muted canary yellow, the back door always open to keep the room cool and bright. Then, when my father joined the army, we moved to Fort Gillem in Forest Park, Georgia. There, I ate Trix cereal and Flintstones vitamins at our round wooden kitchen table, and microwave nachos after I'd come in from playing outdoors.

When my parents divorced, things got tough. We moved to a different apartment seemingly every year; and because my mom often worked late, I cooked for my sister and me: frozen fish sticks and chicken nuggets, instant mac and cheese, canned corn, spaghetti. Next, a townhouse in Riverdale, where I taught myself to make alfredo sauce from the *Betty Crocker Cookbook*, and perfect cheese eggs. Then off to my dad's in Jonesboro, a house in Savannah, another in McDonough, back to my mom's in Snellville—three total that year.

During this time of instability, I returned often to my second Puerto Rican kitchen. Struggling financially, Mami sent me to Puerto Rico for the summer. I relished my time in the kitchen with my grandmother, whom I called Tata, mashing garlic in the pilón for yuca con mojo, squeezing dozens of small juicy limes for her famous pie de limón, sautéing her homemade sofrito—brimming with earthy culantro and ají dulce—in simmering olive oil. That kitchen cemented my Boricua identity, the smells and flavors reflecting the hybridity of my lineage: Taíno, African, Spanish, and American. It also forced me to reckon with the class differences in my family; the concrete apartment next to the caserío where we began, Tata's modest but elegant suburban Puerto Rican home, the low-income housing where I lived in Atlanta.

But things got better. My stepdad was also in the Army and got stationed in Holland. We moved into a modern Dutch home with the smallest and loveliest kitchen I'd ever seen. Light bounced off white walls, floors, and ceilings, the fridge was the size of a hotel minibar, the oven too small for a Thanksgiving turkey. Because we couldn't store much, we made frequent trips to the neighborhood farmers' market for local meat, produce, and fresh eggs. I'd never eaten that way before, and I came to understand that my kitchens, and the ingredients and tools therein, reflected how well my family was doing.

More than a dozen kitchens would follow, due more to my own wanderlust than family instability: eight in Atlanta, one in Oakland, three in New York City. My Oakland kitchen sat in the back of a tiny railroad apartment. Its location and huge windows kept the rest of the house cool and brought sunshine streaming into glass cabinets that I filled with heirloom tomatoes, plumcots, and nectarines.

And then I moved to East Harlem, where my front door opened into a five-by-seven-foot, L-shaped closet of a kitchen. The stove was a tin box that broiled the apartment and was *also* too small for a turkey (I know, I tried). I had to move the fridge into the living room. But the space had a spirit, no doubt fueled by a neighborhood brimming with Puerto Rican culture: salsa and reggaeton streaming in from neighbors and cars; pasta de guayaba and banana leaves for wrapping pasteles at the bodega on the corner. While living there, Tata passed away (complications due to Alzheimer's) and I dedicated myself to preserving her memory through food. I inherited some of her tools—the decades-old lime press I had once used in Puerto Rico, a wooden tostonera. I lit candles and burned sandalwood incense before starting to cook, asking her hands to join in a ritual that honored her and nourished others.

I left New York for Durham, North Carolina, some years ago. My home has both an indoor kitchen and outdoor grill and firepit with every imaginable tool, gadget, and spice. Although we were never close, I honor my grandfather by frying in a heavy cast-iron skillet. And even though I drain the fat when I'm done, I recognize he reused oil as a form of resilience—each dish lending its flavor to the next while preserving precious resources.

My grandmother lives in this kitchen. Her portrait—a hand-dyed sepia-toned photo from the 1960s—rests in a silver mirrored frame. Her tools are here, as is her favorite cookbook, *Cocina criolla*, along with other books and magazine clippings peppered with handwritten notes, her elegant cursive jumping off the pages and into my pans. My kitchen is both studio and sanctuary, a place where I often get lost, where time stops, where I find myself dancing, spinning, and kicking my legs in a kind of boisterous elegy to my ancestors. The food I cook here is the best I've ever made. I believe it's because each of my cocinas has been a bridge, linking me to the ingredients, tools, and techniques that have kept my people alive for centuries; coalescing in a space where I can now conjure their magic to heal past wounds.

Dahlma Llanos-Figueroa

Dahlma Llanos-Figueroa *(b. 1949) was born in Carolina, Puerto Rico, and raised in the Bronx, New York. Her first novel,* Daughters of the Stone, *was a 2010 finalist for the PEN/Robert W. Bingham Prize. Her essays and short stories have appeared in* Kweli *journal,* Narrative Magazine, Latino Book Review, Afro-Hispanic Review, Pleiades, *and internationally in* Puñado *(Brazil) and* Wordetc *(South Africa), among others. She was awarded a 2021 NYSCA/NYFA Artist Fellowship in Fiction and, also in 2021, the Inaugural Letras Boricuas Fellowship from the Andrew W. Mellon Foundation and the Flamboyan Arts Fund. This is an excerpt from her novel* A Woman of Endurance *(Indómita), published in English and Spanish.*

Port of San Juan, Puerto Rico

November 1836

When she was taken from her Home Place, she had been Keera, a comely young woman with rounded hips, strong legs, and a flash of a smile. The woman, now renamed Pola by her captors, arrived on this other shore, this Puerto Rico. She now had three broken fingers, four missing teeth, and had been brutalized by every member of the crew. After the full moon had come and gone four times and the floating hell had made three stops, less than half of the original group of captives remained. Pola was taken to the upper deck for the last time.

She had been below for so many weeks that the sun was blinding. When her eyes finally adapted to the light, she looked out on a new world. This, it seemed, was to be her destination. The ship had docked in a place where the sea had taken a huge bite out of the land. And on the land was a strip of wood that jutted out into the water.

Pola and the rest of the captives were herded on the deck under guard. Earlier they had been hosed down and scrubbed clean under the careful eye of the crew. They were given makeshift clothes that barely covered their nakedness. Women were given cloths to cover their matted and tangled hair. Men were shorn of their matted beards and their heads were shaven. Food had become more plentiful in the past few weeks and now they were fed a last meal on board. During the voyage they had been separated by gender, but now they were chained in specific configurations including men, women, and young boys.

The group was suddenly in the midst of more commotion than Pola had seen since leaving home. Suddenly, there were unchained, shirtless Black men toiling in the morning sun. Most of these workers took care not to look at the captives directly, as they stood in rags and chains. The workers simply walked by, intent on unloading the crates that were taken to the squat buildings lining the shore. Some stepped carefully around the chained group, hoisting large, oddly shaped bundles and huge sacks that went directly into waiting wagons. Not one of them said a word, pretending not to notice the band of half-naked, bony Black people, mostly men who stood to one side.

One young boy tripped, dropped his load and bent down to retrieve it. As he stood up again, he looked directly into Pola's eyes for a moment. She stared back and held his gaze. There, she read all she needed to know about his life and she could see that he read all he needed to know about hers. Pola recognized the sadness she felt pressing against her eyes alive in his. His was an infinitesimal nod. She slowly pulled at the rag that barely covered her naked breast. Someone called. The boy was jostled. The moment passed, and they went on to face their lives in this place neither of them had chosen.

The ship had slipped in beside dozens of others that had already dropped anchor or were moored at the harbor, their masts a collection of sticks prodding the low-swung blanket of clouds. As she stood waiting for the nonhuman cargo to be off-loaded, Pola was shocked by the number of people who filled the area below. It seemed that in this place, the market was right on the shoreline, as though the people couldn't wait until the merchants got to the village center to hold the sales.

But before she could observe much else, a strong jerk on her arm brought her attention back. She was being pulled onto a narrow plank of wood that led from the vessel to the shore. Chained to a line of men and women, she cringed as she imagined one of them slipping and all of them drowning amid the waterlogged, rotting flotsam that floated between the ship and the dock. Decaying food, dead animals, and human waste filled the air with a choking stench. The babble that rose around them as they stood on the pier was deafening. It sounded like no speech Pola had ever heard, the words, jagged, grating sounds that attacked the ear. She realized she was listening to not one but many different languages and recognized an odd word or two of the language of her captors. Their language was as offensive as their behavior.

Then Pola's eyes fell on the white women in the crowd. They wore long dresses covering them from neck to foot, many pointing into boxes and picking their way through open packages—cloth, containers, fruits, fish, metal tools, and figurines—being sold right from the waterfront. She noticed that some had straw-colored hair hanging down to their shoulders. They carried little umbrellas and wore round boxes on their heads with thin netting floating over their faces. Pola was reminded of the beaded and colorful masks worn by believers dancing for the gods back home. But these paled by comparison. They were colorless and flimsy. There was nothing ceremonial about the movements of the women who were focused on grabbing and exchanging paper for the objects before them.

White men stood by waving sticks and gesturing to the Black bare-breasted men who hoisted and heaved roped cargo. From the bridge, they had looked like black worker ants, running back and forth around the freight that had already been unloaded. But up close, Pola could see the weariness, the straining bodies; smell the sweat of laborers who, much like herself, had no time to care for themselves.

The line of captives snaked through the harbor crowds and on to an open area full of men in hats who stood yelling and waving their arms; laughing and passing jugs around. She was herded to a corner of the square to await her turn at the stake in the center, where one captive after another was exhibited to men waving pieces of paper. There was much back and forth, and then paper changed hands and the purchase was dragged away.

When it was her turn to stand at the block, Pola was released from her chains and dragged up onto the platform to the pole where she was tethered once again. *Mother Yemayá, where are you now that I need you most?* Pola closed her eyes. She thought about all that had already been taken from her; her lovely fingers, her teeth, her body, her untouched womanhood, her laughter. But they hadn't taken everything. She clung to her faith, her soul, and her secret—the seed she knew was growing deep within her.

She smelled tobacco, sweat, and rancid breaths as fingers poked, hands examined scalp, squeezed breasts, and slapped buttocks. Someone pulled back her lip and dug into her mouth. She bit down as hard as she could. The loud male cry was followed by a stinging slap that knocked her down, leaving her hanging from the ropes that bound her to the stake. She was dragged up again. And then hands rubbed at her belly and below, digging and jabbing at her bruised insides. Men laughed, then argued. The hands went away and they were done.

One man, short, fat, and self-satisfied, seemed especially pleased as he walked up. The others laughed and clapped him on the back. Satisfied smiles, money exchanged and pocketed.

The auctioneer jabbed at a young boy hanging back behind the platform. He was dressed in breeches and shirt, much like some of the men at the back of the crowd. "¡Apunta tú ahí! La Negra Pola, now the property of Don Sicayo Duchesne, master of Hacienda Paraíso. Next!" The boy scribbled something on a long piece of paper. And then it was over.

Now Pola's chains were replaced by thick rope around her wrists. The man bought five Africans that day. As he watched, they were pulled up into a wagon. His white shirt stretched across his ample belly and shone in the sun. His tightly woven straw hat covered most of his long hair, which brushed his collar. His dark moustache framed thin lips, and his pointy, white teeth bit down hard on his cigar as he took charge of his new possessions. She did not know it then, but he had bought her as he would buy a breeding mare. Her true nightmare was about to begin.

Nastassia Rambarran

Nastassia Rambarran *(b. 1981) was born in New Amsterdam, Guyana. She is a poet, writer, researcher, and LGBTQ activist. She was the winner of the 2021 Frank Collymore Literary Endowment Prime Minister's Award for poetry. She self-published* Time Jumbie, *a chapbook of poems exploring love, ancestry, and Queer thoughts from the Caribbean.*

Which Land?

When I was small
I was fiercely patriotic
Burnham chile
Drenched in national songs
And wrung in redblackgoldwhiteandgreen
Scoffing at backtrack and merica
I would never leave

Then one trip lead to another
Farin was nice,
But I would never stay
Decades later I end up straddling a sea
Choking up when landing on both sides
Confused more than ever

Guyanese was a dutty word
Scorn, mockery, and smirking its companions
Accent too sprawling to be sexy
Clothes too sparkly to be cool
One step above Haiti as only source of pride

Things change some since
Or maybe I juss doan notice anymore
Decades of proudly correcting people
Relishing the surprise when they hear the words
Ize Guyanese

Food, games, smells, language, and navel string support this
But when I fly over
A green so dense
Or lie under
A savannah sky so neverending
And walk through the bush
That could easily hide me forever
I not so sure

Three generations have walked these flats
Planting and mud seeped into pores
In a new country
Becoming one with the littoral
But claiming much more
Land unseen and incomprehensible
Indifferent to the struggles of those who live in that bush
What do *they* call themselves?
Ize Guyanese
But where exactly is Guyana?

Ana María Shua

Ana María Shua *(b. 1951) was born in Buenos Aires, Argentina, and is well known for her microfiction and children's literature. Among her novels are* La muerte como efecto secundario, Hija, *and* El peso de la tentación; *her collected works are* Que tengas una vida interesante. *Among her microfiction novels are* Fenómenos de circo *and* La guerra. *She is a recipient of a Guggenheim Fellowship, Spain's Premio Nacional de Literatura, and Mexico's Premio Iberoamericano de Minificción Juan José Arreola. Her books have been translated into fifteen languages. "Duality," "The Ballad of Snorri Gunnarson," and "Joan of Arc Hears Voices" were translated from the Spanish by Steven J. Stewart.*

Duality

What a strange race. I've personally spent time in the radiation rooms in their hospitals, where the soft ozone smell reminds one's olfactory organs of the beginning of a storm. With wonder I've contemplated the complex, expensive, and precise apparatuses that humans have come up with to delay the death of other sick members of their species, treating them one by one, while they simultaneously knock out artifacts capable of destroying hundreds of thousands at once. They're admirable and also scary. I advise you to avoid their world, which, with no enemies in sight, they're intent on destroying all by themselves.

The Ballad of Snorri Gunnarson

Snorri Gunnarson has fallen on the battlefield but isn't dead. Snorri Gunnarson has a sprained ankle. Snorri Gunnarson has decided not to get up.

Atop their giant wolves, the Valkyries arrive. They come searching for the warriors who have died heroically in battle, to take them back to the Banquet Hall of Valhalla. There they will stay until the end of time, until the moment they will fight for Odin in the final battle. There are seven Valkyries, they're goddesses, they're beautiful, with a kiss of death they finish off the warriors who suffer.

The head Valkyrie advances toward Snorri Gunnarson with Wagnerian majesty. Snorri Gunnarson watches her approach, terrified.

Snorri Gunnarson isn't interested in the prize. Snorri Gunnarson imagines the Banquet Hall of Valhalla, imagines feeling sick from the mead, the smell of boar fat and drunken sweat, the brutal jokes, the lying boasts of the heroes, always the same until the world's end. Snorri Gunnarson doesn't want to be in the Banquet Hall of Valhalla. Snorri Gunnarson has a wife and kids. He's not a heroic warrior. Snorri Gunnarson wants to go home, to enjoy his brief human life.

Instead of kissing him, the Valkyrie spits on him with infinite disdain. Snorri Gunnarson breathes a sigh of relief, of joy—he breathes. And the air he inhales and exhales with his trembling lungs gives him the greatest pleasure that he'll feel the rest of his long, long life.

Joan of Arc Hears Voices

Joan of Arc hears voices. For her, for the French, they are the voices of God and his angels. For the English, they are the voices of the Devil and his demons, one more proof of her witchcraft or heresy. Mental-health specialists today consider the possibility of a hallucinatory psychosis. Meanwhile, between sanity and madness, Joan of Arc leads the French army with undeniable strategic and tactical skill, in addition to encouraging her troops with her presence, with her fervor, with her white armor. Joan of Arc hears voices or maybe not, maybe she doesn't hear anything, maybe she needs the voices like she needs her maidenhood, just because she's a woman, maybe she goes to war just because she likes it, using patriotism and the supposed help of God as excuses, like any man.

Yvette Modestin (Lepolata Apoukissi)

Yvette Modestin (Lepolata Apoukissi) *(b. 1969) is a writer, activist, poet, and storyteller, born and raised in Colón, Panama. She is a coeditor of the anthology* Women Warriors of the Afro-Latina Diaspora *and a contributor to* The Afro-Latin@ Reader: History and Culture in the United States. *Her work also appears in* Afro-Latin@s in Movement: Critical Approaches to Blackness and Transnationalism in the Americas. *She is a contributor to the essay collection* The Trayvon Martin in US: An American Tragedy *as well as the anthologies* Psychological Health of Women of Color, Rapsodia Antillana, *and* Antología de la poesía colonense 1900–2012. *Her poetry book* Nubian Butterfly: The Transformation of a Soulful Heart *was published in Panama in 2019.*

Black Spirit

Black Spirit,
Whispering resiliency, sweet child,
Rise up in the light I shine upon you.
Black Spirit
Walks by,
That scent
Oh, that scent
Sandalwood
Lines up my spine.
Black Spirit,
Serenades me,
Walk tall my child.

Black Spirit,
Be telling me
Esta gente no saben na,
Colón es Africa!
Libre Somos!
Jah!!!
Black Spirit,
Guides me
Protects me
Sustains me
Dances with me.
Black Spirit, is love
Reminding me,
I am never alone!
Ase!

Carmen Boullosa

Carmen Boullosa *(b. 1954) was born in Mexico City and is the award-winning author of nineteen novels, four books of essays, eighteen collections of poetry, and ten plays. Much of her work has been translated into English, including* Texas: The Great Theft, The Book of Anna, *and* Before. *Her first poetry collection to appear in English was* Hatchet, *translated by Lawrence Schimel. "The Rice" comes from her chapbook* La impropia, *about the students from the Ayotzinapa Rural Teachers' College in Iguala, Mexico, who were killed or abducted and disappeared. It too has been translated from the Spanish by Lawrence Schimel.*

The Rice

Oh! I've burnt the rice!
I'm distraught!
The stench has left my soul
reeking like a smelly dishcloth,
never dry, never clean, always at hand.

Each grain of rice has been framed
with a black border by the flames,
which joins it to its siblings.
All the little rices are now one,
a single disaster,
scab of an open wound.

What shall I give my guests for dinner?
I'd set my hopes

on a major rice entrée,
multiple independent grains,
soaked in coconut milk,
overflowing with shrimps and scallops.

Now the pot seems a torso with neither head nor neck
that would hang exhibited at some pedestrian bridge.
The platter like a gringo jail,
like a bullet shot on purpose against a Black
child.

Dismembered or imprisoned the bodies
that should be a living set.
Squished together, blackened.

This was not a rice to devour
but one to live, laugh, talk, enjoy.
Before it,
we would have felt eternal.
At the least
we would have chatted with friends,
and, meanwhile, we'd have filled with grandkids.

Now we have only bereaved relatives.
Parents burying their children.
Grandchildren burying their parents
after exhuming them.
Human rights dig
to identify
cadavers lost in the mass.
On the shared table, there is only burnt rice
and silence.

AQUEOUS MOON

This moon has the energy of the spirit of water, the first medicine, all healing.

Mikeas Sánchez

Mikeas Sánchez *(b. 1980) is an Ajway, Chiapas born Zoque poet, translator, radio producer, teacher, and land defender. She inherited her poetic sensibility from her grandfather, Simón Sanchez, a shaman, musician, and Zoque dancer. From him she learned about the rhythm and musicality of the ancient chants and prayers. She is the author of six poetry collections and has won the Premio Estatal de Poesía Indígena Pat O'tan. Her works have been translated into English, Bengali, Italian, Mayan, Mixe, German, Portuguese, and Catalán. "We Will Return to the Path" ("Volveremos al camino")
is from her poetry collection* How to Be a Good Savage and Other Poems (Jujtzye tä wäpä tzamapänh'ajä/Cómo ser un buen salvaje). *"Naming Things: Three" is from the eleven-poem series "Wejpäj'kiu'y"/"Nombrar las cosas," in the collection* Mojk'jäyä/Mokaya. *All of these poems were translated from the Zoque to Spanish by the author and from the Spanish by Wendy Call.*

We Will Return to the Path

At funeral wakes we drink coffee
and the faces of our beloveds
evaporate with each sip.
We will again become
the morning breeze that feeds
the Wind Goddess Okosawa.
The candles' glow will guide us
to the sacred mountains:
the Mokayas' home.

The scent of yellow cempasúchil
will make us forget what we have been.
We will again be
maize flowers,
an offering for Nasakopajk.

Maka' tä' wyrurame ntä' ntunh'omo

Ntä' ujktampa kafel' nyojayajpak' anima',
tese' ponyi'ponyi joko'jinh maka nhkyene
te' ntä' sutyajpapä ntä' ntäwäs'nyeram.
Maka tä' tujk'wyrurame'
naptzupä'sawa
Oko'sawas nhkyut'kuy
Te' no'as syänh'käis
maka' tä' isanh'tzirame' juwure' te Masanh'kotzäjk:
Mokayas'tyäjktam
Te' putzy'jäyäs yoma'jinh
maka' ntä' jampärame' ntä' ijtkuy Nasakopaj'käsipä'na'.
Maka tä' tujk'wyrurame'
Mojk'jäyä
Nasakopaj'kis'wyenhti.

Naming Things: Three

I came, Yaxpalangui, to offer you my words
the sole inheritance of my lineage
I came to sing you this song I learned in my mother's womb
when I still lived in Paradise
Then I recognized your face like I did the path
that led me to your name
Then I kept an altar of palm and bougainvillea
at the center of my soul

Then I was a pepper-scented temple
That is why I came, Yaxpalangui, to offer you my words
my sole talent revealed to me in dreams

Wejpäj'kiu'y: Tukay

Tekoroya mitutzi mij' dziyae' äj' dzame'ram Yaxpalangui
yä' tzajkayajubä' äj anuku'istam
mitutzi' mij' wajne yä' wane' ngomusubätzi äj' mama's chiejk'omo
Tzuan'nak äj' ndäjk
Jiksek' mij' ispäjkpaj'na' mij' winujpajk'
muspajna' mij' ngänuka' mij' näyi'
Jiksek konukspajna' turäjin totojäyäjin
äj' ngojama'kujkmä
Jiksek äjtejna' tumä' masandäjk' moki'ombabä
Tekoroya mitutzi mij' dziyae' äj' dzame'ram Yaxpalangui
yä' tzäki' tziyajubätzi' äj' mabaxi'omo

Catalina Infante Beovic

Catalina Infante Beovic *(b. 1984) is a writer, editor, and journalist born in Buenos Aires, Argentina. She is a coauthor of three books of stories of the First Nation People of Chile. One of the books,* Aventuras y orígenes de los pájaros, *was selected for the Honour List of the International Board on Books for Young People. Other works include a novella,* La otra ciudad, *a picture book,* Dichos redichos, *and an artist's book,* Postal nocturna. *Her story collections include* Todas somos una misma sombra *and* Helechos. *"Green Gold, Blue Gold" was translated from the Spanish by Michelle Mirabella.*

Green Gold, Blue Gold

I'm terrified of winter growing shorter each year until all that's left of it are a few cloudy hours and a couple of predawn rains amid the many days of intense heat and sweat-induced insomnia. Sometimes I think about this dramatically, about how winter will never come again. About the fires and confused trees. About the charred fruit and about us— holed up in the house, seeking refuge from the concrete and the sun. It's winter now; my son is in the backyard smeared with sunscreen, and me, I'm in bed with spring pollen allergies, a spring that's come early. The smell of cherry trees in bloom this time of year distresses me. Today on TV I heard an expert say that within the next three decades the landscape in this region will turn arid and desertlike. I wonder if some will die of thirst. In a movie I saw about the Jewish Holocaust they said that, more than hunger, it was the feeling of thirst that made you go crazy, fall into despair, cry out begging for help. Right now, there's nothing that distresses me more than thirst. It sounds delusional, but it's something I see at night like spasms that come to me from the future, that are happening now, in another dimension. I don't tell my husband so that he doesn't laugh at me. So that I don't feel like an ingenuous, imaginative little girl. But today, a girl from Sweden, with all the ingenuousness and imagination that childhood affords, pointed her finger at those men who govern it all, and spoke of the beginning of the mass extinction of our species—the way it happened with the dinosaurs, except the dinosaurs didn't know it, and it wasn't their fault. Perhaps that's worse, disappearing from the face of the Earth without having done anything to deserve it. We deserve it, but that does nothing for my distress. Supposedly there's still something we can do about it, but we're stubborn and ambitious, and we won't.

The demand for water is skyrocketing globally.
The world population continues to grow.
The aquifers are stressed.

I see a story on the news about the Petorca province in Chile, a little to the north of Mostazal, where I'm writing from; it's a snapshot of what's to come. What once was fertile land now is wasteland. And this isn't an issue of climate change alone, this is about the brutal inequalities of *our* America, as Martí would say. In Chile, the vast majority of water rights are privately owned, free of charge, and in perpetuity. Water is severed from its land—as it says in the 1981 Water Code, which was made by the dictator Augusto Pinochet. In other words, landowners don't necessarily own the water running through their land. This makes it so that any company can alter the watercourses and suck the groundwater dry, leaving people without water and making them believe it's due to climate change. That's what's happening in Petorca, the reporter says: water is delivered to the residents on trucks that sometimes don't show up, while the large commercial palta companies—aguacate, as the fruit is called in the rest of America—have their orchards with their avocado-laden trees just a stone's throw away. Their crop dried out 100 percent of the community, the animals are dying of hunger and thirst, and the children can't go to school because they don't have water.

The ice is receding.
The snow isn't painting the mountains.
The cows are collapsing, skinny, unable to get up.

Avocado is tropical; when irrigated it demands enormous amounts of water. Growing it in Chile isn't natural, but they force the land because they say it's "green gold." It's trendy at brunch in New York, also in China, two of the regions that receive the most exports. So trendy that during the Super Bowl alone, the United States consumes seventy-four thousand pounds of avocado. So trendy that an exclusive brand released a sneaker mimicking its colors and texture, and Jimmy Fallon shared a picture of his on Instagram next to two pieces of avocado toast. In China it slipped into breakfast, they call it "butter fruit"; they've come up with a hamburger that uses avocado in place of a bun; and women use it in their face masks (I have one myself). In Latin America, the people are mobilizing en masse to exercise sovereignty over their water resources. In Chile, the students are fighting to change the laws on this matter. Meanwhile, people are taking pictures of their eggs benedict with avocado and posting them on Instagram using filters that enhance their chic, exotic color.

The Paraná is drying up.
The green of the Amazon basin is shrinking in the fires.
The Dry Corridor is migrating.
The Argentine forests are soybeans and cotton.

I sneeze in protest over a false spring, and my son switches out his pants for shorts in the middle of winter vacation. In a few decades, this land will be dry. The landscape we're looking at, the two of us, will become increasingly arid, like Petorca, and the dust will float among the willows that fade as time races on. I wonder if people will die of thirst. Supposedly there's still something we can do about it, but that's even more distressing, because we know we're stubborn and ambitious, and we won't.

Claudia Mera

Claudia Mera *(b. 1971) is a writer, feminist activist, mom, and visual art producer born in Montevideo, Uruguay. She runs Wanderland, a cultural production studio, and is the author of* Humedades, *an erotic novel that explores female vulnerability and sexuality. "Never Letting Go" ("No soltarnos más") was translated from the Spanish by Sandra Guzmán.*

Never Letting Go

I walk the fine line that divides the nonsense from a silly joke that is said to release tension. My heart beats fast because it's just you and me, and I don't know what to tell you.

Rather, I know what to say but I don't know if I can.

I can, but I don't know if I should.

It's you and me and no one else.

And you look at me and I look at you and I think about what the exact color of your eyes will be while I let myself fall into your gaze.

All the elastics that support my body are cut and my body relaxes, fragile. You could knock me to the ground by simply exhaling.

Blow on me with your mouth.

Your mouth, ajar, that says nothing but looks at me as if it wants to eat me. Your mouth that I anticipate, a tongue that I imagine warm, wet, but above all, determined.

You look at me and I at you, and we eye each other increasingly more intensely, because our eyes are overflowing with beginners' eyes, eyes that imagined us without clothes and without histories when we were allowed to be only skin.

One meter twenty separate us, but still I can smell you, so much so that I feel as if you were already inside me, I can smell your heat and my body quivers faintly, an impercetible tremble that only you can feel.

And you come.

You come and you touch me, eat me, and you come.

You ask me how long two people can look at each other like that without biting each other, without fusing, degenerating, splitting in half in profound unity.

I tell you I don't know, but let's try, while I'm a spring that overflows and can hardly breathe.

I don't smile, so you don't copy me, because I know that just a trace of your smile will unleash a waterfall from me.

How long will we be able to look into each other's eyes without shaking, dwelling in each other, coming together, dismembering, melding into one another, and never letting go?

Never letting go.

Angie Cruz

Angie Cruz *(b. 1972) was born in Washington Heights, New York, to Do-minican parents.* She is the author of four novels, Soledad, Let It Rain Coffee, How Not to Drown in a Glass of Water, *and* Dominicana, *which was short-listed for The Women's Prize and won the ALA/YALSA Alex Award. Cruz is editor-in-chief of the award-winning literary journal* Aster(ix) *and teaches at the University of Pittsburgh. Her forthcoming books include the picture book* Angélica and la Güira. *"Luna's Lot" is an excerpt from a novel-in-progress.*

Luna's Lot

Like most of my friends, I live with my mother and have never met my father. Or so I met him, but I still had my eyes glued together. He went off to war and came back messed up. So my mother pretended like he was dead. Or dead to me. Definitely dead to her.

I like to take photographs. My mother likes to be in them. This pretty much sums up our relationship.

I can tell a lot about people when I take their photo. My best friend Siobhan Lee never has a bad face on, angling always in a way to catch the best side of her.

We live on the Upper East Side in the fancy projects. Not Section 8 poor but in a mixed-income building where 20 percent of the apartments go to lottery winners.

My mother is good at playing the lottery. She plays every week. Every time she wins money she plays 20 percent of her earnings. This is her in-vestment in our future. "But money is not everything," she says. "Having an affordable apartment in New York City is better than winning a few thousand dollars in a lottery."

"I won the lottery!" she says every time she shares with me how she defied some terrible statistic.

More than half of the women and girls migrating into the US by way of Mexico are raped.

My mother was not raped. Even after traveling on foot, on bus, on train. Her journey from El Salvador to the United States took over three months. She carried almost nothing: a bottle of water and an extra shirt. She was a teen when she took the trek with a caravan. When we turn on the news and see the children in cages, she says, "It was easier back then." She didn't lose a limb jumping on and off the trains like so many have.

On her wrist she wrote with permanent marker the name and number of Tía Maria just in case they found her body thrown on the side of a road somewhere. "Someone who loves me should know I am gone," she said. ·

"Look at these feet—how big they are. They earned their size. I walked thirty miles in one day."

"When I die, I don't want a funeral with crying. Promise me that you'll incinerate me and throw me in a pot of soil and grow a plant that comes back every year. Maybe orchids? They look like they're done with life and then they surprise you; flowering more beautiful than before."

I guess my mother is a prepper. Or she likes to prep me for the inevitable. Unless we somehow defy the inevitable; then we celebrate.

When I turned fifteen, I didn't get a big party to welcome me into womanhood; instead my mother took me to a clinic to get me birth control pills. Did you know that 25 percent of teens become pregnant between the ages of fifteen and seventeen? Some things we can't control like being raped, for example, but pregnancy is avoidable. After we went to the clinic and picked up the pills at the corner pharmacy, she took me and Siobhan to celebrate science. She even allowed us to have one shot of sake at my favorite ramen restaurant.

One shot is medicinal. Two shots is another story. That night my mother had six shots.

Once in the United States, one out of six—or is it one out of five, some-times the study comes out with one out of four—women are raped, or someone attempts to rape them, or assault them, or molest them without consent . . . often by someone they know. "Even grandfathers are capable of such things," she'd say.

"Tell me you won the lottery," she asks often and looks straight into my eyes to see if I am keeping any secrets. Her eyes and mine are a solid ce-dar brown like our family back home, who spent most of their lives work-ing with cedar because cedar is termite proof. Me and my mother both have a speck on the top left of the left eye. She calls that speck inheritance.

"Of what?"

"Who knows? Something your grandmother didn't want us to forget."

"Tell me, querida, did you . . ."

"Yes, Mami, I won the lottery."

In the bathroom my mother hung up a sign: OUR BODY, OUR RULES. She made it with colorful markers that she found in the trash in a backpack full of supposedly "used" supplies. "Back home, a kid would kill for these markers," she said, adding them to my extensive collection of art things.

"Did you know that more than half of us become pregnant before the age of twenty?"

My mother didn't have me until she was twenty-four years old. My grandmother thought she would never get a grandchild from my mother. And like it happens in the movies, the day my grandmother died, I was born. We overlapped on Earth, three hours and twenty-two minutes. Enough time so her spirit can take my body.

"Does that make me your mother?" I asked my mother.

Then she lifted my arm and smelled my pits. A long deep breath, she would take, and look up as if she could remember exactly her mother's scent. If Abuelita is inside of you—do me a favor—live an adventurous and pleasurable life because all she knew how to do was suffer.

Stephanie Elizondo Griest

Stephanie Elizondo Griest *(b. 1974) is a globetrotting author born in Corpus Christi, Texas. Her books include* Around the Bloc: My Life in Moscow, Beijing, and Havana; Mexican Enough; *and* All the Agents and Saints. *She has also written for the BBC, the* New York Times, Travel + Leisure, *and* Oxford American, *and her work has won a Richard J. Margolis Award for social justice journalism. An associate professor of creative nonfiction at the University of North Carolina at Chapel Hill, she has also performed as a Moth storyteller.*

Otoño

When the surgeon called—presumably for my post-op check—Mom was busy coaxing Dad out of the kitchen, but by the time I hung up, she was kneeling beside me while he ate every chocolate in the pantry. We stared at each other, too stunned to speak.

Seven days before, the surgeon had dredged a tumor the size of a basketball from my womb. A team of pathologists had declared it benign while I still lay open on the operating table. Now that they'd studied the tumor more carefully, however, the verdict had changed. I had stage one ovarian cancer, the surgeon said, and must now undergo chemotherapy to prevent it from spreading.

Back when I was healthy—just two weeks prior—I conceived of my body as a harmonious whole. But the first thing you realize as a cancer patient is how many of its parts are expendable. Loyalties are instinctively drawn and viscerally felt. The moment I learned what my ovaries had grown, for instance, I wanted them gone. No matter that I hadn't yet birthed a child, or that, at age forty-three, I'd be instantly menopausal. I felt no mercy for those organs. Ditto with my breasts. When a geneticist screened me for the BRCA gene, I vowed to have a double mastectomy if she found a trace.

But losing my hair to chemo was another matter entirely. Not only did I associate it more with my womanhood than either my breasts or my uterus, but it was also the most visibly Mexican thing about me. I had the blue eyes and light skin of my paternal Griest family, but my pelo was puro Elizondo: thick, dark, and curly. One of the last things anyone remembers my maternal abuela saying before she committed suicide at age twenty-five was that she didn't ever want her youngest son's curls cut. Las tías upheld that wish until he was refused enrollment at elementary school because of it. Having few other connections to my abuela, I started wearing my hair halfway to my elbows in high school and had kept it that length ever since.

My ovaries, my uterus, possibly even my breasts: none of those losses would make me any less than myself. But my hair was my identity. My ancestry. My inheritance. I wouldn't feel part of this lineage without it.

Suddenly, I was hyperventilating. Mom steered me out onto the balcony, grabbing Dad along the way. He had reached that stage of Alzheimer's where he was largely self-absorbed, but he still enjoyed excitement. For the moment, we were more intriguing than the pantry.

Mom sat me down in the Adirondack chair and ordered Dad to hold my hand while she punched numbers into her phone. I thought she was calling the surgeon, but then the voice of my sister, Barbara, resounded through the speaker. All of our nuclear family was now here.

Yet breath did not return. My body had been absorbing one trauma after another for fourteen days straight, and my lungs had apparently declared una huelga. Mom held the phone and Dad held my hand as I held my pelo and heaved.

It was late September in Chapel Hill, North Carolina. The oak tree above us was already autumnal. As a breeze rustled through it, golden leaves began to fall.

"You see that?" Mom asked. "That's you. You are going to lose your hair just like this tree will lose its leaves."

As the wind intensified, more leaves swirled around us. I stared up at the branches as they slowly denuded like my body soon would, not only my pelo but also my eyelashes, my eyebrows, my leg hair, my arm hair, and my pubic hair, until I was wholly naked, until I was a middle-age woman reborn.

I shifted my gaze from the oak tree to the increasingly vacant eyes of my father. At seventy-nine, he had lost his prostate, a segment of his colon, most of his mind, and nearly all of his hair, but there he was, comforting me. Behind him stood my mother, who would spend the next four months caring for us both with ferocious tenderness. Her own curls had whitened long ago.

"And then spring will come," Mom said.

Still clenched in her hand was the phone projecting my sister's voice. Named after the abuela whom none of us had known, Barbara was home in San Antonio with the daughter and son who would someday scatter all these stories.

"Spring will come, and you will grow it back again."

With this promise came the gift of breath that our three generations exhaled.

Natalia Toledo

Natalia Toledo *(b. 1967) was born in Juchitán de Zaragoza, Oaxaca, Mexico, and writes in Isthmus Zapotec. The award-winning poet has written six books of poetry, all bilingual (Zapotec/Spanish). "A Seer's Path," "Don't Forget the Vine Turned Serpent Wrapped Around Your Infant Heel," and "I Wore My Huipil's Fronds into Winter" come from her forthcoming* Decree bitoope/El dorso del cangrejo *(Carapace dancer). They were translated from the Isthmus Zapotec to the Spanish by the poet and from the Spanish by Clare Sullivan.*

A Seer's Path

How many times did I stick my head into the basket's heart
so that they wouldn't forget me.
In my hiding place I ate warped tortillas
so I'd marry an old man.
I played with the dog's tail and became a liar.
Beneath our household altar I ate a brittle turtle egg
that dried out my lips.
A buzzard cast a spell on my slingshot when I lost myself in the dance
of his flight.
It rained at all my weddings because I licked the cooking pot clean
ahead of time.
I crossed two knives over my eyes
to slice up the eye of shame.
How could you ever approach me if every night
I hung a string of garlic in my bedroom

and in my window a shirt full of salt,
from my uncle, who got mermaids pregnant.

Xneza ni ruuya'do'

Ana panda bieque guluaa ique' ndaani' ruba
ti cadi gusiaandacabe naa ya'.
Naga'chi' ritahua' gueta naxubi ruaa
ti guichagana'ya' nguiiu yooxho'.
Gudxite' xubaana' bi'cu' ne biziide' gusiguiee'.
Xa'na' mexa' bidó' ritahua' dxita bigu bidxi
de ra bicuidxe' guidiruaa'.
So'pe' bicaa xiguidxa' tiniyaala xtinne' ne binite'
lade saa xhiame.
Guirá xquendaxheela' biaba nisaguie
runi bindiee' ndaani' guisu guendaró.
Bichuuga' guielua' ne ti gudxíu ne bixuxhe' lu xtuí.
Paraa chi guidxiñu' naa ya' pa guirá gueela'
rugaanda' ti ludoo aju ra guse' ne ti gamixa' dxa'
zidi,
xti' xa xtiua'ya', bisiaca xiiñi'ca gunaa benda.

Don't Forget the Vine Turned Serpent
Wrapped Around Your Infant Heel

Can I tell you something?
all that's left of that innocent creature who caressed
a deer beneath the almond tree's darkening shadow
is a scorpion that bites her veins.
A mark plastered on her clothing
trapped in brackish water.
When I was a girl
I loved to walk in the mud,

my mother roasted chilies and placed them between my toes
to heal my wounds.
In those days I had no memory of time
because my people spoke with the clouds.
I'll tell you one thing more:
I loved you because you weren't content with my image
in the well and you went to my umbilical home
you understood why I changed and became someone else.
You knew me as I was and that among so many brambles there
        could also be happiness.
You said:
Tell me what lullabies sang you to sleep.
Yes, I said:
There are many serpent words upon my back,
but I no longer speak with anyone,
I stopped speaking the language of the silent,
I have revealed my sign,
I have erased my face.
My portrait speaks with all the dead,
the wind has winnowed my seeds.
When my root went crack
I started walking without looking back.

Qui chigusiandu' lubá' naca beenda
yaniñee ca dxi gucu' ba'du'

Zabe lii xiixa lá?
Xa badudxaaapa' huiini' guxubiná ti bidxiña
xa'na' bacaanda' xiñá' rini sti' yaga biidxi qué
napa ti ngolaxiñe cayoyaa neza rini cuxooñe' ladi.
Ti duuba' na'si' ndaani' xhaba
nutaaguna' nisa sidi laa.
Dxi gúca' ba'du' nabé guyuladxe' saya' ndaani' beñe

jñiaa ruquii guiiña' ruguu lade bicuini ñee'
ti gusianda ra gucheza beñe,
nganga ca dxi guiruti qui nuguu bia' naa
purti binni xquidxe' tobisi diidxa' guní' ne ca za.
Zabe lii xti' diidxa' lá?
gunaxhie' lii purti qui ninalú' ñananeu bandá'
biluí' bizé xtine lii
ne guyelu' ndaani' yoo ra ga'chi' xquipe'
bie'nu' xiñee bichaa gúca' stobi
binibia'lu' tu naa ne laaca gunnu' zanda chu'
guendanayeche ra naxhii.
Na lu':
Gudxi naa xi saa bisiasi ne cabe lii
ya, gunie':
Nuu jmá diidxa' naca beenda'
galaa deche' caní' huahua',
ma giruti rinié niá',
ma bisiaanda' diidxa' guní' ca ni qui ñapa diidxa',
ma bilué tu naa,
ma bixhiaya' lua'.
Bandá' xtine riní' ne guirá ni ma guti
bi bixhele' ca xpiidxe'.
Ne dxi biluuza xcú bisuhua necabe naa
nisi guzaya' ne ma qui ñuu dxi nudxigueta lua'.

I Wore My Huipil's Fronds into Winter

On the other side of the world they have snow on their eyelids.
Even though the lights shine bright, the sky shuts down.
No matter, here I am,
my nanny brought me. I am my own family
and whatever hell I may land in
I am my only daughter.

Yeniá' yaga naga'xti' ca xoidaane' ra cayaba nanda

Deche gudxilayú daapa xubaguí ique lagaca'
neca reeche xtuxhu biaani' da'gu' lú guiba'.
Gasti naca, rarí nuaa',
bedané mani' bizidanda xtine' naa.
Laaca naa nga jñaa ne bixhoze'
rizayaniacá' lidxe'
ne ratiisi gabiá guxatañee'
tobilucha xiiñe' naa.

Mary Seacole

Mary Seacole *(1805–1881) was born in Kingston, Jamaica, to a Scottish soldier and a free Black Jamaican mother. A nurse with wanderlust, she traveled extensively throughout the Caribbean and Europe. During the Crimean War she offered to serve as an army nurse but was rebuffed because she was Black. Instead, she set up a hotel and sold food supplies and medicine to British soldiers. By the end of the war, she was destitute and bankrupt. In London in 1857 she published her autobiography,* Wonderful Adventures of Mrs. Seacole in Many Lands, *excerpted here, and it became an instant bestseller. She went on to gain recognition for her war efforts in England, France, and Turkey.*

Chapter 1

My Birth and Parentage— Early Tastes and Travels—Marriage and Widowhood

I was born in the town of Kingston, on the island of Jamaica, some time in the present century. As a female, and a widow, I may be well excused giving the precise date of this important event. But I do not mind confessing that the century and myself were both young together, and that we have grown side by side into age and consequence. I am a Creole, and have good Scotch blood coursing in my veins. My father was a soldier, of an old Scotch family; and to him I often trace my affection for a camp-life, and my sympathy with what I have heard my friends call "the pomp, pride, and circumstance of glorious war." Many people have also traced to my Scotch blood that energy and activity which are not always found in the Creole race, and which have carried me to so many varied scenes; and

perhaps they are right. I have often heard the term "lazy Creole" applied
to my country people; but I am sure I do not know what it is to be indolent.
All my life long I have followed the impulse which led me to be up and
doing; and so far from resting idle anywhere, I have never wanted incli-
nation to rove, nor will powerful enough to find a way to carry out my
wishes. That these qualities have led me into many countries, and brought
me into some strange and amusing adventures, the reader, if he or she
has the patience to get through this book, will see. Some people, indeed,
have called me quite a female Ulysses. I believe that they intended it as a
compliment; but from my experience of the Greeks, I do not consider it a
very flattering one.

My mother kept a boardinghouse in Kingston, and was, like very
many of the Creole women, an admirable doctress; in high repute with
the officers of both services, and their wives, who were from time to time
stationed at Kingston. It was very natural that I should inherit her tastes;
and so I had from early youth a yearning for medical knowledge and prac-
tice, which has never deserted me. When I was a very young child I was
taken by an old lady, who brought me up in her household among her own
grandchildren, and who could scarcely have shown me more kindness had
I been one of them; indeed, I was so spoiled by my kind patroness that,
but for being frequently with my mother, I might very likely have grown
up idle and useless. But I saw so much of her, and of her patients, that the
ambition to become a doctress early took firm root in my mind. As I grew
into womanhood, I began to indulge that longing to travel which will
never leave me while I have health and vigour.

I shall never forget my first impressions of London. Of course, I am not
going to bore the reader with them; but they are as vivid now as though
the year eighteen—(I had very nearly let my age slip then) had not been
long ago numbered with the past. Strangely enough, some of the most
vivid of my recollections are the efforts of the London street-boy's to poke
fun at my and my companion's complexion. I am only a little brown—a
few shades duskier than the brunettes whom you all admire so much; but
my companion was very dark, and a fair (if I can apply the term to her)

subject for their rude wit. She was hot-tempered, poor thing! and as there were no policemen to awe the boys and turn our servants' heads in those days, our progress through the London streets was sometimes a rather chequered one.

I remained in England, upon the occasion of my first visit, about a year; and then returned to Kingston. Before long I again started for London, bringing with me this time a large stock of West Indian preserves and pickles for sale. I spent some time in New Providence, bringing home with me a large collection of handsome shells and rare shell-work, which created quite a sensation in Kingston, and had a rapid sale; I visited also Hayti and Cuba. But I hasten onward in my narrative.

Returned to Kingston, I nursed my old indulgent patroness in her last long illness. After she died, in my arms, I went to my mother's house, where I stayed, making myself useful in a variety of ways, and learning a great deal of Creole medicinal art, until I couldn't find courage to say "no" to a certain arrangement timidly proposed by Mr. Seacole, but married him, and took him down to Black River, where we established a store. Poor man! He was very delicate; and before I undertook the charge of him, several doctors had expressed most unfavourable opinions of his health. I kept him alive by kind nursing and attention as long as I could; but at last he grew so ill that we left Black River, and returned to my mother's home at Kingston. Within a month of our arrival there he died. This was my first great trouble, and I felt it bitterly.

Alfonsina Storni

Alfonsina Storni *(1892–1938) was a feminist modernist poet, essayist, and playwright born in Sala Capriasca, Switzerland, to Italian Argentine parents. She returned to Rosario, Argentina, when she was four years old. Her books include* La inquietud del rosal, El dulce daño, Languidez, *and an experimental collection of poetry,* Mascarilla y trébol: círculos imantados. *She was diagnosed with breast cancer and underwent a radical mastectomy. When cancer reappeared a few months later, she died by suicide by throwing herself into the ocean in Argentina's Mar del Plata on the South Atlantic coast. "Little Man" ("Hombre pequeñito"), from her 1919 poetry collection,* Irremediablemente, *was translated from the Spanish by Sandra Guzmán.*

Little Man

Little man, little man,
Free your canary that wants to fly.
I am the canary, little man,
let me fly.

I was in your prison, little man,
little man, a grand cage you made.
I say little because you don't understand me,
and you never will.

I also don't understand you, but meanwhile
open the cage, I want to fly;
little man, I loved you for a half-hour.
don't ask me for more.

Sara Gallardo

Sara Gallardo *(1931–1988) was a master of mystical realism born in Buenos Aires, Argentina, who was, until recently, rarely lauded or mentioned along- side her male contemporaries, including Gabriel García Márquez.* Enero; Pantalones azules; Los galgos, los galgos; *and* La rosa en el viento *are among her six novels. She also wrote children's books and was a correspon- dent for* La nación. *"Nemesis" is a story from* Land of Smoke, *a complex and multilayered book made up of eight groups of stories, and is the first of her works to be translated from the Spanish by Jessica Sequeira.*

Nemesis

The truth is that I didn't cry for my husband. Thirty years of discord. Or rather: ten of discord, and twenty of hate. That's a yoke if there ever was one.

I inherited from him. I had always wanted assets of my own. I in- vested, bought land—I know how to accept good advice; I took out money in loans.

I became happy, even started to notice colors in the sky. When I moved into my new house, two rooms with carpets and vases overlooking a park, I drank champagne alone and laughed.

Every Friday I invited friends over for bridge. Old married couples and a pederast to round it out.

One Monday afternoon the servant left. She'd been useless and rheu- matic and was going to check into a hospital. A relief.

I asked for help from the doorman, who sent his son.

I don't know how it happened.

I've started to think about stories I never believed. About Cupid, with his arrows and blindfold.

He came in my house and looked at me, and for a minute my tongue didn't respond.

I've read about that happening in novels, but not to me!

I find myself thinking of more mystical things too, sorcerers, and gods. I've grown sick with love.

Ten days ago, I would have laughed listening to this story.

He knows what afflicts me but isn't compassionate. Just the opposite; he hardly conceals his contempt.

He enjoys—like me—money. He builds a little house in a suburb for his girlfriend.

"Like me?" I said. Trembling, I crawl to his feet, bring my hand to his knees. I give him my money.

I still invite people over for bridge, although now I can't tell the faces of my grandchildren apart. Every afternoon I dress the way I believe I used to, and make visits where I talk about films, politics, fashion.

I return at night, without looking at myself in the mirror of the elevator, burning.

Standing in the kitchen, there he is, indifferent. I run to find him.

What was the world?

Diannely Antigua

Diannely Antigua *(b. 1989) is a Dominican American poet and educator born and raised in Massachusetts. Her debut collection,* Ugly Music, *was the winner of the Pamet River Prize and a 2020 Whiting Award. She received her MFA from NYU and is the recipient of fellowships from CantoMundo, Community of Writers, and the Fine Arts Work Center. Her poems can be found in* Poetry *magazine, the* American Poetry Review, *the* Washington Square Review, *and elsewhere. She resides in Portsmouth, New Hampshire, where she is the city's 2022 poet laureate.*

Sad Girl Sonnet #10

I've only been away for a month,
and already three men, two pills, two
countries to watch me swallow. I let myself

sing a sad song in the shower today—Toni Braxton's
"Un-Break My Heart," soap running down my legs. I shave
my armpits while I cry, feeling for the bumps, a kindness

to my most neglected. No one loves
an ingrown. When I was 11, my mother hid the razors, hid
me from the men outside, forgetting the one who shared her bed. I press

the blade down to remind myself I could
be alive, if I try hard enough. My mother says
ma' pa'lante hay gente—yes, there are more people ahead

to do damage. What is it to be *un-broken*? I un-cry,
I un-sex, I un-become this.

Naima Coster

Naima Coster *(b. 1986) is a Dominican American writer born in Brooklyn, New York, and is the author of two novels,* What's Mine and Yours, *a* New York Times *bestseller, and her debut,* Halsey Street, *which was a finalist for the 2018 Kirkus Prize for Fiction. In 2020, she received the National Book Foundation's 5 Under 35 honor. Naima's stories and essays have appeared in* Elle, TIME, Kweli, *the* New York Times, The Paris Review Daily, The Cut, The Sunday Times, Harper's, *and* Catapult. *"Reorientation" was originally published in 2017 in* Cosmonauts Avenue, *where it won a nonfiction prize judged by Roxane Gay, and was republished in* SohoNYC *in 2020.*

Reorientation

The hallways at Spence were blue and narrow. They wound one into another, and I followed the tour guide and peeked into classrooms. Inside, girls in navy blue skirts and white blouses were learning. They sat in chairs arranged in circles or squares instead of rows, and I could imagine myself among them—lighting Bunsen burners, reading aloud from *A Midsummer Night's Dream*, figuring algebraic equations.

PS 11, my elementary school, was official and plain, a brick building in Clinton Hill, Brooklyn. My parents wrangled me into the school, the best in the district, even though I had been zoned for another. I liked the tire swing in the playground, the bodega where I bought potato chips and quarter waters, the library down the block where I waited sometimes for my father to pick me up. I was a favorite of my teachers and selected most mornings to recite the Pledge of Allegiance over the loudspeakers followed by the school motto.

We are proud to be learning and learning to be proud.

The school was run entirely by Black women—teachers, school safety officers, the principal, and assistant principal. The school was a shield to me, a place where I felt safe and as if I belonged. Spence was less than ten miles away across the water in Manhattan but farther than I knew to expect.

After my tour, I interviewed with the head of the Spence Middle School. She had cropped blond hair, droopy eyes, and a pleasant, clear expression. I must have told her that my favorite subject was Language Arts, and I had composition notebooks filled with the beginnings of novels. I probably mentioned that I spoke Spanish, my parents were teachers, I had a grandmother in Bushwick, a grandfather in the Dominican Republic. I might have said I'd been working toward a school like Spence my whole life without ever knowing that Spence existed. Every spelling bee, city-wide test, and book report had been so that I could land here, across a desk from a dignified white woman like her. She seemed amused by me, and I remember being hopeful that I'd won her over.

When I left her office, I waited on the corner for my parents to collect me. It was my first time alone in the city. I watched the high school Spence girls coasting around the block in unsupervised packs, laughing, and sipping sodas. To me, they were glamorous, these older girls in dainty ankle socks, uniform skirts rolled up to their thighs. I wondered if I would ever be like them, if they'd decide, after all, to let me in.

✦ ✦ ✦

The idea of Spence was both problem and promise for my family. My aunt warned my mother against sending me to school with rich kids. They got themselves into the kind of trouble that would slide off them and stick to me. Upper East Side kids had cash for drugs, keys to their parents' liquor cabinets. They had sex in empty Park Avenue apartments, cheated, and stole, talked back to their parents, didn't believe in God.

My parents were used to protecting us in our neighborhood, Fort Greene. They kept me and my younger brother inside and promised one day we'd thank them for protecting us from something big, like getting shot, or something small, like picking up curse words and the crude habits my mother called malas mañas.

Even at my grandmother's railroad apartment in Bushwick, I was relegated to the couch, where I watched cartoons or novelas while my grandmother cooked, and my brother played basketball down the block with our cousins. My grandmother's logic for keeping me inside was simple: the street wasn't for girls.

I was not a prized child in my home, but I was beloved by my maternal grandmother, aunts, and uncles. I was the first grandchild and first member of the family born in the US. They wanted the best for me, and so they warned my mother, "Don't let her go. You won't be able to watch her. She'll change."

My mother had dropped out of high school to work in Brooklyn factories at seventeen. She finished college in her thirties after she was a mother of two. My father was a high school teacher in East New York, one of the roughest neighborhoods in Brooklyn. He had a sober sense of what might await me after PS 11. When the Spence acceptance arrived, they agreed to let me go. I stepped off the ledge of my old life, and they dropped into a freefall too.

✦ ✦ ✦

On the day of orientation, there was an annual family picnic at a park by the East River. My mother was much younger than the other parents, and she likely wore a blazer with enormous shoulder pads that accentuated that there were just over one hundred pounds of her. She brought my brother along, too, and I stuck with the other new girls, making jokes and telling lies to win them over.

Elle, a girl with rust-colored hair and an explosive laugh, approached me first. Then Cate, who, like Elle, was a Survivor—she'd been at Spence since kindergarten. She was a milky skinned ballerina whose sisters also went to Spence. And, finally, Kristen, another new girl, who was transferring from another private school. We sat on benches and strolled around the AstroTurf, and I felt surprisingly free, making corny puns and relying on evasion and exaggeration to explain my life in Brooklyn. It was easy to spin a story about myself, to feel as if my new life was already underway.

We met my father afterward. I don't remember whether he drove from Brooklyn just to pick us up or whether he had parked somewhere and waited in the car while we were at the picnic. When I asked him why he hadn't come, he said, "You don't understand, Naima. If people see me, they'll treat you differently."

My father was a tall and heavy Black man, not yet fifty. He had a long beard and mustache, usually wore a baseball cap and smoked a pipe. I was used to having a father who others considered intimidating. A pair of older twin boys at PS 11 had bullied me until my father came up to the school to set them straight; later, the boys I would date would defer to him, look down at their feet in his presence, then rave about how cool he was, how scary. My father's parents were from Cuba and Curaçao, my ancestors on both sides of the family from the same cluster of islands in the Caribbean. But my mother was light-skinned, slight. She faced a different set of problems—underestimation, innuendo, trouble with the language. I had seen my father harassed and mistreated by shop owners, airport security, and white strangers enough to understand. To be Black was different. And yet, I wanted my father to join us. I wanted to tell him he hadn't seen how nice all those Spence girls were, how they had warmed to me already, how their parents had smiled.

✦ ✦ ✦

Before Spence, I might have said that I knew how to swim, dance, play an instrument, and sing. I learned quickly that compared to my classmates, I was no good at anything I loved. I'd spent summers swimming in the ocean in DR, but I couldn't swim laps the way they did; I danced at a ballet school in Jamaica, Queens, while girls in my class had trained at the School of American Ballet; I played alto saxophone for a few years in the PS 11 band, but my classmates had been taking piano lessons since they were three. I liked to sing, but I didn't know how to read music, and I faked my way through choral classes. I relished that I could at least compete with my classmates in my academic subjects. I knew how to find an image in a poem and say what it meant. I knew how to string words together, imitatively, to say back to a teacher what they wanted to hear. Class was a way to earn my place among them even though my courses were different here. I took Latin, Drama, Public Speaking, a listening class in classical music. I avoided painting and drawing, where the gaps between what I had learned at PS 11 and what they had learned in lower school at Spence were too obvious.

Soon I became an expert observer of my classmates. I tried to decipher the ways they inhabited their bodies, the world. I watched how they peeled clementines with their fingernails, unwinding the orange skin into a single reel. I watched them wrap their bodies around their chairs in class, one foot up on the seat, the other leg folded underneath them. At lunch, they shredded bagels with their hands and ate only half; they devoured crackers and tea or shared a plate of iceberg lettuce and balsamic vinegar. They ran their fingers across their scalps, scooping thin strands of untangled hair into a ponytail. More than once, I untied my own hair, and tried to wind it up the way they did. But my hair was too heavy, and I could never put it back up. I'd spend the day with my hair wild and large around me and make up a story when I got home about how it had come undone in PE.

I spent so much time observing the girls in my class that I remember mostly them. I can recall so much about the many bat mitzvahs I attended—at the Plaza Hotel, in manicured gardens, wearing a little-girl dress with pouf sleeves while my classmates wore high hems and black sequins, and where I felt swift camaraderie with the hired dancers who were so often Dominican—but I have no memory of how I celebrated my own thirteenth birthday. When I think of that first year, I see everyone but myself.

✦ ✦ ✦

My close study of the girls in my class, and its steady effect on me, wasn't lost on my parents. When I wasn't at school, I was writing out the class gossip in my diary. I started listening to pop radio. I requested my parents buy me the leather bomber jacket the school sold with the Spence *S* on the back before I realized no one wore them. At night I clipped a clothespin to my nose, hoping it might narrow. And there was my speech, peppered with likes and elongated vowels. "School" became "schoo-ool," hungry became "hung-ray." Once, my parents overheard a girl from my class promise to call me the next day around "nineish," and after that, they started calling me "Spenceish" and referring to my friends as "Spenceish girls."

Behind their teasing, I sensed growing ambivalence. My mother had picked me up from enough Spence functions to know that she hated the way some of the girls sat with their legs wide-open, or wrote on their hands in pen. Once, she witnessed a girl tell her mother to shut up in public, and she turned to scold me.

"Maybe those white parents will take that kind of behavior, but I won't. Try me."

She was right to think the Spence girl sense of entitlement was catching. Suddenly, there were things I felt I deserved. I wanted privacy to do my homework although we lived in a one-bedroom. I wanted them to lower their voices while I spoke on the phone. I didn't think they had to scream at me if I was already listening. My bids for power were promptly shut down, but I still tried to claim my independence in small, unseen ways. I recorded forbidden thoughts in my diary, slouched in class, talked back to my parents in my head since I couldn't out loud. I shook my hips at the white boys at parties, told lies to the girls at school about my life, hiked up my uniform skirt an inch or two.

I may have been losing a sense of a common world with my parents, but I wasn't sliding easily into the world of Spence. There were dozens of girls I knew would never invite me to their homes, whose invitations to birthdays never came. To me, all my classmates were rich, and I didn't understand the intricacies of class among them. I saw no difference between a country house in Montauk and one in the Hamptons, an apartment on Second Avenue and a penthouse on Park. All I knew for certain was that in the social strata of the seventh grade, I was at the bottom.

In a class of fifty girls, only six of us weren't white, half of us new that year. Plenty of girls had asked me, "What are you?" and "Where are you from?" They asked if my hair was real, whether I was Black. A substitute drama teacher cast me in a sketch about a subjugated Black child, which struck me as patently unfair—why did the other girls get to be whoever they wanted?

One of my best friends, another new girl named Kristen, told me a story once about her father's misadventures on the subway after he decided to take a chance and ride the train. Her father had been going down the stairs, rounded a corner, and bumped right into a big, Black man. Kristen laughed, and I realized I missed the punch line, the end of her story—the Black man her father had run into on the subway. I don't know what I did, whether I laughed or stood silent or asked her what was so funny, but I do know that the figure who came to my mind, the man I pictured in the story, was my father, in a plaid, long-sleeve shirt, his silver pens tucked into his pocket, and his deep brown skin, the color I'd called "burnt sienna" as a child, after the crayon I would use to draw him, and he had called me "peach brown," although it wasn't quite the right color for me, it was a little too white.

✦ ✦ ✦

The tensions with my parents reached a head one night when they were driving me home after a school event. We rode along the highway, the city lights churning. My father smoked his pipe, the sweet tobacco smell floating out the window, my mother looked despondently toward the East River, her chin in her skinny hand. I remember my brother only as silent and small.

I suspect the fight started with my mother: my power struggles were chiefly with her. If I sighed more dramatically than was allowed, or if I rolled my eyes, or disagreed with her, her anger would surge quickly, and she'd shout and threaten and beat. She would turn red, a vein in her forehead would widen and pulse, and I'd wonder whether her rage would be enough to kill me, or her, all of us. What was wrong with me? Who did I think I was? I was useless, ugly, spoiled. Once she'd started, I knew that nothing I said could spare me, and so sometimes I spoke up to say what was happening was unfair or I hadn't done anything wrong. She'd only rage louder. This time, she screamed, "I am taking you out of that school!"

She likely said that the way I behaved was unacceptable. It was a word that bounced in her mouth, the roundness of *p* and *b* identical on her lips. "If you think I'm one of those Spenceish mothers, you're wrong. I won't take this from you! I'll take you out of that school!"

Through my tears and her screaming, I felt as if we were careening out of control. The traffic seemed too fast, and I worried we would slam into another driver or the median and die in a pileup, an accident caused by our inability to get along, my new insistence on not being squashed down. We didn't crash. And so I answered her.

"You would do that to me? You would ruin my future? If you take me out of Spence, I'll never forgive you."

My mother turned to me and repeated my words, her voice shrill and disbelieving.

"That's right," I said. "If you would do that to me, if you would ruin my future, I wouldn't forgive you."

After that, her screams swelled to a higher pitch, and I don't remember whether my father joined in or not, whether she took off her seat belt to reach back and slap me, but I remember the sensation of being outnumbered, and finally cowering in the back seat to cry as quietly as I could. But I couldn't unsay what I had insisted on—that one day I'd have the power to protest, to scorn them, to leave.

My parents talked about that night for years. They brought up my outburst, my threat to never forgive them, as proof I'd become an absolute brat at Spence, disobedient and ungrateful. If I ever raised my voice or hesitated to do something they wanted me to do, my mother would lower her eyebrows in disgust and say,

"Don't think I forgot about the time you said you would never forgive us! I didn't forget. I remember."

I remembered too. I remembered the way it felt to talk back, my voice steady, expanding, answering. I remembered the strain of the seat belt strap across my chest when I leaned forward in the car. I remembered that for an instant I'd refused to accept what my parents decided for me as a sentence. I didn't feel sorry for what I'd said—I wouldn't let anyone take away the future I felt was mine. Unacceptable. I was a Spence girl now, my old life already behind me.

Julia Alvarez

Julia Alvarez *(b. 1950) is a Dominican American New Formalist poet, essayist, and novelist born in New York, New York. She is the author of* How the Garcia Girls Lost Their Accents, In the Time of the Butter-flies, Yo!, *and* Afterlife. *She teaches creative writing at Middlebury College.*

My Sister's Restaurant

Ciudad Trujillo, 1959

They say we are born who we are.
I can't speak for myself, since I began
losing my voice after a brief career
reciting poems for my mother's friends,
a quieting all the more disquieting
of the noisiest of a noisy bunch
of a dozen cousins, running riot
in and out of our neighboring houses.
The cause was unknown—most likely
a case of nerves, a classic female response
to the horror, the horror that surrounded us.
So, I can't speak for myself, but I still recall
the pretend meals at my sister's restaurant,
evenings, on the patio, with the long shadows
already casting our shapes into the future.
The lights were weak, often the power was out—

"El Jefe at work!" The tíos winked at us.
Children of drama, we liked it better this way.
We sat at the long table in an island of light,
a backup gas lamp flaring at the center.
Above us the stars were outdoing themselves,
Each vying for our attention like beauty queens
in flashy evening gowns, but we couldn't care less,
because we were paying attention to the sister
who would later become a chef as she recited
tonight's menu of specials at her restaurant.
After the midday dinner laden with platters,
sancochos bobbing with víveres, arroz blanco,
suppers were simple fare, a buttered waterbread,
a bowl of avena with a stirring stick of cinnamon,
but to hear my sister recite the delights you'd think
the whole Cordon Bleu was sweating away in our kitchen.
Sometimes our clowning cousin, the oldest boy
and heir apparent (so he got away with stuff)
would order up an elaborate meal: a platter
of arepitas de yuca, buñuelos de calabaza,
pudín de batata, a specialty of the house;
snapping his fingers like the spoiled scion
of one of the dictator's cronies' families.
But my sister, who already knew where she was going,
would not be hurried and made him wait his turn.
Night after night, we forgave her when instead of refrescos
tinkling with ice and topped with tiny umbrellas,
she'd set down our milks, as Mami looked in from the parlor
where she and the tías were drinking their whiskey sours,
bracing themselves, as the dictator's dragnet tightened.
The milk, sweetened with sugar, was required
to build up our bones, make us tall as Americanos.
The trick was to stir it quick before drinking it down

as the best, richest part always sank to the bottom,
like the pirate treasure the tíos sent us to find
on wild-goose chases, summers we spent at the ocean,
so they could safely conduct their secret meetings—
who would be giving the signal, who would be
driving the car as another shot through the window—
the king must die, the code name for their plotting.
After the milk came the cereal or pan de agua—
most definitely not the pizza we had ordered.
But that wasn't the point, the point was to partake
in a make-believe world where we all got what we wanted.
She never said, No, or dismissed our wild choices.
Impossible! A chocolate sundae at this hour!
This was her art, night after night, she convinced us
tonight was the night we would not be disappointed.
As she carried her tray professionally on one shoulder,
she looked like a graceful dancer or sequined artist
about to step out on a spotlit stage or high wire.
How could this be the sister we had ignored,
the timid one who wouldn't amount to much,
so the family seers predicted, advising she be
married off young, get the next generation going?
She didn't know any better, like a princess
under a spell, compelled to play out her nature.
But already a tiny chef like a bottled genie
was cooking her future self, and the rest of us
like minor characters in a storybook obliged.
It was her chance to show what a dreamy girl
could do when the noisy ones shut up.
I remember her bending down, her hair on my face,
her solemn nods of approval or confirmation,
her Para servirle, as she moved to the next patron.
It was why I kept coming back to her restaurant,

despite the previous night's mistaken orders.
I was learning from her the art of how to listen,
to dive down deep, recover a hidden treasure.
It's why I keep coming back, half a century later,
each time I sit down to work at my writing table.

ETHEREAL
MOON

The energy of this moon embodies
the spirit of air.

Nicole Cecilia Delgado

Nicole Cecilia Delgado *(b. 1980) is a poet, translator, and book artist born in San Juan, Puerto Rico. Her latest book of poems,* Periodo especial, *explores the socioeconomic mirror images between the island states of the Greater Antilles in light of Puerto Rico's ongoing financial crisis. Her work has been translated into English, Catalán, Polish, German, Galician, and Portuguese. She is codirector of La Impresora, a poetry press and Risograph print shop dedicated to small-scale editorial work in Puerto Rico. "Translation" was translated from the Spanish by Urayoán Noel. It was first published in* Guernica *magazine in 2021.*

Translation

America I've given you all and now I'm nothing.
—Allen Ginsberg

America I spent it all and now I'm nobody.
America 2015 January 2nd zero dollars + tax.
My head hurts.
Fuck you transgenic America.
I won't write this poem until I feel okay.
When are they showing the new Star Wars?
América when will you be dactylic?
Why don't you get naked already?
When will you look at yourself in the shop windows?
When will you listen to our million dissidents?
America why are your libraries leaking?

America why don't you send Haiti your collected leftovers?

I'm disgusted by your mad ambition.

When will I be able to steal supermarket wine without the alarm sounding?

America after all I'm as perfect as you. One need not go far.

Your economy is too much for me.

You made me want to become a Barbie.

The ones who were worth it all went to New York. They're not coming back.

We all know it.

Do you do it out of evil or as a cruel joke?

What I want is to get to the heart of the matter.

I'm not giving up the game.

America don't fuck with me I know what I'm doing.

America the citrus fruits are moldy.

I haven't read the newspapers in months. Every day a man kills a woman.

America I have a soft spot for janitors.

America I've been a communist since I was a girl and hadn't realized it.

I smoke hashish whenever there's any.

I feel the urge to stay home and clean obsessively.

I get drunk in Santurce and no longer go back with my ex.

I've made up my mind, this is not going to be easy.

You should have read feminist theory.

The lady from the botánica says I'm doing great.

I got tired of praying the Lord's prayer long ago.

Now I light candles, I go to peyote ceremonies.

America didn't I tell you what you did to my dad when he started on crack.

Listen to me when I talk to you.

We're obsessed with FB.

How can we let FB control our feelings?

I'm checking it all the time.

FB follows us from every window every gadget every security camera.

I look at it at work and also in airports.

Even my mom has FB.

FB reminds me that big brother is watching.

That's why I should be more responsible. My childhood friends are all mothers and fathers. Or doctors. Or engineers. Or lawyers. Or filmmakers. All of them more serious than me.

My middle name could have been America. Nicole America.

I'm smoking alone again.

I long for Asia so.

But I don't have the means.

I'm better off staying here taking stock of my national resources.

My national resources are a gringo passport, a hydroponic egg, thousands of digital photos, 300 miles of bioluminescent beaches and the weight of colonialism.

I won't mention the political prisoners or the scads of us on the dole of federal funding.

We abolished Cuba's whorehouses now let's go to the Dominican Republic.

I want to be president even though I'm Puerto Rican.

America how does one write haiku with your bad blood?

America I sell you poems at the dollar store.

I give you a discount in exchange for your unpublished poems.

America free Oscar López and Nina Droz.

America bring back Los Macheteros.

America Marigloria and Anjelamaría must never die.

America domestic violence and sexual abuse.

America my mom never took me to El Grito de Lares. In 1998 I went for the first time.

They sold avocado and rice and beans ice cream. The disobedience of 2001. After Vieques they all quieted down a bit. When the FBI murdered Filiberto I was already living in New York. There were always too many undercover agents on the island.

America do we seriously need war?

America are we sure the Arabs are the bad guys?

America you're your own worst enemy.

The extraterrestrials ate us alive already.

The turmoil of power and the hunger for oil.

The cars are going to rust in the garage.

The pharmaceutical companies are going to leave the island.

Angel of speculation, ruin of gas stations.

And it won't be good.

We're going to have to work the land and write by hand. How terrible.

You may even need slaves.

Then we'll see if early to bed, early to rise, makes the man healthy,

wealthy, and wise, and if necessity is the mother of invention.

Help.

America this is no joke.

Though it's hard to believe I don't have a TV but I always find out.

America will you be okay?

I should probably mind my own business.

Don't count on me.

I won't work in fast-food or join the US Army.

Anyway I'm vegetarian and nearsighted.

America I offer your History my big ass.

Virginia Bolten

Virginia Bolten *(1870–1960) was an anarcho-feminist union activist and journalist born in San Luis, Argentina. She denounced the deplorable status and condition of women. A worker in* La Refinería Argentina de Azúcar *and later a shoe factory, she edited by night with other women* La voz de la mujer, *the first feminist newspaper of the Americas, which was financed with their meager earnings. The paper was first published on January 8, 1896; the last issue on January 1, 1897. The short-lived paper that came out "when they could" encouraged women to rebel against male oppression without abandoning their working-class struggle. The paper's motto was "Ni patrón, ni marido" (No boss, no husband). She was deported to Uruguay even though she was Argentinian in 1909 during an anti-immigrant rash of laws (her partner was Uruguayan), where she continued her feminist activism, including contributing to* La nueva senda, *a feminist newspaper in Montevideo. "Nuestros propósitos" (Our Purposes) was on the front page of the debut issue of* La voz de la mujer. *This excerpt was translated from the Spanish by Sandra Guzmán.*

Our Purposes

And well: fed up with so much crying and misery, fed up with the eternal and heartbreaking outlook our disgraced sons offer us, those tender pieces of our hearts, fed up with asking and begging, of being the toys and objects of pleasures of our cruel exploiters or vile husbands, we have decided to raise our voices in the public sphere and demand, we repeat, demand, our part in the pleasures of life's banquet.

Dolores Veintimilla

Dolores Veintimilla *(1829–1857) was born in Quito, Ecuador, to an aristocratic settler couple from Spain. She was a Romantic poet, and her work is charged with pain, loneliness, and frustrated love. Her most famous poem was "Quejas." After witnessing a series lynchings of Indigenous men and women, she wrote "Necrología," a manifesto against the death penalty. After a campaign of harassment against her, led by the highest-ranking clergy of the land, she was found dead eighteen days after she had published the manifesto, allegedly as a result of drinking cyanide. She was twenty-eight years old and left a young child. "Obituary" and "To My Enemies" were translated from the Spanish by Cecilia Rossi.*

Obituary

Dated before May 5, 1857

It is not over the grave of a great, powerful, or wealthy man that I shed my tears. No! I weep over the grave of a man, a husband, a father of five, who had no more for his children than the labor of his hands.

When the voice of the Almighty sends one of our fellow humans into the house of the dead, we see them vanish from our sight, are overcome with feelings, but say nothing. And their friends and family find solace in the belief that it is the Creator who has commanded it, and that His right over the life of humans cannot be contested.

Yet it is not the same when we see the will of one or a handful of our fellow humans, who have no rights over our existence, wrench an individual from the heart of society and the arms of his family, to sacrifice him at the altar of a barbarian law. Ah! Then humanity itself cannot but rebel, as it witnesses, petrified with pain, the execution of the law.

How bitter life seems once seen through the bleakness awakened by the death of the Indigenous man Tiburcio Lucero, executed on the twentieth of this month, at the Plaza of San Francisco in this city!—life, which can itself be constant pain, an endless desertion of the dearest attachments of the heart, the erosion of all our hopes, in brief, life, which is a more or less long chain of misfortunes, whose heavy links are made to feel even heavier by social discontent.

And what can we say of the heartbreaking thoughts the hapless victim would have had at that moment? . . . It is impossible not to weep the bitterest tears, like those that fell from the eyes of the unlucky Lucero! Yes, you wept, martyr of human opinions; but this was the last evidence of human frailty. After that, brave and magnificent like Socrates, you hurried down in big gulps the poisoned chalice, and in peace you descended to the grave.

May your body rest in peace, poor member of a persecuted class; while your spirit, looked upon by angels as their equal, may enjoy the divine inheritance Our Heavenly Father had in store for you. Pray in your grave to the Almighty, that soon a more civilized and humanitarian generation than today's may come to erase the death penalty from the Code of the Motherland of your ancestors.

To My Enemies

What have I, unfortunate woman, done to you,
traitors, who now spit on my face
the poison from the infamous slander
and thus kill my youthful soul?

What shadow can she cast on you,
a fool throwing the laments of her troubled soul
and the tears from her eyes in the winds
to the farthest corners? Poor me!

Do you envy the jasmine giving
its perfume to the calm breeze?
Do you envy the birds their song
when the sun begins to rise?

No! You are not mocking me but the sky,
that in making me so sad and melancholy
has given me a gentle ray
to sweeten my misfortune!

Why, why do you want me to suppress
what my thoughts dare bring to life?
Why do you kill the joy in my soul?
Why, cowards, do you treacherously hurt me?

The woman, wife, loving mother
show no respect to your evil tongue . . .
You brand me with the impure's mark . . .
Ah, there is nothing, nothing you respect in me!

Luisa Capetillo

Luisa Capetillo *(1879–1922) was a journalist, essayist, labor leader, and pioneering women's rights and abolitionist activist born in Arecibo, Puerto Rico, to a Corsican father and a Basque mother. She fought for free love and women's equality. She was unmarried and the mother of two who worked as a reader in a cigar factory. In her essays she encouraged women to spread justice for the benefit of future generations. She considered organized religion a form of prison. Among her most notable works are* Ensayos libertarios *and* Mi opinión: Sobre las libertades, derechos y deberes de la mujer. *During a 1915 visit to Havana, Cuba, she was arrested for wearing pants and "causing a scandal." Her response to the judge at trial, published widely in in Havana, Cuba's* El Mundo*, was translated from the Spanish by Sandra Guzmán.*

Response to the Judge

July 1915

—What do you have to say about what the vigilante said, the judge asked Luisa.

Well, simply, that I was walking on Neptuno and Consulado Street dressed in a jacket and pants without causing any scandal whatsoever, when I was surprised by this prudish vigilante. I always wear pants, Señor Judge [and lifting her dress showed white, puffy pants that almost reached her ankles], and during a night of "autos," instead of wearing them inside, I wore them just like the men do, on the outside, as is my perfect and free right to do.

—So, you always wear pants?

Yes, Señor, always, in one way or another. The same way I was dressed Saturday night I have done in Puerto Rico, Mexico, and the US, and I have never been harassed. Pants are the most hygienic and comfortable suit. It would be more comfortable to go without clothes. But no more hygienic.

—Well, you are acquitted.

Alejandra Pizarnik

Alejandra Pizarnik *(1936–1972) was born in Avellaneda, Argentina, to Russian Jewish parents. She is considered one of Latin America's most powerful lyric poets.* Among her collections are La última inocencia *(1956),* Las aventuras perdidas *(1958),* Árbol de Diana *(1962),* Los trabajos y las noches *(1965),* La extracción de la piedra de locura *(1968), and* El infierno musical *(1971), before her death by suicide. Her prose essay* "La condesa sangrienta" *(1971) was a meditation on a sixteenth-century Hungarian countess responsible for the torture and murder of more than six hundred girls.* "On This Night, in This World" *was translated from the Spanish by Cecilia Rossi and was first published in 1971 in the literary magazine* Revista árbol de fuego.

On This Night, in This World

—to Martha Isabel Moia

on this night in this world
words from the dream of the childhood of death
never this what you want to say
the mother tongue castrates
the tongue is an organ of cognition
of the failure of every poem
neutered by its own tongue
which is the organ of re-creation
of re-cognition

but not of resurrection
of something like negation
of my horizon as maldoror with his dog
and nothing is promise
between the speakable
which is equivalent to lying
(all that can be said is a lie)
the rest is silence
only that silence doesn't exist

no
words
don't make love
they make absence
if I say water, will I drink?
if I say bread, will I eat?

on this night in this world
extraordinary silence this night
what's wrong with the soul is it can't be seen
what's wrong with the mind is it can't be seen
what's wrong with the spirit is it can't be seen
whence this conspiracy of invisibilities?
no word is visible

shadows
viscous enclosures where hides
the stone of madness
black corridors
I have walked them all
oh will you stay with us a little longer!

my person is wounded
my first person singular

I write as if holding a raised knife in the dark
I write as if I'm speaking
absolute sincerity will continue being
the impossible
oh will you stay with us a little longer!

deterioration of words
uninhabiting the palace of language
the knowledge between the legs
what have you done with the gift of sex?
oh my dead
I ate them choked on them
I can't go on not being able to go on

concealed words
everything slides
towards black liquefaction

and maldoror's dog
on this night in this world
where everything is possible
save
the poem

I speak
knowing that's not the point
it's always not the point
oh help me write the most dispensable poem
the one that's no use even
as useless
help me write words
on this night in this world

Jumko Ogata-Aguilar

Jumko Ogata-Aguilar *(b. 1996) is an Afro-Japanese pocha writer and film critic born in Veracruz, Mexico. Her work explores identity, racialization, and racism in Mexico. She writes fiction and essays and has been published by* Revista de la universidad de México, Vogue México, *and the British Council of Mexico. Her essay "Las historias que nos construyen" was featured as part of the feminist anthology* Tsunami 2 *(2020). She is currently a columnist for Coolhuntermx.*

My Name Is Jumko

My name was carefully chosen by my parents for me. It means honest woman or honest child in Japanese and was chosen amongst a variety of options of Japanese and Spanish names. My name is Japanese, just like my father's, my grandmother's, and my great-grandfather's, Jimpei Ogata, who migrated from Miyako Island, Okinawa, to Mexico during the beginning of the twentieth century as a coolie worker. Coolies were Asian workers (mostly Indian, Chinese, Japanese, and Korean) who migrated voluntarily or by coercion to various countries in the American continent as well as the Caribbean islands, mostly because, after the abolition of slavery, a new source of cheap labor was required for capitalist production. My great-grandfather was a nineteen-year-old who made the mistake of being in the wrong place at the wrong time; he went out drinking and signed a paper handed to him by some soldiers at a bar. The next day he was put on a ship towards an unknown country, never to return to his homeland or see his family again.

Historian María Elena Ota Mishima estimates that over ten thousand

Japanese men migrated as workers to Mexico from 1900 to 1910. Their labor was mostly required in the construction of railroads throughout Mexico, in the mining industry, and on sugarcane plantations. Jimpei arrived at the port of Salina Cruz on June 17th, 1907, and was promptly enslaved in coal mines in Coahuila, northern Mexico. However, he was fortunate enough to be able to escape towards the south—a small town along the border with Oaxaca called Otatitlán, also known as the Sanctuary of the Black Christ. Thousands of pilgrims travel to the town each year in search of a refuge or as thanks for a miracle granted, which is just what my great-grandfather found.

I was born in Xalapa, Veracruz, eighty-nine years after he migrated to this country, and I was bestowed with a name that determined my destiny in life. I am to speak of the truth, our truth.

When I was a child, I remember being embarrassed every time I had to introduce myself to others. I'd say my name and be met with confused faces that repeated my name back to me, mispronouncing it or saying a completely different one, as if they'd misheard. One day I asked my mother to call me Jasmine; I loved the *Aladdin* movie and thought that if I had a "normal" name maybe I wouldn't have such a hard time introducing myself. Luckily, she caught on quickly:

"Oh, okay, Jasmine. How are you doing, Jasmine? What do you want to do, Jasmine?"

"Mom . . . I think I don't wanna be named Jasmine, I think I like my name better."

Even though I had a "weird" name, I realized that that was who I am, and any other name just didn't feel mine.

My great-grandfather Jimpei married an Afro-Mexican woman named Lupe, and together they had seven children, including my grandmother Namiko, whose name means child of the waves. She says our names are some of the only things her father left for us, and she never let anybody call her out of that name.

"They tried that at a doctor's office once. Calling me Isidora (her middle name) Aguilar (her maternal last name). 'Isidora! Is there an Isidora

Aguilar around here?' Oh, they must have called it out a good five min-
utes. I waited until they went on to the next patient and sauntered over to
the receptionist. 'Now, ma'am, I haven't been called yet and I believe it's
my turn now. Yes, my name is Namiko Ogata. Oh? You called it already?
Well, I think not, because I was paying attention and you said something
else. My name isn't Isidora Aguilar, it's Namiko Ogata, it says there plain
and simple. Can't you read? It's not hard to say, Na-mi-ko.' You gotta tell
them, baby, otherwise they call you whatever the hell they feel like, and
that's not right. You have a name, and they have to learn to say it."

Namiko.

Namiko.

Namiko.

When I was twenty-two, I visited a prestigious academic who stud-
ied Japanese migration in Mexico, because I wanted to ask for help in
finding more information about my great-grandfather and our family
history. I informed one of the secretaries of the institution that I had an
appointment; she asked my name so they could let me in and grumbled
when she heard my answer: "I don't get why people give their kids these
difficult names."

Difficult names.

Difficult names.

Difficult names.

I stared at her, disappointed but not in the least surprised. I felt the fa-
miliar rage that these types of comments sparked, a sharp ache that bursts
in the back of my throat while I did my best to resist the urge to cuss her
out and storm out of the building. She carefully avoided my gaze and said
that I could go into the office.

It wears me down, little by little, like waterdrops falling on rocks,
having to justify my existence to others. To dread the moment my name
is said out loud, feeling the tension build up in my shoulders, my neck,
my throat. I used to apologize when I had to correct anyone that mis-
pronounced it. "I'm sorry, it's just that you're saying it incorrectly—it's
pronounced Jumko, yes, like that." Though I've dropped the apology, I

still feel slightly guilty, like I'm being overly aggressive or demanding of others.

Every reaction to my name has taught me this: that I should try to minimize myself, take up as little space as possible, apologize for every breath of my body. I feel like I must constrain every vowel, transform and suppress every letter of the name that has carefully survived four generations. I have no way of knowing the names of my African ancestors who were kidnapped and brought to the Mexican Caribbean—I name my blackness in other ways. In the music my ancestors created, the way we dance, the rhythm of the Spanish we speak, the recipes my grandmother teaches me, and, above all, the recognition of community I feel with other Black people throughout the diaspora.

Colonial violence eats away at our stories, heritage, the languages we speak and our ways of life. They teach us that our names are "weird," that our food is "gross," and slowly we are shamed into changing these things, making them more palatable for whiteness, assimilating into the mestizo identity imposed upon us.

My Afro-Asian identity is kept in the way I guard my name, how I care for it like it has its own life—because it does. It carries the memory of my great-grandfather and the love of my great-grandmother, the ways in which diasporas connect and join, creating vibrant communities that knit their stories about home.

Before I go to sleep, I carefully braid my hair while reciting the names of my ancestors so that I can carry a part of them wherever I go, recognizing myself in their lives and remembering that the violence we have faced does not define us.

Araceli

Nisao

Namiko

Armando

Guadalupe

Jacoba

Jimpei

Pedro

Shigue

Isabel

Kanguido

I was blessed with a name that foretold my purpose as a teller of truth, however painful or uncomfortable this truth may be. These exercises of truth began as stories passed on to me, beginning with the story of my very own name. These are reminders of who I am, who we are, and the careful words we preserve despite the colonial effort to devour them, like so many other things that have been taken from us already. I use it boldly and unapologetically as the destiny bestowed upon me, telling the stories that have passed from one generation to another, beginning with the story of my own name.

Aída Cartagena Portalatín

Aída Cartagena Portalatín *(1918–1994) was a poet, novelist, essayist, and scholar born in Moca, Dominican Republic. She studied at Universidad Autónoma de Santo Domingo and École du Louvre in Paris for a postgraduate degree in fine arts. She was a member of La Poesía Sorprendida, a movement as well as an avant-garde literary journal. Her works include the novels* Escalera para Electra *and* La tarde en que murió Estefanía, *and eight poetry collections.* "Una mujer está sola," *from her poetry collection by the same name,* "A Woman Is Alone" *was translated from the Spanish by Sandra Guzmán.*

A Woman Is Alone

A woman is alone. Alone in her power.
With eyes wide open. With open arms.
With her heart open like a wide silence.
She waits in the desperate and despairing night
without losing hope.
She thinks she is on the admiral's vessel
with the bluest light in all creation.
She has lifted sails and let herself be carried by the North wind
with her figure accelerating at the sight of love.
A woman is alone. Holding on to her dreams with dreams
that remain fast, and under the entirety of the Antillean skies.

Sober and quiet before the world that is a human rock,
supple, adrift, lost in the meaning
of her own word, of her wasted words.

A woman is alone. She thinks that now is everything and nothing
and no one speaks of the feast or the sorrow
of the blood that jumps, or the blood that runs,
of the blood that bears or dies in death.
No one comes forward to offer clothes
to dress a voice that is sobbing, naked, spelling itself out.
A woman is alone. She feels, and in her truth she drowns
in thoughts that explain the beauty of a rose,
of a star, of love, of man, and of God.

Lolita Lebrón

Lolita Lebrón *(1919–2010) was born Dolores Lebrón Sotomayor in Lares, Puerto Rico. She fought for the independence of Puerto Rico her entire life and served twenty-four years in prison for leading three male freedom fighters and storming the US House of Representatives in 1954 to denounce US colonial oppression of the archipelago on an international stage. Holding a Luger pistol, she rained bullets on the US Capitol yelling "Viva Puerto Rico libre!" "Long live a free Puerto Rico!" Five members of congress were injured. She was pardoned by President Jimmy Carter and continued her political activism, writing, and delivering speeches at the United Nations and other international venues, protesting US military occupation and exploitation, which began in 1898. She was arrested twice protesting the US military occupation of Puerto Rico in Vieques. She is the author of* Sándalo en la celda, *a collection of revolutionary poetry published in 1976, a year after being released from prison. "Cesen dardos!" (Cease the Darts) has never been published and was penned on the first day of her fifty-year sentence in 1956 in Alderson, West Virginia. Translated from the Spanish by Sandra Guzmán.*

Cease the Darts

Cease the darts!
Already life
over time
rises!

Cease the darts . . .
that did not maim!

With my blissful light
I only know of my own song!

Cease the darts,
they no longer heal the wound.
The heart has been sacrificed.

Silence is my agony
My ordeal is redemption.
Night no longer torments
nor is the day shadow and death.

There is no longer fear in vigil,
nor at dawn does my lyre
shiver from trembling!

Cease the darts
I've washed the dirt off my feet,
and walk through paths
of lilies and sun.

I have done this in my agony!
Sweet life of martyrs
in the altar of pain!

My passion is ablaze!
A flaming throbbing rose
in the temple of my love!

Alê Motta

Alê Motta *(b. 1971) was born in São Fidélis, in the state of Rio de Janeiro, Brazil.* *She is an architect, graduating from Universidade Federal do Rio de Janeiro, and the author of two collections of short stories,* Interrompidos *and* Velhos. *She is a regular contributor to* Vício Velho, *a literary magazine. Her work has also appeared in* 14 novos *autores Brasileiros, edited by Adriana Lisboa, and a special edition of the magazine* Qorpus *called* Brazilian Translation Club State University of Santa Catarina Press. *"He" and "Lives" were translated from the Portuguese by Elton Uliana.*

He

Every day he shouts that I'm worthless, stupid, pathetic. Slaps me on the neck, on the head. Tells me I can't do anything right.

He's never washed a single glass. Never once has he helped me with the dirty laundry, let alone pushed the vacuum around the house. Never given me a present. Never remembered my birthday or taken me on a holiday.

I live this life of making everything perfect for him, doing everything for him, taking all sorts of insult from him, being slapped by him, stuck at home waiting for him.

I put the fries he asked for on the plate. When I enter the room, he jumps up to celebrate, he's drunk, he loses his balance, hits his head on the edge of the bookcase and falls to the floor. Now he's groaning, fallen. And he says that he loves me. He has a hole in his head. It's only a question of minutes before he dies.

On the TV, they zoom in on the smiling face of the player who scored the goal. On the carpet, the blood is seeping, I sit on the sofa, cross my legs, and devour the fries. When he stops groaning I'll go to the neighbor to ask for help.

Lives

As it was in the middle of the pavement, people swerved and carried on.

It was starting to stink. The Fire Brigade came and removed the forty-seven kilos of a man who was hugging his knees. A small crowd gathered. It only lasted the time it took to put the body bag in the fire engine.

By the end of the day, it had rained and the pavement was squeaky clean. No stench or stains from the body. People no longer needed to divert from anything.

Pepita Granados

Pepita Granados *(1796–1848) was an irreverent Guatemalan feminist poet, intellectual, aristocrat, and political journalist born María Josefa Granados y Zavala in El Puerto de Santa María in Cadiz, Spain, and taken to Guatemala City as a child. She was a mother of six who often wrote under an assumed male nom de guerre, Juan de las Viñas, and advocated for Guatemala's independence. She had friendships with some of the most influential men of her time and wrote scandalizing texts criticizing the Catholic Church and her class (other Spanish colonizers). Modernismo founder and Nicaraguan poet Ruben Darío declared her the most ingenious woman Central America has produced. Among her works are* Hymn to the Moon, A la ceiba de Amatitlán, The Resolution, To a beautiful girl—unfortunately engaged to an old man, *and* Plegaria, *among others. She also created the newspaper* A hundred times one *in response to a newspaper of a bitter enemy called* Ten times ten. *A fragment of "El Sermón" (The Sermon) was translated from the Spanish by Sandra Guzmán.*

The Sermon

"Oh fuck or die, oh blessed cunt!
for a beautiful, tender, and virginal offspring,
is worth more than life and glory
which only serve to adorn history."

So said a pagan philosopher,
Octavius Augustus, Roman emperor;
Oh you, negligent boys who are

a laughingstock to the living
spending time in such deep idleness
as if there were no pussies in the world!

You, in the bosom of nothingness,
who waste your youth
disdaining the gifts of the Eternal
and meritlessly earning hell . . .

You who perhaps when nature
awakens your blood and urges you
to seek some pleasure in the flesh,
smear your hand with disgusting oil,
shrouding your lust,
in a sad and bland wank.

And you, deceitful and unclean sex,
what do you do with the flower God has given you?
Silly virgins, I speak to you,
you are neither for God nor for the Devil.

Now, puffed up with eloquence
in preaching fornicating science,
I feel more like Bossuet and Fénelon,
females and males, listen to my intonation.

Benefit from my words and my reasoning,
let each man grab his balls
and the women their pussy and two tits
which haul more than twelve thousand carts.

And in this possession, devoutly
invoke the omnipotent Saint Priapos
and Virgin Magdalena the Jewess,
saying out loud: Ave María . . ."

Nancy Morejón

Nancy Morejón *(b. 1944) is an award-winning poet, critic, essayist, and translator born and raised in Old Havana, Cuba. She is the best known and most widely translated woman poet of post-Revolutionary Cuba. She graduated with honors from the Universidad de la Habana, where she majored in Caribbean and French literature. She is director of the journal of the Unión de Escritores y Artistas de Cuba, where she also served as president of the writers' section. She is the author of* Piedra pulida, *which won Cuba's Critic's Prize, plus in 2001 she won Cuba's National Prize for Literature, the first time a Black woman won the award. Among her notable works are* Looking Within *(Mirar adentro) a panoramic anthology of forty-six years and ten volumes of her work.* "New Women" *and* "Black Woman" *were translated from the Spanish by Gabriel A. Abudu.*

New Women

The arrow from the equator
still lost under their eyelids.
Wildflowers on their chests,
burned by all the saltpeter in the world.
The crowing of the rooster in the mountain.
The whistling of smoke in the city.
And their hands, coming from very far,
from times long past,
kneading the recent substance
that makes us live
between the sea and the shores,
between fishes and nets,

between windows and the horizon.
These women are holding things high up,
walking,
sewing,
hammering,
weaving,
sowing,
cleaning,
conquering,
reading,
loving.
Oh, simple new women
simple Black women
bringing the fresh breath
of a new light
for everyone.

Black Woman

I can still smell the sea foam that they made me cross.
The night, I cannot remember it.
Not even the ocean itself could remember it.
But I cannot forget the first gannet that I spotted in the distance.
The clouds, high above, like innocent eyewitnesses.
Perhaps I have not forgotten the shore that I lost nor my ancestral
language.
They left me here and here I have lived.
And because I worked like an animal,
I was reborn here.
The many Mandinga epics that I tried to turn to.

I rebelled

His Lordship bought me at a public square.
I embroidered His Lordship's dress coat and I bore him a male child.

My son had no name.
And His Lordship, he died at the hands of an impeccable English lord.

 I walked on.

This is the land where I suffered beatings and whippings.
I rowed along all its rivers.
Under its sun I sowed, picked the fruits, and I did not eat the harvest.
I had slave barracks as my house.
I myself brought stones to build it,
but I sang to the natural rhythm of the native birds.

 I rose up.

On this same land I touched the warm blood
and the rotten bones of many others,
brought here, or not, just like me.
Never more did I imagine the road to Guinea.
Was it to Guinea? To Benin? Was it to Madagascar? Or to Cape Verde?

 I worked much more.

I strengthened my thousand-year-old song and my hope.
Here I built my world.

 I went to the mountain.

My true independence was the slave settlement
and I rode among Maceo's troops.

Only a century later,
together with my descendants,
from a blue mountain,

 I came down from the Sierra

to put an end to capital and moneylenders,
to generals and the bourgeoisie.
Now I am: only today do we have and create.

Nothing is foreign to us.
The land is ours.
The sea and the sky are ours.
The magic and the dream are ours.
My equals, I see them dancing here
around the tree that we planted for Communism.
Its abundant wood now resounds.

LUMINOUS MOON

This moon's energy celebrates
the first rays of the sun and the power
of coming out of darkness.

Victoria Margarita Colaj Curruchiche

Victoria Margarita Colaj Curruchiche *(b. 1986) is a Kaqchikel poet, painter, and photographer born in Guatemala City. She writes in her mother tongue, Kaqchikel, and Spanish. A member of the writers collective Ajtz 'ib ' de San Juan Comalapa (Chi Xot) and the artistic movement Ruk 'u 'x, she cofounded IxKot, a group that works to protect traditional weaving. She is the author of two poetry books,* Como agüita de tuj *and* En el vientre del universo. *Her work has appeared in literary journals in Mexico, Colombia, and Peru and in several anthologies, including* Mujeres *del viento. "Atit akuchi e k'o, atit'?" (Where are you, grandmother), "If I Die," and "Untitled" were translated from the Kaqchikel by the poet and from the Spanish by Arthur Malcolm Dixon.*

Atit akuchi e k'o, atit'?

Atit akuchi e k'o, atit'?
Today abuela speaks with the fire and the plants
She realized it has been many moons since the owls sang.
Death will take us in her arms. She says.

In the smoke she washes her face with epazote
Praying to the christ who's nailed above the door.
Huuuu, huuu, huuu
She burns eucalyptus, to protect us from evil
With her woman's eye, she brings the souls back home.
With the pom she guides them.

We are the forgotten, those who die by the instant and at every instant.
Our skin peels off and no one cares.
Death will take us in her arms she says.

She holds the ruda between her hands
Hands familiar with green universes.

Shhh, shhh, shhh
Blows the voice of the wind.
Abuela's kitchen lit up by the fogón
Her pupils lost in the coals.
And the deep gaze that inhabits her.
She sighs.
All that belongs to us is anguish, bitterness,
Silence and now confinement.
Shhh, shhhh, shhh
She sprinkles rosewater at every corner of the house
To wake up the guardians who chase away fear
And the demons who now have us trapped.
We wake up little by little
With so many unconsoled mournings.
Abuela carries on shaking the herbs
Death will take us in her arms, she says.
For us, every day, every night
Is those 500 endless years.
Atit akuchi e k'o, atit'?

If I Die

You can read my story, in the threads interwoven
By these hands of clay on my huipil.
He can tell you of my pains, my sorrows, the deep agonies
And the infinite joys.
He can tell you of the glances of scorn, disgust, and hate cast by some.
He will tell you also of the warm embraces, the meetings of beating hearts,
The smiles that give you goosebumps.
He can tell you that life wasn't easy
And that more than a thousand times we had to mend ourselves

And keep walking.
If I die
I hope only that my huipil hugs you so tight, so tight.
That you can smell the scent of his flowers.
Hear the song of his birds.
Vibrate with the pulse of each one of his threads.
The haven of his mountains,
That his stars light your way through the darkness
And his red blood gives you life.
If I die
My huipil will remind you
Who I was, who I am, and who I will be.

ri ruxe' ri ramaj

Ri jun aq'a' ri' xinok oq'ej, chirij ri' tikirib'äl, chay, kotz'I'j.
Chuqa jun molaj q'axomal pison chupam jun kuchb'al ri b'anön chi
    chupuy qäq'
¡Saqowan! job', k'ulq'ij, ruyik'lunil ri q'ij ri nupub'aj q'aq'
Ri jun ch'umil ri awoyob'en, ri jun tiqaq'ij richin kikotem ri woyob'en
Ri wain ri jani toqa ta, ri alaj awän, ri kumätz ruximon ri'
chupan rupach'un ri awi'
Ja, keri' nin nataj.
Nikiq'äj ki ri b'aqil pa ki jujunal richin ninututej ri' ri b'ey
Richin yealäx chik jun b'ey ri qak'u'x chikipan ri b'o'j taq sutz'
Xinok paxin taq achike chupan ri yakona'ob'äl
Xinok sub' ri xerumalama' ri achi'
Ri jun mank'isel aq'a ri'
Akuchi xejotayin pe ri waq' chuqa ri ruxe' ri ramaj

Untitled

With my toes I touch her
With my blood I feed her

With my tongue I get her drunk
Oh lovely earth!
Hug me, wrap me up, keep me safe in your belly
Oh lovely earth!
From you I was born, to you I will return.

Untitled (Kaqchikel Version)

Kik'in ruwi waqän ninmäl
Rik'in nukik'el nintzuq
Rik'in waq' ninq'ab'arisaj
¡Ruwach'ulew!
Kinaq'etej, kinapisa', kinamatzej pan ak'u'x
Ruwach'ulew!
Chawäx xinaläx, awik'in xkitzolin.

Doña Felipa Pica

Doña Felipa Pica *(ca. 1865–1920) was a cantaora of bomba y plena born in Guayama, Puerto Rico. She was one of the most renowned voices of the musical genre created by Africans who were enslaved during colonial times from 1502 until the 1873 emancipation. According to Nellie Lebrón Robles, music teacher, singer, and founder of the bomba y plena group Paracumbé, women are traditionally responsible for singing bomba. Most of the popular bomba y plena songs sung today were likely written by Black women, who never received proper credit. Bomba y plena music was the people's newspaper, and besides sharing news of the community in these songs, women demanded equality and respect. The chorus of the songs is learned by everyone, and the cantaoras improvise the rest of the song, which last anywhere from three to ten minutes, sometimes more. "Palo e' bandera" was written while Doña Felipa was nursing her thirteenth child. She was home when friends told her that her husband, Don Juan, was in the village plaza dancing bomba and that a young woman was hitting on him. She wrote the song in response, and during a bomba y plena session in the village plaza a few weeks later, she sang the song publicly. The young woman was never seen in town again.*

Palo e' bandera

Ya' flag pole
Rod of an old cot
Don't try it with me
Your face is beat 'n' long
like a ragged mule's clothesline
And you got bony legs
like a' old maid beach vine.

Norma Elia Cantú

Norma Elia Cantú *(b. 1947) is a daughter of the borderlands, born in Nuevo Laredo, Tamaulipas, who grew up in Laredo, Texas. The Chicana poet, novelist, translator, and folklorist is the Murchison Endowed Professor in the Humanities at Trinity University in San Antonio, Texas, where she teaches Latinx and Chicanx Studies. Her novel* Canícula: Snapshots of a Girlhood en la Frontera *won the Premio Aztlán Literary Prize.* Teaching Gloria E. Anzaldúa: Pedagogy and Practice for our Classrooms and Communities; *the novel* Cabañuelas; *and* Meditación Fronteriza: Poems of Love, Life, and Labor *were finalists for the International Latino Book Awards in their respective genres.*

Telling Tales of the Tejas Borderlands

Tejas. La Frontera. The Border; a region, demarcated by official state lines, a geopolitical designation. My home. Our home for at least three hundred years. The stories, the tales, tell of suffering, of violence, and at the same time of joy. Of life!

I am rooted in this land, connected to all sentient beings—the turtles on the Gulf, rattlesnakes, thousands of birds and butterflies, monarchs and others—that migrate through this land. The Coahuiltecan people whose many groups crossed the river and lived off the flora and fauna of the region, our ancestors, still live in us. Someone asked me once: where are the native people? *We are here*, I answered. We may not have tribal designation, or be recognized by any government, but we are the people who have survived the ongoing attempts to erase us. The border: that space in between. Nepantla. Gloria Anzaldúa borrowed the concept from the Nahua people, who during the conquest survived by being in between, holding on to their Indigenous ways and adapting the European ways. As a Tejana, I am a nepantlera, an in between, a survivor.

We, people que por circunstancias particulares, nos auto-denominamos Tejanas/os/es, we inherited cultural and physical codes that surface here and there; these codes evident in our traditions and in our language and cultural expressions mark us. Our bodies bear the marks of our history. We are marked by our mestizo complexion. Our folklore constitutes a historical record. The violent lynching and murder of hundreds of Tejanas/os/es live on in legends and in songs. Our folklore becomes our history, a history not included in history books: "El Corrido de Gregorio Cortez," the subject of Américo Paredes's book *"With His Pistol in His Hand": A Border Ballad and Its Hero* and the legend of Josefa "Chipita" Rodríguez (1799–1863), who was convicted of murder and hanged in San Patricio County, to name two of many. If as Anzaldúa wrote, "The US-Mexican border es una herida abierta where the Third World grates against the first and bleeds. And before a scab forms it hemorrhages again, the lifeblood of two worlds merging to form a third country—a border culture," then in some ways, my work in folklore is an attempt to heal that wound. I seek to walk the path with courage, con coraje. For us in South Texas "coraje" also means "anger." Anger at the loss, the injustice, the dreams and hopes that shattered at that border. I channel the anger into action. I was furious in 1982, in Laredo, when I realized the level of illiteracy. What we needed was an English literacy program for adults. I rallied women from our group, Las Mujeres; we formed an affiliate of the national Literacy Volunteers of America. The group is ongoing, teaching English to many who are only literate in Spanish. One statistic I cannot forget is that when women's literacy rates go up, infant and childhood deaths go down. It's not only the family's economic situation that improves when you have a literate community.

As Tejanas/os/es we walk the paths our ancestors walked and re-cover the memory that lies embedded in our DNA. As we weave, quilt, bake, build homes, write poems, tell stories, we are part of a long line of creatives, those whose dreams and imagined futures we are now living.

Cantando y Bailando en Spanish o English? Or Both?

I use "Tejas" with a *j* so that it is read in Spanish. Why? Because in English "Texas" brings forth memories of the racist Anglo who spat "dirty spic" at me in an elevator in Austin. Texas in English is the white teacher who doubted I had written a paper, and the indoctrination in elementary school singing "The Eyes of Texas"; it's children pledging to Texas every morning in Texas public schools, even today. But Tejas is my mother and her cousins laughing and proudly claiming their tejanidad. Tejas is arroz con pollo and enchiladas con chile con carne as well as enchiladas callejeras. Tejas is the sound of the mockingbird and the chicharras on hot summer days.

I come from a very specific Tejas—South Texas. Our language signals tejanidad. Our Spanish has inklings of older terms and we also use Indigenous terms. For "child" we may say "chaval" or "chavalita," or "huerco" or "huerca." Each of these has an etymology in old Spanish, while other terms for "child" come from Indigenous languages: "esquincle" from the Mechicas' Nahuatl, used in Tejas, and "buki" from the Yaqui widely used in Arizona. We use "espauda" for "baking powder," for instance, a clear borrowing from English. Our language is a linguistic mestizaje that suits our discourse needs perfectly. We love to play with words:

¿Qué hace un pez?

¡Nada!

¿Y una manguera?

¡Sells mangos!

Dance also signals tejanidad, both religious and social dance. Do you dance in English? The question surprised me. "No," I answered, "I'm dancing Tejano and it doesn't feel as if it's in English." Dancing to Little Joe or Selena, that's dancing Tejano. The matachines for certain don't dance in English. They may dance in Spanish with Indigenous elements, though; these folk Catholic sacred dancers who, in Laredo, honor the feast of Our

Lady of Guadalupe—as matachines do throughout Mexico—also dance to honor the Day of the Holy Cross.

The stigma of the mainstream that deemed our cultural work as less— less intellectual, less important, less worthy of study, and less interesting— taints the word "folklore." After all, the folk are the people, la plebe, not really worthy of study. But folkore is in my genes. It is in the yerbitas— ruda, estafiate, yerba buena—my grandmother would grow in our yard to heal an earache, a stomachache, or a headache; it is in the foods—caldos, sopas, and guisados—she and my mom prepared to feed our large family. It is in the celebrations—quinceañeras, bodas, bautizos—marking life stages and bringing community together in mutual respect and mutual assistance. "Hoy por ti, mañana por mi," my father would answer when someone thanked him for a favor or for sharing a tool or food.

The borderlands, that specific geographical region and ethos, is at the center of my scholarly work and at the core of my creative writing. In my folklore work, I have found space to do activist work within the academy. Working with quilters like Sra. Solis in San Ygnacio, Texas, in the '90s and clay workers, ceramicists, like NEA's National Heritage Fellow Verónica Castillo, in San Antonio, I have found that in affirming their work, I am honoring the long line of costureras, seamstresses, and knowledge bearers like my grandmothers. Tales are often more telling than statistics. In the storytelling cycles we held in Kansas City, I found rich and important narratives from a number of immigrant communities.

Our "work" is not always our jobs but the larger life project. What matters is the work that honors who I am and what I came to do. What matters is that I work to dismantle oppressive structures, racist practices, that I question the way things are to make them better for Tejanas/os/es. For all.

Marie Arana

Marie Arana *(b. 1949) was born in Lima, Peru, and is the author of the* memoir American Chica *and the novels* Cellophane *and* Lima Nights. *She also authored the biography* Bolívar: American Liberator *and a sweeping history of Latin America,* Silver, Sword, and Stone. *She won an American Academy of Arts and Letters Award in Literature in 2020, plus she is the inaugural literary director of the Library of Congress and the former editor-in-chief of* Book World *at* The Washington Post.

Prayers of the Mandona

I blame it all on my older brother. It was his idea to play Conquistadors and Incas with him as the triumphant Pizarro and I as his captive, Atahualpa. Or Cowboys and Indians with him as the dazzling Lone Ranger and I as his Comanche, Tonto. We were on the north coast of Peru, far from the capital of Lima, where the dizzying aroma of sugar coiled through our senses and a hacienda's factory belched smoke into a lowering sky. We lived between the sugar fields and the threshers, with an angry Pacific pummeling the nearby shore and nothing but desert rolling out as far as the eye could see. In our imaginations, however, we were fighting for life on a soaring plateau of the Andes or galloping through the mythical brush of the American southwest. We were wherever victories were being won and empires were being forged; we were seekers of glory.

My brother would come at me—swift as a Chan Chan lizard—with a tin bowl on his head and a plastic sword in his hand, or a black mask on his face and a wood gun in his fist. He was always the radiant victor; I was always the doomed Indian. We never stopped to think, nor did anyone think to remind us, that we were both children of the Indigenous, with deep, ancestral roots in that land. It was power we were negotiating; a power I came to crave.

In time, there were other games. When my father decided to build us a tipi out of sugarcane, twine, and heavy Peruvian blankets, my brother announced that he wanted to use it as a neighborhood club. He would be president. I would be vice president. The children down the road would be our tribe. I balked at my subaltern role, stamped my feet, shouted that I had enough of being relegated to the lower rung in his high-flown dominions. We fought during the day, I prayed during the night. And lo, the apus—the gods of the huacas—came to my rescue and answered my prayers. With Solomonic wisdom, my brother decided I could command the other members: it would be I who decided who could join our tribe and who couldn't; and it would be I who would delegate everyone else's roles. The president would make speeches, lead campaigns, prosecute wars. The vice president could rule all the rest. I would be the one who gave the orders, told people when they could talk, held a gatekeeper's power. I would be the cacique, the gerente, the unimpeachable mandona. It was then that a seed was planted. It was then that I began to view the world as a man.

I didn't realize it until much, much later, of course. At least half a century later, at least. But looking back at it now, I see that from that time forward, it never occurred to me that I couldn't do anything a "man" could do. I was easily a bossman, a foreman, a tribesman, a happy member of mankind, an inheritor of the Earth and everything that's in it, un ser bien planteado, with two boots on the ground. I could "walk like a man," as my father directed my brother to do, if I really wanted to. I could certainly talk like one, even maybe think a little like one. And finally, as years went by, I began to write like one.

As I say, none of this bubbled into consciousness until many decades later. A whole career went by before I looked back and saw the evidence. In truth, I only see it now, sitting down to write this essay. But there it is, and I offer it here as a testimonio: The memoir of my childhood is—if I look at it squarely—truly about my father. My novel set in the Amazon jungle is told from the point of view of the patriarch of a large and unruly family. My flinty, hard-nosed novel about a blighted love affair between an elite, white-skinned Limeño and a dark-skinned shopgirl from the slums is seen through the eyes of the male. Then there's my biography of Simón Bolívar—el culo de hierro, the iron ass, as his soldiers called him—liberator of six republics, whose singular machismo won him as many lovers as battles, a figure who stands as the very personification of the Latin male.

Finally, there is my history of Latin America troubles, a book which starts in the fourteenth century and runs to the present day. When I read the first draft of the introduction to a circle of friends, I was surprised by one woman's observation that every one of the three contemporary characters I had chosen to feature was a man. I had managed to see a thousand years of Latin American history through a gender not my own. I corrected that lapse, added a woman to the heart of that book, but I remained blind to the fact that this had always been my modus operandi. Not until I reached the last page of that book's first draft did I go back and re-see my world. History books always tell of Pizarro . . . *and* Atahualpa; Cortés . . . *and* La Malinche; Columbus . . . *and* the Taíno; Cabeza de Vaca . . . *and* the Guaraní; the conquistadors . . . *and* the conquered; Bolívar . . . *and* his thirty-five mistresses; the westward pioneers . . . *and* the invisible peoples of the land. Where are the powerless, the voiceless, the women, the Indigenous, the erased, the "ands," the lower rung in someone else's high-flown dominion? Looking more closely now, I see that the people of the lower rung have always been there in my books— indomitable, valiant, resilient—lurking in every work I have conjured. I see that they are the builders, the defenders, the pillars of strength. Much as my brother once saw that I was braver, bossier, more bull-minded, than any boy down the road. Very possibly even more ferocious than he.

How clear this is to me now! My memoir may have been ostensibly about my father, but it was really about the power struggle between my mother and grandmother. My novel set in the Amazon jungle only appears to be about the patriarch; it is his no-nonsense wife who really rules the roost. My stark, urban love story involving the rich, well-born Limeño is actually about a gutsy young Indigena putting her foot down and getting her due. The women are there all right, making demands: they are there in my larger-than-life grandmother, my defiant mother, in the spirited jungle matriarch, the gritty girl from the barrio, the fiery lover who saved the liberator's life no less than three times, in the indomitable widow scrabbling for gold high up in an Andean no-man's-land. These are the strong of spirit, the tireless warriors. It was always in them that the power lay.

Carolina De Robertis

Carolina De Robertis *(b. 1975) was born in Cambridge, England, to Uruguayan parents. She teaches creative writing at San Francisco State University. She has authored both poetry and novels, including* The President and the Frog, Cantoras, The Gods of Tango, Perla, *and* The Invisible Mountain, *and her books have been translated into seventeen languages. She's received two Stonewall Book Awards, a Northern California Book Award, and Italy's Rhegium Julii Prize. De Robertis is also an award-winning translator of Latin American and Spanish literature. She is editor of the acclaimed anthology* Radical Hope.

A Song for Queers in Public Bathrooms

Tell me true, tell me queer
what is your joy? Where is your body?
Are you inside yourself, delicious, pure, made new
by each breathing now? Are you awake?
Each moment a door through which
to know yourself. To touch.
To be here in all your
folds and curves
and gleaming.
Breathe.
Begin.

Tell me true and tell yourself—
for every conversation turns us home—

has it not been wounding,
this life? This world?
Tiring to the soul?
Restroom,
we call it.
Perhaps.

Tell me true and tell me queer
as you wipe your tender body
will you remember to say *love*?
Will you remember to say *ánimo*
or *órale* or *praise be* or *amen*?
Will you linger in the lushness that you are,
even here, yes, where City speeds and flushes
and dizzies past the glitter grit inside the song
of you that rose before your dreaming?

Will the mirror spark
as you gloss and lick and smooth and brush,
open what you promised to your deepest self
so long ago, when you said Yes
to the breaking of the chains?

Because inside that Yes
is everything you need.

For here you are,
glowing.

And there they are
in the mirror:
your eyes,
and in your eyes the everything,
all it took to make the fierce and lovely
creature you become again

now
right now
with each breath
in this public temple of wipe and wash and sing.

Come in.
Shine on.
Be home.

This Very Moment I Am on the River

leaving Buenos Aires
where I, the prodigal queer cousin, found embrace

This very moment I am on the river
Rushing from the shore, over thick brown water
Away from you—my family—all of you—again.

What impossibly good fortune
This chance to break my heart
Over the Río de la Plata
The way a soft container breaks when water pours
From relentless jugs.

A broken heart can pour into this river.
A hungry heart will long for what it loves.
If a heart were strong, then it could
Fill and burst and break and fill again,
Missing you already, rushing over waves.

This too will pass—this moment on the river,
Water will never take this shape again,
And we, too—all of us will change,
The baby will be born, people will couple,
People will sing and weep and strive and eat

And kiss and fight and yearn and touch and
Run and build and weep and eat again,
Hair will pale to silver or to gray,
Steps will slow, the infants will grow tall,
All of us will pass to wherever death might take us,
But before that, some of us (impossibly
Good fortune) will live to watch
The changes, to watch each other
Change, to watch as our own faces
Crease with infinite stories
In the mirror, the child inside
                                    surprised
At the sight, the skin's long story,
The waves we made along the way.

Juana Borrero

Juana Borrero *(1877–1896) was a poet and painter born in Havana, Cuba, to an aristocratic family of Spanish intellectuals and revolutionaries. As a teen, she began publishing in journals, including* La Habana elegante, *and was part of the Kábala, a modernist movement of the late nineteenth century in Cuba. She authored five volumes of poetry, including* Rimas. *She is beloved for her wide epistolary with two poets/lovers, Julián del Casal, who died nine months after meeting her, and Carlos Pío, who was killed in combat with the Cuban Liberation Army. Her family was exiled in Key West during Cuba's War for Independence from Spain, where she died two months before her nineteenth birthday. Her letters to Carlos, sewn into his combat uniform by his aunt, and signed with his pet name for her, Yvone, remain one of the most beloved love stories in Cuba. "Letter 17" was translated from the Spanish by Carla Bauzá López.*

Letter 17

Carlos, my angel: this morning I awoke very early and left my bedroom, disregarding higher orders because, as you should know, I am very unwell as of late and have been ordered to stay in bed.

But I was expecting a letter of yours, and what advice could dissuade me from waiting for it? Listen, I don't mean to blame you . . . I don't do so, because any fault is in itself indicative of a lack of affection or, at the very least, a voluntary forgetfulness of sacred promises, and I do not want to believe that your attitude towards me responds to voluntary reasons of your own but rather circumstances regarding which there was nothing you could do.

For the record, I forgive you and absolve you . . . It would pain me so to see clouds loom over this sky just as dawn awakens . . . You know I'm very sensitive . . . Every injury pains me like a wound . . . and the triple deception of these days has pained me so, so much!

These words are not born of my own selfishness . . . Not at all! The desire to know of you, the longing to see your handwriting, the grief of seeing me far from you, oh my love, are all feelings that elicit grievances from my lips and fill with despair this my poor heart that loves you so! Forgive me!

I've felt so sad these days! How I anxiously awaited your letter! Oh, my love! Do you know what it feels like to love and not know if you are loved back? Don't you know? Then you do not understand my torment . . . I long to hear you apologize for your forgetfulness. I will even believe the first excuse you utter because I don't want to doubt you just as I started believing you to be sincere . . . But I beg you to be compassionate . . . I want to be honest with you because pride leads nowhere in times such as these . . . So, I beg you: forgive this morning's letter and see that you are true to me. Every time you forget me is a new sorrow in my poor soul! Goodbye, my dear! Have mercy on me! Oh, love me! Love me!

—Yvone

Carolina María de Jesús

Carolina María de Jesús *(1914–1977) was born in Sacramento, Minas Gerais, Brazil. She is best known for her diary, published in August 1960 as* Child of the Dark: The Diary of Carolina María de Jesús, *which became an international bestseller and was translated into twenty-seven languages. "Favela" is an autobiographical narrative published posthumously in* Onde estaes felicidade?, *edited by Raffaella Fernández and Dinha. It was translated from the Portuguese by Elton Uliana with the support of University College London.*

Favela

It was the end of 1948, the owner of the land on Antonio de Barros Street where the favela was located showed up. The owners insisted and demanded they wanted the land empty within sixty days. The favelados became anxious. They had no money. Those who could leave or buy land, they left. But it was the minority who had the conditions to leave. The majority didn't have resources. Everyone was worried. There were policemen going around the favela to make sure that the favelados leave. All we could hear people saying was what will become of us?

São Paulo was becoming modern. All of her old houses were being destroyed to construct skyscrapers. There were no more cellars for the poor. The favelados talked, and thought. And vice versa. Until someone suggested.

Let's go and speak to Dr. Adhemar de Barrós. He is a good man. And Leonor is a saint of a woman. With a good heart. And she feels for the poor. Dr. Adhemar de Barrós doesn't know how to say no to poverty, he is a Godsend. I'm sure if we go and speak with Dr. Adhemar de Barrós, he will solve our problem.

And so, the favelados calmed down. And they slept peacefully. They still hadn't gone to speak with Dr. Adhemar de Barrós. They trusted this great leader. They gathered and went. And they were all well received by Dr. Adhemar, who doesn't make any distinctions. He opened the doors of the palace to the whole group. It was through Dr. Adhemar de Barrós that the common people got to see the rooms of the campos eliseos palace. They reported their distressing problems to Dr. Adhemar.

Within three days I will arrange a place for all of you.

Every night I did two trips. I used to go by tram and come back on foot with the boards on my head. For three days I did two trips carrying the planks. I was going to bed at two in the morning. By that time I was so tired I couldn't sleep. I made my little shack myself. 1.5 meters by 1.5 meters. [. . .] It was a Sunday the day I built my shack. There were lots of men around and none of them helped me. I was left with a forty-centimeter-wide board—it was on top of this board without a mattress that I slept.

I was always very tolerant, I thought: better days would come, God willing. I started to prepare my João José's baby trousseau. I was doing the prenatal treatment at Hospital das Clínicas. I felt dizzy and fell on the floor semi-unconscious. People walked past and didn't look at me. Others glanced at me and said:

Young Black woman she could work but she prefers to get drunk.

Little did they know that I wasn't well, deficient nutrition, moral, and physical aggrievances. When I felt I had the conditions to hold myself upright, I would stand up and continue. Sometimes I would go to the Church of the Immaculate Conception to ask for bread. How many times that child turned in my womb. When I got to my miserable hovel, I would lie down.

The neighbors whispered. She's single she must be a whore. It is a general belief in Brazil that Black women are all whores. But I've never let myself be affected by what people think of me. When these people came to me with their funny business, I said:

I'm a poet. I ask for a bit more respect.

Do you drink?

No! And I don't approve of people who drink. I also hate those who offer me drinks. My stomach is noble, I'm not going to destroy it with toxins.

Nobody would get to me. On the 27th of January of 1949 I realized I was going to be a mother. I asked Dona Adelia my neighbor who knew all about childbirth to keep me company. She said:

I can't!

And I liked her a lot. Everything nice that I had at home like fish I gave to her, everything I bought I shared with her. Faced with her refusal, my affection for her went cold. I would moan in pain. And none of my neighbors showed any interest in me. The ex-wife of Adalberto, Marina, who is now dead, did feel sorry seeing me there alone, only me and God. She called for assistance and took me to the Hospital das Clínicas. I was registered there. They accepted me. The pain multiplied, I spent three days in agony. On February 1st, 1949, at five o'clock the boy was born. The midwife Dona Amelia brought the boy to me and said:

Look, here is your bulge-eyed boy!

✦ ✦ ✦

How am I going to have another child in this one-and-a-half-meter-wide shack, there was no space. Oh! I can't! He only gave me twenty cruzeiros a week. He said you earn more than me. Inside I rebelled. The day after I got up determined. I went to work with the objective of saving money for me to build my new shack. At that time I was collecting waste paper for Senhor Estefenson. I collected paper from seven to eleven. When I went to get paid, he said it amounted to twenty cruzeiros. The following day I gathered more paper. I thought: today I'll earn more. He said it amounted to twenty cruzeiros. I started to send the paper to the other place in Guarapé Street. The first day, I earned forty-five cruzeiros. I was very happy. The following day fifty-five cruzeiros. I thought: Now yes! Now I can get the shack built.

Lola Rodríguez de Tió

Lola Rodríguez de Tió *(1843–1924) was a poet, feminist, abolitionist, and revolutionary who fought for the independence of Puerto Rico. Born in the town of San Germán, Dolores Rodríguez de Astudillo y Ponce de León was the daughter of Spanish colonizers and dedicated her life to fighting against the Spanish empire as well as for the abolition of slavery. After she was exiled from the island, she lived in Venezuela and Cuba, where she died. Among her poetry collections are* Mis cantares, Mi ofrenda, *and* Noche buena. *She penned the patriotic poem "La Borinqueña" as a call to arms. Since it was considered too revolutionary, tamer lyrics were written by a Spaniard before it was adopted as Puerto Rico's national anthem decades later. Rodríguez de Tió's original version of "La Borinqueña" has been translated from the Spanish by Carla Bauzá López and Sandra Guzmán.*

La Borinqueña

Wake up, Boricuas
the call to arms has rung!
Wake up from this reverie
The time has come to fight!
Doesn't the patriotic flame
fire up your heart?
Come! We'll be one with
the firing cannons.
Come, Cubans will soon be free;
the machete will free them . . .
the machete will free them.

The war drums
rumble their song,
that the jungle is the place,
the meeting place . . .
the meeting place.

El Grito de Lares
must be repeated,
and then we will know
victory or death.
Beautiful Borinquén,
we must follow Cuba;
you have brave children
who want to fight.

We can't remain indifferent,
and timid
and continue to be subdued.

We want
to be free now,
and our machete is
sharp,
and our machete is
sharp.

Why then are we so tired
and deaf to the call,
to the call, to the call?

There is nothing to fear, Riqueños,
to the cannon's call:
the cannon's call, the cannon's call.
We must save our motherland
It is the duty of all our hearts!

We no longer want despots,
let the tyrants fall;
our unconquerable women
will also fight for all.

We want freedom
and our machetes
will give it to us . . .
and our machete
will give it to us . . .

Let's go, Boricuas,
let's go now.
Our freedom anxiously awaits.
¡La libertad! ¡La libertad!

Ivelisse Rodríguez

Ivelisse Rodríguez *(b. 1975) was born in Arecibo, Puerto Rico, and raised in Holyoke, Massachusetts. Her debut short story collection,* Love War Stories, *was a 2019 PEN/Faulkner Award for Fiction finalist and a 2018 Foreword Reviews INDIES finalist. She is a contributing arts editor for the* Boston Review. *She earned an MFA in creative writing from Emerson College and a PhD in English creative writing from the University of Illinois at Chicago. "Before We Became a New People" is a chapter from a novel-in-progress.*

Before We Became a New People

Ponce, Puerto Rico
July 25, 1898

The sound of gunfire is what draws everyone to their porches. Loida steps out barefoot onto her porch to see the humid, black night light up. Shouts from neighbor to neighbor of "¿Que? ¿No se? ¿Que carajo? No te oigo. Quédate adentro, mi'ja" volley through the sky. Curiosity more than fear seems to draw them out. There had been rumors that the Spanish would invade. That the rumblings in Cuba were enough for the Spaniards to come back across those seas like they did in 1493, and so many centuries after that. And these Ponce residents wonder now if they have come, come from shores away to re-stake their claims on Puerto Rico, deciding that their four months of autonomy were enough.

Loida sees the intermittent red tip of her neighbor Santos's cigar—the most light in the dark other than the gunfire. The small, square, wooden houses in her Vista Alegre neighborhood are so close to each other that women pass to each other cups of coffee in the morning, arms barely extending through the open windows. Loida speaks to Santos the most out of all the other neighbors because, like her, he wishes to be left alone. He doesn't drink with the other men, he doesn't stand in the doorway and comment on the women going by. He opens his house in the morning, like everyone else, but he won't call out to his neighbors like the women across the road who seem to sweep out their houses at the same time and take the opportunity to gossip with each other. Noticeably, he and Loida open their doors all day, to let the sunlight in, but not to let the noise and conversation and life of the neighborhood seep in.

Vista Alegre is comprised mostly of gente de color, a new catchall group formed out of a dash of libertos and huge doses of free people of color, the ones who had never been slaves but had cautiously looked at the slaves and quickly looked away. How many people could say they had the opportunity to see what their lives could have been like but for the capriciousness of fortune? Loida has always wondered about that—the flippancy by which these consequential things are decided.

But like most of the people in Puerto Rico, they are not really a community; people adrift on this island with no way of returning, a culture in abeyance, a people in abeyance on a tiny plot of land, floating in the ocean, 110 by 39 miles that somehow sobrevive. The island itself knows about survival much more than the people.

As the gunfire continues, it becomes clear that the sounds come from the harbor. What is absent is the volley of back-and-forth gunfire or the shouts of men from two sides. There is gunfire and silence. Loida realizes the gunfire is an announcement, an introduction. And so, a winner can now be easily declared, even if the win doesn't come tonight.

Loida steps into her slippers that rest on the porch every night, and she does what none of her neighbors do, she goes off in search of that gunfire, that light. She wants to see what destructions are being brought upon the shores of Puerto Rico.

Luisa Valenzuela

Luisa Valenzuela *(b. 1938) was born in Buenos Aires, Argentina. She is one of the most powerful literary voices in twenty-first-century Latin American letters. She has published forty books, including novels, short and flash fiction story collections, essay collections, and anthologies. Among her most recent works are a novela,* Fiscal muere, *and newspaper articles "La mirada horizontal," "Los tiempos detenidos," and "Encierro y escritura." Her books have been translated into more than seventeen languages and her essays included in numerous anthologies. She has honorary degrees from Knox College in Galesburg, Illinois, and Universidad Nacional de San Martín, Buenos Aires. A member of the American Academy of Arts and Sciences, she is a multiple award winner and in 2019 won the Premio Internacional Carlos Fuentes. "Between Two Waters" ("Entre dos aguas") was translated from the Spanish by Suzanne Jill Levine.*

Between Two Waters

As if caught between two bodies of water, I the author was swept away by the unfolding, the doubling that plagues those of us engulfed in the magma of writing, which more than a profession is an abyss, a chasm that gives birth to stories. A bottomless pit, or gouffre in French, which might sound like a ravenous mouth, or the gates of hell with its brimstone vapors.

My language skills hound me when I venture into these godforsaken places. I would rather pass this gift along to Masachesi, which he refuses to accept, and I respect him for it. As a character, Masachesi has his own voice and knows what he wants. He even took me by the hand, obliging me to record moments of his life.

This morning I wrote to a friend, "I couldn't answer you before, because I am totally involved with Masachesi . . ." A second after sending this message I realized the linguistic trap into which I had just fallen, from my youthful days, when "totally involved" is synonymous with being or almost being in love. However, it's all clear to me. Masachesi is not my unavailable lover nor even my invisible friend. He is my informant, my inspiration.

And so it was, exactly at dawn on June 12, 2021, when he tossed or handed me the gift of his remarkably realistic premise about the falsely controversial death of Attorney General N, a plot rigged and financed by the secret police so that he would follow the tributaries to wherever his investigation led him, so long as it was useful to them. Only that the attorney general ceased to be useful to them when he tried to cut loose and be his own man, in which case it was preferable to get him out of the way. I understood the whole thing, sketched out the plot, wrote to my close friends that I felt like the extraordinary Macedonio Fernández for having written a novel before lunch and for having solved the N case.

With that sketch outlined, the novel took me several months to write. Its first title was *The Deduction* but the publisher changed it on me for the more convincing *Attorney General Dies*. "The Deduction" as title was then free to alight upon the story rediscovered later, which initially was called "Two Birds." Two birds with one stone . . . but there was only one shot that supposedly assassinated N—if, given the inaccessible setting, we discard the suicide theory—if, at that distance, only one shot was plausible. It would seem that not just any person, even if instigated by the current government, would be capable of such a precise and subtle maneuver.

Who benefits from this death? is the first question to ask, as recommended by seasoned detectives when they investigate a crime. I have just come to realize this, but Masachesi, that mysterious swarm of neurons folded within my cerebral synapses we call Masachesi, understood it right away.

And so "The Deduction" as a title, remained free. And flying around and around, it came to alight upon the old story, unfinished because of the lack, precisely, of deductive closure.

Speaking of which, this is where the circle would close if not for a big pressing unanswered question that continues to require more extensive introspection:

Where are stories born?

Or, at least, for now, out of which crevasse did this tenaciously lucid, imaginary character Masachesi crawl?

Idea Vilariño

Idea Vilariño *(1920–2009) was a poet, essayist, and literary critic born in Montevideo, Uruguay. She was a member of the literary group Generation of '45, which included Juan Carlos Onetti, Mario Benedetti, and Amanda Berenguer. She was the author of twelve books of poetry, among them* Nocturnos *and* Poemas de amor. *Her collected poems,* Poesía complete, *was published in Uruguay in 2002.* "Not Now" *is from the bilingual edition* Poemas de amor/Love Poems, *translated from the Spanish by Jesse Lee Kercheval.*

Not Now

Now it will not be
not now
we will not live together
I will not raise your son
I will not sew your clothes
I will not have you at night
I will not kiss you before I leave
you will never know who I was
why others loved me.
I will never come to know
why or how
or if what you said
was true
or who you were
or what I was to you
or how it would have been

to live together
to love each other
to wait for each other
to be.
Now I am nothing but myself
forever and you
now you won't be for me anymore
only yourself. You are no longer there
a day in the future
I will not know where you live
with whom
or if you remember.
You will never embrace me
like that night
never.
I will not touch you again.
I will not see you die.

Danielle Legros Georges

Danielle Legros Georges *(b. 1964) was born in Gonaïves, Haiti, and grew up in Boston, Massachusetts. She is the author of several poetry collections, including* The Dear Remote Nearness of You, *winner of* New England Poetry Club's 2016 Sheila Margaret Motton Book Prize, *plus the translator of* Island Heart, *a poetry collection by Haitian French writer Ida Faubert. A professor of creative writing at Lesley University, she served as the poet laureate of Boston from 2015 through 2019. "The Afternoon" was originally published in the summer 2021 issue of* Ibbetson Street.

Little Farou

They are all gathered together,
a black family at Archis Bay Beach Resort,
for the birthday of little Farou, who is two,
and the father gives an elevated discourse in honor
of the éblouissante fille,

which seems, éblouissante, like an adjective one
would use to describe a debutante or an evening
of diplomats,

and little Farou is running around the pool
in a pink-and-green bikini contrapuntal to her
brown, brown skin and presenting her round belly
to the world which mirrors her father's own rotundity.

I'm just hanging back with my ex-husband because we're
friends like that, and vacation together from time to time.

He's lounging on a chair, looking like a sated baby. Handsome.
Why there is a rotting banana next to him, I don't know.
The banana is not a metaphor. It's just there, but weird,
right?

As I was saying, there is Farou and her family,
and the sea not far, now éblouissante: so many points
of light in the distance, the sun so in sync with the water's
movement that all but blue is obliterated.

Things should end here. Really, they should.
I am a black woman in a black country watching
a black family just being. So marvelous a thing this is.
So marvelous. DuBois's double consciousness be damned.

The Afternoon

—after Mahmoud Darwish

If I were told:
By evening you will die,
So what will you do until then?

Of course, there would be a flurry of emails
Or perhaps one email sent to all. No, that would
not do. The flurry then. Of where to find the keys,
the passwords, codes, the papers that sort a life. Meaning.
Meaning.

I would want to see the round faces of the soon-
to-be-mourners of my love, family, shining moons against a dark
backdrop. Friends. I would wish to view the sky in whatever mood it's taken.
Bright like this morning's or thunderous. Something's happening: why
not bolts of light thrown by some god.

I would call my great love of youth when pain and beauty were
one thing, who is married to someone else, whose number I do not
have, but would try for a half hour to find before forsaking

the task to futility. Flowers would be necessary,
white tulips, white roses, the afros

of hydrangea, in vases set throughout the apartment. The time
would pass too quickly with this work. I would walk down the stairs
to bid adieu to my neighbors. Goodbye, I would say to them
all. Back up, I would regard my dead relatives in photos,
to let them know I was on my way.

I would bathe, brush my hair into a bun, paint my nails indigo.
Frankincense would burn, drift up in plumes. I would lie on
the couch with the music of drums—yanvalou—and call
out to them *I am ready.*

SHAMANIC
MOON

This moon's energy is favorable
for disentangling problems.

Daniela Catrileo

Daniela Catrileo *(b. 1987) is a Mapuche poet and professor of philosophy born in Santiago, Chile. She is a member of the Rangiñtulewfü Colectivo Mapuche and part of the editorial team for* Yene, *a digital magazine featuring art, writing, and critical thought from across the Wallmapu and the diaspora. She is the author of two poetry collections, including* Río herido *and* Guerra Florida; *two chapbooks,* El territorio del viaje *and* Las aguas dejaron de unirse a otras aguas; *and a book of short stories,* Piñen. *"I Look in the Mirror" and "They Inseminated Our Sisters" were translated from the Spanish by Edith Adams.*

I Look in the Mirror

I look at the Indian women
I look at the colonizer
I spread my legs
and shove
    flowers
    cactus
    animal
    god

the cosmos inside me

I explain to the god
with a female bird's face
that I have nothing inside
that it's just a creator's fantasy

that in me no one can be born
because nothing survives

They Inseminated Our Sisters

They made us their slaves
in the Circle of Stones

We escaped drunk
dancing with our rapists

Then
we broke open their intestines
to share with the peaks
of the Andes.

Vicenta María Siosi Pino

Vicenta María Siosi Pino (b. 1965) was born to the Apshana clan of the Indigenous Wayúu people in Colombia. She received the Comfamiliar del Atlántico Prize for Children's Literature and the Colombian Institute of Culture's documentary prize-grant in 1995. She is the author of five books in the Wayuunaiki language, aiding in the conservation of her mother tongue. Her short stories have been published in French and English, and her book Cerezas en verano *was translated into Danish. In 1982, she became the first Indigenous woman to be published in her home country. "Owl's Voice" was translated from the Spanish by Arthur Malcolm Dixon.*

Owl's Voice

Three stones broke the roof tiles. The woman woke up to the commotion with her heart beating like a drum and could not go back to sleep. She will have no rest tonight, again. Her eyes stay open in the darkness. The moonlight slips in through the holes in the roof.

Two weeks ago, they shattered the window and took fifty books they then left scattered down the street, all the way to the avenue where the taxis go by; the week before that, they poured boiling water over her patch of medicinal plants.

In that district of Riohacha, she found four resigned teachers and a potbellied principal. She thought she was going to die there, like the dreams of those who dwelled in that neighborhood of adobe houses.

She requested 150 million pesos from the teachers' co-op. Its architecture was contemporary: a jutting terrace on the second floor, mirrored picture windows, an open-plan built-in kitchen, a library with mahogany shelves, a garden with oregano, lemongrass, bushy lippia, mint, and balm. She was sure her days would end in that place, far from the hustle and bustle of downtown Riohacha. The locals dubbed the property "the mansion."

Her everlasting daily schedule went school, mansion, mansion, school, school, mansion, mansion, school. So much lying around reading, eating cheese with guava jelly, left her the size of a cow. When she looked at herself in the mirror she said, "Mooo, mooo." Her pleasures were simple, and she asked nothing of life, until the fat-bellied principal started inviting himself over to her ample abode. He would stay until the wee hours of the morning, talking about things that meant nothing to her. She would yawn to get rid of him tactfully, and if that didn't work, she would go on the offensive, eyes closing, head nodding, and snoring. When he left, she would hear the street dogs barking at him in the distance as he trekked off down the dusty side streets of that forgotten suburb.

One splendid afternoon, looking out over the tops of the mango trees from her balcony, the fat-bellied principal declared his love for her. "What made him think I would take him?" the Wayúu teacher wondered. One day on the ranchería, on their way to the water well, her wrinkly handed, calm-walking mother had advised her never to play love games. So, to deal a quick killing blow to his hopes, she rejected him, cuttingly and stone-faced. Within twenty-four hours, the pot-belly's tantrum had begun. Meetings were called and attended over nonsense, he demanded all planned classes be filled to capacity in advance, he blamed the teaching staff for the students' incompetence at parent meetings, and he institutionalized endless commemorative events: Desertification and Drought Day, Tree Day, Water Day, Singles Day, Memory Day, Origami Day, Veterans Day, etc., etc. The teachers creaked under their workload.

One dark night, the thunderous stones came, the garden was reduced to stubble, and her books succumbed, defiled.

It was after a torrential rainstorm, when the Wayúu heart is happy, when she asked her father's permission to earn her high school diploma in the city. She sought lodging at her Arijuna godmother's place,* in exchange for help with the housework. It was hard but she was up to it, and her host, who provided her used clothes and shoes, encouraged her to carry on to a degree at the university. When asked for this second round of permission, her father said only, "One day you'll come back to your people." She was twenty-two when she graduated. She no longer wore her incandescent tunics and her heart, amid so many books, had been Arijunized. When she went to show her degree to her family, her father said, "You're old, but I have found you a husband." Said husband had no steady job and had been born a generation before her; she was vibrant and beautiful like the purple morning glories after the rain. She knew the traditional Wayúu law, learned in the ritual enclosure of her puberty, and so she fled, flying down the narrow path lined with divi-divis. Her supportive godmother got her work as a teacher in that neighborhood full of families displaced by the country's violence.

One gray afternoon her father hanged himself from a leafless trupillo tree. He could not take the shame of breaking his solemn word to a friend, not handing over his daughter in marriage. She did not go to the wake. She swallowed the pain. And her clan did not want to see her.

As soon as the door to her house shut behind her, she would cry like a solitary owl. If she escaped, cowardly, to some other distant land, she would lose the 150 million pesos it would take her twenty years to pay off. But while she melted in tears, her mother's words of advice came back to her: "Don't go where you're not wanted."

---

*   Arijuna: non-Wayúu person.

Adela Zamudio

Adela Zamudio *(1854–1928) was born in Cochabamba, Bolivia. She was a pioneering feminist poet, essayist, novelist, and educator who also went by the pen name Soledad. Her books include* Ensayos poéticos, Ráfagas, Cuentos breves, *and* Íntimas, *a romantic epistolary novel exposing the hypocrisy of the upper classes. She compiled a spelling book and wrote several poems in Quechua, including her most famous, "Wiñaypaj wiñayninkama" (Forever). "To Be Born a Man" was translated from the Spanish by Sandra Guzmán.*

To Be Born a Man

She works so hard
To correct the clumsiness
Of her husband, and at home,
(Pardon my surprise)
As inept and as vain,
He is still the head of house.
Because he's a man!

If verses are written,
a poet must have penned them,
but she only transcribed them.
(Pardon my surprise.)
If unclear who the poet is,
Why assume it was he?
Because he's a man!

A wise woman
in elections can't vote,
but the biggest crook can.
(Pardon my surprise.)
If he can learn to sign his name
Any idiot can vote,
Because he's a man!

He sins and drinks, or gambles
and is on the wrong side of luck:
She suffers, struggles, and prays.
(Pardon my surprise.)
She is called the weaker sex
and he the stronger sex.
Because he's a man!

She must forgive him
when he cheats,
but he can seek revenge.
(Pardon my surprise.)
In a similar situation
He's allowed to kill her,
Because he's a man!

Oh, privileged mortal
How perfect and complete,
You surely enjoy respect!
In any case, to get all this,
It is enough for you
To be born a man.

Josefina López

Josefina López *(b. 1969) is a Chicana playwright born in East Los Ange-les. She is the artistic director of the Casa 0101 Theater in Boyle Heights, which she founded in 2000. She is best known for the play* Real Women Have Curves, *which was made into a film in 2002.*

Being a Screenwriter in Hollywood

In 2015, I met with a very successful movie producer, who shall remain anonymous, who was interviewing me for a job adapting branded material from another country. I was as pleasant as I could be, but after listening to a project that I felt was somewhat derogatory to Latinos, and then hearing this producer talk about how African American women were doing so well in society, but "African American men were just a mess and couldn't get their act together," I had to take a second to think.

In that moment I knew if I spoke up about her subtle racism that I would not get hired, but if I didn't, I wouldn't be able to sleep that night and live with myself for the rest of my life. So, I took a deep breath and proceeded to educate her as kindly as possibly how "slave masters" con-sciously and purposely crushed the males so that they could not be the leaders of their families, and by breaking up their families and humiliating the men they could keep them under control. I explained to her how what looks like African American men "not getting their act together" is about hundreds of years of oppression, police brutality, and a prison system that targets them.

I left the meeting knowing I would not get the writing job, but I didn't care because I knew that if I kept quiet to get a job then I was not being a real writer and it was not worth losing my dignity. Yeah, maybe like other writers who keep quiet I could have earned this producer's trust and slowly educated this producer . . . But why is it my job to have to educate so many people in Hollywood who only see Latinos and People of Color as the help? Aughhh!!!

A few days later my "representative" asked me if it was possible for me to "tone it down" with my activism when I went out on meetings. The producer told her I was very creative and intelligent, but I had a "chip on [my] shoulder." I told my "representative" what happened and said, "Funny, I'm the one with a chip on my shoulder, but this producer doesn't think they're being racist with their choice of projects and their comments. I am not going to tone it down! I became a writer so I could speak the truth and especially about injustices. My whole life society has told me as a Person of Color to be quiet and tone it down—well, I'm not! And if it means no one is going to hire me, then oh well! I'll produce my own plays and films and publish my books independently." My "representative" apologized and admired my stance even if it was challenging for her to get me jobs.

It was amazing for me to see the thousands of outraged people marching on Hollywood Boulevard for Black Lives Matter in protest to the police's killing of George Floyd, yet it's ironic that Hollywood is completely guilty of perpetuating stereotypes and racism. I've been in this industry for over thirty years and as a Person of Color I can tell you that I didn't need to see the WGA Inclusion Report Card to know that white males control the narrative of the reality that the rest of us have to live and experience in film and real life. When I became a writer, I chose to be the protagonist of my life. Yet Hollywood keeps telling me that I have to be a "supporting character" in a white man's story and that my life doesn't matter. Well, no more!

Let's rewrite this story so that all of us can see ourselves as heroes and heroines. We all want and need to see ourselves as heroes, not just white men. If we are professional writers writing about protagonists making difficult decisions to do what is right, then we must tell the truth and speak up about all the racism and sexism we know is real in this industry that people excuse so they can make their mortgage payments. I challenge writers to rewrite this story and make it a beautiful one where it's not US versus THEM—but US versus our mutual understanding. How much longer do Writers of Color and women have to wait to have equality in this industry?

I wanted to share this list to inspire other people to contribute to it so that those who need to look in the mirror closely can open their eyes. If people are really outraged, then let's look at ourselves and see how we can all do better by becoming aware of our blind spots.

"White Writer Privilege" Means:

- Never having to consider whether a heterosexual white male/ female protagonist will eliminate your screenplay from being considered "commercial" and ever getting made.
- Always having your white male/female protagonist be the hero/ good guy/gal or the cool "antihero" even if the story is about People of Color.
- Never having to ask if you're the best writer for a job about a story surrounding People of Color that clearly could be done justice by a person from that community.
- Never having to write People of Color in your story, and never having anyone question you as to why there are no People of Color, and being able to say, "Back in the '50s/Middle Ages, women, People of Color, didn't have those jobs or weren't around."
- When you make a grammatical error, no one questions your right to be a human being who makes mistakes, and they don't assume that you didn't go to college or you're a foreigner who studied English as a second language.
- Never having to understand that when you write about People of Color you automatically speak about a community and can damage that community—even get people killed—with your

ignorance, because white characters get to be individuals and you have the privilege of seeing yourself as an individual, not a sea of whiteness.

- Never having to understand white privilege because, after all, you're a writer and you are the mirror to society so nobody can hold a mirror up to you.

"White Male Writer Privilege" Means

- Never having anyone question your right or merit to be on a writing staff or to be a producer or director.
- Never having to write about women characters over fifty because "they're not sexy anymore" and you can't have your fifty-year-old male protagonist sexually involved with a woman in his age range or older.
- Never having to see storytelling from another perspective but a linear, masculine, Western point of view.
- Never having to consider that "rape" as a plot point can be used in a story concerning a male protagonist instead of overusing it in a female protagonist story.
- Never having to consider that perhaps the "White Man saving the world" plot is propaganda and that it's been so overdone that it needs to be retired.
- Never having to consider that perhaps a story about a young guy wanting to lose his virginity is not that important to anyone but him and that story can also be retired.

Grisel Y. Acosta

Grisel Y. Acosta *(b. 1970) is an Afro-Latine poet born in Chicago, Illinois, to Cuban and Colombian parents. Her poetry collection* Things to Pack on the Way to Everywhere *was a 2020 finalist for the Andrés Montoya Poetry Prize. She is also the editor of the anthology* Latina Outsiders Remaking Latina Identity, *a professor at the City University of New York, a Macondo Fellow, and the creative writing editor at* Chicana/Latina Studies Journal.

χ (chiasmus)

—after Julia de Burgos

you can be certain	there is no assurance
I will pile on more bracelets	in community, choose a single ring
marry reckless blush to sparkle	solitude, safety in its low tones
be gauche like Gaudi, boldly	be elegant, like landscaped gardens, muted
blurt in too loud a voice	whisper in a euphony of song
La Lupe fighting	Dolores Del Rio at peace
legs kicking wild swings	arms posed in precise arcs
sweat trailing hot black sequins	cool, crisp flowing white satin

this venturesome queen desires the unwanted everyday stability: her to
relinquish the wild night to embrace the gentle dawn

Britney's shaved head speaks to   Angela Bassett's lush mind
everything I want, angry   seems impossible for me, joyful
fierce energy destroying capital   statuesque fixedness, priceless

I am unstable, mercurial   I want to be solid platinum
dangerous, like blood poison   secure, like a holy ritual
and I love this innocent freak   but I hate this worldly aficionado
yet I wish to be the exact opposite   and I am absolutely this thing
the woman who will always choose camp   the queer who will never be
                                           frumpy

       so why the chiasmus . . .
          let the overalls meet the manicures
       hello braless eccentric, meet the madam
wearing a pillbox hat and Doc Martins
      may your inner Siouxsie hash it out with Schomburg
          let Jimenez Román argue with the Dead Kennedys
in your head filled with dollar store art and Basquiats and Lalique tchotchkes
          dance with B-Boys and Baryshnikov, sing
     with monks making chartreuse, Zola Jesus, and Bad Bunny
        make grilled cheese with brie and Wellington with quinoa
dress your home in cheap velvet and expensive books
     treat woven bags from Colombia like relics
         put designer junk in drugstore lot drop boxes

               embrace the contradictions
               they are your superpower

The Fools (Historia 2.0)

Para todas que me oigan y me comprendan
Nuestra historia no la enseñan
Pero vive en los árboles
Y en estrellas que iluminan las noches
Ella vive, ella vive, ella vive
Y volverá
Y volverá
Y volverá

Once there was a land that grew stories . . .
they grew like cantaloupes and mangoes and guavas
huge, epic stories that everyone feasted on
como una pachanga, sharing all through the night
you could visit your best friend and she'd share
a story, then she'd join you and you'd visit Doña Encarnacion
y she would tell the most heartfelt story and everyone cried
the stories got bigger with each telling, todos adding to them

then the story killers arrived
they slashed fields of stories and jailed stories that survived
the massacre, the stories were cold and hidden underground
but all the people kept wanting to share stories, so they did

then the story killers banned the stories
if you think of this in environmental terms, they burned
the stories—there were fires of words floating up to the sky
everywhere, when the people lit candles, whispered stories
tickled their ears and they knew the stories were still alive

then the story killers decided to kill people
anyone with velas or a memory was sent to the slaughter
but that didn't work because esta gente made so much love
and the stories lived in their children
little ones tilled the land to make more stories

then the story killers thought to steal
the stories, taking them from anyone who had one
putting their name on it, twisting its meaning
and saying, "Look! This is your story!"
At this point, the people laughed, knowing full well
these were not the stories their land fed them

then the story killers decided to kill the land
and this is when the land itself laughed
along with all the people of the tierra who were
always of the tierra, because the tierra could not be killed
and its stories could not be killed, so the land roared
with laughter and called the story killers *fools*

soon, the fools all died because the tierra
wasn't happy with their attacks and, of course, the stories
lived, in the trees, the dirt, the stars that swallowed the fires,
and the stories grew, like guanábanas and piñas and tamarindos . . .

Estella González

Estella González *(b. 1967) is a Chicana novelist born in East Los Angeles, California, her literary inspiration.* Her work has appeared in anthologies such as Latinos in Lotusland: An Anthology of Contemporary Southern California Literature *and literary journals* Kweli, The Acentos Review, Asteri(ix), *and* Huizache. *Her writing has been recognized with awards and honors, including an International Latino Book Award, Cornell University's Philip Freund Prize in Creative Writing, a Pushcart Prize "Special Mention," and as a "Reading Notable" from* The Best American Nonrequired Reading. *Her first book,* Chola Salvation, *a collection of short fiction, was a finalist for the Louise Meriwether First Book Prize and a finalist for the James D. Houston Award for Western Literature.* "La Malinche and La Llorona" *is an excerpt from her novel-in-progress,* Huizache Women.

La Malinche and La Llorona

Blue, blues, every shade of blue can be found in the bathroom: powder blue on the walls, baby blue dots on the white tiles of the shower stall, royal blue towels, sky blue outside of the windows. The sink, toilet bowl, cabinets, and built-in wooden vanity all gleam porcelain white while knobs on the drawers and medicine cabinet sparkle sapphire blue. The white hexagonal floor tiles outlined in thick black goo cool me down after school while I wait for my abuela Merced to come home from her shift at El Yuma. Sometimes I lie on the floor in my bra and panties while I listen to KROQ, the rock of the '80s. Richard Blade's sexy Australian accent rambles out of the transistor radio about some concert at the Greek or "Fabulous Forum." His voice bounces off the floor, onto the walls, and out through the thin panes of glass, out into the concrete courtyard. Then he spins the latest hit, like "Shiny, Shiny" by Haysi Fantayzee or "Time Zone" by World Destruction. Weird but danceable.

Sometimes a song's beat makes me jump up and twist the volume all the way up so I can lip-synch while I watch myself in the built-in mirror of the vanity. I lean in close, pretend I'm singing to John Taylor of Duran Duran or my boyfriend, George. Before we started seventh grade at Griffith Jr. High, he was Jorge with the corduroy vest and thick accent. The Fourth Street School boys made fun of him and called him a TJ. Not because he was from Tijuana but because he was a Mexican. Never mind that all of our parents are Mexican, we're American and, somehow, better. But at Griffith, it's all about first kisses, dances, and the "babes." According to my girlfriends, George was now a babe. No longer a TJ, it's okay for George to be my boyfriend.

During these summer nights, I need George the most. After dusk, when all of East LA cools down, I open the little bathroom windows for fresh air. Sometimes, especially on hot June nights, the stink of rotting pig blood drifts in through the windows, filling up the bathroom with gross death smells.

"That's the Farmer John Slaughterhouse," George says.

"Like the one from Carrie?"

"Same one," he tells me.

The moment he says this, the stink becomes glamorous. It's from Hollywood. I remember the scene with John Travolta killing the squealing pigs after Nancy Allen, his güera girlfriend, gives him a blow job. George and I kiss a lot but he never asks or makes me give him a blow job. He just tells me to never hold his hand or kiss him in front of anybody at school. Now he comes to stay with me in the little yellow bungalow house until Merced comes home from her bar job.

"Don't come to my locker after class," he says more and more these days.

I know why. He's after Yolie Zamudio, the güera queen bee of Griffith Jr. High, who won't give him the time of day. The boys call her Miss 69, whatever that means.

✦ ✦ ✦

"Chillona is more like it," my abuela Merced quips during one of her drunken rants. She's missing her boyfriend, Leandro, again, and once she gets started, she destroys anyone who tries to stop her. This time she's coming after my runaway mom, Alma, and Tía Suki, who moved out months ago to be with her lawyer girlfriend, Lily.

"No use crying over your children. What for? Puras ingratas."

Am I ungrateful too? True, I don't give Merced any of the money I earn from working at the Jack in the Box but at least I'm not pregnant like some of those other girls who come to Suki's house for abortions.

Suki and Lily had been running a partería from their home in Santa Monica for a year now. Lily was making enough money to help cover expenses even when some of the women didn't have the cash for a doctor and were too embarrassed to go to Planned Parenthood. At the kitchen table, Merced tells me that Suki and Lily are the worst ingratas because they do not share their good fortune after all she has done for them.

"La cuidé," Merced mumbles, fumbling with her Marlboro packet before shaking out its final cigarette. She catches it before it hits the floor, then floats it slowly to her mouth. I try to focus on the beans simmering in the clay olla but I'm afraid she'll throw the Bic lighter at me like she did last time. After three flicks, a flame shoots up to meet the tip of her cigarette. She closes her eyes, taking a deep drag. I open the window above the sink to clear the smoke stink. A slight breeze blows. I roll my eyes but turn back to the stove, stir the now bubbling beans, listening for another voice, or the ringing of the telephone. George said he would be calling me about getting together to study but I know all he wants is to make out, which I love but I also really want to pass my algebra class. And if I say no, he'll go to Yolie. I set the heavy iron skillet on the stove, turn up the burner, then grab the half-empty red box of Farmer John's lard from the refrigerator.

"I took good care of Alma and Suki," Merced shouts as she reaches over the table for her bottle of brandy. "¿Y que hacen? They leave me for a broken-down old man and a malflor."

At least they have love, I think as I spoon the manteca onto the griddle and watch it melt, then ripple like the little waves at the park lake. Slowly, I spoon in the beans. Thick fatty steam rolls up into the cracked ceiling. I stand back and watch droplets hang from the pale-yellow paint, ready to fall. I think of Merced's face, then Yolie's, as I mash the beans into the griddle until they start to cream.

"¿Me oistes?" Merced shouts.

"¿Mande?"

"I told you to start warming up the tortillas."

As I crouch down to pull out the warming drawer for the comal, the phone finally rings. I jump up, but even though she's drunk, Merced's faster. She's been waiting for Leandro to call her for days and quickly picks up the receiver on the wall.

"No, she can't," Merced shouts. "She's busy." Then slams the receiver into its cradle.

For a moment, I'm tempted to throw the pot of beans out onto the concrete stairs outside the kitchen door. For a moment, I want to throw them into Merced's face. But I don't. Instead, I bite the inside of my cheeks, feel the burning stone in my throat as I turn up the flames under the comal and watch them dance around its thin, sharp edges.

"It's too hot, inservible," Merced yells. "You're going to burn them."

I lower the heat. My throat tightens, my eyes keep swelling and burning. Don't cry. Don't be a pinche llorona.

But the tears drip anyway. Mocos fills my nose until I use the back of my hand to wipe it away. I want to run out the door, jump on my purple bike, and book it to the park. There I can cry by the lake in peace until my body just dries up. Maybe that's what La Llorona was all about. Just crying until nothing of herself was left. Maybe she just wanted to lie on the riverbank and wait for her cheating lover to come back to her. Yes, I would wait for George to find me, pick me up and kiss me until his spit mixed with my tears. But who was I fooling? He hadn't kissed me in weeks, not since Yolie had been hanging out by his locker.

"Are the tortillas ready?" Merced squawks.

At this moment, I want to slap her mouth shut. Just make her stop talking until this sadness blows out the window and into the purple dusky sky. At this very moment, I understand why La Llorona chokes children. I go to the refrigerator and the cold air rolls over me. The thought of Suki and Lily near the ocean, the salty breezes that carry the seagulls over their house, flicks through me. My face cools at the memory of throwing pieces of tortillas at them.

"I can enroll you here at SAMOH," Suki said. SAMOH was her favorite name for Santa Monica High.

I said no then because I couldn't leave George. I loved him. I still do. You can't leave someone you love. At least that's what the songs say. I know I'm only fourteen, but I feel empty whenever he's gone. How did that happen? But now that George exists, life at Merced's house is bearable, even without Suki.

The corn tortilla sizzles on the comal, heat waves warping the air above it. Corn and cigarette smoke mix with steaming beans, killing my hunger. As the edges curl away, I pinch the tortilla then carefully flip it over. After finishing her bowl of beans and tortillas, Merced finally goes to work her job at El Yuma bar. I jump up at the phone and call George, who tells me he's "studying" with Yolie. Then I call Suki.

"I miss the seagulls," I say, trying not to cry into the receiver.

✦ ✦ ✦

"Your abuela's like Madonna," Suki tells me the morning after I come to visit.

I laugh. What a joke. How can she compare the coolest queen of dance to a mean old woman who never wants her daughters or grand-daughter to have a life much less sex?

"She's a pura sin vergüenza," Suki says. "And she doesn't care what anybody thinks."

We listen to Richard Blade, who's been broadcasting from the Live Aid concert in Philadelphia. According to Richard, Madonna told off the men in the audience chanting, "Take it off! Take it off!"

"I ain't taking off shit today," Madonna said. Outside, the waves roar with audience. Haha! Just because that gross man from *Penthouse* published her naked photos she took when she was a struggling dancer doesn't mean she's going to do it now.

Too bad Merced couldn't make money off of her shamelessness like Madonna. After bartending at most of the cantinas along First Street, Merced is known as La Reina de la Primera by her customers, especially by the men.

"They call me the queen for good reason," Merced explained to me one day. "Staying loyal to one man keeps you decent. Too many men makes you a puta."

So does not splitting money with your mother. Merced thinks Suki is shameless for running a successful botánica business out of the house she shares with Lily.

"She could've done it from here," Merced fumed.

Today I help Suki move her jars from the garage to one of the guest rooms in the little beach house.

"What are all these for?" I ask Suki, who's labeling little jars filled with dried plants and powders. One of them looks like a little man who has sprung roots all over his body.

"That's ginseng," Suki says, holding the jar closer to my face. "It's supposed to heal the whole body, especially its immunity."

Suki climbs the stepladder to the top shelf of her medicine hutch where she keeps the best and rarest plant samples.

"Immunity from what?" I ask as the jar hovers then lands on the top shelf with Suki's other strange herbs.

"From anything," Suki says.

"AIDS?" I ask. She looks at me funny but I have to know because George's been bugging me about having sex with him. And I want to but I know AIDS is out there. Even Madonna has a commercial about AIDS. Suddenly the ginseng jar drops, explodes at my feet. Suki scrambles down and holds my shoulders. Her hands squeeze me so hard I pull away.

"You having sex with that kid?" she asks.

"No," I say. Suki's eyes widen.

"Do you want to?"

When I don't answer, she yanks open one of the skinny drawers from the hutch marked "SIDA." She hands me a purple plastic square with the word "Trojan" on it. The square has little white figures of men in those Greek soldier helmets all around its edges.

"Here," she says, putting the square in my palm. "This will protect your body from AIDS."

"What . . . ?" I start, but Suki's now laughing.

Before I know it, she's taken the square from my hand. She rips it open and jerks out a thin plastic circle. She pulls the little balloon tip, stretching it out until it snaps hard into her hand.

"It's a rubber," she says, suddenly serious. "Make sure he wears it on his pito before you go at it."

Little streams of sweat drip from my pits. She plucks out a couple more of the purple plastic squares, shoving them into my back pocket.

"If you're both virgins, then you're gonna need a couple of these."

She pats my butt and smiles down at me.

"Now let's sweep this mess up," she says.

In the background, Richard Blade introduces New Order, who start playing "Temptation." It echoes off the garage walls and through the boom box but the waves roar louder.

✦ ✦ ✦

La Malinche, Suki's new botánica on Whittier Boulevard, has it all. Love potions, charms, sacred waters, statues of saints, lo que sea. She bought it last month from the owner, who was moving back to her home in Chihuahua.

"She was the best," Suki says. "I'd always go to her with questions and she finally told me to stop being a pest. So, I became her apprentice."

I guess curanderas have to learn from somebody.

"There are no schools for curanderas as far as I know," Suki continues. "Except in East LA."

Suki not only makes her own stuff, she also uses it. Mainly on women. Mostly they're women who want a lover or a baby. Sometimes neither.

"For the ones who want a baby, I give them this special candle and water," she tells me. She pulls out a little brown bottle with a dropper. The water smells faintly of lilies and honey.

"They just place a few drops in their té de yerbabuena for twenty-one days." Suki wraps up the bottle in wax paper. She ties a gold elastic string around the top. It looks expensive.

"Is the woman supposed to drink it every morning?"

"After she makes love," Suki says with a wink, placing the wrapped bottle on the top shelf of the glass showcase where she keeps the most powerful and precious of her charms and potions.

"I call it moon water," Suki says, turning the lock. "The moon is the mother of water and love."

Later, a woman with sunglasses like Jackie O. comes through the glass door and asks for the moon water. A shiny black scarf with little gold G's covers her puffy brown hair streaked with copper highlights. Her black-and-white checkered suit looks tight but new. She smells like the makeup women at the nice stores in the Pasadena mall. I go to the little back room in search of Suki. I almost bump into her as she hunches over the copper coils sending little waves of heat up into the skylight. The faint smell of roses makes me a little dizzy.

"Some woman in a scarf wants the moon water. Where's the key?"

Suki pulls it out of her back pocket and walks with me to the front.

"Hola, comadre," Suki says, smiling. "You're back for the moon water?"

The woman smiles back but does not pull off her glasses. Her lips glisten a soft pink even under the fluorescent light of the store.

"Yes," she barely whispers. "The lover's potion worked."

"Good." Suki nods as she opens the case and places it on top of the counter.

"Three hundred dollars," Suki says as she writes up the receipt. I suck in my breath and try not to widen my eyes. The woman keeps smiling as she reaches for her quilted leather purse hanging over her shoulder by a gold chain. She snaps open the two big gold *G*'s latching the purse. She pulls out a wallet, a flatter, slightly smaller version of her purse and delicately picks out three bills that look ironed and starched. This is the first time I see Benjamin Franklin up close and personal. Suki recounts the bills and hands her the package.

"Does that potion really work?" I ask after the woman walks out the glass door and slips into her tiny, shiny gray car.

"What matters is the love," Suki answers, tilting her head sideways like a bird. "Do you want to try it on Jorge?"

I don't bother with correcting her this time. Jorge will always be Jorge, not George, no matter how many güeras he cheats on me with. Still, the thought of him sitting by the lake with Yolie, kissing her neck like he kisses mine. It's too much.

I take the potion Suki offers me but I hand back the condom.

"I don't think I need this," I say.

Suki shakes her head and pushes the condom back to me.

"Just in case."

Soon, another customer walks in. It's Lily leading a girl by the arm. She looks like Yolie Zamudio from the side but I'm not sure until she turns her face.

"She needs help," Lily says. "I found her at the bus stop down the street."

Yolie looks like she's been crying for days. Her greasy light brown hair looks stinky. The moment Yolie recognizes me she trembles. Lily wraps her with the rebozo she usually wears around her shoulders and holds her tight.

"You're like ice," Lily says. "Can you get the té de yerbabuena?"

Suki nods at me and I head back to the little kitchen. I pour water into the little enamel saucepan and put it on the hotplate. From the giant refrigerator, I find the jar of fresh mint leaves and rinse them under the faucet. I tear the leaves off the stems and drop them into a blue mug. Their sharp green freshness clears my head. When I see the little man in the jar, I grab a grater. As the water boils, I follow the steam up to the skylight. Tiny droplets float up into honeycombed glass and fade into the sky.

I pour the water over the leaves and grated ginseng, then head back to the front of the store. When I hand the cup to Yolie, I crack a small smile. Her freckled nose wiggles at the minty smell.

"Drink it," Suki says. "It'll calm you."

As she drinks, I can hear Yolie's breath slow. Soon, I'm breathing along with Yolie. I know then I will still love Jorge.

María Elena Cruz Varela

María Elena Cruz Varela *(b. 1953) is a journalist, novelist, and poet born in Colón, Cuba. She won the Julián del Casal Prize (UNAC) for her third collection of poetry,* Hija de Eva *(Daughter of Eve). Among her novels are* The Daughter of Cuba *and* Juana de Arco: El corazón del verdugo *(Joan of Arc: The executioner's heart). Her poetry books include* The Exhausted Angel, La voz de Adán y yo *(The voice of Adam and I),* Afuera está lloviendo *(Outside it's raining), and* Mientras la espera el agua *(While the water awaits). She publishes testimonies of her political experiences in her native land, including* Dios en las cárceles de Cuba *(God in the prisons of Cuba). "Helena's Variation" and "The Jump" were translated from the Spanish by Ignacio Granados Herrera.*

Helena's Variation

—*to Alex*

The war unleashed in my favor was hardly an offering.
A resource of hatred where my skin was not.
Grieved. Icy. Of vaporous gauzes. Distant. I didn't rest.
Screams. Spears. Carriages smashed my dream.
Not a single nightingale. Not a single song. Not a pleasant word.
Slight. My pleading went nowhere. I was
the banished. It was only my name that wandered.
In my name the men killed themselves. Proof of my innocence
was the white region where I implored a thousand times and cursed

a thousand times to exterminate the male. His absurdity. The steeds.
The blood shed for my spectrum. The men didn't hear me.
The men. The clumsy listeners felt happy. They fought.
My skin was not there. "I was never in Troy. I
was only a phantom."

The Jump

Jump again, Antinous. That is your vocation.
Unveil among rocks the pressing mystery of your flesh.
Liturgy that escapes. Incomprehensible detail.
Shatter the beauty.
Show the flesh without love. Bloody.
Splashing the cliffs.
Antinous is jumping. He crashes into the depths of himself.
With him we all jump. And all the misery of nonbeing.
All the gentleness. All the revulsion. All this littleness
fits in your beautiful captive body.
Jab the adjective. Jab is the poverty of naming you.
Yes, when I hug a man, I embrace the oldest of this myth.
I embrace his past. Splattering the beasts
of the future and the present.
So, as long as you jump, I contemplate you.
Everything jumps with you. I contemplate you. Pushing you
with the sinister force of our entire race without destiny.
It's just jumping. As if nothing.
Learning paths.
Despondently irresponsible. The hot gun
in the half-open mouth of the captive.
At midnight the jump.
It's always the same jump towards the same thing.
Antinous is jumping. With him we all jump.
Suicides have a sweet language. Let yourself be devoured.

Jump with you in a succession of possibilities.
My jump is not newer with the centuries.
When a man jumps, with him we all crash.
We are all broken. Scattered.
The purity is achieved with the jump.
Below are the stones. The tempting stones of the abyss.

Celeste Mohammed

Celeste Mohammed *(b. 1976) is a Trinidadian lawyer-turned-writer, and the author of* Pleasantview, *which won the 2022 OCM Bocas Prize for Caribbean Literature and the 2022 CLMP Firecracker Award for Fiction. She holds an MFA in creative writing from Lesley University and received the 2018 PEN/Robert J. Dau Short Story Prize for Emerging Writers, the 2019 Virginia Woolf Award for Short Fiction, and the 2017 John D. Gerner Memorial Prize for Fiction. As a "half Indian," Celeste hails from a line of humble but resilient Indo-Trinidadian women, who faced a post-plantation culture that viewed them as possessions to be supervised and controlled by intimate-partner violence.*

Sundar larki*

Yesterday, while she'd watched Raj cooking dinner, Salma, whisked into a kind of madness where she thought she could have everything she wanted in life, had run into the bathroom, called her sister and pleaded, "Just cover for me a li'l while longer, nah?"

But Yasmeen, in her typical big-sister style, had lectured, "Look, pull your ass home, eh. It bad enough you hornin your husband and involvin me in this chupidness. But now you takin things too far. You have three chirren, or you forget?"

---

* "Sundar larki" is a term commonly used in traditional Indo-Trinidadian culture to mean "a beautiful girl." It is the Trinidad Bhojpuri cognate of the Standard Hindi "Sundar ladki." The difference in spelling is because some phonetical sounds used in Hindi are difficult to transcribe into Standard English, or to replicate with an English-speaking tongue.

Salma had returned to her senses then, hating herself for this whole sweet, sticky weekend away from her children. She'd hated herself so much that she'd made Raj hurt her during last night's lovemaking. She'd made him pull harder, bite deeper, squeeze tighter, and in the darkness, he'd filled her with enough pain to dilute all her motherly shame. But now it was morning, and sunlight streaking through his dusty glass louvres made her dress on the floor seem as two-toned as her heart.

Raj wriggled forward, gliding his hand over her stretch-marked tummy, then down between her legs. "Oh gosh, stay nah. One more day? I really need you to stay," he said.

Salma pincered her muscles, refusing him admission. "How I could do that?" she said, her voice sharper than intended. She resented how he'd phrased it as his need. What about what she needed? Did she need him bearing down on her? Forcing her to apportion her guilt between him and the children, the way she shared one sandwich between three hungry mouths at home, whenever money was tight and Shiva, her husband, hadn't sold enough lettuce at market.

"I have to go and organize them chirren for the first day of school," she said.

"But they father there. He could handle them."

"Their father?" Salma grunted. Shiva? A half-blind drunkard, thirteen years her senior, who was more loving to his crops than to his children, who interacted with them only to teach and beat. Salma had promised her son, twelve-year-old Anil, a big reward if he'd take care of little Amelia and Aarti himself, keeping them out of their father's way this weekend. Ten whole dollars, she'd promised. She'd stooped that low. Yasmeen was right: she was a bad mother, a "selfish bitch in heat," and now it was time to re-tie this Let-go-beast Salma, pull her ass back home and become nothing but "Mammy" again.

"The man manage for these two days. What's one more?" Raj asked, and the sureness of his tone made Salma's skin flush with annoyance. But then, she remembered, much of his ignorance was her own fault. She'd never told him how hard-won this weekend was, how much planning and collusion had been involved, and how desperate a lie she'd told Shiva ("Yaz beg me to come Barrackpore to help them for Eid ul-Adha holiday"). It was a cardboard lie that needed Yasmeen to continue propping it, and last night, she'd declined.

Salma had kept much from Raj, over their year of "friending" and two weekend trysts. Partly because she liked to pretend Shiva didn't exist when she was with Raj, and partly because Raj was so hungry for her—young engineer like him, he could've had any young, single, educated girl, but he'd wanted her, the office cleaner with three children. And she'd wanted his desire to remain just so: pure and pity-free. It made her feel she was worth something, even though she had nothing to offer him.

What she needed right now, though, was for Raj to help her leave this apartment—even though she longed to stay, even though he was heading out tomorrow for a rig in the Gulf and they wouldn't see each other for two weeks, even though she had no idea when she'd be able to arrange another weekend like this. She needed to leave with the assurance that he'd continue to make do with whatever she could spare of herself, whenever she could safely spare it.

She'd never told Raj her deepest fear: Shiva would kill her if he found out she was horning. In fact, he'd threatened to kill her for less: when the man in Central Market had smiled at her too long and she'd smiled back, when he'd come home early from the garden and found her watching TV with the neighbor and accused them of "gossiping," when she'd asked him point-blank if he was really screwing the Chinee woman in the hardware, when she'd put too much garlic in his tomato choka.

It wouldn't take much for Shiva to turn her into another front page sad story.

And yet, she'd come to Raj. Twice. She'd come and never told him these things, for fear of scaring him away. She'd come feeling not an ounce of married-woman guilt, feeling only that she deserved this pleasure and was justified in taking it, because one day Shiva would kill her and she would die without ever having lived in her body . . . and that seemed to her the greater sin.

But she couldn't get greedy and take stupid risks—Yasmeen had reminded her—not with the children still so small, they needed their Mammy.

"Look, I done tell you: we could have we fun and thing, but I have my responsibilities," she chided Raj now.

A small space opened between their damp bodies, the fan's air replacing his lips on her spine.

"So where your 'responsibilities' was since Friday?" he dared over her shoulder, which still stung from the imprint of his teeth last night.

"You know what?" she sat up and wheeled on him. "You damn right. I was wrong to come, and in future, Mr. Gentleman, I will never make the same mistake."

She stomped her nude self all the way into the bathroom. She locked the door, turned on the shower, made fists in her hair and pulled. She cried in that heaving but noiseless way that had become second nature at home, so the children wouldn't hear. Now, though, crying silently seemed more difficult. Especially when she wanted Raj to barge in and say something like, "I sorry. I know this hard for you. Don't worry 'bout me. I go be here whenever you need, nah." Just as he'd done in their first real conversation, when he'd been the only person in the office to notice her swollen lip, and he'd sought her out in the cleaning supply closet—her little hideaway— found her sitting on a bucket sobbing, and he'd knelt on the floor amongst all her brooms and mops and gallons, to share the same bleach stink air and to listen to her story. That was the time she'd answered-back Shiva and he'd dunked her head into a barrel of water and held it there. She'd come up sputtering and gasping, her lungs, eyes, nose, burning, greedy, and grateful for air. These weekends with Raj—two weekends out of her whole suffocating life—had felt the same; they were air. And he could restore that feeling right now—he could give her back the air, if he stopped asking her to be a bad mother, to risk more than she could.

But as Salma soaped and lathered and tried to rid herself of Raj's scent, she couldn't help wondering how different life would've been had she been a bad daughter, the type everybody called "force-ripe" and "own-way." She might've fared better. That type of thirteen-year-old girl might've uttered a steups and walked right out of Tanty Nazroon's shop when the curly haired stranger in coveralls and rubber boots had aimed his chin at her and called her beautiful.

"Hello, sundar larki," Shiva had said. "You look just like your Mammy."

Both she and Tanty Nazroon had blushed—as much at his mistake as at the compliment. Then Tanty had pushed his two dollars change across the cracked laminate counter and turned to admire Salma. "Nah, this is my sister daughter," she'd said proudly. "She helping me for the holidays."

"What you name?" he'd asked Salma, who sat perched atop a stack of sweet-drink cases, swinging her legs and braiding her hair into a thick black Rapunzel rope.

"Answer the nice Mister," Tanty Nazroon had urged.

"I name Salma."

"Well, I's Shiva. From the road crew, nah. So I go be around for a while, comin to buy we li'l snacks and thing. Like how I's the youngest, they does always send me."

He'd been as old then as she was now. So, at twenty-six years old, Salma could see plainly what had been her mistake. She'd demonstrated to Shiva that day, and over the next few weeks of that fateful July, that she was wife material: a "good" little Indian girl who'd always listen to her elders. Her Mammy, her Pa, her Tanty, her big-sister Yasmeen, and even him.

But somewhere along the way, over the last thirteen years, she'd changed. She no longer wanted to be good, she ached to be happy. It was probably too late, though, she had the children to think about.

While she dressed and packed her bag, Raj flitted around her, droning apologies.

"Look, I sorry. I not used to this . . . sharing. I never deal with no marrid-woman before. It does mess with my head, nah. You slaving behind that asshole when . . ."

"When what?" Salma heaved her canvas tote, which bore the name of the company where they worked, onto her shoulder.

"When I should be your man. Your real man. Why you don't just leave him?"

Her arms fell so limply at her sides that the tote slid off and landed at her feet with a dejected thump. In a whole year of friending, Raj had never spoken like this—commitment talk, leave-your-husband talk— and she'd never let herself hope for it.

"Yeah, I saying it with my whole chest. Leave the damn fool. This is love, girl."

He snaked his arms around her waist and drew her close, looking into her eyes in a way that made her think she'd never seen him nervous until now.

"Leave him and go where?" she said, in that weary tone she often used when one of the children asked a question too many times. Did Raj actually think she could just saunter out of Shiva's house and go pay a rent and mind three children on a cleaner's salary?

He laughed and threw his head so far back she saw straight up his nostrils. He could laugh, yes, because he'd never heard all the times Shiva had threatened her and all the times he'd mocked her, "Go where? Back by your mother-and-them to shame them? For the whole village to laugh? Go where? Nobody go want you 'round with that string-band of chirren behind you!"

"Come here, with me," Raj said, with a winning smile that told her he was sure of himself after all, and more than that, he expected her to be grateful to him for this offer. That's what he was searching for on her face now, she guessed. Gratitude.

"Well, what you waiting for? Say yes, nah girl?"

Salma's anger revived, like a noise that had always been there in the background, like the sound of Shiva's old Weedwacker whenever he moved from the garden's depths to the roadside grass. She tried to tear herself from Raj's grip but couldn't, and they ended up struggling, pulling and tugging, arched backs bounding from wall to wall like one organism with two hard shells.

She wailed openly, and Raj kept asking, "What the ass wrong with you? What you getting on so for?" And, every time he said it, Salma cried harder because it became more and more apparent how little he understood her situation.

Finally, Raj pinned her against the fridge. "I love you, Salma. That's what I trying to tell you, girl! Why the hell you can't understand that?"

His words had that ring of condescension, in tune with what she'd always heard from Shiva: Look at all I do for you! Take you from the country and bring you in Town. But you's still just a duncey-head li'l coolie girl.

And did he say "Love"? The only love she was certain of was what she felt for her children. They'd been scooped from her flesh, and yet she belonged to them. Salma shut her eyes and set Raj a final test.

"If you so love, then tell me bring the chirren and come, nah?"

She needed him to prove Shiva a liar, to whisper something that would drown out the thirteen years roaring in her head. She needed to know that Raj loved all of her—not just the Let-go-Beast Salma who'd ridden him like a demon all weekend but "Mammy" too.

For a love like that, she'd be prepared to risk her life.

She held her breath and waited, but then, suddenly, Raj released her and bared his palms as if her skin had scorched him.

"Okay, go," he said. "Go see 'bout your chirren and the man who try to drown you and thing. That's the life you like, eh? Well, gone from here!"

She grabbed her bag and half ran to the front door, half blinded by tears and hating herself for daring to believe—even for a second—that Raj's love might be real. He followed and caught her in the gallery, prized open her fist. "At least take this for taxi money, nah."

She fled down the stairs with only the vaguest sense of dollars sloughing from her, like fish scales. She flagged the first taxi to come along, and got in without so much as a look-back.

She found two dollar-notes then, softening in her sweaty grip.

Two red dollar-notes. That's how it had started with Shiva, too. He'd pushed the change from Tanty Nazroon back across the counter. "This is for the larki," he'd said.

From her seat on the crates, Salma had blinked down at the money.

"Take it nah, girl," he'd insisted.

Salma had looked from him to Tanty Nazroon, who nodded encouragingly, back to him again.

"But why you—"

"Because I feel you deserve it."

With that, Shiva had left the shop. When he was out of sight, Salma jumped down and claimed the cash. It was hers, and the thought had made her pores swell and prickle. Then she did a "big-woman" thing—crumpled the bills and shoved them deep into the too-big brassiere she'd inherited from Yasmeen.

Later, somewhere along the last thirteen unlucky years, she'd come to understand that she should never have accepted Shiva's money that day. It had been a shop transaction, in a way. By accepting his fake generosity, she'd made him feel he'd actually done something for her. And that's why she hadn't wanted to accept taxi fare from Raj today. It was chicken feed compared to what he could've done for her today, if he'd really loved her.

But all he'd said was: Just leave him. Easy as that? And just leave the children too? Raj might as well have asked her to leave her soul.

And yet, he wouldn't have been the first to do so. Unfair exchange is robbery, her Mammy and Pa had always said. And yet, look, they'd still given her away at thirteen years old, and exchanged her whole life, for only the three thousand dowry Shiva had paid. Of course, they'd also made him take shahada—accept Islam—so an Imam could perform the marriage quick, quick. But while it had cost Shiva nothing to lie to God, it had cost Salma everything, every blasted day since then.

She was tired of paying debts that other people had thrust upon her. Paying, paying, paying, and getting nothing in return. This emptiness was what it meant to be "good"?

As the car pulled into The Croisée, she surrendered the two dollars and boarded a maxi-taxi heading to Port of Spain. Her phone rang. She felt its vibration through the bag on her knees. But confined as she was in the back seat, between the door and the middle passenger, and unable to spread her elbows, she got to the device too late. It was Yasmeen who'd called. Salma jammed her thumb and switched off the phone. She was not in the mood for another lecture about her responsibilities, when she knew them all too well.

The last time she'd made this exact walk, her body had still been warm from Raj. She'd glided along this same broad Port of Spain pavement not noticing the sleeping vagrants, not wrinkling her nose at the smell of human excrement and unwashed flesh—as she did now. Instead, she'd marveled at how pretty the place looked at 6:00 a.m., and at how the retreating chill of night and the oncoming warmth of day had combined to harden her nipples and make her wish to return to Raj's embrace.

Now she saw nothing but people crowding her like bamboo in the Barrackpore forest, felt nothing but shoulders and elbows scraping her like jointed branches. She walked in a straight line, though, making no effort to avoid collision. Why couldn't they move around her for once! A nuts vendor interrupted his own chant—"Salt-and-fresh, salt-and-fresh!"—to heckle her, "Baby, fix yuh face, nah?" She scowled deeper. A Jehovah's Witness standing under the bank shoved a magazine in her face and said, "Smile, God loves you." Salma cussed him under her breath instead of taking the book, as she'd often done, to learn about how the meek would inherit the earth.

She was not in a believing mood.

She dropped her gaze and hitched her eyes on the person ahead. From his back pocket, the fringed end of a rag waved as he walked, its fabric so white that it glowed almost blue. The thing was either brand-new or this man had a good wife who scrubbed her knuckles raw with blue soap on a jookin board. Did he even care? What a shame that, any minute now, he was going to pull it out and wipe his greasy face, streaking her sacrifice brown.

Raj had spoiled everything. He had sullied Salma's saving grace, revoked the one thing she'd had to look forward to and fantasize about: her times with him. She could never go back. Not now, not knowing what he wanted from her. And worse than all that, Raj had proven Shiva right: she'd been a fool to think she could set her own terms with a man.

Even Pa had once said similar. That morning when she'd gone to him at dawn, when he was seated at the dining table, drinking his coffee before heading out to the field. Twisting a finger in her cotton nightie, she'd stood at eye-level with her father and said, "Pa, I don't want to marrid Shiva. Yasmeen like him. So, why you don't marrid she to him?"

"But he don't want Yaz. He want you, Sally."

"But I not ready, Pa. I want to go back to school. I feel I go do better this time."

Pa had shaken his head and wrapped his fingers, with halting tenderness, around the arm of the mug. Salma had stood there, wishing it could be her. She'd wanted him to cradle and baby her like he used to, a few guava seasons ago, before she'd gotten breast-swells and underarm hair—by her estimation, that was when he'd abruptly surrendered her to Mammy and Tanty Nazroon and their endless lessons on how to balay and sakay and clean and wash for a future husband.

"School is for bright chirren, Sally. Otherwise is just wastin' time. So, I send you to wuk in Nazroon shop, look, only couple weeks and this Shiva come sniffing behind you. More will come, and more will come, until braps! you make a mistake and let some chupid li'l fella spoil you. Nobody go want you then, you go remain on my hand, get over-ripe and rotten. I can't let that happen. It better you marrid now. This Shiva say he go carry you in Town, where it have plenty white-people and rich-people and thing, where you could live free as a big-woman in your own place."

With his boldfaced lies, Shiva had charted her whole life, Salma mused, as she ducked her head and climbed into the empty twelve-seater maxi-taxi idling on the stand. It would take a while to fill up, she knew. But the wait would give her chance to collect herself and to rehearse her story—one last time—to make sure it matched what she'd said to him and the children during calls over the weekend: It was a real big bull. Uncle Kazim and the other brothers in the mosque kill it. I spend whole weekend helping Aunty Yasmeen cook for visitors. She drop me by the bus place early this morning. I didn't bring none of the beef 'cause it woulda thaw out and drip blood all over the place.

This would be her last lie, Salma swore to herself. By the time Raj returned from the rig, there would be nothing but vapors left between them. She would no longer encourage him, and she sure as hell wouldn't listen to him talk about "Love."

Trudging the dead-end street to the base of the mountain, Salma craned her neck, knowing that at a particular angle, she'd glimpse the house. Over the years, Shiva had changed out the raw plywood walls and replaced roofing sheets blown off during rainy season, but the structure had remained substantially the same: a wooden box on stilts, teetering on the side of a bushy mountain. They did not own the land. Like all the other squatters, Shiva had simply cleared a space and, with pine lumber he'd credited from a hardware on the Main Road, he'd made a marital home.

But Salma had never gotten to be a big-woman in her own house; only a servant-girl in Shiva's. Still, she reminded herself now as she drew closer, there'd been some good days up there, in that box. That was where her children had been born. Where they were now sleeping. Salma felt a ripple of excitement at the thought of seeing them, smelling them: Aarti like baby oil, the other two like Lifebuoy soap—except, in Anil's case, there was the musky promise of teenage boyhood. She had missed them this weekend. Despite all the ramping with Raj, she hadn't forgotten her children.

She came to the foot of the mountain, where the village standpipe stood. Its brassy head was once attached to a length of PVC that would often break and cause a fountain her children enjoyed. But recently, some Good Samaritan had encased the raw plumbing in a concrete tower, and made a level platform underneath, so buckets could stand without tipping. Tomorrow, at this hour, Salma would be jostling neighbors to fill water for the children to bathe before school. But today, she used the concrete as a bench, to rest and gather courage for that steep unpaved trek to her home. She had to admit, she didn't want to climb that hill.

If only Raj had said, "Bring the chirren." If only he'd loved her that much, she would've loved him back for the rest of her life. She would've gone straight to the police station on the Main Road and asked them to come back here with her—Shiva could keep everything else—all she would've taken was Anil, Amelia, and Aarti.

And how long before he find you? she chided herself. How long before he showed up on her job brandishing a two-by-four as he'd done the last time she'd worked late? How long before he showed up at the children's school?

A flock of wild parrots squawked overhead, taunting her with their lofty green freedom. A sadness fell upon Salma. It wasn't the same old hurt she'd carried since thirteen years old, this was fresh and unexpected, like bird shit. If only she had somewhere to go with her children, someone to protect them from Shiva. Not even Raj could ever do that, she had to concede, and maybe he'd been honest not to offer to.

She drew the phone from the canvas tote, switched it on, and saw no missed calls from Raj, but five from Yasmeen. She dialed and then aborted the call. She knew exactly what Yaz would say: No! You can't come here, girl. What Kazim will say? Within a few months of Salma's marriage to Shiva, the same Imam had found Kazim to marry Yaz. The sisters grew closer during their first simultaneous pregnancies. And closer still after Shiva's accident: somebody on the road crew had been using a jackhammer and something had pitched up and hit Shiva, taking half the vision in that right eye. Government didn't want him no more. He went from sulking at home to drinking at the rumshop down the road. He wore an eyepatch—put it on every day, like a uniform, before picking his way down the mountain—and people sympathetic to his injury bought him drinks. Anil was a year old then, Salma had needed milk and Pampers, she'd tried to talk sense into Shiva one day. "Get a next work, or go plant garden and sell," she'd said. That was when everything changed. Instead of the few slaps she was accustomed to receiving—the normal way she'd seen Pa fix-up Mammy—Shiva had beaten her that day like she wasn't a real flesh-and-blood person, like she was a straw-filled Good Friday bobolee; beaten her till her face was twice its size. It became a hobby for him after that.

And after every beating, Yasmeen had counseled, "Girl, that's how all them Indian man is. Kazim does well cut my ass, too, when he drink he rum." In that way, the sisters, though distant, became each other's confidantes. Chatting every day, detailing the joys of motherhood, along with the horrors of wifehood, knowing full well that they'd never find sanctuary in each other's homes, and would have to make do with only some sympathy in each other's hearts.

The front room-combined living room and kitchen was empty. The children's bedroom door was closed—they were still asleep. The door to the smaller bedroom, the one she shared with Shiva, was open. Salma walked bravely toward it, not knowing what to expect, but he was not there. Probably in the garden. She unpacked her clothes and put on an old house dress. Then, she tiptoed into the children's room, stood over the king-size mattress—something her boss had been ready to throw away— and studied the children. How Anil and Amelia formed two sides of a capital H while the steamroller, little Aarti, formed the bridge in between. They were worth more than any man's love. Their happiness was fair exchange for hers.

She closed the ill-fitting door slowly, to reduce its dragging, and crossed to the kitchen. From the lower part of the rust-freckled fridge, she got eggs, but had to fight the freezer door, which was iced shut. She used an ice-pick to dislodge a pack of chicken-feet to thaw for lunch. She was supposed to defrost the fridge this weekend. She would do that today, she decided. Along with ironing school uniforms, and making some cheese paste for the children to take tomorrow. She'd already covered their books with brown paper. And she'd left instructions for Anil to pack everybody's schoolbag and scrub everybody's school shoes. He'd complained, "But Mammy, my toe squeezing in these," but Salma knew it was just a trick to get new shoes. She chuckled now, remembering his cheekiness.

"What have you so happy, girl?" Shiva's voice came from behind.

She wheeled to see him sitting in the doorway, removing wet boots, garden coverall peeled down to his waist, muddy cutlass on the floor.

"I ain't hear you come up the steps, nah. I not-too-long reach. The boil egg almost done. You want Milo tea? Or coffee?" She talked fast and moved even faster, grabbing the small pot, filling it with water from the plastic barrel next to the sink, taking it to the stove. She wanted to appear busy and dutiful.

"Coffee," Shiva replied.

While the water boiled, she peeled eggshells. There was silence, except for the sound of metal on metal, him using a file to scrape mud from the cutlass blade, as he usually did after a damp morning in the garden.

Back to normal. In his box, as if the whole weekend hadn't happened. This was her lot—she'd just have to accept it—but at least she'd had those few times with Raj.

"So where you was?" Shiva asked.

"How you mean? In south, by Yasmeen-them for Eid . . ."

"I say: where the fuck you was?" He raised his voice. "I call there this morning. To tell you pass in the bank-machine and take out forty dollars for me. The daughter answer. She say she ain't see you whole weekend. She say you was never there."

Salma felt her face reddening, her pulse quickening as she tried to recall whether there'd been a missed call from Shiva on her phone. She kept her back to him as she scraped the eggshells into the trash and replied, "That li'l girl over-dotish. Let we ring Yaz now, now. She go clear up everything."

"I done talk to she. She lie like wind . . . till she tie up she-self . . . and then she confess it: you wasn't there."

"Shiva . . .," was all Salma could say, turning slowly to face him, convinced now that there had been no call to her phone. Had he suspected her for some time and simply waited for today? Or had Yasmeen—her sister, her own sister—betrayed her?

In one lunge, Shiva crossed the kitchen and grabbed her neck.

His eyes searched, then landed on her shoulder. "W'happen? Dog bite you?" he asked.

Raj's teeth marks. They'd been so far from her mind—like something from another life—she hadn't thought to wear sleeves.

With his free hand, Shiva ripped down her housedress as if it were made of Anil's kite paper. "And w'happen here?" he asked, pointing to her breast, "Soucouyant suck you?"

He released her neck then, and sure enough, on the pale flesh beside her nipple, there was a purplish bruise.

He slapped her. She stumbled backward, but the sink caught her.

"You feel I stupid! You feel I dotish! Since you get that office wuk, you feel you better than me. Which one of them you fuckin'? Eh? Who it is? Is a nigger man, nah? Or is the boss, the white fella?"

Normally, Salma would just stand there and take the loud cussing, or curl up like a congoree on the floor and take the heel pounding. But normally she was innocent; today she was guilty, and it made her determined that Shiva should not take her life a second time, leaving her children motherless, without a bloody-good, ring-down battle for her soul. She owed her children that much, and, after thirteen godforsaken years, she owed it to her own damn self.

She dashed to the stove, reached for the pot of boiling water, but then her arm fell away, like a broken stem, and hung at her side. She glanced down to see why it had disobeyed her. When she looked up, the cutlass was coming at her again. In her mind, she raised the same arm to block, but in real life nothing happened, so she shut her eyes.

The children's door grated open and Anil shouted, "No, Daddy, no!"

She cried, "Go, son!" knowing he would remember what she'd drilled into his head, like schoolwork, so many times: If I ever tell you go, leave everything, take your sisters, run next door and tell them call police, you hear?

But Anil didn't move, he just stood there screaming, "Somebody come! Daddy killin' Mammy!"

Shiva turned away from her then and moved toward the boy, pointing the cutlass. "Hush your mouth! Your mudder is a old 'ho! She look for this! Is she who make me—"

Bleeding, Salma raised her good hand and retrieved the ice pick on top of the fridge. She measured the broad expanse of Shiva's sweaty back, its skin smooth and gleaming like everything he'd ever taken from her. She moved to his blind side, hoping he wouldn't see her coming. Then, she angled and jammed that point right up inside her husband. He gasped, and she withdrew, satisfied that she'd penetrated him, but suddenly so very tired. She watched everything dissolve into tiny yellow dots, like the chicken feed she and Yasmeen once fed their fluffy little common-fowl pets—stroking, loving, fattening them—knowing full well that, soon enough, Pa would take them away, to be plucked and gutted.

Teresa de la Parra

Teresa de la Parra (1889–1936), the most important Venezuelan novelist of the twentieth century, was born in Paris, France, to a wealthy landowning Venezuelan family. Her father was ambassador in Berlin. She was raised in Hacienda Tazón and divided her time between South America and Europe, where she was a busy socialite and underwent treatment for tuberculosis. Born Ana Teresa Parra Sanojo, she launched her writing using the pseudonym Fru-Fru and penned audacious and funny short stories, rebelling against her class. Her short story "The diary of a young lady who writes because she's bored," published in a local magazine, was the genesis of her literary career. Her two major works are Las memorias de Mamá Blanca *and* Ifigenia, *a novel about Caracas high society, snobby women, racism, classism, sexism, and corruption at the highest levels of Venezuelan government at the beginning of the twentieth century. The following excerpt from* Ifigenia *was translated from the Spanish by Sandra Guzmán.*

A Very Long Letter Where Things Are Told Like in a Novel

During these last four months, Cristina, I have spent many moments of sadness, experiencing unpleasant feelings and exasperating insights and yet despite it all, I feel immense joy because I have witnessed in myself a new person unfolding that I did not suspect and that fills me with great satisfaction. You and me, and all of us who walk this Earth have some sorrows, we are heroes and heroines of our own novella, which is more beautiful, and a thousand times better than all the novels written.

This thesis that I am going to develop before your eyes, will report every minuscule detail, like every good novel, all what has occurred to me since I last saw you in Biarritz. I am sure that my story will interest you very much. In addition, I have discovered that lately I have the genius gift of observation and I am able to express myself with enormous ease. Unfortunately, these talents have been of no use until now.

Sometimes I try to test them with Tía Clara and Abuelita, but they have not been able to appreciate it. Tía Clara has not even taken the time to acknowledge them. And Abuelita, since she is very old, has very outdated ideas, which she has leaned on because she has twice told me that my head is filled with cockroaches. So, you can understand why this is one of the reasons why I get bored in this house that is so big and so sad, where no one sees nor understands me, and why I have a need to feel understood, which is what compels me to write to you.

I know very well that you will understand me. As for me, I don't feel any reservations nor embarrassment sharing my most intimate confidences. You have before my eyes the sweetest prestige to know what happened to never return. The secrets I will tell you will not have any unpleasant consequences in my future life and therefore, I know that I will never regret telling you. It will be "like the secrets that dead take with them to the grave." I'll write with deep affection which feels very much like that time during our tender blossoming, when we thought about those who left to "never return."

Mary Grueso Romero

Mary Grueso Romero (b. 1947) is a poet, children's literature author, and literature and Spanish professor born in Guapi, Cauca, who lives in the port town of Buenaventura, Colombia. She is a leading feminist and Afro-Colombian intellectual whose work celebrates the Black people of the Colombian Pacific coast. The region exports the entire sugar and molasses production of Colombia, 80 percent of its coffee, and has the third largest number of gold, platinum, copper, and manganese mines in Latin America. The town is majority Black and among the poorest in the country. She has been awarded top honors by the Colombian Ministry of Culture for her commitment to lifting the voices of Palenqueras and Afrocolombianas. She is the author six poetry collections, among them El otro yo que sí soy yo, Negra Soy, Tómame antes que la noche llege, *and* Cuando los ancestros llaman. *She has written seven illustrated children's books, including* La niña en el espejo, El pico más hermoso, La cucarachita mandinga, *and the bestseller,* La muñeca Negra. *"If God had been born here" from her poetry book,* El mar y tú, *was translated from the Spanish by Sandra Guzmán.*

If God had been born here
—For Soffy Romero Hinestroza

If God had been born here
he'd be a fisherman,
eat chontaduro
and drink borojó.

María would be Black
big boned like me
and on top of her head would carry a platter of fish
offering at the top of her lungs
through the town's streets

to all the town folk:
"I have silky fish whole and intact;
snapper to eat fried,
ñato fo' stewin,
tollo fo' sweatin'
and canchimala for tapao."

If God had been born here,
here on this coast,
he'd be a farmer
who'd harvest coconuts from the palm
grove with his muscled body
like a Black man from El Piñal,
with jet Black skin
and ivory teeth,
with tight coily hair
like he was a chacarrás.

On the Pacific plain
he'd harvest natos and mangroves
that he'd turn into rollers fo' the rails to rest,
and he'd fish crabs
from the neighborhood caves.

If God had been born here,
here on this coast,
he'd feel his blood rise
at the sound of the drum.

He'd dance currulao with marimba and guasá,
he'd drink biche
in the patronal festival,
he'd feel on his own flesh
the inequality's scorn for being Black,
for being poor,
and for being from this coast.

SINUOUS
MOON

This lunar energy corresponds to
the serpent energy, which is the energy
of Mother Earth.

Amada Libertad

Amada Libertad *(1970–1991) was the literary pseudonym of Leyla Patricia Quintana Marxelly. She was a revolutionary poet born in Santa Tecla, El Salvador. She died in combat on the San Salvador volcano during a solar eclipse at the age of twenty-one. Her mother published posthumously some of her poetry collections, including* Larga trenza de amor *and* Burlas de la vida. Libertad va cercando *was published in Spanish and Italian with the papers she sent from the combat front via clandestine mail. She received the 1990 Wang Interdata and the 1991 Juegos Florales de Zacatecoluca awards. Since 2014, the Festival Internacional de Poesía Amada Libertad has been celebrated in her honor. The following four works were translated from the Spanish by Whitney DeVos.*

Epitaph

When I die
I will not leave this world.
I'll remain in your longings, your ideals
I'll remain in each word I wrote out that day
full of rage.

I'll burst into a thousand dawns, more
and each day awaken
honed sharper in the people's consciousness.

Pueblo

Not even breathing in your absence
will convince me I've left.
The thing is, you're so deeply entrenched
it's impossible to strip you from my face.

You're etched in my steps
my path takes your name
my sun reflects your image
all that's mine
seizes a voice shouting at us
when I name you here
in pain's silence
in this dark and distant place.

Today I resurrect your name,
your sun and your hope.
You, man, child, woman,
sea, air, desert, water:
I name you PUEBLO.

Extraordinary

—to Mae

You know . . . Turn up the radio and listen to the news
go outside and into the street
where my people suffer most.
Go downtown
smash the mannequin windows
and take in the suffering, the sacrifice,
the human anguish.
Today you can cry

unashamed. Not for me.
It's outrage
throbbing in your consciousness.
Yes, *now*
I am your daughter, your cousin, your sister,
your friend and comrade.

In the Past

I used to run through the streets
singing in the mornings
screaming in the evening
sabotaging things at night.
No, it wasn't a routine;
just one of the ways
I defied pain
kept close to the dead
and our communal love of peace
which day by day we weave
with a pain most of us share.

Giannina Braschi

Giannina Braschi *(b. 1953), born in San Juan, Puerto Rico, is a poet who writes radical literature, plays, and Latinx philosophy. She penned the epic poem* Empire of Dreams, *the Spanglish classic* Yo-Yo Boing!, *and the tragicomedy* United States of Banana. *With a PhD in literature, she has taught at Rutgers and published works on Cervantes, Garcilaso, Machado, Lorca, and Bécquer. She has been awarded grants and fellowships from the National Endowment for the Arts, the Ford Foundation, the New York Foundation for the Arts, the Instituto de Cultura Puertorriqueña, the North American Academy of the Spanish Language, and PEN America, among others. Her life's work is the subject of the anthology* Poets, Philosophers, Lovers: On the Writings of Giannina Braschi.

Reservations

—Do you have reservations?

　　—No, I don't. But I don't see the problem. The restaurant is empty.

　　—The problem, madame, is that you don't have reservations.

　　—But all the tables are empty.

　　—You would have to leave in half an hour.

　　—I will leave right now and leave your restaurant empty.

　　—It will be full in half an hour. If you can eat and leave in half an hour.

　　—We will be finished in forty minutes.

　　—Table for one?

　　—I am one but look at the pack who are following me.

　　—Madame, this is an invasion. I was expecting a lonely ranger, but your people are filling up the whole restaurant—and not one single reservation—and bad manners too—eating with their mouths open—talking with their mouths full. You want instant gratification, madame.

You enter my place with ferocious hunger. Demanding food in the spur of the moment because you are a moody compulsive eater. Here and now, for you, is more important than honorable and later. Discipline is the mother of safely wait for your retirement. Wait for the moment to come. Don't take the moment as a rapture. As a rape of time. Because you want to eat now, I have to feed you now the food you want now forgetting all the reservations that were made before. This is a very popular artsy-fartsy restaurant. People come here with high brows, raising their chins and noses, and behave as if they were not hungry. Hunger is substituted by taste. Oh, things are tasteful. And the clients are not hungry. They eat because they have taste, and they like to taste. They don't eat because they are hungry. That is why they make reservations. They can wait and they wait.

—You're giving more importance to the people who are not here than to the people who are here. Absence, for you, is more important than presence. Future more important than moment. Predictability more important than improvisation. I refuse to reserve what I can grasp in a moment. I refuse to predict every step I take. I refuse to carry an iPhone in my pocket even though I got stuck in an elevator last night and couldn't call 911. I refuse to forsake my right to be here and now and now what I want is to be here and how, free to act on the splurge of the moment. I hope all of you who make reservations find something better to do than fulfill the expectation of the reservation. I hope all the seats stay empty. And a pack of wild cards and cats enter the restaurant with guitars and mandolins—and break the expectation of the reservation. I hope they speak loud with a heavy accent. I hope they break dishes and start screaming and insulting each other, and a wife hurls a glass at her husband—and he ducks the glass by an inch—but it awakens his sense.

—Yes, I am hungry. I want my food now. Hunger exists. I won't reserve to eat. I won't let my anxieties fulfill your expectations. Do I have to wait for the waiter? The waiter waits—yes, too much he waits. No tips. No tips. Because he believes in reservations, he reserves his opinions to himself, and his silence is his unconformity. Tired of waiting? Become a waiter— then you'll really know what reservations are all about. I have my reservations. And then I criticize the waiter for accepting more reservations than needed. He is really a reserved gentle soul—too many reservations made him forget that he had something to do in life that was not waiting for the waiter and the reservation to reserve. Very reserved—he died with all his reservations inside. Oh, all you tasters, moving your tongues like snakes—and saying: Uumm—*it's tasty*. It's tasty because you are not hungry. If you only knew what hunger is you would not have any kind of reservations. There would be no hesitations—should I—or should I not. There would be no impotence—and right now there is no impotence in me—no reservation—I am not reserved. Please don't reserve a seat for me. And don't tell me where to sit. Who is the decider? You? I happen to like deciding for myself where I want to be seated. Even that you want to rule out of the constitution of my fancy.

And then the millennials say: What's your problem, lady? Sit and wait for the waiter. You've waited all your life. You might have to wait a little longer. Without procrastination. With determination. And anger doesn't get you far enough. We were born after the facts. We are all the information you need to pack in your bag. We are conceited. We know what you don't know—the smell of time—as Donald Trump Jr. says: It's disgusting! Tasteless we breed pigeons and smell bird shit all the time, but we wait and procrastinate for other times. Will we understand. Will we enter space-time? Will we, will we. Sure, for sure. Who has time to doubt—when all the time of the world is waiting upstairs at the bar. Ha, Ha, Ha, Ha! Look at the phone, pick a dish, trash the other, click here, click there. Take a selfie. Take your time and click me a like.

—Take a step further. And back away. The President is arriving in his limousine. The credit cards are all in order. Step aside. The First Lady is arriving in the second limousine—with no reservations—no procrastination—no hunger to taste the food that without hunger tastes like documents to be turned over to the investigators of the procrastination that is taking too long—448 pages long—and no decision on collusion, nor obstruction of justice. I have my reservations. Why did you make reservations? You have taste not hunger. If you were hungry and you had nothing to eat, you would take the bullshitter by his horns and rip his balls off.

Virginia Brindis de Salas

Virginia Brindis de Salas *(1908–1958) was a poet, journalist, and Afro-Uruguayan activist born in Montevideo, Uruguay. She was one of the few Latin American women writers to publish in the first half of the twentieth century and the first Black woman to publish in Uruguay. She was a member of El Círculo de Intelectuales, Artistas, Periodistas y Escritores Negros (CIAPEN), a Black Uruguayan cultural group.* Pregón de marimorena *and* Cien cárceles de amor *are her most notable works. "Mi corazón" (My Heart) was translated from the Spanish by Sandra Guzmán.*

My Heart

I said to my heart:
you are tired
as a caged eagle,
you hate life.
You think your dreams
have faded in history's shadow . . .
Yet I know you as a fighter,
giant and brave;
in your body runs—
a slave's blood.
You are strong
solid as steel.
Why do you beat your wings so weakly?
Why don't you free yourself from your prison?"
And my heart replied:
"—I love and I wait . . ."

Natalia Trigo

Natalia Trigo *(b. 1990) was born in Puebla, Mexico. Earning a PhD in creative writing in Spanish from the University of Houston, she specializes in bilingual creative writing, immigration literature, and literatura fronteriza. She won the international Aura Estrada Prize in 2019 and is currently an assistant professor at the University of Texas at Arlington. She has also collaborated with Houston's Writers in the Schools (WITS), Inprint Poetry Buskers, as well as the Houston Public Library and was a resident writer at the Ucross Foundation in Wyoming (2021) and Art Omi in New York (2022). "The Caregiver" was translated from the Spanish by Sylvia Garcia-Palauro.*

The Caregiver

Cut the deck, she says, putting her scrawny index finger on the deck of cards she has been shuffling for the last fifteen minutes. The old lady's nails are red and peeling at the tips. Her eyes are full of the mascara the neighbor buys her with the emergency money. Luisa responds, no, Señora Maca, no, but the old lady insists, and she pinches her arm when Luisa gets up, and she tells her, come on, cut the deck. Before looking up, Señora Maca acts as if she is focusing on the deck of cards instead of studying Luisa.

Luisa hesitates because sometimes she thinks her bad luck began the day she accepted this job. Go on, girl, Señora Maca says, and Luisa finally gives in and chooses a card with a bent corner: the figure of the hermit. Another, pick another, she says, and Luisa picks the tower card. Ahh, the old lady remarks, and Luisa shivers. Her hands begin to sweat, so she discreetly hides them beneath the table, hoping the old lady won't notice. But Señora Maca smiles. Her blackened gums remind Luisa of the first prediction, the broken flowerpots, scattered, Tamara's arm covered in soil and blood, and the visit to the local emergency clinic for stitches. One of the legs of the ladder had bent during the fall and they had not been able to use it again.

Luisa gets up. She picks up Señora Maca's plate full of leftover lentils and tells her, you didn't eat anything. The old lady frowns and waves her hand as if she were swatting at flies. Luisa had thought about canceling, but she needed money more than ever, the hospital bill, now that Tamara's delivery was so close. So she said yes, she'd be there at eight just like last month. Don't worry, she had said to the raspy voice on the other end of the phone. It had to be the son, or the grandson, calling at the worst times—when Luisa was cooking or bathing Daniela—and she'd have to ask Tamara to take over while she copied Doña Maca's medications and schedule onto the electricity bill.

Luisa throws the rest of the lentils into the sink and lets the water wash them down the drain. She puts a blood pressure pill on a napkin and brings Doña Maca a glass of water so she can swallow it. But the old lady ignores her. She says for the new baby to survive, she'll have to get rid of someone, that it does her no good to carry the burden of another woman. Luisa turns to look at the purse she left on the armchair because she thinks the old lady might have been rummaging in it while she fixed the bed, but the purse doesn't seem to have been moved. Look, pay attention to the card, the old lady continues, raising the tower card. Do you think this card lies? she asks, looking at her intently, and Luisa notices the glassy pupils of the old lady, and she feels a chill run down her spine. Doña Maca, we're going to take your medicine. The old lady doesn't shift her gaze, and Luisa fears for Tamara, for Daniela, as if the old lady could hurt them.

She takes the pill between her fingers, hoping the old lady will forget her reading. Take your pill, she says, rubbing Señora Maca's back as she does with other patients. The old lady resists. Go on, take it. She presses it against Doña Maca's lips. The old lady closes her lips and twists her head away as if it were a game. Please don't be like that, Doña Maca. The old lady responds she will swallow the pill only if Luisa picks another card. No, no more cards, Luisa replies. She doesn't want to listen to the old lady anymore. She just wants to finish the day as soon as possible and take her pay from the ceramic jar. She takes a few steps back, but when the old lady holds out the deck of cards, it becomes impossible to say no. She watches her hand move involuntarily, her fingers bumping into the old lady's hand, knuckles pulled tight under her skin. The hanged man.

Doña Maca smiles and says, see, it was nothing, and Luisa leans against the table because she feels weak. The old lady sips a little water and slams the glass down on the table, and Luisa jumps. Now, the pill, she demands. The old lady turns her head, and makes a circle with her lips, and leaves Luisa's fingers slimy as she sucks in the pill. She shows her tongue to prove she swallowed it. No doubt, you will need to make a sacrifice, get rid of someone, that's what the hanged man means. Enough with the games, Luisa says. She dusts off her sweater as if dusting off the words of the old lady. Doña Maca bangs the cards against the table and repeats, for the baby to live, someone needs to die. Luisa desperately wants to call Tamara, ask her how she feels, run to the daycare to see how Daniela is doing, but then she sees the old lady hunched over, the effort it takes to lift her cup off the table, and she tells herself, she is only instigating.

Let's go to your room, she suggests. She holds out her arm to help her get up, and Doña Maca clings to her body as if she fears crashing onto the floor. Don't worry, Luisa reassures her, I've got you, and the old lady huffs until she manages to get up completely. Luisa laughs at herself. Her mind must be playing tricks on her. They walk through the hallway, and Doña Maca drags her feet with the filthy, red slippers that she lets no one wash. Luisa suggests she leave the cards on the table. The old lady presses them close to her chest and says, no, girl, the cards go where I go.

In the hallway, behind yellowed glass, there are two photos in frames coming apart at the corners, colored photos, of a man with the same smile, the same thin body covered in expensive fabrics Luisa could never buy her own family. Even less so with Tamara's treatments, the monthly bills they still need to pay. Your son is very handsome, she tells the old lady and strokes her arm as if wanting to comfort her. Doña Maca replies no, she doesn't have a son. But how? Luisa asks, and she stops in front of one of the photos, and the eyes look back at her from the other side of the glass. This isn't your son? Luisa asks, pointing at the boy in the middle, a boy with dark skin and chin-length hair. No, that's me, the old lady responds. She says it with such confidence that Luisa doesn't try to correct her.

Come sit down, she tells her. Luisa thinks Doña Maca might like looking out the window, watching people pass until nightfall. Let's put on your pajamas so you can be more comfortable, she suggests, and Doña Maca agrees. She asks her to lift her arms up so she can take off her blouse, revealing Doña Maca's lace bra and good-luck, amber necklace. She pities the old woman, naked and exposed, and feels embarrassed for having been afraid of her. She embraces her to unfasten the bra, then she puts the flannel pajama on her. She thinks she feels Doña Maca sniffing her hair when she bends down to remove her slippers. What are you willing to do to save her? Doña Maca asks while Luisa pulls up her pants and adjusts the elastic band around her waist. Save who? she answers and grabs the armrest because she feels her heartbeat accelerating. The baby, Señora Maca responds. For her to live, someone must die, she reminds her. A pair of cards fall on the rug, and Luisa picks them up. They are the fool and the moon, both printed with a faint ink, almost imperceptible. For my daughter, I would do anything, she says. The old lady smiles. You must be a very good mother, she answers, and she grabs her hands, and Luisa doesn't resist until the old lady's grip begins to hurt. You are hurting me, Señora Maca, and she tries to free herself, but her body fails her. Then, a blackout, a pain in her spine that forces her to bend toward the old lady's foul face. Doña Maca smiles with another mouth. And she looks at her hands, now with red, chipped nails. She attempts to lift herself but doesn't have the strength. The caregiver watches her from above, looking down at dry patches of hair. She takes a pillow from the bed and presses it against the withered face until there is no breath left to resist. She pushes her hair behind an ear and walks in silence toward the door, the deck of cards in the right pocket of her pants.

María Hinojosa

María Hinojosa *(b. 1961) was born in Mexico City, Mexico. She is a journalist with more than thirty years' experience reporting for CNN, NPR, PBS, CBS, and WGBH, and anchoring and executive producing the Peabody Award–winning show* Latino USA. *She is a frequent guest on MSNBC and has won several awards, including four Emmys and a Pulitzer. In 2010, she founded Futuro Media Group, an independent nonprofit newsroom and production company. Her critically acclaimed memoir,* Once I Was You, *was named a best book of the year by NPR and BookPage, and was published as a young readers edition in fall 2022.*

The Lessons de Victoria

I met Victoria in the back of a smelly school bus as it transported me and dozens of others to a protest in DC, or as the saying goes, el pan nuestro de cada dia.

It was 1983. We were on our way to a demonstration against US intervention in El Salvador. Every month or so my girlfriends and I were protesting one thing or another.

This was during a period in my life when I was embracing my full rebel Latina self in NYC, having left mi querido El Paso (and Juarez) behind. I was a fronteriza in deep ways, but NYC made sense to me from the first time I visited. Here you find border crossers not just from Mexico but from all over the world.

I could tell that Victoria was new to New York, even though I had only been in the city a few years myself—I left El Paso to attend NYU. Victoria looked a little fragile and, well, the city can be a lot. She was sitting alone and looking out towards the highway. Something moved me to lean across the aisle and introduce myself.

NYC was overwhelming, she agreed, but she loved meeting all the new people the city presented her with. Victoria loved people. But she needed to look into their eyes when she spoke. So many people in NYC didn't seem to have the time or patience to do that. Or maybe they were scared New Yorkers who didn't want to look into Victoria's eyes because they were just too intense.

Her eyes were light blue and brown at the same time. How was that possible? They were almost phosphorescent, but it was that same lightness that drew you into the darkness of the iris. That's where you might get lost in the sadness.

Then there was Victoria's crooked smile, which also drew you in because her mouth was always slightly ajar and appetizing. The left side of her lips turned down just a bit, creating an expression that combined sensuality and sorrow. Of course, some people turned away. It was too much. I liked it though.

On the bus, we spoke to each other as if we were lovers, though we weren't. We became glued to each other. We walked the length of the protest together and I introduced her to all my Salvadoran homies who were like family to me. She loved that I was Mexican and from El Paso and that I had never let my Mexican citizenship go.

"¿Y tú, de donde eres?" I asked her, looking straight into those hypnotic crystalline blue and dark brown eyes.

"¡Nunca sabrás definitivamente! Porque soy de dos países que se quieren y se odian. Chile y Argentina."

It's true. Her accent at times sounded clipped like it was from Santiago, sometimes guttural because of the Indigenous languages she grew up hearing, and other times it had that sophistication of the Buenos Aires drawl.

"Es mejor que no sepas, de verdad, de donde vengo."

We laughed but she wasn't joking when she said I shouldn't know where she was born. Later she would tell me that the CIA had a file on her because she had been going to protests—for better wages, for unions, for the poor—in both Chile and Argentina as far back as her own childhood. It was no mistake we met on a bus to a protest.

What we did talk about in those first days of falling into friendship was what had happened to her there, though she would not reveal the country. The men came from behind and pulled her and a friend off the street in a small-size city while they were walking to a cafe. They were taken to a secret jail where they could hear other women yelling and pleading for help, but they could see nothing because they were blindfolded the entire time.

The men had tied the blindfolds so tight it gave her a headache. The soldiers joked that she and her BFF were their guinea pigs. Victoria later wondered whether the blindfold was actually a gift. She never saw them take her friend away instead of her or what they did to her. Was it a blessing that she only heard her best friend's muffled screams and the scuffle of feet and legs hitting the floor, the sound of her kicking the thighs and calves of the prison guards who dragged her away?

Victoria saw nothing. Not even a glimpse of a shoe. Who were their torturers? Were they prison guards? Were they police?

The morning after they had taken her friend, Victoria woke up in the gutter on a side street in a barrio and city she did not know. She eventually learned its name when she asked a local walking down the street, but she would not reveal it to me.

"Porque es mejor asi. Mejor que no sepas los detalles." Better that you don't know certain details, she would whisper to me.

I'd never heard a story like that before. I felt honored that she shared it with me and I was moved by her sadness. I wanted to show her solidarity. That was the word of the moment in the '80s. And I was trying to live it.

✦ ✦ ✦

Victoria, my amiguita, became a kind of teacher, a role model, a madrina in real life, and a spiritual guide to me. She was thirty and I was twenty-two; she had lessons to offer me and there was more to come.

I'd arrived in NYC to go to school at NYU, but I didn't last long there. The girls were too rich and prissy. They didn't eat the cafeteria food hardly ever. They could afford to eat at the cute cafés along 8th Street and Astor Place. But I had to eat the cafeteria food because it was covered by my scholarship. Well, you know how stupid eighteen-year-olds can be. So yeah, I quit because I hated the food and my prissy roommate from Long Island.

I made sure I wasn't one of those statistics that say Latinas never graduate from college, though. There was no way I could go back to Ysleta High School and show my face if I had dropped out. I took a year off and then went back to school, this time to Yale—take that, prissy NYU girls. Except, of course, I had to encounter the prissy, WASPy girls from Yale. But the trees and the birds helped me deal with them, and I stayed until I got my PhD in English.

My degree gets me all the cred I need back home, but let's just say my writing has become a bit more escandalosa since then. My poor familia, les da mucha pena that I am such a mal-hablada. The way they put it delicately: tiene una vida sexual tan abierta. They inevitably look down and away.

Yes, I write about sex. I talk about it and discuss it openly with almost anyone. I mean, my side gig is as a sex writer and columnist so, yeah, I guess I can do this with anyone brave enough to bare their own soul and maybe something else. It was Victoria who opened my eyes and gave me the confidence to explore my sexuality in the first place.

I was much more private when I first met her. Victoria was not. She told me about her lovers. Sometimes she talked so openly about sex that I thought it was an act. As if she was showing off, como le gustaba tirar, how much she liked having sex and how often she was giving and getting it.

There was the Puerto Rican guy with the beard, thick Bronx accent, and lightly toasted brown skin who worked as a prep cook. The first three times he slept in her bed he did nothing. He wanted to prove to her that sex wasn't the only thing he wanted from her. He didn't know that was all Victoria wanted from him. Sex.

Then there was the Peruvian guy, the PhD historian at Columbia who was a descendant of the Quechuas and who, she pointed out with glee, ate her out like no other man had ever done. He started slowly, rubbing her toes first, she explained, and then made his way up her legs and her inner thighs until she couldn't stand it any longer and she was arching her back and needing him to touch her right there, right now! He knew how to stay away from her little hilltop at the tip of her perfectly sliced durazno, papaya, manguito, her popona, her sweet pussy, a term she used with trepidation and delight, until the time was right for him to descend on her hilltop with tenderness and precision and a tongue like a gentle whip.

She talked about her older lover, a Brazilian human rights leader and lawyer in his fifties who was in NYC for meetings at the UN. He fell in love with her after what she thought was a one-night stand in his Midtown hotel—but then the affair continued. He may have been a rebel, but he was a proper man from São Paolo with a wife and family and, mind you, a very distinguished career. She liked that this middle-age man was prepared to challenge the government of Brazil for human rights abuses under its military dictatorship. Something about this made her want to do for him what she rarely ever did for other men. Suck his cock.

Victoria felt such tenderness towards him and such gratitude and even she didn't know why it was manifesting in wanting to snuggle up next to his crotch and smell him, his manliness, his sperm, his bajo. Anyway, the man fell in love with her, or was it that he fell in love with the thought that a woman could be so moved by her feelings towards a man that she would want to put her lips around what is usually a pretty gross and unattractive organ?

I heard these stories and marveled at them. No one I knew had ever spoken about sex in this way. It's just not what we did in my home. My dad was a prude. And mom too. No naked bodies. No discussion about sex ever. Victoria taught me to no tener pena por el sexo and it's thanks to her that I have this career as a sex columnist. She taught me to speak about sex sin pelos en la lengua.

One morning Victoria and I went for a late breakfast after a very late night out dancing salsa at Casa Nicaragua. I was sipping a perfect café con leche with leche condensada, so you know how good it was, when Victoria said she needed to share something.

"I have a partner that I want to tell you about . . ."

"¡Orale! Cuentamelo todo . . . en detalle," I said, excited to hear about another one of her sexual escapades. I leaned in to hear what Victoria was about to reveal.

"My new partner is a woman. I'm bisexual," she said.

Victoria had fallen in love with a woman, a Cuban artist. And after that day, she basically disappeared. I mourned the loss of our friendship, but I understood. I knew her blue-brown eyes could suck you in.

✦ ✦ ✦

We lost touch for a few years. I assumed Victoria was enjoying the bliss of her new relationship, and I had launched into my own sexual adventures, which I'd started writing about. One day in the city I ran into her again.

She was visibly pregnant and glowing. She was getting married to a man, her child's father. I was confused. My head was spinning. What had happened to her woman lover? How could she be so open to change? How could Victoria just give herself over to love, to one man, to starting a family and even jumping in with the institution of marriage when she was anything but conventional?

Then she clarified, as if it were a throwaway line, that she was still bisexual and that her relationship with this man was going to stay open. Victoria became a mother, had several more kids, and who has time for sex except to make kids, which can be some of the best sex you ever have. But I didn't know that yet.

Our difference in age was showing. I was in my midtwenties and had slept with many more men. I had made sex my friend and had started to experiment. I had one-night stands. I had different kinds of sex with different kinds of men. I had a threesome, and though it made me feel left out, I realized I was totally into watching other people have sex. In fact, it might be the thing that brought me the most pleasure besides being eaten out or having sex outdoors—also things I learned by experimenting.

Taking my cues from the sexual fluidity I learned from Victoria, I ended up in an open relationship myself. It was a lot of work, but if I wanted that pleasure of watching, I had to check my ego and insecurities. That's the hard work of an open relationship, or in my case, our permanent threesome. My lover is a poet from El Salvador and his wife is Afro-Garifuna from Honduras but was raised undocumented in Nola. We share the man and the bedroom in a cottage in rural Connecticut. I thrived.

Victoria taught me well. But while I was free in my quaint Connecticut threesome life, she was off making babies in a hetero marriage to, it turns out, a rich man.

Years later, she sent me a postcard from Rome. It arrived inside an envelope along with a ten-page letter explaining her life to me, as if she needed to. I was curious to see what she had to say—Victoria had been such an influence in my life.

She and her husband had four kids, she said. They were incredibly high performing and enrolled in the best schools in NYC. She had been living the Brooklyn wife life essentially.

Her letter continued, written in beautiful legible cursive like she was taught as a niñita, and it all came tumbling out. Even though Victoria and her man were married with a family, she and her husband had never had a follow-up conversation about being in an open relationship. She started to smell other women on her husband.

I mean, seriously? You didn't have the follow-up setting the rules after marriage? That is part of the bible of open relationships! But Victoria assumed that since she was busy having children, one almost after another during a five- to six-year period, and was not interested in having sex outside of her marriage, that her husband was probably feeling the same thing too.

Except he wasn't.

He was feeling pussy wherever and whenever he could get it. He took their lack of a follow-up conversation as a signal that nothing had changed. That they remained in an open relationship where they did not discuss each other's lovers. That they could have as many partners as they wanted as long as it didn't inflict a problem in their marriage.

Well, Victoria had just given birth to four kids. Do you think she was interested in taking on a lover as well? She was glad she could muster up the energy to have sex with her husband every two weeks, okay, sometimes three. That and her newfound toy, a clit vibrator, kept her satisfied. She imagined her husband was satisfied as well.

Actually, he was. He was satisfying himself across NYC. And now he had broken the golden rule. He had fallen in love and was moving to Panama to start a new life with one of his lovers. That was it.

Her husband was wealthy, so he asked her what she wanted. There was nothing he could do to mend her broken heart, which was not just broken but ripped into shreds. There was blood everywhere, she wrote, there was blood everywhere.

I noticed something shifted in the words she had written. Victoria was no longer telling the story of her broken heart and the husband who abandoned her for a hot Panamanian woman. No, in her letter to me she was now writing the story of her broken body. She was remembering what it was like back in that prison after she had been taken from the street with her friend. Something *had* happened to her in that prison. Something horrible. She thought nothing had happened because she had no visual memory of it. But in her letter, she revealed that she had gone into shock after they dragged her friend away. The guards took advantage of that moment. They took turns holding Victoria's arms down as they forced themselves into her deeply, ripping her open and making her bleed. There was blood everywhere, she wrote.

The blindfold never came off as they assaulted her. It brought them extra pleasure, and for her, extra terror. Not physical but mental pain. The blindfold was about that—psychological terror.

When they dumped her and her head hit the sidewalk, the blindfold finally came off and she saw the blood on her belly, just under her ombligo, so much blood that they had wiped themselves off on her belly along with their cum. This was another form of degradation, a way to let her know she was just a warm pussy. That was all.

That's why they threw her away in the gutter after they were done. She was trash to them. Not even worth the time and effort of killing her.

I put the letter down. I cried. I waited till I could focus again through the teardrops and then I continued reading.

Victoria was doing therapy now. She was living in Rome in a gorgeous two-floor loft that came with a terrace overlooking the old city center. "The sights and sounds, the little flickering lights everywhere, the resistance of this place," she wrote, "a place like Rome where there was once so much horror perpetrated on humanity and yet here I am, finding joy."

"No tengo rencor. Tengo tanto amor," she continued. "Lo siento en mi corazon. Estoy en terapia. Estoy meditando. Estoy haciendo ejercicio y comiendo bien. Estoy abierta otra vez. El se fue a Panama y me dejo libre de nuevo."

"Sex after motherhood," she wrote, "is even better than before it. Something happens when you realize how precious these moments of joy are in life. And I have so much to be thankful for. I have four kids. They are all in boarding school and they are happy and know that I love them. They even know that their father loves them and somehow are mature enough to understand that if men are not careful, they will end up thinking 'con la cabeza chiquita y no con la grande.'"

"I'm using my head, my heart, mi cuerpo y mi popona, mi manguito, mi montañita, my little hilltop of love and ecstasy, to heal myself," she wrote. "My focus now is on alegria. Joy and alegria."

I folded up the letter and put it back in the envelope. It was made of rice paper, the kind that gets mailed internationally with the "par avion" wings emblazoned on it, delicate and strong at the same time, an envelope meant to be sent around the world. Holding it and her words made me think. What Victoria had taught me was to be full in my sex. Full in my joy. Full in my rebellion. Full en mi Vida. Y con miedo pero adelante.

Delmira Agustini

Delmira Agustini *(1886–1914) was born in Montevideo, Uruguay. She published her first poetry collection as a teenager and was one of the few women of the Generación del 900, a Uruguayan literary movement at the end of the nineteenth and beginning of the twentieth century. Her modernist feminist work explored women's sexuality, which she found a source of power. She wrote a column for* La alborada *under a pen name Joujou. Among her works are* El libro blanco, Los cálices vacíos, *and* Obras completas, *published posthumously after her tragic murder at twenty-seven years old. A month after divorcing her husband, he killed her and then himself. "The Ineffable" is from* Cantos de la mañana *(Morning songs) and was translated from the Spanish by Cecilia Rossi.*

The Ineffable

I die strangely . . . Life does not kill me,
Death does not kill me, Love does not kill me;
I die of a mute thought like a wound . . .
Have you never felt the strange pain

Of a thought so immense that it roots into your life
devours flesh and soul, and never comes to bloom?
Have you never carried within you a sleeping star
burning you whole but emitting no glow?

The summit of martyrdom . . . To carry into eternity,
piercing and barren, the tragic seed
biting into one's entrails like a fierce tooth . . .

But to pluck it one day from a flower unfolding
miraculously, inviolably! Ah, nothing equals this
not even cradling the head of God!

Laura Restrepo

Laura Restrepo *(b. 1950) is a Bogotá, Colombia, born novelist and journal-ist who covered the drug trade for twelve years. In 1984, after being invited to join the Peace Commission bringing together the Colombian government and the guerrillas for talks, she was forced into exile. Restrepo wrote* Isle of Passion, *the first of ten internationally acclaimed novels and novellas pub-lished in over twenty languages, including the prize-winning novel* Leopard in the Sun *and* The Angel of Galilea. *Her novel* Delirium *won the Premio Alfaguara and the Premio Grinzane Cavour, and was short-listed for the Prix de Meilleur Livre Étranger and the Independent Foreign Fiction Prize. A Guggenheim Fellow and an A. D. White Professor at Cornell University, she travels with Doctors Without Borders.* "Hairs" ("Pelos") *was translated from the Spanish by Layla Benitez-James.*

Hairs

A thick bush of hair was what Courbet emphasized most when painting his *The Origin of the World*, a defiant close-up of a woman's exposed sex. "Bush, bush!" the audience yelled at *strippers* during Mexico City's popu-lar striptease shows. That was what they came to see. But something has changed, and human beings, strange, self-denying creatures, now hate what remains of the body hair that completely covered them at the be-ginning of time. Sexual attraction seems to focus on a shaved pubic zone, or the pubis angelical, as Manuel Puig called it. What are they after? Do women want to look like the porn stars who did the most to spread the style, or on the flip side, are they attracted to the idea of seeming vir-ginal and childlike? Many a theorist has spilled ink on the subject, but I've done one better and asked Aurora for her opinion. She's an employee of Conejo's, a salon specializing in hair removal. She doesn't ask why, but she knows everything about how.

She explains: Everyone likes to take care of their appearance. It's no crime, and I've never seen the harm in it. It's natural and comes with culture. Leave hairiness to the beasts. Nobody likes to walk around with a jungle between their legs, and that's where I come in. Perfectly professional after twenty-two years of experience (though I've only been at Conejo's for three years) my role is to help people. The owner chose that name because it's also what people call their *pussy* (because it's furry like a bunny rabbit, I guess). One client from Panama says la araña, some la cosita, it depends.

As for me, I follow all the proper hygiene protocols for comprehensive and careful treatment. After all, this is an intimate business. Just imagine, there you are locked up in a teeny-tiny cubicle stall with a client laid out on the waxing table just as God had her enter the world. Of course, there are some very calm, very polite, dear little clients, and with them there's no fuss. But there are others who get hysterical straightaway, yelling at you and cursing you every time you accidently cause a bit of pain. An extremely rude lady comes in here every month. If you even barely touch her, she comes out with such foulmouthed curses that none of us want to work on her. But since the owner would kill us if she knew we refused anyone, we flip a coin to see who wins that honor.

I'll tell you about another case. A while back, a very young woman came to me, a redhead. She asked me to do a full job, that is, her whole body. The moment I saw her I said to myself, Aurora, we've got a problem. Do you know why? Because redheads have very delicate skin. Listen up, and I'll tell you. I did everything with the utmost care, so she left happy, and I relaxed. But what do I get the next day? Shouting: in comes the mother like a fury with, *What did you do to my daughter? You've left bruises all over her body!* We had no right to do it, the lady shouted, and she was going to report us to Health and Human Services, and motherfuckers this and sonofabitch that.

Of course I try to be understanding of people, because I know it can be a painful process. Let's say the wax is too hot, so it burns. Pulling the waxing strip is an art, you know? You've got to do it sharp and fast to avoid hurting them. Pulling from the bottom up, just like that, sharp and fast. But with really hairy people, this business gets more complicated, and each pull of the strip can be an ordeal. Imagine going to the dentist but without anesthesia and, to top it all off, we're talking *down there.*

Although most people handle the treatment pretty well, some turn pale from the pain, others tremble, others almost pass out. Now, when that happens, you've got to pause the session, bring the client a little chamomile tea, talk to them for a while, let them calm down. It's impossible to work if there's a bunch of drama. Others shiver not from fear but from cold. As you can imagine for a full job they're naked, and they've got to lie still on the table for about an hour, and sometimes the room temperature isn't the best. In that case, I turn on the heater and wait for them to feel comfortable.

Some get embarrassed, let's say those who come in for anal waxing (which is also very popular among male clients). And you can see why. Just put yourself in the client's shoes who has to position himself bent over on all fours like this. I tell you one thing, this is where the use of a bit of psychological control plays a key role. I have co-workers at Conejo's who play it safe and make it clear from the start that when it comes to anal waxing, they won't do it. Not everyone is cut out for it, and some will do it and then complain afterwards, saying, "Euf, that old lady made me wax her all the way up to her *ju-jummm.*" As I've got no qualms of that nature, I flow with the human body like a fish in water.

You see it all in this job. Some clients are so chill they even fall asleep while I wax them. They put themselves in my hands, so to speak. There are others who spend the hour talking on their phones. They barely acknowledge me at first, just "Hello, Aurora, how are you, I'm here to get my legs and armpits done," in short, whatever cursory greeting, and at the end they say goodbye, "Thanks, Aurora," or "Ciao, Auri," depending on how friendly we are. We don't exchange any other words because, apart from that, they forget about me and devote themselves to chatting with their boyfriend or friends, planning what they're going to do next. Because one thing's for sure, every waxed woman has plans. Whether it's for a party, the beach, or someone's bed, no one waxes to stay home alone. I mean, I don't know if you get me, but after every waxing, something is sure to be happening. It's also not uncommon for the client to talk about it while getting ready. For example, she may chat to her boyfriend, "Oh, babe, I'm taking it all off just the way you like it, see you tonight." As I say, you hear it all in this job.

More ornamental waxing involves more, let's say, "sophisticated" styles. Some clients like to adorn themselves with a bit of whimsy in their pubic zone. Some styles are already standard, like "the Mister T," that is, with a crest down the middle; or "the love heart," which needs no explanation; or for example a very popular one is "the diamond." Also "the postage stamp," and another less frequent one, "the nerd," which is parted in the middle with the hair combed out to both sides. There's also "the landing strip," and there are some women (also men) who ask for letters, the initials of their boyfriend, for example, or who knows who. They don't always say.

When they want a number, it's almost always for an anniversary. Let's say they're celebrating six months of dating, so they ask you to do a 6 down there—6 and S are tricky because of their curves. Letters like F or H are a cinch, while something like R is a nightmare. I don't recommend it. A client once came into Conejo's with a boyfriend who had the initials RR. I remember it like it was yesterday, because I was royally stuck. The first R was half crooked, and I got so nervous that the second one was a total mess. So much so that when I showed her in the mirror, she told me to shave it all off. Better to have nothing than that.

It goes in trends. These days lots of people want us to take everything off, especially the younger ones. A really pretty client (a well-known television actress, obviously I can't use her name) always asks me to leave her *clean*, without a single hair, because her husband likes to see her like an eight-year-old girl. For others we do dye jobs. Red, blond, that kind of thing. And black? No! Not black, I don't know anyone who gets their hair dyed black. Quite the opposite, everyone wants lighter hair, because dark body hair is for primates.

Our tragedy here at Conejo's has been the laser. We don't offer it. We don't have that cutting-edge technology, stuck in the age of wax. And since today everyone demands laser, we've lost a lot of customers here. We had to relocate from a good, upper-class neighborhood to this, a more modest one. And what can I do about it? I don't know how to do anything else. I'll be what they call a bikini wax traditionalist till the end of my days.

Nicholasa Mohr

Nicholasa Mohr *(b. 1938) is a pioneering, award-winning Nuyorican writer born in Manhattan. She was the first Latina writer to have her literary works published by major US publishing houses. Her writing explores Puerto Rican communities of the Bronx and El Barrio through the lens of girls and women. Among her most notable works are* Nilda, *which traces the life of a teenage Puerto Rican girl facing racism in New York of the 1940s,* Rituals of Survival: A Woman's Portfolio, Going Home, *and* El Bronx Remembered, *which was picked as one of the* New York Times*'s Outstanding Books of the Year. The following excerpt from the short story "A Matter of Pride" is from the collection* A Matter of Pride and Other Stories.

A Matter of Pride

I was born in the Bronx and, although I had never been to the island, my parents often spoke longingly about their homeland. Like Charlie's folks, they, too, had held the dream of returning home someday. They would refer to their region of Barranquitas, in the highlands of Puerto Rico, as nuestro paraíso. Growing up, I shared my parents' sense of displacement and loss. After they died, my sorrow was intensified by the reality of their unrequited dream, and I developed a longing to see Puerto Rico. I felt that on this trip I might somehow make it up to my parents by visiting their beloved homeland. I didn't need much convincing. Going to Puerto Rico seemed like a perfect idea.

Besides, I was accustomed to having Charlie dictate my life. We met when I was seventeen, right after my father died. I was still a virgin and had never seriously dated. Charlie was twenty-four and had a reputation of being wild and chasing women—a much admired macho. Soon after we began going steady, Charlie settled down.

People said I was good for him. As our relationship developed, Charlie assumed a paternal role. "Baby, it's only natural," he liked to tell me, "that I be the one to guide and protect you. I'll teach you what you need to know, Mami. You gotta listen, Paula, and do like I say, because I'm older and wiser, so I know what's good for you." As I got older, I began to disagree with Charlie, which resulted in quarrels, lots of quarrels. In fact, it seemed that with each passing year our arguing increased.

In those days, I worked as a receptionist in a major insurance firm. At night I had enrolled in City College, determined to get my degree in business administration. As for having children, that was somewhere in the distant future, "My college degree comes first." I was clear on that point and said so. "No way am I staying a file clerk or a receptionist forever, Charlie. I've got better plans for my life."

At school, one of my teachers recommended I read an anthology about women who helped to change American history. I read with awe about the lives of Sojourner Truth, Jane Addams, Margaret Sanger, and other powerful women. I was amazed by these accounts of female independence. My newly acquired knowledge about the issue of women's rights and freedom provoked our worst disputes. Charlie dismissed my assertions and refused to acknowledge my views.

Once, I decided to share a section from *The Second Sex* by Simone de Beauvoir with Charlie and quoted from the chapter on "The Independent Woman": "It is through gainful employment that woman has traversed most of the distance that separated her from the male; and nothing else can guarantee her liberty in practice. Once she ceases to be a parasite, the system based on her dependence crumbles; between her and the universe there is no longer any need for masculine mediator."

"You're reading crap again! What do you mean, that women should have the rights like guys? Don't be comparing yourself to me because you still need what I got. Do you pee standing up, girl?"

I wasn't about to walk away from that argument so easily, especially when I had proof positive. "No," I shouted, holding up De Beauvoir's book, ". . . but I don't use what's between my legs for no meal ticket either. I work for what's mine and I do what I like! I'm a free agent and YOU don't fucking own me!"

And so it went a good deal of the time.

Charlie was also a jealous man who repeatedly insisted that I not wear tight clothing or show cleavage. That was when I would tighten my belt an extra notch or undo another button on my blouse. In spite of my Latina upbringing, I always found it difficult to conform to the demands of males who declare themselves to be in charge. This is probably because being passive was never part of my nature.

Whenever Charlie became too overbearing, I argued back and threatened to leave him. Once, I even packed up all my things and went to stay with a friend. It took just a few hours until Charlie found me and begged me to come back, promising to alter his ways. "Come on, Paula, I like your spirit. Give me time to get used to some of your crazy ideas. Look, I don't want to dish rag for my old lady. You're smart and beautiful. I want my feisty baby. I can't live without my baby. I can't live without my baby. I love you, Mami . . . don't hurt me like this. I love you!"

Jovita Idár

Jovita Idár *(1885–1946) was a Mexican American journalist, civil rights leader, and suffragist born in Laredo, Texas. With her family, she helped organize the first Mexicanist Congress, which gathered Mexicans along the border to support the Mexican Revolution. She wrote for* El progreso *newspaper, which published an op-ed against President Woodrow Wilson's decision to deploy the US Army to the border. She famously stood her ground in front of the doors of* El progreso, *refusing to allow the Texas Rangers entry in their attempt to shut down the paper. A few days later, they violently shut it down. She returned to run* La crónica, *a newspaper owned by her family, when her father died, penning pieces that condemned lynchings and supported civil rights and women's right to vote and right to an education.*

The obrera recognizes her rights, proudly raises her head and joins the struggle, the time of her degradation is over, she is no longer a slave sold for some coins, she is no longer a servant but the equal of a man.

Ada Limón

Ada Limón *(b. 1976) was born in Sonoma, California, to Mexican parents. She is the author of several poetry collections, among them* The Carrying, *which won the National Book Critics Circle Award for Poetry,* Bright Dead Things, *a finalist for the same National Book Critics Circle Award for Poetry,* Sharks in the Rivers, Lucky Wreck, *and* This Big Fake World. *She earned an MFA from NYU and is the recipient of fellowships from the Guggenheim Memorial Foundation, the New York Foundation for the Arts, and the Kentucky Foundation for Women. She teaches at Queens University of Charlotte in their low-residency MFA program. In 2022, she was named US poet laureate.*

Ode to the Hair Clip

You are asked
to do so much

small clasp sharp
teeth metal jaw

how much you
hold black plastic

not even bone
but human made

cheap fodder
for landfill still

you bear the weight
of furious strands

hair like tripwire
like horse hair

without you I am
chaos crested

like lion your pleasure
in pressure small

star in black sky
of mane small star

you are asked
to do so much

If I Should Fail

The ivy eating the fence line
each tendril multiplying
by green tendril, if I should
fail the seeds lifted out
and devoured by bristled
marauders, blame only
me and the strip of sun
which bade me come
to lie down snakelike
on my belly, low snake
energy, and be tempted
by the crevices between
the world and not world,
if I should fail know I
stared long into fractures

and it seemed to me
a mighty system of gaps
one could slither into
and I was made whole
in that knowledge of
a sleek nothingness.

Sylvia Rivera

Sylvia Rivera *(1951–2002) was a New York–born Puerto Rican and Ven-ezuelan transgender and gay liberation activist. With her close friend Marsha P. Johnson, she cofounded STAR, Street Transvestite Action Rev-olutionaries, an activist collective that also provided shelter for homeless teenage drag queens and trans women. In 1972 she penned a ground-breaking essay,"Transvestites: Your Half Sisters and Half Brothers of the Revolution," on trans lives for* Come Out!: A Newspaper By and For the Gay Community. *She delivered the following speech at New York City's Christopher Street Liberation Day Rally in Washington Square Park in 1973, which was a seminal moment in the Gay Power movement. In it she addressed racial, gender, and class issues. She is considered the Rosa Parks of the modern transgender movement.*

Y'all Better Quiet Down

June 24, 1973

Y'all better quiet down. I've been trying to get up here all day for your gay brothers and your gay sisters in jail that write me every motherfuck-ing week and ask for your help and you all don't do a goddamn thing for them.

Have you ever been beaten up and raped and jailed? Now think about it. They've been beaten up and raped after they've had to spend much of their money in jail to get their [*inaudible*] and try to get their sex changes. The women have tried to fight for their sex changes or to become women. On the women's liberation and they write "STAR," not to the women's

Daughters of Latin America

groups, they do not write women, they do not write men, they write "STAR" because we're trying to do something for them.

I have been to jail. I have been raped. And beaten. Many times! By men, heterosexual men that do not belong in the homosexual shelter. But do you do anything for me? No. You tell me to go and hide my tail between my legs. I will not put up with this shit. I have been beaten. I have had my nose broken. I have been thrown in jail. I have lost my job. I have lost my apartment for gay liberation, and you all treat me this way? What the fuck's wrong with you all? Think about that!

I do not believe in a revolution, but you all do. I believe in the gay power. I believe in us getting our rights, or else I would not be out there fighting for our rights. That's all I wanted to say to you people. If you all want to know about the people in jail and do not forget Bambi L'amour, and Dora Mark, Kenny Metzner, and other gay people in jail, come and see the people at Star House on 12th Street, on 640 East 12th Street between B and C, apartment 14.

The people are trying to do something for all of us, and not men and women that belong to a white middle class white club. And that's what you all belong to!

REVOLUTION NOW! Gimme a *G*! Gimme an *A*! Gimme a *Y*! Gimme a *P*! Gimme an *O*! Gimme a *W*! Gimme an *E*! Gimme an *R*! [*crying*] Gay power! Louder! GAY POWER!

LIMINAL MOON

The energy of this moon opens the
threshold to communication with our
loved ones on the ancestral plane.

Irma Pineda

Irma Pineda *(b. 1974) is a bilingual poet and Indigenous activist born in Juchitán, Oaxaca, Mexico. She is the author of twelve bilingual Diidxazá and Spanish poetry collections, including the award-winning* Naxiña' rului'ladxe'/ Rojo deseo. *A faculty member at the National Teachers' University, she was the 2020–2022 vice president of the United Nations Permanent Forum on Indigenous Issues. Her poem was translated from the Diidxazá by the author and from the Spanish by Wendy Call.*

Darkness ends here
You are the Fire Goddess
You spark new life
You create all beginnings
You are blessed light
Our great creator
And I bring you
my bare feet
anointed by mud
my hands
purified by work
my skin darkened by your love
I am here in your presence
with sacred words
inherited from my ancestors
I am here
reciting ancient prayers

descended from my grandmother's lips
I am here with you
with flowers from earth's garden
with water made holy by your gaze
with the same song
with the same eyes
with the same heart
where your sacred name is engraved
in the lost memory of my people
who now simply call you: Sun.

✦ ✦ ✦

Rari' riluxe guendanacahui
Lii nga bido' guí
Lii rudiilu' xidxaa guiele' guendanabani
Lii biza'lu' nirudo' guirá xixé
Lii nga biaani'
Guzana ro'
Ne rari' zedaniá neza lulu'
ca xieebata stine'
ni guca nandxo' ndaani' beñe
nia' naya'
ma bisiá dxiiña' laaca'
guidilade' bisiyaase xquendaranaxiilu' laa
Rari' nuaa neza lulu'
ne diidxa' nandxo'
ni bidii ca bixhoze' gola naa
Rari' nuaa
Cuzeeruaa diidxa' yooxho'
ni binadiaga' bieteti lu guidiruaa jñaabida
Rari' nuaa ne lii
ne ca guie' ridale ndaani' le'

ne nisa ni guca nandxo' dxi biyadxilu' laa
ne ngueca riuunda
ne ngueca bezalú
ne ngueca ladxido'
ra cá dxiichi' lalu'
casica cá ni lu xquendabiaani' binnixquidxe
ni rabi lii yanna: Gubidxa.

Reyna Grande

Reyna Grande *(b. 1970) was born in Guerrero, Mexico. She is the author of the bestselling memoir* The Distance Between Us, *a National Book Critics Circle Award finalist and the recipient of an International Literacy Association Children's Book Award. Her other books include* Across a Hundred Mountains, Dancing with Butterflies, *and* A Dream Called Home. *She coedited with Sonia Guiñansaca* Somewhere We Are Human: Authentic Voices on Migration, Survival, and New Beginnings, *an anthology by and about undocumented Americans.* A Ballad of Love and Glory, *excerpted here, is a novel set during the Mexican-American War and inspired by real events.*

A Ballad of Love and Glory: Chapter 1

El Frontón de Santa Isabel, Gulf of Mexico
March 1846

When the three steamships came into view, undulating on the shimmering waters of the gulf, the villagers grew quiet and still, in the way Ximena had seen meadowlarks freeze when hunted by a hawk. Standing on the shore of the Laguna Madre, the water soaking into her skirt, she squinted from the glare as she watched the ships passing through the entrance of the inlet, the smoke rolling out of their funnels dark as storm clouds. She trembled inside. These vessels were not traders or merchants bringing goods to market.

The port of El Frontón de Santa Isabel, just north of the mouth of the Río Bravo del Norte, was a lifeline for the small settlements and scattered ranches in the area and the nearby city of Matamoros. Ximena loved swimming and fishing in the bay, the cool salt air and rolling waves, so whenever her husband went to the port to sell and trade supplies from their rancho—cowhides, tallow, wool, livestock, and crops from the last harvest—she eagerly joined him. As the steamships anchored in the harbor, she caught flashes of red and blue in the air and something glinting on the decks in the afternoon sunlight. Though she couldn't see clearly what they carried, an image formed in her mind: bronze cannons and blue-clad soldiers.

For eight months, she'd been hearing rumors of war, ever since US and Texas soldiers had been encamped in Corpus Christi Bay. But as long as they remained two hundred and fifty kilometers away, their presence hadn't disrupted her daily life. Three months before, in the last days of 1845, the Republic of Texas had become the twenty-eighth state in the Union, and a dispute had erupted over this strip of land between the Río Bravo—or the Río Grande, as the norteamericanos called it—and the Río Nueces to the north. She, like everyone, knew it was only a matter of time before the Yanqui president, James Polk, would order his troops to march south to take possession of the disputed land. These warships, Ximena realized, were bringing an end to what little tranquility had existed in her region.

"We should go," she whispered, turning to her grandmother, who was standing beside her in the water. Nana Hortencia's silver braids hung loosely at either side of her head, and although the years had bent and twisted her body like the limbs of a mesquite, her hands were firm and steady.

The old woman sighed with worry and said, "Let us go find your husband, mijita."

Tolling church bells shattered the eerie silence that had descended upon the small community. All at once, mothers pulled their children out of the water and rushed them home, fisherwomen snatched up their baskets, and fruit and vegetable vendors hastily loaded their crates onto their carts. Out in the Laguna Madre, the fishermen were rowing their boats back to the wharf. Then bugles sounded the alarm, and the handful of Mexican soldiers protecting the port hurried to their posts.

Ximena waded out of the water and guided her grandmother to the storehouses. Her wet skirt clung to her legs, her sandals squished, but there was no time to change. She quickened her pace, but as Nana Hortencia struggled to keep up, she forced herself to slow down, to not panic. Clutching the old woman's hand, they wove through the throng of frightened villagers, her eyes searching for her husband, Joaquín. She sighed in relief when she spotted the ranch hands at a storehouse rushing to finish loading the sacks of coal onto the carts. But Joaquín wasn't with them, nor could she find him inside.

"Stay here, Nana," she said and hurried back outside.

As Ximena whirled around into the street, a party of Texas Rangers rode into the plaza from the rear of the port, shouting their wild cries and firing their revolvers into the air. The villagers screamed and ran for cover. The Mexican soldiers guarding the customhouse hastily fired warning shots, and the Rangers retaliated.

The grass-thatched roof of the customhouse had already begun to smoke, and then, suddenly, burst into flames.

"Joaquín!" Ximena cried out, pushing past the crowd, her heart flailing like a seagull trapped in netting. Seeing her husband run out of the building, she rushed to join him.

"Vámonos," he said, taking her hand.

The air reeked of smoke. Ximena could hear the crackling of the burning timber and thatch as the villagers' huts burned. Flames licked the rafters in the plaza church even as the bells continued to toll. People ran out of their homes with whatever they could carry. A fortunate few loaded their wagons and carts and fled. The rest followed behind on foot in a frantic pace, seeking shelter in the prairie beyond.

The Yanqui cavalry suddenly burst through the smoke, led by a peculiar old man dressed like a farmer and wearing a straw hat. They shot their pistols into the air, and in the shocked silence that followed, the man in the straw hat pulled his horse to a halt and held up one hand.

"My name is General Zachary Taylor, commander-in-chief of the

Army of Occupation of the United States of America," he declared. "Do not be afraid."

No one waited to hear the Yanqui general say more. Joaquín handed Ximena her horse's reins, and as soon as Nana Hortencia sat safely on one of the canvas-topped wagons and the ranch hands took the reins, they rode out of the village, eluding the general and his mounted troops along with the Rangers.

They made their way across the broad plains, but encumbered by wagons and carts loaded with sacks of rice, wheat flour, coffee and cacao, crates of piloncillo and dried fish, and other provisions they had picked up at the port, they couldn't get away fast enough. As the gathering dusk gave over to the fireflies twinkling over the prairie, Ximena, struggling to see in the deepening twilight, wondered how long it would take to cover the remaining nine kilometers to the rancho.

She glanced back at the village in the distance and saw it was covered in an orange haze.

"War is coming," she said.

"No, mi amor," Joaquín said. "They will negotiate. I'm sure it won't come to war."

He was only trying to ease her worries. But it was futile to try to shield her from what she had witnessed that day. What else could this be, if not an act of war?

She remembered that ten years before, when Texas rebelled against Mexico and declared itself an independent republic, it proclaimed that its boundary would then extend two hundred fifty kilometers south to the Río Bravo, even though the Río Nueces had been the established border even before Mexico had achieved its independence from Spain. Mexico had never recognized Texas's independence or its claim to the Río Bravo and the region between the two rivers, and it had warned the United States to keep its hands off its lands.

Looking to the sky, Ximena thought of the single star on the flag of the Republic of Texas, realizing that it was now part of the American constellation. If the United States was now ready to destroy everything in its wake, what would become of her and her family?

Ana Paula Lisboa

Ana Paula Lisboa (b. 1988), born and raised in a favela in Rio de Janeiro, Brazil, is the eldest of four siblings of Black parents. She currently lives between Rio de Janeiro and Luanda, Angola, where she directs the cultural and arts centers Aláfia and Casa Rede. She started writing when she was fourteen and has published short stories and poetry in Brazil and abroad. She defines herself as a textual artist, using the written and spoken word on different platforms to promote Black narratives and language throughout the world. She contributes regularly to Cabeça de sardinha, *a newsletter of* O globo's Segundo carderno. *"A Hole Where Your Name Is" was translated from the Portuguese by Emyr Humphreys.*

A Hole Where Your Name Is

There's a hole, a hole where your name is.

It was the year she died, '93, I think. I say I think because I was five. I wasn't old enough to understand, that's what the grown-ups said. I didn't have the eyes to understand. I didn't have ears to understand. But I understood, I understood everything, because understanding doesn't just come through the eyes and ears. I had Black skin, which covered my whole body, even if it was small and so young. It had the Black skin the grown-ups had, which covered their bodies. That much I understood. Each one of my pores could hear the moans of despair, each one of my pores could see the tears, each one of my pores could smell death.

But I couldn't measure time, even though so much of it passed. I remember the burial: I remember being hugged by many people, I remember my father who stuck with me for nearly the whole thing because my mother just cried and cried. Every grown-up was crying around a high table and there I was with my little body. I didn't know what was on the table, my eyes couldn't reach, but my pores knew. Then my father lifted my little body up, I can still feel my father's hands holding me by the armpits and then my eyes saw.

It was a woman, with Black skin, Black hair, and a short white dress. She had cotton up her nose and under her closed eyelids. She looked like she was asleep, but that wasn't the expression of a sleeping person, I think she was frowning, as if she was worrying about something.

I say I think she was frowning because I don't know if I actually saw her with her eyes open or closed. For a long time, how long I can't say, I dreamt of the woman. It wasn't a nightmare, five-year-old me wasn't scared, it was just a dream, a memory. I think it was my pores trying to understand.

Something else I don't know if I'd seen or if I'd dreamt was the sunflowers. The woman on the table who looked like her sleep was troubled was in a bed made of sunflowers, not just a bed but a blanket too. Perhaps that was why I wasn't scared, the sunflowers calmed me and helped me realize that it was a good dream.

Even after growing up a bit, nobody told me anything, I had to come to understand everything on my own. Not much was said, at a party or at lunch, when once in a while stories of the woman would come, they spoke of her with longing, that she hadn't deserved to die. And people became teary-eyed, and their voices faltered. There wasn't just love and longing in those eyes and faltering voices but also the pain and anger of someone demanding justice, someone who wants to scream out. I understood them all, but if I had asked, nobody would have told me anything.

And there were the photos: through them I understood that the woman looked happy, though she wasn't very smiley: she had a half smile, like she was keeping a secret, or even a sort of melancholy in her. And there was the music: on Sundays, when someone put a samba record on the turntable, people were always reminded of her.

And there were the objects: she was the kind of woman who liked pretty things, clothes, makeup, wigs, souvenirs, records, plants.

And there were the lovers: they said that all the men fell in love with her, they told stories of conflicts between them, but at the end the voice of the person telling the story would become quiet and sad and say: "she of all people was the one who ended her life."

My pores remember him, he was tall and slim, he had grayish-Black skin and wore a little cap. What a waste of memory, that I remember more of him than her. Of her, I only have the sensation, which stayed in my pores, I remember hugs, but I remember them in my body, there aren't images; what there is, is a hole.

There's a hole, a hole I can't understand, Grandma. Not a single cell in my body understands this hole of longing where your name is, the same name as mine. There's a hole that I fall down and you're not there, but my mother is, I see the way she sits and that half smile of hers, I see the same foot with its curled toes, I see how her eyes are full of love as she holds her children. I also see myself in the hole, they say we have the same loving way of being in the world, the patience to listen to others, which I inherited from you. Yes, there's another time for us to be.

But there's a hole where your voice is, which my pores can't hear, there's the smell and taste of your food, which the stories can't feed me. There's the hole for all the things I should have learned, like how to sow and how to braid my hair, I wanted to learn them from you. I would give anything to hear you sing Fundo de Quintal. If a part of us comes from the world within my grandma, then I stay here with this hole of mine, totally nameable.

Nelly Rosario

Nelly Rosario *(b. 1972) was born in Santo Domingo, Dominican Republic, and raised in Brooklyn, New York. She is the author of* Song of the Water Saints, *winner of a PEN Open Book Award. Her fiction and creative nonfiction works appear in various anthologies and journals. She holds an MFA from Columbia University and is an associate professor in the Latina/o Studies program at Williams College. "Umbilicus" is from her medical storytelling project* How the Medicines Go Down.

Umbilicus

The navel, where revolutions start and end.

My first wound is an outie. A belly button that sticks out like Cain's not Abel's, as they say my mother feared. They also say she didn't raise me, and that her name is Eva. Supposedly. Everything about my origins is a "supposedly" and a "di'que." A lip curl and a shrug, palms held up. The worst is my grandmother, calling me Di'que whenever I ask about my father, her saintly son. He'd already been out of the country a full eleven months before Eva gave birth to me.

"Women like her eat apples and spit out snake bones," says Granma G.

Women like Granma G don't respect a mother who leaves the curing of their newborn's umbilical cord to her mother-in-law, in this case Granma G. Or a mother who disappears before her baby's terrible twos, leaving it to nurse on dry breasts, in this case Granma G's. But women like me question women who question all women, in this case Granma G.

Why, for example, did she sell off my umbilical-cord blood without my mother's consent? Are my stem cells sitting in a cord-blood bank some-where, still waiting to be hematopoietically transplanted? Whose bone marrow did my stolen blood replenish? Am I now more related to them than I am to my supposed grandmother?

Granma G may have always doubted my blood, but in the end, she was the one to rub the stump at my belly with coconut oil, press it under gauze and a coin bearing the face of Juan Pablo Duarte, then tamp it all down with surgical tape and a prayer. But not even the father of our country could stop the umbilical hernia caused by my crying fits.

"I did my best with the curing," she says, "so blame that outie on them."

Them. Neither Eva nor my father, Tomás, ever came for me. When I was born, my supposed father was out in MedIsla, probably delivering ba-bies himself. As to Eva, another lip curl and a shrug. But love from a child is pure, infinite. I'd lie awake beside a snoring and hacking Granma G, drowning in fantasies of my mother dressed in snakeskin pants, paring apples with my father's scalpel. In the moments before sleep would finally come, I'd feel my belly swell with light and my outie extend like an an-tenna towards the noise outside. From all the honking and barking and sirens and shots and laughter and fireworks, I'd try to isolate the metallic tenor of their voices. Their silence I welcomed too.

"Granma G, you ever get a funny feeling in your belly-eye at night?"

"¡Mira, muchacha!"

In my teens, when I took to wearing crop tops and waist beads and navel rings, Granma G could only shake her head and mumble, "Ese ombligo," as if my navel were a live wire in need of grounding.

After kissing it, my lover Milton will one day tell me that Leonardo da Vinci used the navel—mine!—as a center of a circle and a square to simultaneously contain the human soul and body. But no matter how spread-eagle I lay on the bed now, I can no longer see from my belly-eye.

I go to a bruja.

I describe feeling as if I'm excreting thick light through a circle and a square.

"It's your first mouth," she says, "your spirit gate."

"Am I suffering from soul emesis?" I ask.

Her eyes narrow at mine. A breath later, she says not to worry, that the variety of bacteria in my navel rivals the biodiversity of the Amazon.

After my birth, back in DR, Eva buried the placenta, along with a book, at the foot of a siguaceiba in the backyard of Granma G's house. No one knows how that mutt of a tree came to be, born as it was from the ceiba and the siguaraya. People would come to see it, pray it, sing it, cry it—so many pilgrims that Granma G began to charge a "tree fee." Tongues started wagging about her businessified ways. So she let the toilet overflow in hopes that people would understand: each time pilgrims came, the roots of the siguaceiba would swell and invade her septic tank. The tree fees went towards paying the brujo-plumber Tefo, who would ceremoniously prune the swollen roots from the septic, careful not to disturb the ancestors.

"Placenta? Who came up with that word anyway, Granma G?"

"Di'que, it's Greek for 'uterine cake.'"

"Whoa. Then what would they call the frosting on—"

"Now go to sleep, carajo."

"So if I ate a fruit from that siguaceiba, Granma G, would I be a cannibal?"

"¡Mira, muchacha!"

"And what was the book Eva buried, Granma G?

"¿Y qué sé yo? You have to write that yourself."

Wrapped in a plastic bag, inside a metal box, wrapped in two plastic bags, inside of our toilet tank, Granma G hoards a stack of letters from my father. During sleepless nights, to the sound of her snoring and hacking, I read them all. They arrive each month through Fat Franklin, a courier from MedIsla who Granma G only receives during the day, when I'm at school—this I know because I'm not at school but off with Milton. We go to Free Radical meetings on the roof of one of the neighborhood buildings. From up there, I see Fat Franklin park his motorcycle across the street, at our building, then Granma G throwing down the keys from our bathroom window because she can't figure out how to buzz him in.

Rumors have been spreading in the building. That she cooks for him. That he leaves with gifts. "Good, let them talk," she says. "Revolution should look like love." Through Fat Franklin, she will keep sending medical contraband to her son in MedIsla, the only man who's ever had her heart. "I should've been my son's daughter instead of you," Granma G once told me. But in this life, all she can do is nurse her bizarre sibling rivalry by hiding his letters to me where she thinks they belong: beside the toilet's fill valve. In those letters, her son, Dr. Father, hides his own grief behind the four valves of the heart through leaky anatomy lessons addressed to me.

Dear Ms. Irma Castillo Torres, MD2B:

You're stamped with the memory of Eva through a second navel. It's a mark the size of my thumbprint and located in the right atrium of your heart. We all have this beautiful scar: the fossa ovalis.

Albalucía Ángel

Albalucía Ángel *(b. 1939) was born in Pereira, Colombia. In 1964, she moved to Europe and lived there many years. A folk singer, novelist, playwright, essayist, and poet, she was an innovator in the Latin American literary boom and a pioneer of Latin American postmodernism. Among her novels are* Los girasoles en invierno, Dos veces Alicia, *and* Estaba la pájara pinta sentada en el verde limón, *which explores violence against women.* Misiá señora *explores the profundity of a woman's soul and essence;* Las andariegas *is an epic novel about women from other galaxies who come to tell the history of the world from their lens; and* Tierra de nadie *is a groundbreaking science-fiction novel. "The Eagle Woman" was translated from the Spanish by Cecilia Rossi.*

The Eagle Woman

With faith in your wings
you will cross
surprising hollows
forbidden heights
peaks sealed by the gods
almost impossible
to comprehend
by someone who relies
on their breath alone

and wants for no reason
to overcome the unfathomable

infinite distances
erase the map
of destiny
and hoist flags

without expecting trophies
in return.

Helena Urán Bidegain

Helena Urán Bidegain *(b. 1975) is a writer, political analyst, and human rights activist born in Leuven, Belgium. She is the daughter of a Uruguayan mother and a Colombian father and has a master's degree in Latin American studies, linguistics, and media from the University of Hamburg in Germany. She is the author of* Mi vida y el palacio, *a political autobiography told from the perspective of an eleven-year-old daughter of a judge murdered by the military during the 1985 guerilla siege of the Palace of Justice in Bogotá. This fragment of the book was translated from the Spanish by Andrea Rosenberg.*

Writing About Everything I Wanted to Forget

I wanted to be like the other girls. I was eleven years old, and I didn't want to have to lug around the burden of a tragedy of political violence. Nor did I want to be the new girl, the foreigner, the outsider; I just wanted to forget. I fought to fit in, to speak English fluently, to mimic codes and customs. At first it seemed like I might pull it off, but as in everything in life, once you start to understand the mechanism, you also start to see how it's held together.

In 1980s North Carolina, as in the rest of the United States, longstanding discrimination preserved vestiges of the official racial segregation of decades past; the enduring marks left by the principle of "separate but equal" were plainly visible. Everybody knew who was supposed to be on one side or the other, so my schoolmates found my neither very dark nor very light complexion unsettling. I frequently was asked, "What do you think you are, Black or white?" I imagine they were looking for a response that would help them define me, situate me, and label me in society. A simple children's question, nevertheless freighted with great power and violence, which none of my friends at the time understood. But for me, who heard it constantly, it caused deep confusion.

Latinos were not visible in that part of the United States back then, and the few who were there worked mostly as agricultural laborers. My school had only a set of Puerto Rican twins whose African features clearly signaled which side society had assigned them to. But what about me? Who was I? Where was I from? Where was I going? To what group did I belong? How should I act? *How would they have viewed my father?* I wondered sometimes. It was in him that I saw myself the most; it was with him that I shared my skin color and my identity. Would the adults have asked him these questions too, if he were with us? And how would he have responded? Yet again, I felt the keen pang of his absence.

After my father was murdered and my family fled Colombia in the face of threats made against my mother, my life was never the same. According to the official account, the one the entire country unques-tioningly accepted, a group of guerrilla fighters, financed by capos from Pablo Escobar's drug cartel, attacked the heart of the government's judicial power in an assault on the Palace of Justice in Bogotá. And the Colombian army had valiantly defended democracy.

My father was working in the Palace of Justice when the attack took place. He was an auxiliary judge and had turned up dead afterward, along with many other judges. The final tally was nearly one hundred dead and eleven missing.

I had seen the smoke, the photos of the ruined building, the site cordoned off by soldiers, the snipers, the helicopters, the tanks wag-ing a battle in which nobody considered the consequences for innocent civilians, victims of the clash between a few dozen guerrilla fighters and more than five thousand soldiers who participated in the military operation. Nobody cared about the lives of those who were caught in the crossfire because the objective was not to rescue them.

I didn't understand the claim that the men who were constitution-ally provided with weapons had saved us from war by attacking the very society they purported to serve. I found the explanation too abstract, and my experience of grief and injustice too concrete. Nothing made sense; it was impossible to comprehend an account that was half truth and half lie. Lacking any alternative, I did my best to forget. The only thing clear was that my life had been forever altered.

I did not feel afraid or see suffering on street corners in Durham as I had in Colombia. Nevertheless, not only had the war taken away my father and, in a way, my mother, who spent little time with her daughters because she was working hard to support us, but we had also lost our daily lives, our sense of being at home in our surroundings, our everyday language and, with it, an ability to react naturally and spontaneously; we had lost the simplicity of gestures, the understanding of every code, joke, and comment. I found contending with the new universe I had been plunged into immensely challenging.

My family was different now. My mother was lost in silence. My sisters, too, seemed preoccupied, and little by little we developed a sort of scab that seemingly protected us from the brutal blow we'd been dealt.

Though I learned to fake it in my new home, partly because the place bore no resemblance to the city nestled in the Andes where I had watched tanks rumble past one November day, there was always something heavy, like a boulder I was dragging behind me that caused me great pain every time I became aware of its presence. Though I longed to scream and weep, I chose instead to expend huge amounts of energy to quell my grief, to keep it from slipping out; I wrestled with it as if it was an enemy to whom I refused to concede any ground. Quite deliberately, I blocked myself out: ceased feeling, left the past behind, forgot in order to endure.

More than twenty years passed, and we discovered that those who claimed to be defenders of institutions had actually been the ones who had executed my father and other administrators of justice as revenge for their investigations. The dead had paid the price for pursuing justice. The people who called themselves heroes were in fact the most vicious aggressors against democracy and destroyers of justice itself.

Finally, after thirty years, in the face of my son's questions, I began to grapple with all that I had tried so hard to forget. I began to remember, to feel, forcing myself to resist my old, learned instinct to block things out. For the sake of my son and the suffering of my father and everyone else who died there, I decided to write. I feared I might fall into a dark pit next to the pain of my memories, a pit like the mass graves into which the soldiers dumped many of their victims from those grim days in November 1985. But writing showed me the path I'd traveled; it showed me solidarity, shared struggles, hope, and the love implicit in every letter I traced. It gave me back my identity. I no longer wish to forget, and so I write.

Salomé Ureña

Salomé Ureña *(1850–1897) was a poet and feminist educator born Salomé Ureña de Henríquez in Santo Domingo, Dominican Republic, and among the most celebrated poets in her native land. She opened Instituto de Señoritas, a school of higher education for young women in the Dominican Republic, in 1881. Among her most notable works is "Anacaona," a lyric poem divided into thirty-nine parts telling the violent story of the Indigenous people of Ayiti during the time of the Spanish Royal Crown. This portion of the poem was translated from the Spanish by Carla Bauzá López.*

Anacaona

IX

Proud of his victory
from Maguana the hero goes,
and the Indian crosses the jungle
singing of his liberty.
From the waves of Guayayuco
he crosses the threshold so,
and he greets his domain
where everything, as he goes,
the mountains and the valleys,
the forests, the streams, the birds,
seem to, all on their own,
wish him well on his way.
Crossing hills galore

he finally makes it home
where love and glory
eagerly await his return.
The elders of the tribe
go meet their hero,
and pay tribute with honors,
and their faces inclined in reverent bows,
and lead his procession, proud
in pomp and circumstance.
Then, radiating bliss,
beauty and majesty,
Queen Anacaona,
wife so honorable and true,
approaches, surrounded by lovely virgins,
who deftly dance a diumba,
maguey strings echoing along
to the beat of the timbal,
on to receive the cacique,
they walk with zealous delight,
waving palm fronds and feathers,
perfuming them as they go by,
and singing in sweet voices,
in harmonious cadence,
the areito that his queen,
proud songstress without match,
of Caonabo's greatest victory,
lifts high praise to the wind.
All is jubilation and joy
all rejoicing and peace;
the Indian returns to his dances
free of anguish and grief,
and believing his bliss eternal,

and eternal his liberty;
and Anacaona, in the arms
of Caonabo in gentle desire,
sighs, dreaming love,
dreaming happily.

Miluska Benavides

Miluska Benavides *(b. 1986) was born in Lima, Peru. She is a writer and a literary translator specializing in poetry. She authored the short story collection* La caza espiritual, *and her translated works include Arthur Rimbaud's* A Season in Hell, *translated from the French to the Spanish. In 2021,* Granta *named her one of the twenty-five best young Spanish language writers in the world. "Calles" (Streets) is a chapter from* Hechos *(Facts), a novel-in-progress, and was translated from the Spanish by Michelle Mirabella.*

Calles

First

She asked the maize to reveal the whereabouts of Salomón. The colorful and black kernels rolled away; the white ones stayed close. The woman looked at them, puzzled, and didn't answer. She—who knew the kernels and the coca leaves—was now incapable of reading them. The silence unsettled her. She asked to see where Salomón was walking. "I wouldn't know what to tell you because I don't see him," the woman said. She showed her a black kernel that fell at the edge of the manta. "There he is," she said. She didn't ask any further questions. She didn't know if she was asking the right ones. "He doesn't walk among us," she assured her before closing the door.

The last time she spoke with Salomón, he told her that he'd had several dreams about a fox climbing up a pirca. It didn't strike him as a bad omen. When she returned, she found the house's only room burned to the ground—the clay pots overturned, the fardos, their bundled fabric, slashed. They came looking for her; she knew it.

She'd gone on foot to visit an oracle in a valley on the coast. She followed the guanaco path that runs from the puna down to some wetlands. On her way back she had only half a piece of bread as a snack for the journey. A woman at the entrance to the town warned her not to go in. "They've laid waste to your house," she said. She thought the woman was exaggerating because she found the fields to still be damp. Once inside, she realized the true state of things.

Two people reported having seen Salomón. One told her that he saw him going up a stone path toward San Cristóbal mountain. The other warned her that he went off with some arrieros. The latter seemed unlikely to her, so she decided to be off. Without Salomón in Santa Lucía, she had no reason to stay.

AT NIGHT SHE'D LOOK TO the constellations, trying to make out the shortest path to the mountain. With the heavy clouds she was uncertain of the route. She told herself it was difficult to give up without saying goodbye. She'd imagine Salomón's steps on that path, a path that grew increasingly uninhabitable as it gained in elevation. She'd lost the ability to pass away, but that didn't mean it didn't hurt when others did. She arrived at San Cristóbal mountain nearly breathless. Penetrating the side, she admitted herself to the mountain through an opening that was like a narrow, unknown street. She dragged herself toward a small cave frequented only by animals. She was destined for the mountain's depths, a womb that, for her, would simulate the darkness of the realm of the dead.

Second

She emerged from a dark street and clutched her purse to her chest. The avenue lights made it so that she could spot who was trailing her: a woman with dyed hair, a long coat, and a lonely face like hers. She wound up in the street to avoid the people rushing across the main avenue. Home, she went up to her place—everything was in shadows. In another time, her mamá would be there waiting for her with the lights and TV on.

She wanted to boil water in the kettle. The burner didn't light. She called up the gas delivery guy. While she was waiting, she answered some missed messages. A friend told her off because it'd been months since she'd gone out. "You can't live like this forever," she said. "I lost my mami, and I was the same way." She listened closely to what her friend was saying, though her responses were vague. She lied, saying they'd see each other soon. She started answering the WhatsApp messages she'd put off, then the young guy showed up with the gas. Distracted, she paid. She got into the shower like she did every night, to kill time before going to bed.

In the bathroom, enveloped in steam, she recalled how her mamá would smoke in the afternoons next to a picture of her late brother. She'd summon him with a cigarette and a candle. She'd smoke two or three at a time. She'd sit at a little wooden table where she sewed for many years. She'd place a faded ID photo on the table then open a pack of cigarettes. "What are you doing?" she asked her the first few times. And she'd respond: "I'm summoning my hermano." She only told her once how her brother had died. He was a ten-year-old boy. They sent him out to sell some chickens. He went with the town's only teacher, who was headed to Cusco. She was going with her young daughter on horseback, he was on foot. Along a steep section of the path, she asked the boy to carry her daughter. "At the puna you run out of oxygen," her mother explained. "At some point he got tired on that long stretch. That's where they left him. A schoolboy found him that night talking nonsense, delirious from the fever." She'd had nine siblings; she'd lost two, but she'd only summon that boy on certain afternoons. "Forget about that already," she'd tell her. "Sometimes he comes," she'd say. "A street appears to me." She'd point at the window. "Then he comes. I can see him in the cigarette smoke."

She awoke from the memory. She didn't know how long the water had been running. The steam prevented her from seeing herself in the mirror as she changed. She left the bathroom, turned on the burner, and put the kettle on. Then she sat down at the small table. She took two cigarettes out of the pack that she hadn't dared to throw out yet. She lit them at the same time. They were more bitter than she'd imagined; her tongue began to go numb. Her eyes began to burn. The thick ash was falling on the table, though she wasn't able to read anything in it as her mother often would. The smoke enveloped her; she wasn't able to see any street either. At some point she realized the water in the kettle never boiled. She'd turned on the gas without lighting the flame. If she'd gotten up from the table, she would've been able to smell the gas moving toward her. She blinked, turned around, trying to see.

She didn't know whether to set the cigarettes aside. Putting out the fire was now a question of survival.

Anjanette Delgado

Anjanette Delgado *(b. 1967) was born in Santurce, Puerto Rico, and now lives in Miami. She is the author of two novels,* The Heartbreak Pill: A Novel *and* The Clairvoyant of Calle Ocho. *She is also the editor of the anthology* Home in Florida: Latinx Writers and the Literature of Uprootedness. *A Bread Loaf alumni, her work has appeared in the* New York Times, Vogue, *and* Kenyon Review *and on NPR and HBO.* "Lucky," *first published in* Pleiades *magazine, was nominated for a 2020 Pushcart Prize.* "Lucky" *was inspired by the true events that occurred in Cleveland, Ohio between 2002–2013. I first came to the story as a journalist and television producer, and yet, to really look at the horror of a predatory world as a woman, as the girl I once was, the only possible tool was fiction.*

Lucky

We are lucky, people say, when we emerge wrapped in decade-old dusk, our eyes squinting in pain, our pale skins raw in secret places we dare not look.

Paramedics offer us food and water. Police drop blankets in front of us, their expressions stern, suspicious. Other people appear, without identifiers on their clothing, each one a stranger to the three of us.

They take our blood pressure, listen to our chests, and ask if we are pregnant, or could possibly be pregnant. We could be. Of course, we could be.

But we can't speak or even nod. Instead, we look at our bodies, learn the devastating truth: we are separate. Not one girl, not three sides of the same taken slave, the other two always there to keep the one who'd just collapsed alive. That illusion is gone. What we are: three Eves searching memory for the "we" in which we lived all the life we could remember.

The questions continue, but how can we answer? We only know that Mina's dirty dark hair grazes her waist in clumps and we should figure out a way to cut it even though we have forgotten the feel of scissors, of kitchen knives, of glass.

We know Emily is glad for the blanket hiding the small breasts he bit purple just that dawn, the pants in which she peed the pain and did not have a chance to change when police commanded us to come out.

And we know just how petrified we are because Abby's whole face darts to the right again and again and again and again. And again.

But that's all we know. All we have. Everything else, even our voices, is still down in the room hidden from view, below the basement of the house in Hanging Rock. Outside the trap door where he placed our food. On the floor where he chained and choked us when we were defiant.

Now a police officer drags him out of the house and handcuffs him. He's just a few feet away and spume escapes his mouth as he twists himself into a piece of rope to look at us one last time, blaming us, we know, for being found.

He struggles against his own kidnapper, but a second officer brings the length of his arm thick against the back of his head and he falls against the ruptured sidewalk in front of the house. Then the two officers who'd been watching us run over and jump on his body, kicking and punching. His response: quick, successive staccato-sharp grunts we hear as commands: Look at what you've done!

The sound muddles our memory, dissolves it into a puddle of mercury and we obey, looking even as our too-slender arms lift and intertwine around each other like the branches of fall, dry and silvery and quivering with winter. Where are they taking him? How will we survive all this sunlight without him?

Now a female police officer says, "Let's get back to this. Did you know him?"

But we no longer know. We have forgotten how to remember.

"Did you ever try to escape? To get out when he went to work?" presses another, as if to say she needs an answer, any answer.

We look at each other in search of words. On the sidewalk, some of the officers talk while leaning on black patrol cars with summer beach blue letters parked every which way, blocking traffic, barricading the house from neighbors we've never met. One of the cars leaves with him in the back seat. We try to look away then, to speak. But there is no language left in us. We can only part our lips, move air summoned from within, up and through them and at the women asking us questions. Nothing comes out, of course, but we do it to show obedience, a willingness to cooperate with our new captors.

That morning, it never occurs to us to go back to the bottom of bottoms where we lived and rescue our voices. To think of how much they would have liked the sun, its warmth, the sight of summer beach blue letters on cars, now that our breath flows unrestricted, free of the bones and fumes of him.

Maybe because there are too many voices out here, too many I's asking questions and we lack the tools of rescue, having been girls, giggly and ignorant and silly, when we were taken. Girls even now bewildered, unsure of where they've landed.

It will be later, after he's strangled in his cell with a piece of rope like the one we'd just seen him morph into as he was arrested. After his only daughter, once our classmate, goes to jail for slashing her own baby's throat. And much after our families, having kissed and hugged us and told us we're heroes for surviving pore triumphantly over the evidence of our "living" remains, then withdraw when they realize those girls, their girls, all three of them, died of fright years ago on the cold, damp floor of a room hidden from light. That we're just songless stand-ins and there's no redemption in the saving of souls too damaged for music.

We, too, will see it then: that these salvaged bodies just aren't enough to live on this earth as victims, groaning, nodding, shaking our head in answer to the mudslide of questions, so many questions.

And that's when we'll go back. Sift through the ribs of memory still strewn around our jail, all while trying not to look too closely at the other pieces of us still there. We'll search until we find them, our voices, then grab them, emerge again to ask, at last, a question of our own: How dare you? How dare you call us lucky?

Lila Downs

Lila Downs *(b. 1968) is a Grammy-winning singer-songwriter born Ana Lila Downs in Tlaxiaco, Mexico, the daughter of Mixtec singer Anita Sánchez and Allen Downs, a Scottish American art professor and filmmaker. She was raised between Oaxaca and the US, where she eventually studied voice in New York and anthropology at the University of Minnesota. Among her albums are* Pecados y milagros, Balas y chocolate, *and* Al chile. *"Free Woman" is from a book-in-progress and was translated from the Spanish by Sandra Guzmán.*

Free Woman

La Tacha was a very beautiful girl. She was dark brown like the color of the ocote tree, and with skin velvety as river rocks in winter. She had in her eyes the power of freedom, eyes as black as an Asian ancestor, smooth and slanted. She was the daughter of Matilde, a woman as beautiful as she was a hard worker. One of three brothers and one sister. Tío Lolo, Tío Jose, and Tía Nanda.

Matilde had been the eldest, which had made her the caretaker of all her younger siblings when the plague came and took her own mother while she was still young. From her eleventh birthday she became the mother of her siblings and her father, who died several years later. Her mother, as thousands of people, had died during the plague at the beginning of the 1900s. Matilde had lived through the aggressions of the Mexican Revolution. She spoke of the soldiers. When she was eighty years old, she would describe them with terror.

Since Matilde sold pulque on la raya between Chalcatongo and San Miguel, she knew many men. Not all were good to her. Especially when they were drunk. She was such a beautiful woman that when she passed by San Andrés Xinicahua, the cacique of the pueblo summoned for her. The townsfolk saw that she entered a huge house and the cacique's men arrived to knock on the door. Neighbors alerted her and that is how she was able to escape through the back door and ran to the mountain, going around a hill until she arrived at San Miguel. Because it was nighttime, she hid along the road. She walked alone.

Young Tacha would get angry. "Why does that man stay with you? He does ugly things with my mother." That is why La Tacha believed that sex was violent, and something done by bad men. She never trusted men for this reason.

Surely that is why La Tacha was always sexually free, unlike other puritan Oaxaqueños. Sex was there to enjoy, a need, and that is it. She spoke of sex as if it were one of the human questions, that it is necessary to have a lot of it to get rid of it from the body—to clear oneself to do important things. That was how she was and that was her life plan. She found a foreigner, very educated, artist, biologist, lover of sex, and decided to live her life with him. She told me, you must enjoy life, hija, and that is how she liberated herself from the chain of abuse.

That is how La Tacha was; the daughter of La Tilde, the pulquera of la raya.

Claudia Salazar Jiménez

Claudia Salazar Jiménez *(b. 1976) was born in Lima, Peru. She is one of the most outstanding contemporary Peruvian voices of her generation. She studied literature at the Universidad Nacional Mayor de San Marcos and holds a PhD in Latin American literature from NYU. She's edited several anthologies, among them* Escribir en Nueva York *and* Pachakuti feminista. *Her debut novel,* Blood of the Dawn, *won the Casa de las Américas Prize for best novel in 2014. She is a poet, short story writer, and novelist, authoring the story collection* Coordenadas temporales *and the young adult novel* 1814: Año de la independencia. *She lives and works between New York City and Los Angeles. "In the Afternoon" ("En la tarde") was translated from the Spanish by Gabriel T. Saxton-Ruiz.*

In the Afternoon

Sliding slowly
almost
sticky.

Tracing
shadows
on a whim.

The dry
air
wrung out the afternoon.

Warming up
the solitary
grates.

The wheels
worn out
seething.

The plastic traveled
through many hands
already forgotten.

You did what you had to.
Everywhere.
Always.

The Californian sunrays
(in their own way)
remember.

MAGNETIC
MOON

This lunar energy encompasses
the four cardinal points.

Elsa Cross

Elsa Cross *(b. 1946) is a poet, essayist, and translator who was born in Mexico City, Mexico. She has authored more than twenty collections of poetry, winning the Premio Nacional de Poesía Aguascalientes for* El diván de Antar, *the Premio Internacional de Poesía Jaime Sabines for* Moira, *and the Premio Xavier Villaurrutia for* Cuadernos de Amorgós (Amorgos Notebook). *She has a PhD from the Universidad Nacional Autónoma de Mexico, where she is a professor of philosophy of religion. The below is an excerpt from* Napantla, *translated from the Spanish by Lawrence Schimel. "Nepantla" is a Nahuatl word that means "in the middle of," and it represents a concept of "in-between-ness," or straddling different cultures, borderlands, and mestiza identity.*

Excerpt from Nepantla

Nepantla is a moment
where death prowls

It grows
toward a silent touch
toward the center of the dream

It awaits
and vanishes
or huddles together
in fleeting space

Nepantla

between the light and the blink
between the bull's-eye and the arrow
between the flying fish
and the seagull

Nepantla
between the days
and their codex—

Oh shadow of memory
dancing
in the green depths of summer.

Denise Phé-Funchal

Denise Phé-Funchal *(b. 1977) is a writer, professor, playwright, and sociologist born in Guatemala City, Guatemala. She is the author of three novels,* Las flores, Ana sonríe, *and* La habitación de la memoria; *a short story collection,* Buenas costumbres; *and a poetry book,* Manual del mundo paraíso. *When she was a sociology student, she took part in the exhumation of the remains of thousands of Indigenous people killed during her nation's civil war. The remains were identified by the unique belts and pants that each wife had woven for her beloved. Her work explores historic memory and the Guatemalan Civil War. "The Earth Was Opening Up" ("La tierra se abría") was translated from the Spanish by Arthur Malcolm Dixon.*

The Earth Was Opening Up

The earth was opening up and roots, stones, bits of wood that had slept for years were coming out. Dry earth and wet earth were coming out, bugs were coming out, small stones and big stones. The men were digging and we women were trembling, hidden in the trees, up there, on the mountain. The fields were filling up with holes, down there, over there. They had told us and some of us didn't believe it until it was here. They brought them there, where you all first opened the earth and they shouted at them to make big pits like the ones you make and then came the terror, then came the blows, the insults, the raised machete, then came the blood, the crying, the fire. I ran, I ran with the children, my feet beating against the earth, hiding ourselves in the raindrops that were falling fat like tears. We ran and all we could hear were the footsteps of others as they slipped between the trees. We ran and I thought we would never stop, until my baby boy stopped short. Over there where those trees are he stood, still as the saints in church, still with his eyes staring, staring at the houses that were screaming, turning orange, red, yellow. He was crying, his feet were hurting and my heart was coming out of my mouth. Others were passing close by but they were so scared they did not see us, as if their open eyes, entirely open, round, could see nothing but the unmarked path we all knew up the mountain. I was trying to pull my little boy away but I could not, his feet had turned to stone, to stone and roots. He seemed lost with his eyes looking down at the ground, and I was afraid. I could not carry him and no, it was not because I was holding my little girl against my chest, but because his feet were made of stone and his eyes were staring, staring down at the village, at the houses that no longer exist. I was afraid because there, standing in between the trees, they might have realized that we had run away and some of those still passing close by us were saying to me move, run, you're putting all of us in danger, but he was not moving. Someone passed by me saying leave him there, let him turn to stone, if they come for us it will be your fault and they tried to push me but my little girl and I had also turned to stone and we were looking down and I was asking my great-grandmother for no one to see us, for us to take the shape of a tree until my little boy could move. The others were still passing by but nobody said anything to us now. We were trees and there we stood for a long while until the smoke rose and came with us, it slipped into our lungs and my little boy said let's go, Papa is sleeping without sleeping now, he's not smoke, he's not coming, he'll wait. My baby girl began to move and nurse and I could move my feet, my legs, and the smoke walked with us. If they had wanted to catch us, if they had known how to read the wind, they would have snatched us up in a moment, but the smoke, the smoke that smelled like people's flesh, like people's clothes, like people's teeth and hair came with us. With us came the smoke of my father, my father-in-law, my husband's grandmother, the smoke of those who could not run with us. Their smoke reached us and spun circles, hiding in the fabric of my skirt, in the stitches of the blanket wrapped around my sweet girl. I knew we were not trees anymore, and if one of them turned around he would see us. I was afraid and my little boy was not moving and I was asking my great-grandmother, asking the smoke of my new dead to help us. A thin, playful plume of gray smoke spun circles around my little boy, who closed his eyes and moved. Papa is not smoke, he said and he ran. He ran and I ran with him. Night fell over us and the mountain swallowed us up.

We came back later, much later, when the smoke sloughed off our clothes and whirled around us. My little girl, who was walking now, would say the smoke sang to her like her great-grandmother, and I, who heard her too, knew it was time to come back, so we followed the smoke, we came back down the mountain, afraid but with our people's smoke whirling all around.

He, my little boy now almost a man, was walking up front. I thought he would not remember the path, but he ran, he ran with his eyes clear and full of water. Others were already here, others had already picked up what was left, others were already crying for sorrow, others for joy, and I, I could not cry. I came back there, back there where you all were making the pits, there where they opened them up and I lay down, I lay down on the earth and women, sons, fathers, mothers, daughters came, looking to be close to those who did not turn to smoke. The earth filled up with water that was falling from our eyes and we fell asleep. Together.

Life began again there where we had been with them, the market there, life over there, the dance just there, prayers right here, with them sleeping close by, with them telling of the last thing they saw before falling into the little abyss, before the earth fell over them, before they felt their head bones break and their life leak out red. It hurt but there they were, together, until they came, this time at night, and we trembled. Stay inside, we said, everyone inside, and once they've gone away we can come out. The fear came back, with them the fear came back, the sorrow came back, my little boy's feet made of stone came back and he stood glued to the door for three days when all we could hear was the roar of a machine and the screams of the earth as it pulled out stones, roots, old bits of woods and their screams too. It was raining and the water was washing away the machine's tracks, drowning the screams of the earth and the open earth was closing up and they were not there anymore, there was no place left to leave flowers, to leave tears, to leave words. Silence.

Silence. It was silence, not them, who told us the machine and the men had gone away. Silence for years, and then you all who came, who came and asked in your language where they had been, and there you opened up the earth again, just to find it empty of them, empty of bodies, full of stones, of old roots, of bugs. The earth was opening up there where they were until the machine pulled them out and then the dreams came, their voices came and their smoke came back, their smoke that on the wind had seen it all and slipped into my lungs, into my children's lungs, into the lungs of others who took shelter in the mountains, in amongst the trees, and then we knew where the machine had opened up the earth again, where the bones had returned to her, been covered up again by her, by the earth that you now open up heeding the dreams of women, the dreams of children who had taken few steps in this life when the terror came. Now you all open up the earth and stones come out and bugs come out and roots come out and bones come out, bones dressed in scraps of fabric that we sewed, bones with ribbons full of birds that used to speak of love and children, bones with shirt hems in the colors of the mountain, the colors of water. Bones that raised their voices and snuck into dreams to guide us toward them, so that the earth would open up once more, so that the earth would open up and we would see on their bodies the machete blade, the bullet hole, the prison of the rope that cut their voices short. Bones that clung to our woven cloth so that we could say he is my husband, he is my father, she, my grandmother, my daughter, my little boy. Bones that will rest one day, with names, with a place for prayers to come back to, for flowers, for life that hopes to one day, once again, meet death.

Reina María Rodríguez

Reina María Rodríguez *(b. 1952) was born in Havana, Cuba, and is a poet and author of more than thirty books. She's the winner of the Pablo Neruda Ibero-American Poetry Award (2014), two Casa de las Américas Prizes for Poetry (1984, 1998), the Alejo Carpentier Prize for Cuban literature (2002), and Cuba's National Prize for Literature (2013). France named her Chevalier in its Ordre des Arts and des Lettres in 1999. Among her most notable collections are* Achicar, Luciérnagas, El piano, *and* The Winter Garden Photograph/La foto del invernadero. *The Princeton University Library holds her papers.* "Success" *was translated from the Spanish by Kristin Dykstra and originally published by* The Common.

Success

I

Of all that has come to pass
explanation was the worst.
A mother is not a day
for going shopping.
A mother coughs,
catches cold
and asks questions to which
you will never respond.
That's how this series works:
it is disloyal.

I touched her fingers, so thin,
waving goodbye to me,

but in my head you're still a young woman
in the sea wearing underclothes,
black and yellow ones,
belly spread with red flowers.
The worst of all is explaining what we gave,
or what we couldn't give,
a thing uninhabited,
and it protects itself
with no further explanation.

II

I hear her voice
calling me
when through the window
I see her playing in waves
that soon will not return
—even if the undertow
brings her
to the stairwell with the soup bowl—
or gives back all the money
she loans me
which I will never return
with the map of cloth left over
even if this time I can't
stretch it any farther,
can't get the blouse to fall,
the raglan,
over her shoulders need
buttons sewn
some above others
reasserting something
in orange thread
that she can't see.

III

Someone plays the piano,
and next to him someone pauses,
it's her, the woman who sewed dresses
neverending as keyboards
over finite
chords.
It's me, the woman who made poems
inadequate
for giving any explanation
but the cheapest:
one dress, one color, one button,
the trail (secondhand store),
"Red, White, and Blue,"
which we women used to call:
"Success"
and we wouldn't tell anyone
where it was
so we could be complicit
and keepers of mystery.

IV

A tilted kiss
slips off one cheek,
heads for the highway
and sidetracks
toward the side mirror marking
innocence,
from the time in a life
when we believed ourselves intelligent.
Those were our voyages
and our discords.
I will die without you

—as she will die without me.
It's written in the dream
with old shoes.
It's the destination
a repetition
of the hand, open
with its fine
controversial lines.

If I were born again
to have a daughter and a mother
I would ask for them to be you both.
I would tell them what is not explained
in the explanation
at the exit door
where one neither knows nor says
how much one can give
or deserve.

Yasmin Hernández

Yasmin Hernández (b. 1975), born and raised in Brooklyn, New York, navigates notions of motherland/otherland in her work. She studied art at Cornell University, has worked as an educator with Taller Puertorriqueño in Philadelphia, El Museo del Barrio in Upper Manhattan, and the Studio Museum in Harlem, and has exhibited her art in the United States and Puerto Rico. Rooting her creative practice within a liberation praxis, Hernández in 2014 moved with her husband and their two children to Borikén, her parents' birthplace. "El charco" is a fragment of her rematriation memoir-in-progress.

El charco

The frigid, green-brown waters of the Rockaways were always brutal, unwelcoming to me. As a child I feared their forceful waves. Their white foam crashing against my chest as boulders, knocking me over, rolling my little body back to shore, elbows, and knees sand-scuffed. The burning in my nasal passage from having drunk too much salt. The pressure and soreness in my chest of having been battered by the sea in the name of a fun summer activity.

This was me: never dunk my head without pinching my nose. Never enter farther than where sand could touch my toes. I spoke of fearing the ocean the way people fear God long before ever being claimed by the energy of Yemaya. An energy, a force to be reckoned with, respected, I mostly admired her from afar. At night after those family childhood visits to the sea off the shores of Queens, I'd lie down to sleep but would see waves crashing over me. One by one sweeping over my head, covering me. That side had me drowning.

I found my sea on the shores of Guánica. Passing Ponce, past the rusting refinería of my abuelo's Peñuelas. Rising through arid, brown brush and the occasional cactus of El Bosque Seco, giving way to the deep turquoise beneath cerulean skies, I met the Caribbean. Family trips to Caña Gorda where the water was warm like my blood, color of clear crystal quartz. Protected by a colony of plants, it was more like a pool, where I could sit soaking in healing salt, or float, curl like a fetus in its womb. Safe. Held. There in those waters was home. Water mother goddess of aqua, turquoise, and teal. Sacred salt waters of the warrior people of Agüeybaná. Waters invaded by Nelson Miles's fleet. Waters of crossroads where sea and desert meet.

Charco-crossers like myself arrive at a place divided: our bodies on one side, hearts and spirits in another. Our home on one side, work on the other. Many of us have either lived on each side, or travel and work extensively on both sides. Others adhere to one side only, told which side we belong in, expected to choose. I had a gaping hole in my heart and soul, yearning to connect to my ancestral home. Called to her calmer, tepid waters. Two decades of dedicating my art practice and activism to Puerto Rican history, culture, and liberation brought me to the crossroads. I had to transcend. To do so, I had to heed the lessons of el charco.

The myriad ways in which colonial trauma manifests (physically, emotionally, mentally, and spiritually) require constant innovation and imagination to survive and thrive. When we leave our comfort zones to venture out cross-charco, no matter which direction we cross, we run the risk of being denied our identities, having our authenticity questioned, doubted by others, even our own selves. Many of the survival rules and tools we collected along the way no longer apply. We are forced to learn new ones. With this shedding of old ways, taking on new skin sometimes, I found myself identifying more with the sea. From neither here nor there, but a deeper, bluer part of el charco. The nebulous in between, the transcendent middle. The connectivity, fluidity, totality.

"The pond," a term used to describe the Atlantic by the British, is now el charco, another Atlantic separating the colonies-turned-empire

from its colony in Puerto Rico. For Borikén, with its various diasporas
(Indigenous, West African, Caribbean, etc.) there are many charcos be-
tween many ancestral homes. Beyond claiming relatives and communi-
ties in the US and ancestors in Europe and Africa, many of the ancestors
of this archipelago moved around the Caribbean or were brought here
from other islands, other lands of the Americas. Our Antillean ances-
tors know the healing, connective properties of water. The revelation
comes in recognizing our ability to transcend conquest and colonialism
by heeding the lessons of water, by channeling or being of water. As
taught by Borikén, as Bruce Lee told the world, we must go deeper and
"be water."

¿Que misterio encierra el agua que Dios la escogió como elemento
para la transmutación del alma? (What mystery does water hold that God
has chosen it as an element for the transmutation of the soul?)

As a political prisoner at La Princesa prison in Viejo San Juan, Pedro
Albizu Campos wrote these words to his daughter in a 1936 letter and
printed decades later in Marisa Rosado's book *Pedro Albizu Campos: Las
llamas de la aurora*. The title, *Flames of the Aurora*, seems to reference the
radiation torture he would later be subjected to while at this prison, ra-
diation administered in the form of colorful light waves. Foreshadowing
all he would endure, channeling fuel from a higher source, he contem-
plated spirit, reincarnation, and liberation from a cell in this notorious
prison—a meditation on freedom and transcendence that led him to
water. Our bodies, like this Earth, are 70 percent water. We gestate in a
womb of salt water. Cry and sweat salt water. Body, Water: One. Water
of the Oxygen and Hydrogen prevalent in our bodies, in the cosmos,
reflected as rainbow nebulas in the light of stars. Water, Cosmos: One.
We abandon our physical and liquid state to go on as vapor, as spirit
energy transformed. If our very beings mirror the natural environments
of the Earth and of the cosmos, then we are more expansive than the
colonialism that seeks to contain us, than the constricted thinking of the
conqueror whose power relies on their subjugation of another.

As above, so below. The brilliant nebulas shining through the darkness of the cosmos are mirrored in the bioluminescence of the abyss. The light of the sun does not reach the dark depths of the Puerto Rico Trench, the second deepest part of the Earth's crust. Plummets nearly twenty-eight thousand feet beneath the sea, just seventy miles north of the main island of Borikén. But there in the descent are a variety of species that produce their own light or work symbiotically with other light-producing microorganisms. With the intense pressure, lack of oxygen, lack of sunlight, it is an environment that is uninhabitable to us, but perfect for them as they were designed, or have adapted, to thrive in it. We humans think that what does not work for us won't work for anyone. We impose our needs and opinions on others. Think all living creatures need oxygen and sun. Think that this blue dot of the Earth is the only speck of the universe worthy of life, as if the multitude of organisms in the Earth's oceans isn't a micro glimpse into the infinite variety of environments and corresponding life forms across the universe. El charco teaches humility. We enter her waters. Complain of jellyfish. Fear sharks. Litter her beaches. She knocks us down with her waves, rolls us back to shore where we belong.

In the abyss of bioluminescent creatures and fish lie the mysteries of Olokun, orisha of abundance whose domain is unknown to us undeserving humans. We could never know the vastness of the ocean floor, its caverns, its abundance, the diversity of life that thrives there. There are some things that thankfully are sacred and designed to stay that way. If Olokun is the mystery of the abyss, Yemaya, or Yeye Omo Eja, Yoruba for "Mother whose children are the fish," is the orisha of the sea, mother of mothers. Are we, her children, descendants of those forced to cross water, to make like fish, think like fish navigating water?

Still disarmed if my feet cannot touch the seafloor, still unwilling to submerge my bare nostrils, I still struggle in the sea. One rematriated birthday in Borikén in my favorite protected lagoon, an intimate ecosystem of coral and colorful tropical fish, I attempted to snorkel. Though a deeper-water hole, I feel safe there, as it is surrounded by a vast expanse of shallow water and huge boulders and coral protecting it from the rough

Atlantic that pounds the shores off Isabela. That deeper, colder, phthalo blue water rolling in from the trench, crashing, spraying white foam contrasting, shining like the sun against dark surf. There is power in this juxtaposition of peaceful pool of coral, rainbows of fish protected from the turbulent waves. Still, I struggled. Water kept getting into my mask. Suspended over the sand fifteen feet beneath me, I continued to panic my way back to the rocks where I could sit above it. A human in water/fish out of water.

Frustrated by my inability to make it work, but undefeated, I'd adjust my mask repeatedly and go back in. My breathing changed. I stopped fearing water seeping into my mask. I breathed with the pulse of the water currents sweeping past my body. I ceased paddling my legs, up and down. My movement switched to my hips, body wiggling like streamlined fish seamlessly undulating through water. Momentarily abandoning its terrestrial ways, my body opened itself to remembering the soothing salt water suspension of the womb. Schools of fish moved with me, through me, carried and embraced me. I wanted to be them. Remove my mask and suck oxygen from water itself. Move in sacred synchronicity with them. Our scales catching rays of sunlight, refracting rainbows reflected through the water. Surface ripples mirrored in webs of light across the sand. My gift that birthday was to taste transcendence. The magic of immersing ourselves completely in a new environment. Releasing rigidity to embrace new ways of moving, breathing, seeing, being. The essence of living, cycling through existences, over and over in various environments.

How do we carry this transcendence onto the sand? Embody this mermaid existence of half this, half that, whole everything? I return to the water to remember, to honor my journey and what it stands for. Presiding over our waters is Indigenous Mother Goddess Atabey. Mother of God Yucahu, signified by the triangular form mimicking mountains, rising to the skies with a human face representing the living and amphibious feet for the dead. The mother bears a human face adorned with headdress. Where Yemaya's children are the fish, a creation story describes the children of these islands as having turned to toa or frogs.

Atabey's figure is marked by the triangles of her breasts, three moon circles at her ears and over her womb. Together they form an inverted triangle. The circles at the sides and top of her head form another triangle pointing upwards like that of the triangular cemí representative of her son Yucahu. One pointing upward and one pointing down to the triangle of her yoni evoke the balance and harmony that is center to Indigenous art where center itself is one of the sacred directions. Her legs and feet are those of a frog, the triangles of her yoni in between. The natural curvature of these frog legs emulating the sacred, ancestral squatting position of birth. Water is fertility. Frogs and other amphibians transcending land and water are fertility. This goddess has her legs anchored in the elements of the Earth and her head and torso with moons and triangles, anchored in the cosmos. Earth, Cosmos: One.

For thousands of years the Indigenous ancestors of these Antilles navigated from the continental shores of South America, el Yucatán, along the Bahamas, the Leeward Islands and everything in between. Packing their canoes one hundred deep, they crossed water, traded, exchanged, interconnected with other people, other waters, other lands. Indigenous remains on the island of Vieques reveal a four-thousand-year presence of our ancestors on these lands. These waterways carve paths to transcendence. The work of the charco-crosser is to travel from that divided place we arrive at, to the place of transcendence, fluidity, inspired by, working on, and influencing various sides simultaneously.

María Clara Sharupi Jua

María Clara Sharupi Jua *(b. 1964) is a Shuar poet, essayist, singer, and Indigenous and human rights activist, born and raised in Sevilla Don Bosco, in the Ecuadorean Amazon forest. She writes in Shuar and Spanish, and served on a team who translated the Ecuador Constitution into Shuar. She has coauthored seven books and authored the short story collection* Tarimiat. *She also is the director of the Tarimiat Cultura Amazónica Shuar. The Shuar nation includes more than eighty thousand people who live in Ecuador. "Star Women Yaá Numa" ("Mujeres estrellas Yaá Nuwa") was translated from the Spanish by Sandra Guzmán.*

Star Women Yaá Nuwa[*]

Oh, pretty star like a queen you shine for me!
Two hearts sighed with love,
they liberated their minds,
chanted prayers of love,
and made their dreams come true.

In the Shuar world, all species of the universe-sky and Earth are people, the same ones who through disobedience or invocations transform and acquire other bodies (the elements or animals). The stars are women with living energy who listen to prayers, especially from young Shuar lovers who ask to meet them. In the transformation from stars

---

[*] In Shuar Nation they are the sister stars (two of which came down to Earth) invoked by two young Shuar lovers.

to women, they assume a new role in a growing family, putting magic everywhere—the environment, everyday life, and chores. When the time comes, from the wisdom they experience, they return to the heavens.

Arútam Brings Married Love and Originates in the Pleiades-Musach

In old times, our ancestors would frequently visit and sleep on the banks of the great rivers to connect with the spirit of Arútam.* They built a small hut with palm fronds called ayamtai near the beach on a cozy and harmonious place where they would receive visions and/or revelations. Our abuelos told us that once two young brothers, after fasting, drank tobacco juice and lay on the ayamtai to ask Arútam to grant them happy marriages. As they lay, the sky began to be covered with beautiful stars, which grew brighter as the night progressed. The young men admired the splendor with excitement and longing and asked: Who can give a wife from those enchanting stars? Can they really transform into women? One of them affirmed: Our abuelos said that their brightness comes from their lights. Only when they light their fires can we see them. The other enthusiastically added: I would love that one, the most beautiful one. Immediately that star fell from the sky and rushed toward the Earth, flooded with a marvelous light, immediately followed by another, even more luminous star. Two lights came down quickly and landed on the chests of the two young men. They had the face of a maá oruga (caterpillar) and one of the young men quickly wrapped her in his itip.** The other, frightened, threw the star far away in an uncontrolled act of terror. Since Arútam detests cowards, the star immediately returned to the sky even more luminous than before.

When the young man realized his mistake, he was filled with sadness

---

*   Arútam: the supreme male god who lives by the waterfalls in the rivers.
**   Itip: a cotton skirt that reaches the ankles, with vertical lines and dyed with flower and plant dyes.

and pleaded with Arútam for compassion. He fasted for a very long time, but Arútam condemned him to live a life without a partner. The other brother, on the other hand, stayed with the maá-oruga and in an instant, the caterpillar transformed herself into one of the most beautiful women. She whispered in his ear: I am Yaá nua—a star woman—and I feel very bad about your brother's cowardice. It's his fault that my sister returned; she is much more beautiful than I am. My sisters, the smallest stars, are the most beautiful; the larger ones usually have eczema on their skin. You are very fortunate because I will bring you happiness and then I will take you to the sky with me.

The man fell in love with her and took her as his wife. She began to live with him on the Earth but would often visit her mother in the sky. She would accompany her mother-in-law to the vegetable patch, who would continually reproach her because instead of placing the yuca in the chankin to take it home, she would devour it quickly.* She would arrive home empty-handed and would vomit everything she ate in the fermenting pots, muets,** which would transform into a delicious chicha, nijíamanch.*** What she vomited into the hollowed out pumpkin, a pilcher, would transfrom into chicha, or punu.† Her husband would drink the brews very quickly because they had all kinds of flavors. She would swallow peanuts, would vomit them over bananas that would mix with pepper that she would knead into delicious tortillas called michak.‡ With that food and drink her husband was never hungry or thirsty. He felt so energized he never tired at work. He was always full and did not feel the need to dispose of his waste. He wanted to be immortal like his wife, who lived without eating because her body was devoid of a digestive system capable of processing food as humans do.

---

*   Chankin: a basket of the Shuar women that is generally carried on their backs with farm produce.
** Muets: a ceramic fermenting pot.
*** Chicha nijíamanch: chicha made of chewed yuca.
†   Chicha punu: a pumpkin where the chicha is placed.
‡   Michak: food that is chewed and soft.

She made her husband delicious tamales. To prepare them, she used leaves piled under the bed that resembled an armadillo burrow. No one noticed that in the leaves she had hidden three beautiful babies that she had given birth to. Because they were star children, they only woke at night to drink their mother's milk. And they slept during the day.

Yaá nuwa did all her chores at night, and during the day she accompanied her husband on the hunt with the energy of a young girl, even in the days immediately after giving birth. Her mother-in-law would stay home in a bad mood repeating bitterly that she only fed her beloved son vomit and made him sleep on a pile of garbage. One day, tired of her daughter-in-law, she removed the palm fronds to make the bed, threw the leaves in the garbage can, and swept the house carefully.

Yaá nua was hunting with her husband and shouted: Something grave is happening to my children because my breasts are crying! Let's get back right away! She found her babies outside, sitting on top of a garbage heap, shivering with cold, and crying bitterly. She tried to calm them, giving them breast milk and caressing them, but it was useless. There was no consoling them because they were not used to daylight. They cried day and night without stopping until their lips twisted and turned into flattened snails with crooked mouths named uut(a).*

That is why when babies cry abuelas show them a snail and say: Don't cry because your lips will twist like the sons of Yaá nuwa. That is why abuelas, to keep their grandkids from crying, hang uut(a)s in the children's hammocks. When the baby wants to cry, they make sounds with the snails that sound like bells. Don't cry, don't cry. My mouth is crooked from crying so much!

Yaá nuwa had other babies but did not want them to live on the Earth. She told her husband with bitterness, Here I am persecuted and treated terribly; I am going to return to the sky. Her husband tried to console her, showering her with all his love, but she pleaded with him: Hide in my hair and hold on tight and in a blink of an eye you will be with me and our

---

*   Uut(a): a white snail endemic to the region.

children in the sky. But her husband was scared despite loving her deeply. She decided to leave alone. After counseling her children, she placed her husband in a deep spell and began ascending to the sky. Her husband heard in his dreams when she sweetly told him: You will also go up to the sky with my children. I will be waiting for you, and if you don't come, I will suffer greatly.

When her husband opened his eyes, he saw that his beloved Yaá nuwa was in the sky shining with the other stars. The children grew up quickly and, once adults, constructed a raft out of sticks. They spent the day sailing the rivers and exploring faraway places. They only returned at night, telling their father of their adventures. One day they left taking cold meat to eat. They navigated in the direction of their mother, Yaá nuwa, all day and never returned to their father. Concerned, he went to the river to wait, but seeing a raft he began to sail, scrutinizing the snakelike narrowness of the river and casting his gaze far into the great pools of backwaters in the hopes of finding them.

Finally, he saw them, far away and sailing fast, getting farther and farther away. He hastened his navigation to try to catch up to them, he called out, shouting and whistling shuishui shuishui but he lost sight of them.* His sons would rest at night under a shed called aák that they built by the riverbanks.** They ate fish that they harvested and would keep going, leaving food for their father so that he would not fall behind. Their father followed them eagerly. He quickly ate the food that his sons left for him, and after a brief rest, he resumed his march, saying to himself: Tomorrow, I will catch up with them. His children finally reached the edge of the Earth, where the Earth ends. They picked a few plumes from blooming spikes on the edge of the Earth and, throwing them like spears, stuck them into the infinite sky—a celestial vault. Then they climbed up the sky, advancing one after another, holding tightly on to the nailed plumes. Their father, despite all the desire to reach them,

---

*   Shuishui shuishui: whistling using the fingers.
** Aák: a small house in which to rest or meditate.

could not hang on to the plumes and stayed on the Earth. Making his way back amid cries and tears, he became extremely emaciated and arrived at his house exhausted.

Raising his eyes to the sky, he realized that Yaá nuwa also cried with sadness and that his children gathered in the sky, trembled, and twinkled, forming the Pleiades.

These stories were passed down to us by ancestors.

Elisabet Velasquez

Elisabet Velasquez *(b. 1983) is a Boricua writer born in Bushwick, Brooklyn. Her work has been featured in* Muzzle Magazine, Winter Tangerine, Latina, mitú, *and* Tidal *magazine. Her debut novel,* When We Make It, *was named a New Book to Watch For by the* New York Times.

20 Years Later Mami Apologizes

I never talk about this. I was only 17
working a 6 a.m. shift at a bakery in Penn Station.

My daughter had just turned one and had been taken from me or given away depending on the storyteller.

After work, I left the big city lugging with me to Brooklyn promises that I would be a better mother than you.

I don't think you understand.

I didn't want to evacuate
if it meant I lost a day's pay.

I waited one hour to use the pay phone.

So of course, I didn't think anything of the people running past the takeout window because everyone is in a rush to be someone better than who they are.

I only had one quarter. I had a choice to make. Call you or my daughter.

Surely you saw the news & would worry. I just wanted you to know that I hadn't died. I remember your words clearly. You wish I had died. You hung up.

I fingered the coin slot.

Wished my quarter back.

The line behind me

was a venomous snake threatening.

They had people to share the sting of grief with. The subways shut down & I had no home to walk to. Even on that day, I was careful not to center my sadness.

I buy you a new sofa

and we sit side by side

like we've always been this close.

There are the deaths we carry that will never get proper anniversaries. Twenty years later & there is still so much to mourn.

I decide to be alive enough

to ask you if you think you were a good mother.

Forgive me you say and all of the anger inside of me evacuates in search of a pay phone or a home.

One Day I'll Write a Good Poem About Mami

I show up to my performance at the park & peep Mami unraveled on the bench

like a god that has abandoned her anger

to witness her creation drown itself on a stage

Are you gonna read a poem about me?

I don't know what she wants the answer to be

so I smile wide enough for her

to see my childhood, the affection

only the roaches & language gave me but I wasn't gonna talk about that

today, I am someone's daughter

& I give in to the moment of *finally*

but Mami leaves before I can say what I really wanted to say

What I've heard good writers say—

my mom is in the audience tonight.

Anaïs Nin

Anaïs Nin *(1903–1977) was a diarist, essayist, and novelist born Angela Anaïs Juana Antolina Rosa Edelmira Nin y Culmell in Neuilly-sur-Seine, France, to Cuban parents. She spent her early years in Cuba, moved to Paris in her early twenties, and lived out the rest of her life in the US. She wrote journals from the age of eleven until her death, about her relationships, private thoughts, and her numerous affairs. She is considered one of the finest writers of female erotica. Among her erotica are* Delta of Venus *and* Little Birds. *The following are diary entries from* Fire: From "A Journal of Love."

October 30, 1935

Yesterday I began to think of my writing—life seeming insufficient, doors closed to fantasy and creation. I had written a few pages now and then. This morning I awoke serious, sober, determined, austere. I worked all morning on my Father book. Walked along the Seine after lunch, so happy to be near the river. Errands. Blind to cafés, to glamour, to all this stir and hum and color of life, which arouses such great yearnings and answers nothing. It was like a fever, a drug spell. The Avenue des Champs-Élysées, which stirs me. Men waiting. Men's eyes. Men following. But I was austere, sad, withdrawn, writing my book as I walked.

No money. So I close my eyes as I pass the shops.

Henry is working. He cut out the pages I didn't like in New York about "I snooze while you work, brothers." Two things he has to beware of: one, the ranting and moralizing of a second-rate philosopher; the other, the personal, trivial feminine passages—the pretty ones.

It is clear now that I have more to say and will never say it as well, and he has less to say and will say it marvelously. It is also clear that surrealism is for him and not for me. My style is simple in my Father book, direct like in the diary. Documentaire. His is rich and meaningless to the mind.

November 9, 1935

Allendy coming to dinner. Eduardo and Chiquito moving in. I, weakened by the moonstorm, losing blood. Weeping with my Mother in unison, both emotional, she trying to understand my *motives*—ending by believing me innocent although I live with a "homo" and go to Montparnasse. "I believe you can touch filth and not be defiled."

Kissing and feeling very close to her. I explained to her that if society exiled homosexuals they would become dangerous—bad—like the young, guilty of light offenses, who are put in prison and then become criminals. Emotional talk. Why do I keep Eduardo? To give him a home, understanding, faith in himself. All Havana society talks.

November 13, 1935

Everything Henry writes or does is "burlesque." Now he and Fraenkel are writing a burlesque of *Hamlet*. Burlesque: the bicycle on the wall of the studio. *Burlesque* talks, breakfast, letters, relationships. I don't know what I am doing there. Every day I must grin and go hungry. Everything I feel is too sincere, too humane, to human, too real, too deep. I write my book on my Father and I am hungry.

I am terribly, terribly lonely, terribly lonely. Full of rebellion and hatred of Henry. Hatred of the love that keeps me there. Why can't I break away?

Tremendous conflict between my feminine self, who wants to live in a man-ruled world, to live *with* man, and the creator in me capable of creating a world of my own and a rhythm of my own in which I can't find any man to live with (Rank was the only one who had my rhythm). In this man-made world, altogether made by Henry, I can't live as a self. I feel ahead of him in certain things, alone, lonely.

November 15, 1935

Having touched bottom, I sprang up again to reconstruct my life. Woke and wrote fifteen letters to call people around me and create a whirlpool. Then struggled with Henry to understand what was happening, and with his help realized my resentment and storm were due to his sacrificing me—depriving me of New York and of all possibility of expansion and *modern* living (New York kills him). I love him and don't want to sacrifice him. On account of this I began to struggle against Henry himself. I think that is over. I am making the best of it, knowing it is my destiny to love *with sorrow*, and always what is bad for me, to be limited, stifled by love, sacrificed to love, to Henry's lack of modernism, and now definitely stuck inside of his bourgeois life. But I must find compensations, chemins détournés: London. New York in the spring. A feverish life here in Paris. I feel blocked and yet I must expand somehow.

In Henry's arms I can yield. As soon as I leave him my desire is so strong it kills me—my desire for adventure, expansion, fever, fantasy, beauty, grandeur.

Alexandria Ocasio-Cortez

Alexandria Ocasio-Cortez *(b. 1989) is a Bronx-born Puerto Rican elected official who represents the 14th Congressional District in eastern Bronx and north-central Queens, New York. She delivered the following speech on the floor of the US Congress in Washington, DC, in response to the white Republican member of Congress who had verbally attacked her while another white male Republican member of Congress heard it and said nothing.*

US House of Representatives

July 23, 2020

Thank you, Madam Speaker, and I would also like to thank many of my colleagues for the opportunity to not only speak today but for the many members from both sides of the aisle who have reached out to me in support following an incident earlier this week.

About two days ago, I was walking up the steps of the Capitol when Representative Yoho suddenly turned a corner, and he was accompanied by Representative Roger Williams, and accosted me on the steps right here in front of our nation's Capitol. I was minding my own business, walking up the steps, and Representative Yoho put his finger in my face, he called me disgusting, he called me crazy, he called me out of my mind, and he called me dangerous. And then he took a few more steps, and after I had recognized his comments as rude, he walked away and said, *"I'm* rude? You're calling *me* rude?"

I took a few steps ahead and I walked inside and cast my vote, because my constituents send me here each and every day to fight for them and to make sure that they are able to keep a roof over their head, that they're able to feed their families, and that they're able to carry their lives with dignity.

I walked back out and there were reporters in the front of the Capitol, and in front of reporters, Representative Yoho called me, and I quote, "a fucking bitch." These are the words that Representative Yoho levied against a congresswoman, the congresswoman that not only represents New York's 14th Congressional District but every congresswoman and every woman in this country. Because all of us have had to deal with this in some form, some way, some shape, at some point in our lives.

And I want to be clear that Representative Yoho's comments were not deeply hurtful or piercing to me, because I have worked a working-class job. I have waited tables in restaurants, I have ridden the subway, I have walked the streets in New York City, and this kind of language is not new. I have encountered words uttered by Mr. Yoho and men uttering the same words as Mr. Yoho while I was being harassed in restaurants, I have tossed men out of bars that have used language like Mr. Yoho's, and I have encountered this type of harassment riding the subway in New York City. This is not new. And that is the problem.

Mr. Yoho was not alone. He was walking shoulder to shoulder with Representative Roger Williams. And that's when we start to see that this issue is not about one incident. It is cultural. It is a culture of lack of impunity, of accepting of violence and violent language against women, and an entire structure of power that supports that. Because not only have I been spoken to disrespectfully, particularly by members of the Republican Party and elected officials in the Republican Party, not just here, but the president of the United States last year told me to "go home to another country," with the implication that I don't even belong in America. The Governor of Florida, Governor DeSantis, before I even was sworn in, called me a "whatever-that-is."

Dehumanizing language is not new. And what we are seeing is that incidents like these are happening in a pattern. This is a pattern of an attitude towards women and dehumanization of others.

So while I was not deeply hurt or offended by little comments that are made, when I was reflecting on this, I honestly thought that I was just gonna pack it up and go home. It's just another day, right?

But then yesterday Representative Yoho decided to come to the floor of the House of Representatives and make excuses for his behavior. And that I could not let go. I could not allow my nieces, I could not allow the little girls that I go home to, I could not allow victims of verbal abuse and worse, to see that—to see that excuse—and to see our Congress accept it as legitimate, and accept it as an apology, and to accept silence as a form of acceptance. I could not allow that to stand, which is why I'm rising today to raise this point of personal privilege.

And I do not need Representative Yoho to apologize to me. Clearly he does not want to. Clearly, when given the opportunity, he will not, and I will not stay up late at night waiting for an apology from a man who has no remorse over calling women and using abusive language towards women. But what I do have issue with is using women, our wives and daughters, as shields and excuses for poor behavior. Mr. Yoho mentioned that he has a wife and two daughters. I am two years younger than Mr. Yoho's youngest daughter. I am someone's daughter too. My father, thankfully, is not alive to see how Mr. Yoho treated his daughter. My mother got to see Mr. Yoho's disrespect on the floor of this House towards me on television. And I am here because I have to show my parents that I am their daughter, and that they did not raise me to accept abuse from men.

Now, what I am here to say is that this harm that Mr. Yoho levied—tried to levy—against me was not just an incident directed at me, but when you do that to any woman, what Mr. Yoho did was give permission to other men to do that to *his* daughters. In using that language in front of the press, he gave permission to use that language against *his* wife, *his* daughters, women in *his* community, and I am here to stand up to say, "That is not acceptable." I do not care what your views are. It does not matter how much I disagree, or how much it incenses me, or how much I feel people are dehumanizing others. I will not do that myself. I will not allow people to change and create hatred in our hearts.

And so, what I believe is that having a daughter does not make a man decent. Having a wife does not make a decent man. Treating people with dignity and respect makes a decent man. And when a decent man messes up—as we all are bound to do—he tries his best and does apologize. Not to save face, not to win a vote—he apologizes genuinely to repair and acknowledge the harm done so that we can all move on.

Lastly, what I want to express to Mr. Yoho is gratitude. I want to thank him for showing the world that you can be a powerful man and accost women. You can have daughters and accost women without remorse. You can be married and accost women. You can take photos and project an image to the world of being a family man and accost women without remorse and with a sense of impunity. It happens every day in this country. It happened here on the steps of our nation's Capitol. It happens when individuals who hold the highest office in this land admit—admit—to hurting women and using this language against all of us.

Once again, I thank my colleagues for joining us today. I will reserve the hour of my time and I will yield to my colleague, Representative Jayapal of Washington. Thank you.

Angela Morales

Angela Morales *(b. 1966) is a Mexican American essayist born and raised in San Gabriel, California, a suburb of Los Angeles. Her essay collection* The Girls in My Town *won* River Teeth's Nonfiction Book Prize *and the* PEN/Diamonstein-Spielvogel Award for the Art of the Essay. *Her work has appeared in* The Best American Essays *and journals such as the* Los Angeles Review, *the* Southwest Review, *the* Normal School, *and the* Harvard Review. *Currently, she teaches English at Glendale Community College and is working on her second essay collection, a family portrait in essays.*

Family Day

On his days off, my father, wearing only his underwear, would sprawl out on the den sofa, shades drawn, television light flickering in his eyes. Clicking the remote control, he would cycle through all seven channels again and again as if he were searching inside those pixels for the answer to some question that he could not name.

Everything annoyed him: my mother's congealed scrambled eggs, our mountains of laundry, that damned kid banging the theme song from *S.W.A.T.* on the piano. Fed up, my mother would suggest that he take his fat ass off the couch and play with his children or maybe lift a finger and fold some laundry. Then my father would tell my mother to leave him the hell alone. "Get off my back," he'd say.

But with my father, it was all or nothing. Either he was selling appliances at the store with his personality turned on high volume—energetic and positive, joking with the customers, patting their backs, complimenting their wives. Or he was home brooding in the den, deflated on the couch, his hair greasy and uncombed. He wanted nothing more than to eat a half gallon of Carnation Neapolitan ice cream and to be left in peace.

Outside, sparrows tweeted and fluttered beneath the silver arc of the neighbor's sprinklers; the sun shone as brightly as ever. On our cul-de-sac, Mr. Lima was tossing his son a baseball; Mr. Dyrek was maneuvering a lawnmower across their patch of grass; Mr. Britain was painting their garage a brighter shade of white. My dad was sitting on the couch in his underwear, enraged about one thing or another and making our lives miserable.

One Sunday when I was seven years old, my mother suggested that my father get off the couch and that we go for a picnic to one of her favorite places: the Los Angeles County Arboretum. My father loathed such places, though he believed, theoretically, in a "family day" where he could show off his attractive wife and his well-fed progeny. However, take such a man, place him in a rolling green landscape beside a grove of eucalyptus trees beneath a white-hot sun and soft piles of steaming goose shit, and now surround him with crowds of cheerful church-going families; add to that a few soggy bologna sandwiches, a wife who often hates him, five kids who alternately want all his attention or want him dead. Now put this man on a blanket next to a dried-up pond that smells of dead fish, and you've got the makings for a disaster.

But for whatever reason, miracle of miracles, my father agreed to go. My mother prepared the picnic lunch of her childhood dreams: birch basket filled with bologna sandwiches on white bread, Lay's potato chips, and Hostess Ding Dongs and Twinkies. My mother had grown up admiring the processed "American" foods in the lunches of her Anglo classmates and had been shamed by the sneering faces of her classmates when they saw her lunch—typically a burrito filled with leftover dinner scraps inside a paper bag.

Picnic basket ready, my mother set to work changing diapers, wiping dirty faces, cramming toddler feet into unwieldy little shoes, basically trying to wrangle an eight-year-old, a six-year-old, two unstoppable toddlers, and a drooling infant into the car.

Meanwhile, I was feeling sorry for myself about my father ruining our day, about being a child with no legal or spiritual recourse, with no way to control the direction of her life, about being forever at the mercy of adults with their erratic moods and inexplicable whims.

I remember quite clearly declaring, my arms crossed tight: "Well, if he's going, I'm *not* going." Leave it to one kid to upset the delicate balance.

"You most certainly are going," my mother said.

"I most certainly am not," I replied.

"Shut up and get your ass in the car," my father said. By this time, he'd pulled on some Bermuda shorts and a Hanes T-shirt and had wet down his hair. But living in a house with a blaring TV, bickering parents, barking dogs, and shrieking children had left me yearning for solitude, for empty houses, for birdsong. All I wanted was some peace and quiet so I could read my books.

"I'll stay here," I said.

"No, you will not," they said.

"Yes, I will," I said.

"It's family day," they said.

"Family day sucks. I always stay home by myself. What's the big deal?"

"Shut up," they said, "and go put on some shoes."

"Maybe if you knew how to read, you would understand," I said to my father. I held my book up to his face and dangled it there. "Some people enjoy reading," I said.

My father stared at me coldly but, for once, said nothing. Although he was by no means illiterate and was a smart man, he simply had no patience for books, and I'd quickly discovered that I could taunt him with this fact.

Further argument seemed pointless, so I trudged outside, shoes half on, book in hand. I flopped across the back seat of the Cadillac; better, I thought, to preemptively put myself in the back seat by my own free will rather than to be dragged there. Although ours wasn't the pancake-eating family lounging around in their pajamas, I still had my books to keep me company and to shield me from daily skirmishes. How I loved the feel of a book in my hands, the woody smell of the pages, the candlestick *i*'s and the graceful and curvaceous *g*'s. I could wander across a landscape of sentences, soothe myself with the gentle and logical authority of a narrator's voice, so opposite to the chaos of life on Del Loma.

So there I was, lounging across the velour back seat of the Caddy, my nail-bitten fingers grasping my book, *A Little Princess*, sunlight streaming through the car windows with a haze of dust fairies encircling my head.

In all of childhood we are given rare and precious moments when the world for just a few seconds belongs to us, and no adult can intrude. We believe that despite our small bodies and limited experiences, if adults would just leave us alone, the future would shape itself perfectly into what it was meant to become.

The plot had just gotten REALLY GOOD: the protagonist, Sara Crewe, had just been forced to become a scullery maid in her fancy finishing school because her father had not paid her tuition. As I held the book above my head, one foot slung across the top of the seat and feeling that momentary sense that my life belonged to me, my father flung open the car door, muttered, "Goddamn it," and snatched my book out of my hands. In two quick motions, he tore it lengthwise down the spine and then crosswise into quarters.

"There. There's your book, smart-ass," he said, breathing hard, ripping up more pieces, and flinging them back at me. "How do you like that? Maybe now you'll learn to show some respect. Little shit." He breathed hard; his eyes had gone bloodshot. Then he laughed. "You think you're so fucking smart with all your little books?" he said. "You're just a lazy, disrespectful brat."

Ooh, how I hated him at that moment, but I would not give him the satisfaction of seeing my rage. My brutalized book lay in strips and pieces all over the back seat of the car. My book had been murdered. Such behavior was not unusual for my father, a bully who taunted his children for sport—a swipe, a little push—oops, you tripped! And then, what a comedy show! So funny, he must have thought, to watch those chubby little faces contort and get all twisted up, those sweaty baby fists pummeling his thighs, that stomping, that kicking, like mini Muhammad Alis—so hilarious to watch his kids go berserk. I still do not understand the source of my father's bullying, but I suspect that his own father had mocked and belittled him and at the same time encouraged his son to belittle others. Perhaps my taunting that day had struck a nerve and hurt my father's feelings more than I had realized. Maybe I had reopened old wounds and made him feel like a "dumb Mexican," a phrase he'd surely heard his whole life.

In any case, my father must have assumed that he'd seen the extent of his children's rage. But real rage is quiet and seething. True rage bubbles up and stays low, simmering, and simmering, until some later date when it emerges fully formed into some green dragon or into a superpower like flames from the fingertips. That day, seeing my book ripped to pieces, I tried not to show my outrage, worse than if he'd slapped me across the face. I felt more outrage than if he'd thrown my big teddy bear into the fireplace or if he'd driven his Cadillac, forward-reverse-forward, over my new bicycle.

My rage compressed and flattened me, but I had acquired, by age eight, an increased density and mass, and a reptilian skin that would both help and hinder me into adulthood. My father had done many mean things, but in my eyes, this might have been the worst. At that moment, not only had he stolen my tranquility but he had also snatched me out of London, out of Miss Minchin's School for Girls, away from my beloved protagonist. Moreover, he'd deprived me of my escape route, of my disappearing act, of my ability to flee the chaos of 6269 Del Loma Avenue, San Gabriel, California. I can still see that Dell Yearling book, shell pink with lacy flourishes, strewn in jagged strips across the back seat of the car.

I shrugged. "Who cares," I said, trying to keep my voice steady. "I didn't like that book anyway. It was boring."

A little history: That book had cost me $2.50, purchased at Perveler's Pharmacy. My younger sister Linda and I often walked up the street to the drugstore when my parents were working; we'd buy whatever five dollars or ten dollars or whatever we'd scrounged up could get us: a pack of striped gum, a tube of cherry-flavored Lip Potion, a bag of Doritos, a bottle of Love's Baby Soft perfume. Mostly, though, I would browse through the metal revolving display cases stocked with Dell Yearling Classics and other paperbacks. On these very same book displays, I'd found titles like *Go Ask Alice*, *A Wrinkle in Time*, and *Are You There God? It's Me, Margaret.*

My father surely understood what books meant to me; otherwise, why not punish me some other way? Why not order me to pick up dog shit in the backyard? Why not lock me in my bedroom without dinner? He must have known that, for this child (me), the worst punishment meant being forced to live in the "here and now," and not some fantasyland where fathers spoke gently to their daughters and people could be rich without actually having to work. In *A Little Princess*, Sara Crewe and her father were kindred spirits, theirs a relationship of mutual respect. She sat with her feet tucked under her, and leaned against her father, who held her in his arm, as she stared out of the window at the passing people with a queer old-fashioned thoughtfulness in her big eyes. I must have thought that even if my father would never be a gentle and loving man like Captain Crewe, at least I could read about such fathers and imagine what it would be like to have one.

I now realize that books, even children's books, to my father, symbolized intellectualism. A schemer, a businessman, he could not understand how a person could stare at a page for hours at a time. After high school he'd completed two years at a trade college where he learned to be an electrician. When it came to math and rewiring a building, he was a natural. He liked living in the "here and now." Apparently, he'd never had much use for that invisible portal through which you could escape your daily misery. Or maybe he'd tried and failed and maybe this very failure had affected him so deeply that failure and fear of failure had turned him into a Destroyer of Books. Ripping up a child's book might, too, have meant "sticking it to the man" and giving the finger to a (white) society that cherished books with a near-holy deference. He knew that you didn't have to read books or go to college to make a ton of money. He could point to plenty of men who'd read big books and had earned college degrees but still drove crappy tin-can cars or scrounged paycheck to paycheck. What good had books done for those fools?

After my father had torn up my book, my mother appeared, looking distraught with my baby sister in her arms. She hissed, "What's wrong with you, Raymond? Did that feel good? Is that how you get your kicks, by destroying books? Maybe if you ever bothered to read a book, you wouldn't be such an asshole. You might learn something." But it wasn't like he'd hit anyone, not this time; he'd only torn the book to pieces and then stomped on it. This time we hadn't needed to call the police. We hadn't needed to lock ourselves in the bedroom or hide in the backyard. But for me, the day would loom large in my memory, possibly eclipsing other more dramatic and more significant ones.

I've always wondered, though. By ripping up my book, did my father do me a favor? At the arboretum that day, did my life take a turn down a dirt footpath, between the Mexican palms and the banana trees, beyond the giant ferns and into my future, which would one day lead me to writing? Did I know at that moment, even the tiniest spark of recognition, that I would someday need to tell this story? That I would need to pick up the pieces and put them back together again?

If staring eyes could bore holes through a person's body, my father would have been Swiss cheese. In the car on the way to the arboretum, I decided that I would glare at him with all my might. I wanted him to know that I had power too, and that even though he could bully me, I would not let it affect me. I rolled down the windows and threw the pieces of my book into the wind—words fluttering away like feathers. I liked watching them disappear.

Next to the duck pond, I stared at him some more as I chewed my bologna sandwich, the gluey, white bread sticking to the roof of my mouth. I stared at him while my siblings ran screaming after a peacock. I stared at the back of his head as he ambled down the path, a man who would any day choose a casino over a garden. I stared at him as he wolfed down his sandwich in three bites, shoving it in and swallowing huge chunks of it, without chewing, and then he reached for a Twinkie. Bookless, I glared at him from afar as I stomped down fern-lined paths and climbed onto forbidden ledges.

My father brandished the Instamatic like a weapon, laughing, and snapping picture after picture—unauthorized pieces of me. Girl stomping down a path, Girl scowling with crossed arms, Girl atop ledge. In one picture, I look as if I'm walking against a headwind, my hands clasped behind my back, my head turning sharply, my hair frozen into a whorl. I had tried to escape the camera, but it had caught me and immortalized my fury.

A few days later, my mother handed me a ten-dollar bill and told me to walk up to Perveler's Pharmacy and buy a new book. There it sat on the wire shelves, the unmarred pink Dell cover gleaming under the fluorescent lights, the spine, pure and unbroken. But with this new book came an invisible subtext—words so tiny that they bounced off the page, words that I would not understand for decades. The story had new meaning, and thus seemed a different book altogether. Or maybe it was I who had changed.

I finished reading my new copy, though I can never remember the ending. The ending may have been unremarkable, or maybe I have blocked it out. Since that day, I've bought several more copies too. In fact, just about every time I see a copy of A Little Princess, I buy it, perhaps to wallpaper the interior of my psyche, or maybe because a part of me is still sitting in that car, still staring at those strips of words strewn across the seat.

In the years to follow, my father never warmed up to books or to family life, and eventually my parents would split up in a dramatic divorce and we would see him only sporadically in tense, brief visits. Thus, my father has remained an enigma to me. I've wondered, however, if on that day, Family Day, my father gave me a gift that led me to writing: the desire to piece stories together word by word and to reconstruct that which has been torn apart or never fully formed. Maybe writing, then, became my rebellion—not so much the drinking or the smoking or stealing the car, which would happen at ages thirteen and fourteen, all the predictable behaviors of a teenager finding her way into adulthood. My real rebellion, I realize now, were those random words and phrases that I'd pencil into the margins and inside covers of those tattered paperback books, all embryonic versions of future essays:

Family Day Sucks!

Help! SOS! Ray Morales is a lunatic.

Are you there, God? It's me, Angela.

What better way to make sense of my own life than to write myself and my father onto the page, to turn us into characters with distinctive boundaries within my control. But the best stories are not about control; they are about seeing through the smoke of memory. They are about finding answers, and my stories would ultimately help me to make sense of the man and that world from which we came.

Achy Obejas

Achy Obejas (b. 1956) *was born in Havana, Cuba, and emigrated to Chicago, Illinois, at the age of nine. She is a poet, writer, journalist, literary translator, and the author of such novels as* Memory Mambo, Days of Awe, *and* Ruins, *as well as short story collections, including* We Came All the Way from Cuba So You Could Dress Like This? *and* The Tower of the Antilles. Boomerang *is her latest collection of poetry. In the following prose poem, the protagonist is Ana Mendieta, a Cuban performance and multimedia artist who died in 1985 when she fell from her thirty-fourth-floor balcony. Her husband was tried and acquitted of her murder.*

The President of Coca-Cola

Ana Mendieta is the president of Coca-Cola and dresses in yellow, a mother of millions, an international pop star rolling by the riverside covered in spit and feathers. Ana Mendieta is the US senator from Florida, the governor of New Hampshire, four feet ten inches seared into wood, traced with blood, formed from mud and grass and gunpowder. She leans on the bar counter, a Mentirita in her hand. Ana Mendieta is the Grand Duchess of Luxembourg, a prestigious professor of international law at the Geneva School of Diplomacy and International Relations. Ana Mendieta is a shadow play of light in the cornfields of Iowa, a mound of earth outside Havana, cave drawings. She is the mayor of Wichita, the tenderhearted sister of the late dictator, a glamorous fashion model, welfare recipient, emergency case in the emergency room, a soldier, dentist, and historian, the host of a daily talk show on Telemundo who gulps down a milky Black Cow every day before taking calls. Ana Mendieta is the intellectual author of Miami's resurgence, the evil genius behind the bombing of a plane that killed every member of the national fencing team, and the man who ripped out his lover's guts when she moaned the name of another. Ana Mendieta is a power hitter, MVP, and six-time all-star celebrating at a gay B&B on Duval Street with a Chocolate Slam and a tray of cocaine. Ana Mendieta is the president of Coca-Cola and a double agent. She invented the sitcom, the telephone, birthed Amazon, came over with 14,000 kids and got deported with 2,021 others, mostly murderers. Ana Mendieta fears that if she weren't an artist, she'd be devoted to a life of crime. Ana Mendieta is subject and object. She is overwhelmed by feelings of being cast out of the womb, from the island, from exile. Ana Mendieta is the target of racism and a particularly fierce misogyny. She has a wicked cackle, a cruel flutter of hands. She swallows a Dark 'n' Dirty, an Eye of the Storm, a Fucked-Up Float. Ana Mendieta is the goddamned president of Kola Coca and she's both gleeful and embarrassed by the millions she earns but is also keen on what all that money can do. She's on the outside looking in, and so in with the in crowd. Ana Mendieta is alone. She pushes and presses her face against the glass until there's a tiny hairline fracture that snakes back and forth and back and forth and the glass separates so she can pop each piece with her fingers. Ana Mendieta is the youngest of all, the last to open her eyes when Earth was created. She is the feminine ideal, the masculine ideal, the nonbinary ideal and inspires lust and fruitfulness. She loves handheld fans and mirrors and is constantly dipping her fingers into honey jars. Ana Mendieta loses interest quickly. She's a peacock, a sack of bones, a woman dozing on the roof of a deli thirty-three stories down.

SUPREME
MOON

This lunar energy is the highest energy of
the universe, representing both the seed
and the full blossoming of the seed.

Esmeralda Santiago

Esmeralda Santiago *(b. 1948) was born in San Juan, Puerto Rico, and moved to Brooklyn, New York, as a thirteen-year-old. She is the author of three bestselling memoirs,* When I Was Puerto Rican, Almost a Woman, *and* The Turkish Lover, *and three novels,* América's Dream, Conquistadora, *and* Las Madres, *as well as numerous personal essays about her Puerto Rican experience in the United States.*

Mi sangre

I leave my blood in strange places.

In Macún, rusty barbs on a wire fence
scraped across my arms and legs
but couldn't keep me from ripe guavas.

I left blood on the jagged edge
of a can discarded in Luquillo Beach.

As I balanced on a curb in Barrio Obrero,
I slipped without letting go of a glass milk bottle.
My red handprint marked the sidewalk until it rained.

Over the tidal flats of Cataño,
a spike dug into my thigh.
Blood marked the point, the post, the spot;
dark crimson rivulets oozed
through splintered boards
into the black muck.
I still have the scar.

I first bled on my panties in Williamsburg
and left my bloody hymen in Hell's Kitchen.
My blood stained a subway seat in Queens,
my bedsheets,
my lover's towels in the Upper East Side.
It swirled down the drain in Boston
where I delivered my babies.

I've left my blood in forty-nine states,
twenty-seven countries on five continents.

These days, my blood fills test tubes
and spreads across specimen slides.
I bleed to delay death,
a sanguine stream to unutterable regions
while my defiant blood
pulses in the strangest place of all:
my children's veins.

Natalia García Freire

Natalia García Freire *(b. 1991) was born in Cuenca, Ecuador. She holds a master's degree in creative writing from Escuela de Escritores in Madrid and works as a creative writing teacher at the Universidad del Azuay in Ecuador. She is the author of* Trajiste contigo el viento *(You brought the wind with you),* Mortepeau, *and her first novel,* This World Does Not Belong to Us, *which has been translated into French, Italian, English, Turkish, and Danish. She lives in Cuenca, has a garden and a cat, and writes. "Crossing" was translated from the Spanish by Michelle Mirabella.*

Crossing

I was waiting for my father in the forest. Clear light and swirling leaves. Father had told me not to move from there, not to talk with anyone. And I was as obedient as they come. I was also love-crazy and a bit of a pig. And I was hungry. Hungry for buñuelos bathed in their sweet drizzle, for sugared rose petals and suspiros de merengue, hungry for sweet breadsticks with tree tomato jam, for everything Mother would prepare. And Father didn't want to come back or couldn't. Who knows why? I'd been there since sunrise, and all he had to do was go dig up the jewels. Mother had left them in the forest during what happened with the mayor, who went from house to house taking what he could to pay for the debt he said we'd incurred as a village.

But Father never came, not even when my head began to split from the sun. It was two very young guys who came. They were carrying empanadas de viento, fried with their cheese. And there I was, gnawing at my fingers in hunger.

"Head north and I'll catch up to you tonight," one of the young guys said. His teeth were crooked, one was black. The other guy didn't respond, he was just moving his legs like he had to pee. Later he did, over by a small apple tree. He did it quickly, while he was smoking. But at that moment he was still moving around, and the other guy talked and talked at him saying he should head north, set everything up with the woman, the trip, the crossing, and that he'd go with the money the next day. The young guy with the shaky legs was very hesitant and didn't say anything. I was still hiding under the boulder, listening, and eating dandelion, which was the only thing nearby. Then I tried some clover; it tasted raw, like sap. The dandelions, however, had something sweet in their flowers. That's when he went to go pee and the other guy stayed behind counting the money. When he got back, the guy gave him a few bills. "Tell the woman this is an advance and get yourself something to eat," the guy said and left.

I didn't see anything else because by then Jucha was there breathing in my ear. Jucha is my older sister and she's like a tank of gas. She was born a dwarf, square, but has strong arms. She took my hand and led me away quickly, quickly, toward the finca. It wasn't much of a finca anymore, it was more like a chacrita with a dilapidated house. When I arrived, Jucha told me that Father wasn't coming back, that he'd dug up the jewels a while ago and must be on a bus by then, heading to New York. Well, first to the north and then to the Riviera Maya, dressed as a tourist, to then cross over. Everyone was crossing back then and very few came back. Some would come only for their children's first Communion; they'd hold fancy parties with speakers the size of a cow and then they'd disappear forever.

Mother cried for a long time because Father only called once from New Jersey and then we never heard from him again. And Jucha had to go work as a farmhand on a finca a ways away because Father didn't even send money through Western Union like the others, who at least did that.

A few months later I ran into the young guy. The one with the shaky legs. I walked up to him like a fool saying wasn't it that he was

headed north? The question didn't seem odd to him because he imme-
diately answered me saying that the other guy, he called him Chamo,
had scammed him and left him broke up north for a few days with the
woman making him sell blanca, until he escaped and returned to the
village, to his village, which was a bit farther than ours. Then he asked
me for my name; we went off to the forest for a bit and became a couple.
Later on, he went too. No one scammed him the second time. He crossed
and arrived in New Jersey, which is where he called me from every other
day. One day he bought a ticket for me to go live there. He said he had
a lot of work and that we could have kids and even a car. I dragged my
feet for a few months; I told him that I wanted to see Jucha one last time,
and that I wanted to bring Mother to live with us. He stopped calling
and forgot me too.

Mother kept crying every day. I was nearly living in the forest with-
out her even realizing it. I would spend the day there, sitting on the
boulder, waiting for a red fox to appear. Back then, the idea had occurred
to me that if I saw a red fox, I'd know what to do with Mother, how to
console her. I'd sit there still, obedient to her wishes, obedient as they
come. I'd eat dandelions because I wasn't a pig anymore. Mama would
say that I ate like a rabbit, only grass. Sometimes I'd drink aguardiente,
which burns and stings deliciously, and sit there smoking until sunset.
Then I'd go back home and prepare dinner for Mother. I'd take her to
bed and give her some lettuce tea so she could sleep.

When everything was finally silent, I'd go to the forest again, to wait.

Excilia Saldaña

Excilia Saldaña *(1946–1999) was born in Havana, Cuba. She was a poet, essayist, and children's book author. She was one of the most celebrated Afro-Cuban writers of her generation. Her books include* Kele kele, La noche, Mi nombre: antielegía familiar, El misterioso caso de los maravillosos cascos de doña Cuca Bregante, *and* Lengua de trapo y todos los trapoanudadores del mundo. *"Mysterious Poem" ("Poema misterioso") and "Night 1" ("Nocturno 1") were translated from the Spanish by Sandra Guzmán.*

Mysterious Poem

Abuela, what is a river?

The tears of a giant crying for a lost love.

The bridge is such a fool: It thinks that the river was built so that water will flow under it.

Abuela, is it better to be a river or a bridge?

A river, if you want to know the currents; a bridge, if you don't want to go through the cold.

And you, what do you prefer, Abuela, to be a river or a bridge?

To be a river, mi niña, to be a river. To overflow with the rain, reach the sea, and sing in the fountain. Yes, I was born to be a river and not a bridge.

Abuela, I found an umbrella!

I will buy you a radiant sun and fine rain!

Abuela, look at the clouds.

Ay, mi niña, if I could set sail on that boat of lace and tulle, I would rain over you to make your perfume grow.

Night 1

What is the night, Abuela?

She's a sweet-eyed maiden, dressed in ebony, barefoot and tired. She's Black and she's beautiful. She's wise and quiet. She doesn't look like any of her sisters.

She rides a very black colt in her dreams to the lagoon to gaze at her face: What face so Black, the water reflects, what face so pretty, the envy of the world!

Flowers wished they had your scent, the dew that secretly loves her, tells her. If only you would let me wet your Black petals!

If I were a flower, your love I'd accept, the Night says and then, it escapes. Timidly she hides in the tallest branches.

The silent wind song that passes covers and guards, cuddles and lulls her to sleep.

I plucked the feathers from the crow, the ink from the sky, the flight of the tatagua, and the wings from the bat.

You've left the night without a body!

It's so that it's only eyes, Abuela: Your two ebony eyes.

Ingrid Rojas Contreras

Ingrid Rojas Contreras *(b. 1984) was born and raised in Bogotá, Colombia. She is the author of the novel* Fruit of the Drunken Tree, *a First Work of Fiction silver medal winner of the California Book Awards and a* New York Times *Editor's Choice, plus the memoir* The Man Who Could Move Clouds, *about her curandero grandfather and her magical family. Her writing has appeared in the* New York Times Magazine, The Cut, *and* The Believer.

When the Mask Becomes Who You Are

For one tongue that moves there is the other one that remains still. A ghost tongue that waits and surveys and judges, in its own language, what it hears. When we kissed sometimes you kissed one tongue and then the other. Forked, they tell me in one language and then another: everything is a wound. Inside of me, my skin has singed. I let you in so many places. Nothing can grow here, the tongues say, surveying the scene. It's all carbon, here, y aqui, y allá. Wailing is the one language the tongues share. And laughter. Late at night, having grown tired of their daily work of understanding each other, the tongues take turns answering wails with laughter and laughter with wails.

Decades ago, in high school, as we learned English for the first time in Bogotá, Colombia, I discovered in myself an uncanny ability to parrot the sounds I heard. I was a savagely ambitious student, and when our teachers announced that our goal was to speak English with perfect grammar and pronunciation, it was with a singular concentration that I put myself to the task. I delighted our British teachers, after whom I fashioned the words I spoke. And two years later, when the American teachers followed, pouring their efforts into correcting the British accent we had carefully crafted, making us learn to speak with *their own* pronunciation, I was good at that too.

Inwardly, I laughed at the American or British teachers who didn't seem aware of the irony of their small colonizing acts. Did it really matter with which accent we spoke? Was really one accent *more correct* than the other? What I remember is that they each were fond of sharing their experience of our country, introducing the topic by saying things like, "Here in the developing world . . ."

Unlike the large majority of my classmates, I knew the secret to aspirating and softening my *r*'s (the *r*'s that I otherwise let rumble all over my Spanish); to letting my tongue barely alight on the *y*'s and double *l*'s as I came across them so that they were almost whispered out (New York, llama). I knew to pay attention to what syllables were stressed. *Un*believable, the Americans liked to say, contracting their tongue close to the roof of their mouths, making squat sounds. The British, in turn, shaped their tongues so as to make the most room in the mouth cavern, producing words that sounded echoey and full.

The secret to perfect English pronunciation was letting the person I was disappear; making the girl who said things like carajo, que vaina, mi reina, no me diga, who wanted to say not "hello" but jelóu, not "and" but en, not "welcome" but guelcom, vanish from sight. Then, on top of that razed place, I built another, someone who resided in a tinny, headier, nasal soundscape and knew nothing else.

An accent is simply a sonic schematic of the original language from which a second language is understood. When we learn a second language, we use the rules of pronunciation from our mother tongue and enounce in that way, referencing it. An accent is simply the sounds of someone being rooted in a time and a place and an origin.

Not knowing all it would entail, I marched down the road of enouncing English in the way my teachers dictated until, one day, the traces of my natal tongue in my adopted one were gone.

When I emigrated to the US, fleeing violence on a student visa, I saw that speaking English with an American accent when you are born and grew up somewhere else is the equivalent to wearing a mask. (!!) Routinely, I was mistaken for someone who wasn't born, in the favored language of my teachers, quote unquote, in the developing world. I wasn't asked what the foreign-born were asked—"How did you end up here? How do you like America?"—those uncomfortable queries prompting for the sharing of trauma and expressions of gratitude.

I was a brown Latina and when white gringos heard my accent and registered my skin, they asked me what I soon learned all brown people who are born in the United States are asked, which is: "Where are you *really* from?"

There was a sudden switch to pity when white gringos learned I was alone in the United States, far from family. But the flicker of charity I saw in their eyes would then give way to something else, something more pervasive and terrifying, how they invited me to things and showed me off, proudly announcing I was Colombian, like I was a thing to collect.

Back then, I could still hear my *real* accent beneath the *put-on* accent I carefully enunciated and course-corrected for with every vowel and consonant that flew out of my mouth.

Then one year, I stopped hearing it at all.

The danger of wearing a mask is that if you do it long enough, the mask stops being a mask and sets into your face. It is no longer a mask. The mask becomes who you are. Now only I alone am aware of what, with great caution, I buried under layers and layers of corrective modulation.

I have, according to one of those quizzes you can fill out online, a Midwest accent, specifically, a Twin Cities, possibly Madison accent, places I've never lived. I say "kitty-corner" when referencing something that is across both streets from me at an intersection; and "soda" when I am talking about a carbonated drink. When I pronounce "cot" and "caught" they don't sound the same. "Merry" and "marry" are pronounced the same, but "Mary" is different.

I alone am aware of the two women who live in me at all times. For one tongue that moves there is the other one that remains, still and dormant. A ghost tongue that waits and surveys and judges, in its own language, what it hears. Sometimes I am convinced that those who love me do not really know whom they love. When I am kissed, no beloved has been able to tell which tongue it is that devotes itself to their body's architecture. And part of me will always remain out of reach, and inaccessible. Though, sometimes, when I am very drunk, I can hear my real accent emerge, the one who prefers to say guelcom and que vaina, and it is a relief. I am happy it is still there. It feels like a mercy to come face-to-face with what I once discarded so easily. Since, still, it sounds like the truest version of who I am.

Hebe Uhart

Hebe Uhart *(1936–2018) was a novelist, short story and travel writer born in Moreno, Argentina. Considered among the greatest contemporary Argentinian writers, she received Argentina's Fondo Nacional de las Artes prize for her overall oeuvre. Among her most notable works are* Camilo asciende, La gente de la casa rosa, Memorias de un pigmeo, Mudanzas, *and* Enero. *"Just Another Day" is from her collection of stories* The Scent of Buenos Aires, *translated from the Spanish by Maureen Shaughnessy.*

Just Another Day

I wake up at five o'clock and at six I turn on the radio for the weather report. Once a lady I know said in disgust: "People have to be told the temperature just to know whether they're hot or cold." I didn't say anything back, but I'm extremely sensitive to judgments that correspond to the aesthetics of the soul. Besides, I can't help myself: I need to know the temperature and the time. It annoys me when CNN, after each program (every half hour), lists the temperature of all the cities in the world; in Istanbul it's always cold and they always claim it's ten degrees hotter in Buenos Aires than it really is. What a sham.

I want to know what time it is too, and something too strong to resist compels me to look at the clock on the wall. I used to have some idea of what time it was—not anymore. I look at the clock and if it's two o'clock, I say: "Time to sleep again." But if you'd asked me, it might as well have been seven o'clock. To fall asleep I repeat lists of names from A to Z: Abraham, Abdel, Abenámar, Abdocia, Abdullah. And they're all real names. But when I'm happy about something and I feel accepted by the world, I make up a name. When I'm feeling down or really tired, I do it too. (Only one.) If you repeat the same list of names in the same order at siesta, you fall asleep. And then I start to think:

"How interesting the brain is!" That's why it's better not to give it a second thought, because then the sleepiness vanishes. I didn't always list names. I used to use a list of insults and slights from an old boyfriend. I used that list for several years; the idea was to make it to twenty insults. It went more or less like this:

1. He walked out on me.
2. He lost his shit because I told him how a lady had used the term "rest area."
3. He disappeared for two weeks.
4. He told me to go smoke in the other room.

And so on. Trying to think up twenty reasons bored me and I never could so I switched to names; there are so many more of them.

Anyway, every day except Saturdays I turn on Radio Continente at six o'clock and my whole gang of friends are there. They always get there at the same time. The host is Pérez, who's sometimes a bit basic when it comes to his taste in literature—I think he's religious, I'm fond of him in general. Later Antonio Terranova comes on. He's an editorialist who's entitled to reflect on what happens or doesn't happen. Sometimes he's right on, but sometimes he flounders because he thinks he's got the right to make all types of observations about the way things are going in our country and around the world. He asks himself questions like: As a country, are we perhaps going to hell in a handbasket? That puts me off because if there's one thing I don't like it's prophecies: doesn't matter if they're ecological or they're from the Bible.

On Saturdays I leave the radio off because Fernando Cuenca has a three-hour agribusiness program. He says things like "Pregnant cow in disuse," "Remaining balance," "Keeping old cows." He also talks about cattle diarrhea. He interviews people who talk about soybean caterpillars.

When he starts the program he asks for the blessing of Our Lady of Luján and it conjures up the sad sight of inland Argentina where dingy offices that operate out of old houses have an image of Our Lady of Luján on the wall, and outside the cows are pregnant or in disuse. And I don't want the countryside to make me sad. I don't say "cow in disuse." But sometimes I listen to him anyway on Saturdays because he interviews an agricultural engineer—I don't remember his name but it doesn't matter: his voice is what matters. He's an old man and his voice is deliberate, like someone who has gently taken control of his life. He speaks very clearly, as if everyone else were a little childish, and he manages to calm down Fernando Cuenca, who always sounds somewhat rushed, and who ends by saying: "The voice of the Argentine countryside" in a grandiose tone. Who is he to think he represents the countryside? Even if he did live there, he probably got kicked by a horse. And if he was sent to be reeducated in the countryside, I'll bet he got mixed up in all the wrong places. His job was probably to chase the chickens. The agricultural engineer, on the other hand, I could marry him. Well, I don't know if I would get married at this point in life, but I would like to spend a long time with him in a house in the countryside (if he has one) or in a village, so he could explain to me what a lightweight steer is, what "wintering cattle and breeding cows" mean, and stuff like that.

Ten minutes afterwards I'll surely have forgotten it all, but just to hear that voice. But there's more to life than staying by the radio all day. So I tell myself: "C'mon, Catriel, it's polka" (they used to say that to Chief Catriel so he would dance faster), and I pick up the pace. I have to go get a little glass I left on the night table to take a pill at night. My little glasses are beautiful, they're like tiny bells, but they have two flaws: they fall and break immediately, and they have a seam. And I didn't see that. It's as if they were made with the remnants of some sort of material and that reminds me again of the lady who says people need to be told the temperature to know whether they're hot or cold. Once she even argued with me about some little cups or glasses. I said that if I liked the shape of a cup or a glass, it didn't matter to me whether it was ordinary or refined.

Then she said: "You don't appreciate human craft, or the culture that produces porcelain, etcetera." I'm going to appreciate human craft; I'm going to put on some socks that are a little bit nicer. Dear Lord, how do I even go out on the street in these socks?

Today they looked all right to me, but now I realize they're impossible. One day something shifts, and then you see something you've always considered to be acceptable in a bad light. But I'm so fickle that I see it in a bad light and maybe within a couple of hours, I'll see the same thing as good again. So I leave them in a special spot in the closet, which is like a limbo for socks, sweaters, and other trifles. One day I'm going to organize that limbo—I will, but not today. After all, it's nice to hide things, forget that you have them and then discover them all over again as if they were something new. Could this be a trace of old age? I'm always reminded of the myth of Tithonus the sorcerer and the Cumaean Sibyl, who babbled to herself in a bubble. I'm like the sorcerer: I go from the kitchen to the bedroom carrying things back and forth; I forget something and go back to the bedroom. What will old age hold for me? Will I walk pointlessly in circles with no visible objective, or will I search for a potato or a towel with a gesture of heroic determination? Who knows. This must be forestalled: I'm going to go out for a walk, walking renews one's thoughts and strengthens the legs.

Okay, it's time to walk. First I have to decide which direction to take. There's only a few: north, center-north on Córdoba Street until Plaza Serrano, and, if I'm really happy, a few blocks until the strip of bars in Palermo Viejo. By the time I reach El Taller or any other bar, I'm happy: people bask in the sun on the sidewalks, their dogs tied up here and there and a street fair in the square. The happiness doesn't last; even early in the day idle people are about, and that entire neighborhood makes me think of a life of permanent idleness: reading the newspaper in the sun, then taking the dog for a walk in the park, the street fair . . . Besides, the route from my place to Córdoba Street is dark, not even the sun can lighten those eyesores that look like old camels. I can go directly north and end up in Palermo, but I've walked that way so many times and, besides, crossing from Almagro into Palermo is difficult: it's an area where they sell bolts, nuts, and screws, like a no-man's-land. And, anyway, my sense of justice tells me that I can't always take the same path. I'm going to give the west a chance. My sense of justice is like that: a little bit in each neighborhood, a little bit for each shopkeeper, when I haven't been to a shop for a while I remember and I tell myself: I should go there. I'm going to give the west a chance, I'm going to walk down Rivadavia Avenue until Primera Junta—although I'm also reminded of a shop called Designs for the Soul, which is near the Abasto shopping mall, but I don't want to risk disillusionment if I change direction, because it's always closed and the storefront is dark and dirty.

I'm going to Rivadavia Avenue, which keeps getting wider as I walk, reminding me of the pampas; way out west is the countryside. Rivadavia is flanked by eyesores, but they're a lighter shade than the ones in Serrano: reddish, yellowish, and light brown. The avenue is so wide that you can see the number 26 bus from afar. Out here the buses don't hurtle around the corner; they glide along with a certain somberness, almost a gracefulness. The 26 turns onto various side streets, as if to say: "Live around here? I'll drop you off." If I had been born in the neighborhood of Caballito and stayed there my whole life, I would have married a construction foreman who had wanted to be an engineer but never made it, because he had to contribute around the house. But at a certain point, we would have moved from a one-story house to an apartment with reddish walls and a bit of gold on the door (gold adds luster to dreams), and I would be like that woman over there who is heading out now, all dressed up with her dark blond hair. She's well dressed but proud of being working class; in fact, she likes people to notice her worn hands.

They're worn because she worked so hard polishing the brass on the door and took great, great care of her husband, like I would have taken care of the construction foreman until he was a little old man—and the dog too, sewing winter coats for it. Tartan coats, because tartan is refined. And now the dogs are out, the furry little one with legs that go tiki tiki as it struts along, and another one with a rectangular face, the

one I call "ugly mug"; that face astonishes me. I talk with the owner of
one of those dogs and ask her:

"Have you gotten used to it? To your dog's face?"

"Whatever do you mean, he's a saint!"

Virtue surpasses the most improbable appearances.

Aura Estrada

Aura Estrada *(1977–2007) was born in Mexico City. She died in an accident while swimming in Mexico's west coast waters. She was pursuing a PhD in Latin American literature. "An Open Secret," her last finished short story, was translated from the Spanish by her husband, Francisco Goldman.*

An Open Secret

Borgini

José Borgini decided to arrive before the others. And he also decided to come by boat instead of by car or plane. He took advantage of the voyage to scribble some notes in his black leather notebook for the text he would be working on during his stay in M., and which he would read before an audience in just a few days, as an invited guest to the New New Writers Congress (NNWC).

Disembarking in the lonely industrial outskirts of M., Borgini remembered the arrival of his Italian ancestors, armed with the parmigiano cheese upon which they would erect their immigrant future, to this same port that today wasn't a shadow of its past, which—because of his youth, or his nostalgia for a longing aunt's fastidious recounting of that past—appeared to have been glorious, even if it never was. Beneath the purple dawn mists, in the muddy and blackly glittering water, rusting ships that hadn't sailed in months or years floated listlessly. The windows of the buildings remained shut and the streets were mute, except for the hissing of the wind. The sun wouldn't rise for another hour, and Borgini set out walking down M.'s only avenue.

It wasn't his first time in M., though it might as well have been. The last time he was here, his experience had been tainted by the crooked paths of a frustrated love he wanted to forget but could not. Off the avenue he made a right turn onto one of the bystreets, from where he could see, beyond the farthest corner, rusty iron beams that had never become train tracks, strewn through dry, flammable weeds in piles all the way to the horizon, and a wagon loaded with broken windows and old leather seats cracked by the sun. Borgini set his only suitcase down on the cold pavement, pulled a wrinkled piece of paper from his pocket, and confirmed the address: C. De los Bernardinos, No. 15. Between the harbor and the train station.

He found the hostel's lobby small and cozy, perhaps too brightly illuminated compared to the gloomy, silent streets he'd just come in from. After a quick glance around, he approached the desk of the hostel manager. They greeted each other with amiable smiles. Borgini signed a paper, received his key, and climbed the four flights of stairs up to his room. There he unpacked his few clothes, accommodated his books on the shelf above the desk, and stepped out onto the balcony, from where he admired his new landscape and listened to the murmur of the nearby river. He looked at the fog that was beginning to lift, revealing lights in the distance, the domes of M.'s numerous churches, the black roofs of still dormant buildings. A sense of relief went through his body. He slept a little, until it was time for breakfast.

In the lobby, Borgini sipped his coffee and got ready to return to his room, where he would work all day, all afternoon, all night if necessary. His performance at the renowned Congress was crucial—if not for the others, at least it would be for him, dangling in limbo at the border between the old New Writers and the new New Writers. It could be said that he was now a relatively New Writer whose first incursions as a new New Writer had caused a certain sensation, and created great expectations, in the international literary community. He finished his coffee and returned to his room on the fourth floor.

At midday he wrote: *This is not a story. This is not a story either. These*

words don't narrate. There is nothing (there is nobody). The wall is cracked. It has
a yellow stain running in an unexpected, improvised path. It's the humidity, my
mother used to say. It's the humidity that's to blame for human misery. I hated the
smell of humidity, of clothes that wouldn't dry, and I remained saturated with that
blame for human misery. But I found a girlfriend who loved the smell of clothes
that hadn't dried. And the smell of humidity. And of human misery. I won't talk
about my mother. There's nothing to talk about. I mean to say: write. I mean to
say: I write but I don't say anything. I am an eye outside of the world. The yellow
stain of a yellow story that I don't dare to write . . .

He immediately pressed delete and once again the page was blank,
virginal, thought Borgini. He also thought about Goethe and Carver and
Capote—his favorites—intensely staring at the whitish, static page.

Beads of sweat slipped down his forehead. It was possible that he was
suffering from a fever, a result of the anxiety with which he was working.
He took a deep breath and expelled a profound sigh that surprised him like
a sudden change of wind. He stood up and went out onto the balcony. He
watched men and women dressed in white come and go through a door
of wood and stone, certainly ancient like most of the architecture in M.
From this vantage, the world looked small and distant. He went back to
his desk and stared at the screen, which stared back at him like a luminous
eye revealing nothing. He typed a word before leaning back in his chair,
fixing his gaze on the ceiling. In this position, he fell asleep.

On the green, almost phosphorescent grass, amidst giant flowers with
blue and pink petals, they ran naked. It was he without being he; he was
other but that other was he; she was also he. Everyone was he, but there
were only two, and they were running naked under a clear sky where an
enormous white eye shone, within which the same scene in the grass was
occurring—the he that wasn't he but that was he happily frolicking. They
lay on the grass, he (who was not he) and a woman with long hair like
golden filigree and skin like polished marble. She multiplied into hundreds

whom he (who was not he) savagely kissed until arriving at the last woman in whom, horrified, he recognized his mother's face and whom, still horrified, he kept on involuntarily kissing until finally he was able to let go of her lips and take off running over the green, almost phosphorescent grass with such power that he began to fly, at first scared, and then with expert ability. Alongside him flying books appeared, with gold-colored spines, and riding atop them, talking vegetables: peppers and ears of corn with eyes and talking mouths, like in that old TV show, *The Treasure of Knowledge*, which mysteriously always made him cry. And in the same way the flying books and talking vegetables used to make him cry on his mother's bed every time they came on the TV, he was crying in his dream, in which suddenly he'd stopped flying and found himself again in the green, almost phosphorescent grass, but this time reclined against his mother's breast, weeping torrents.

✦ ✦ ✦

He was woken by his own sobbing. He returned to the blank page, the screen glowing like a sign of desperation or hope. He wanted to succumb to the temptation to pour onto the page the oceans he imagined in secret, in lands less cold and gray than M., lands of tepid sands and tyrannical suns whose commotions only calm the temperate waters; to write about the children who populate those lands with their open, mischievous smiles; to write about what it's like to listen to them tell stories about their arithmetic and grammar teachers, who hold up the start of their classes because they're making out with the gym teacher outside the classroom door. To listen over the sand as they compete to recite the alphabet the fastest, which some of them don't even know yet, becoming almost immediately distracted by a deflated soccer ball that they kick vigorously toward invisible goalposts. To write about their parents, conversing in the kitchen that they've turned into a shrine in which they hang some pots but also saints and a crucified Christ to whom they pray every Sunday in a private mass (at which they themselves preside and assist).

His visits to those warm lands were behind him, along with his youth. He rarely revisited his memories of those journeys with his friends, planned in noisy cafeterias dense with cigarette smoke, to places they were separated from by old highways in terrible condition and the discouragement of their parents, suggesting plane flights and family automobiles. But they were determined to win and in a few days, in silent jubilation, they would be on a long and winding bus trip to a place remote from everything that up until then they knew as familiar. After nightfall the highway, in satisfactorily bad shape (the danger lent a flavor of reality to their adventure), wound along the edge of a vast abyss filled with brush and dense woods, from which escaped, now and then, weak lights that seemed to pulse between the trees until they disappeared with the break of dawn in the sky. When they arrived, they looked for a grove of trees to hang the hammocks in which they'd spend their nights, prob-ably by candlelight, staring out at the darkness of the nocturnal ocean with the exaltation of a four-year-old but the introversion of a boy of seventeen. He remembered little or nothing of what they tended to talk about during all those days they spent isolated together, but the fervor with which they'd done so suddenly felt fresh in his memory.

A timid knock at the door returned him to his page, which remained blank, the time blinking in a corner of the screen: 5:16. He'd lost all morn-ing and part of the afternoon in a useless trance. A second knock on the door, no longer shy but adamant, so startled him that he got up with an in-stinctive jump, knocking the chair to the floor. Because of the narrowness of the room he didn't even have to think, *Who the hell is this interrupting me!* or even worse, *Who the hell even knows I'm here!* until he reached the door. He opened it slowly, just a crack. He poked his nose through and saw a chubby, brown face that, though not unfamiliar, he didn't exactly recognize.

"Yes?"

"Borgini?"—among his writer colleagues he was known by his last name—"What's up, Borgini? How are you? Everything fine? I heard a strange noise. Am I interrupting, or are you with a girl? Uy, excuse me, brother, sorry to—"

"I'm not with any girl and nothing has happened. The noise you heard was a chair that fell on the floor. And the truth is, it's not clear to me—who are you?"

"What do you mean who am I? Valaza, man, Valaza." The other writers also called each other by their last names (with the sole exception, confirming the rule of the women).

Just what he needed: Valaza.

Valaza

The bar was the only section of the ground floor that was dimly lit. The sky-blue armchairs and red seats in the lobby shined brightly; small but luminous halogen bulbs hung from metal wires traversing the ceiling. Inside this modern setting, Borgini and Valaza seemed like two oversize, perhaps anachronistic figures, and they climbed uncomfortably atop narrow stools where they didn't fit. Neither said anything. The bar only had some wine and a couple of bottles of hard liquor. The bartender was the same man who worked at the check-in desk, which made his service inefficient and rather slow. They drank in silence. After the second glass they began, shyly, to question each other about their stay in M., their accommodations, and the general state of their lives.

Valaza wrote for various magazines and a newspaper that Borgini had never heard of. He'd come to the Congress not as an invited participant but as a reporter so that people out there (or at least those who read his newspaper) could learn about the latest innovations in the world of literature. Valaza, or El Negro as he was called behind his back, wasn't the type of man Borgini tended to associate with. In truth, everyone mocked him. Few had read Valaza's work because he'd never been anthologized and his only novel, *Devoured Serpents*, had been published in silence and in silence had slipped into oblivion, but when he was drunk, he talked about it incessantly, which was how Borgini knew what it was about. "Thematically," Valaza had explained in a whisper, as if he were explaining the machinations of a singular conspiracy, "it's a sort of genealogical tree whose many branches are brought together by the narrative voice of an Indian"—Valaza's alter ego (or Valaza himself), whose ulterior purpose was to trace Valaza's Indigenous ancestors, but also the Indigenous ancestors of the entire human race. "In terms of structure"—here his voice had pitched into a shrill tone—"it starts in the future, with the last descendants and inhabitants of Earth, and ends in the past"—and this was the part he was especially proud of—"in the *primal soup*, the ultimate source and common ancestor of all humanity. I will prove that somehow, in one way or another, we are all Mexicans; we are all everything, one way or another," he'd concluded, grinning broadly, sweating from the excitement or the alcohol. Nothing was further removed from critical taste and the spirit of the age, Borgini—along with the critics—believed. Too much local color, tints of indigenismo, little objective distance to allow him to narrate a story with assured veracity without running the risk of becoming emotional. Borgini, on the contrary, following the examples of the Great Ones of his personal canon (which correspond mostly to the dictates of the literary haute couture) preferred remote settings and events, such as the Austro-Hungarian Empire or the Franco-Prussian War.

It was here in M. that they'd last seen each other, but that time Borgini wasn't alone. Not only wasn't he alone, he was, as he couldn't help but notice, the envy of the New Writers Congress, because of Cipatli Pérez, the woman with whom he was frequently seen: slender and tall, black hair, silky brown skin, and a slightly lazy eye—the perfect touch of imperfection to accentuate what would otherwise be an intolerable beauty.

"So, are you still with the flirty-eyed lady?" Valaza asked distractedly.

No, their relationship hadn't lasted beyond autumn.

"Man, that's too bad; you seemed really in love."

Cipatli

Cipatli and Borgini had met at a literary event that took place before the one Valaza remembered. More than a Congress, it was the anniversary celebration of a masterpiece by one of the old New Writers, and Borgini, as one of that year's promising young writers, was invited to give the keynote speech, which Cipatli attended by pure coincidence; a friend of hers had dragged her along. Once he was at the podium, about to begin his talk, he raised his eyes to make sure the auditorium was full, as it in fact was, and he saw her come in, illuminated by the dim aisle lights. Her face stood out from the rest like a brilliant shield. From the podium he directed his words solely to her, and met her shortly after, at the closing cocktails. Not being a man of physical attributes, he seduced her the best way he knew: introducing her to the honored author and the other celebrities there.

That first night, Cipatli told him about her errant life, her world travels to places Borgini considered exotic (like Paraguay or El Salvador), and she confessed her ambitions regarding matters of human rights and a more just society. To Borgini all that seemed laughable, but the sweetness in her eyes and a pair of breasts the mythical Amazons would have envied helped him to comprehend the prolonged existence and validity of such adolescent thoughts in a mature woman. At the same time, in those thoughts he also surmised the possibility of taking her to bed.

They became inseparable. They were seen together at every literary event or dinner, in fashionable restaurants, movie theaters, traveling to remote places; their names appeared together in the newspaper's social pages. Curiously, Borgini began to notice, the newspapers made less and less mention of his intellectual labors in order to speculate about the nature and future of his relationship with Cipatli P. (so was her surname abbreviated), a relationship the media found enigmatic. The truth was less simple. Their lives had never achieved real intimacy. Their closeness was a facade that they themselves ended up believing. Apart from a pair of months when they coincided in the same place, the two lived in different countries for most of that year when they were seeing each other. Borgini tended to think about that relationship as a fortunate cluster of coincidental encounters that required from him nothing more than a readiness to let them happen. There were also certain aspects of Cipatli's character that he could not bear (i.e., her voracious intelligence and its inaccessible nonsense) and that she displayed at the worst moments (such as literary gatherings where Borgini was the guest of honor). At the New Writers Congress where Borgini had first met Valaza, his and Cipatli's relationship of coincidences was at its peak. Such a peak could not but signal the initial descent into their final separation. Their coincidental meetings became less frequent until, as easily as they'd begun, they ended without anybody's protest.

The River

"It's night already . . . though there's not much difference between sunrise and nightfall here. It always looks like dawn. Do you want to go somewhere else for another drink, somewhere less . . . less . . . ?"

With a few cheap whiskeys inside him, Borgini assented impulsively. Having spent the day in the hotel, he hadn't noticed the cold and gusty wind sweeping the deserted streets, howling like a wounded animal. There was no moon in the sky. The only illumination was a distant lamp intermittently spitting a faint yellow dust. Borgini pulled on the lapels of his black corduroy jacket to cover himself a little.

As was his habit, Valaza pulled a joint out of his right shirt pocket, stained with ink from a leaky pen, spoiling its blue striped symmetry.

"All right, but you never took it very seriously, or did you?" he said while he sipped at the joint, before passing it to Borgini, who took it clumsily. "It was obvious . . . well . . . you know how things are; it was obvious. It was obvious you couldn't stay with her, like that, in a serious way. No, brother. Here where there's nobody to hear us, one can speak openly. I'd never even thought about it, until we went to that dinner together. Do you remember? After your reading at the last Congress. We were having dinner, and, well, you know how wine loosens the lips; these banquets are the moments for spitting out the truth just like that, the way Rojas showed us all too well, though now nobody even remembers him. Finally, after dinner and a couple of drinks, I went to the restroom to smoke a joint. And while I was there I overheard a conversation I wish I hadn't heard. There were voices coming from the ladies' room. It was dark, I couldn't see, but I heard women's voices talking about Cipatli. They were saying they couldn't believe a man of your ambition would go out with someone like her, with a name like that, and so Mexican-looking, so morena. When I understood, I was already saying in a loud voice, 'But that's racism.' But all I heard was a loud laugh, and then they came out, laughing some more. I just saw them from behind. I guess this is how these things are, an open secret. But what do I know? Are you with anyone right now?"

Valaza's words resonated in the emptiness of the street they were walking down slowly, like old friends. The question was stamped onto the frigid air, and the wind stole the answer. The river interrupted their path, and they stopped for a moment on the damp grass of the bank.

"You know what the problem is with where I come from, Valaza?" Borgini suddenly said.

"No, brother, I don't know. What?"

"There are no rivers. And the ones that used to be there, they made them disappear; silently, without anybody's permission, they put them into concrete tubes. Haven't you noticed? How when you're there you feel like you're dying of thirst and you don't know why? It's because they took our rivers away. Look at how this one gives fluidity and a soul to the landscape. Where I come from, we're being buried, Valaza. We buried ourselves and we don't even notice. Or we do notice but no one says anything."

The words came out of his mouth as naturally as breathing, as naturally as the sob that accompanied them. Borgini wept on Valaza's shoulder just as he'd wept on his mother's in front of the flying books. But unlike back then, Borgini knew that this weeping wouldn't have a happy ending (i.e., his mother wouldn't come to turn off the TV), and he longed for his childhood. Cipatli's image came into his mind, and he cried harder until he was done.

"How did I get here?" he asked desolately.

The walk back to the hostel was silent; they were lost in the anonymity of M.'s gray streets on this night when few souls ventured out.

✦ ✦ ✦

A few days later, at the inauguration of the Congress, Borgini learned from Valaza about an unfortunate tourist beheaded by a piece of sheet metal flying on the wind as he walked along the riverbank.

"That could have been one of us!" Valaza recounted with a morbid but frightened smile on his face.

The news didn't disturb Borgini, who had more pressing reasons to be anxious. After that brief chat with Valaza—very brief, because there were other people Borgini had to see and with whom he had to be seen—a girl with flirtatious green eyes handed him the program of the night's readings. And who, to his surprise, would be sharing the stage with him but Cipatli herself! He would read a nonexistent text; or rather, it did exist, but consisted of only one word: oxen.

The New New Writers Congress

Due to limited time *pause serving as a comma* we regret to inform you that there will not be a moderator at this panel *pause and* the texts will be read one right after the other *distinct pause signifying a period following* the readings *pause intended as a comma* there will be a ten-minute question-and-answer session *pause and* it will be the job of the audience to establish the connections between the two texts *second distinct pause* we hope that you will enjoy the event and join us afterward for a reception in the main hall *third distinct final pause* thank you all for coming. Those were the words of the female voice coming from speakers in the half-darkened theater, which Borgini listened to as in a dream, the drops of sweat running down his temples and dripping uncontrollably from his underarms, soaking his green shirt, which matched, to his humiliation, the color of the tablecloth upon which rested the wrinkled piece of paper supposed to contain his text, which he surreptitiously tried to smooth with the palm of his hand to make it look more official.

To complete his bad luck Cipatli, who'd never been a writer when he'd known her, would be reading last. Then the first to read would be he, Borgini. He took the microphone between his hands and placed it at a moderate distance from his thin, pale lips. With a look, Cipatli urged him to begin. He coughed a few times, accompanied by others from the audience, and then, without taking his eyes from the green tablecloth adorned with yellow pompoms, he read: "Oxen." He lifted his eyes to look out at the packed theater—an uncomfortable silence. But then came a faint clapping, and then another, and another, and yet another, and then a unanimous and sustained ovation was ringing in his ears. Overwhelmed, Borgini smiled timidly; he even, as perhaps Cipatli could hear, laughed a little; and as the ovation slowly continued its natural decline, he released some hard laughs and then some more, until the ovation ended and now in the room only his laughter could be heard. Borgini was no longer Borgini but a giant laughter that was slapping the table, laughing explosively despite Cipatli's frightened gape. She tried to calm him, first with glances meant to remind him of the presence of the audience, and then with words like, "What's going on, Borgini, what's so funny? Get ahold of yourself, please stop this and sit down, it's my turn to read"—but by then, Borgini had already left the table and was leaping around the stage like an escaped orangutan, laughing hysterically.

Valaza came to his rescue. He was the only person Borgini seemed to recognize. He led him away between the curtains, green too, the long legs of the silenced theater. By the time Cipatli started to read, the audience had all but forgotten about José Borgini and was ready for the next show.

Brigitte Zacarías Watson

Brigitte Zacarías Watson *(b. 1961) is a Miskita poet born in Bilwi, Puerto Cabezas, Nicaragua. She writes in her mother tongue, Misquito, and Spanish, and is the author of the poetry collection* Soy multiétnica. *Her poetry has been published in three anthologies, including* Miskito tasbaia/La tierra Miskita. *"My Old Man" ("Mi viejo") was first published in the journal* Wani *and was translated from the Spanish by Wendy Call.*

My Old Man

Don't think I've forgotten you, my dear old man,

No, my heart. It's just that I've been busy going from place to place looking for my true love.

I went to every constellation and no one could give me your phone number, then I went around asking all the Archangels. No one could tell me anything and I couldn't stop sobbing.

One day, my handsome father, I ended up where the gods live. I saw Venus, Jupiter, Juno, and Odysseus himself and none of them knew your number.

Somewhere, there must be someone close by who I could ask how you're doing. But no one could tell me anything.

Exhausted, I finally went to the graveyard and poured my heart and soul into trying to reach you.

Poor me. I had cried a river.

Afternoon had come, clouds filled the sky, rain fell. The yellow-breasted sparrows rested in their nests. I was hopeless.

I returned to the cosmos and screamed with all my might. No one answered. But your sweet scent enveloped me. I realized I was wearing your jacket.

My Papi. My mad love.

Ruth Behar

Ruth Behar *(b. 1956) was born in Havana, Cuba. She is a cultural anthropologist and writer. Her travel books include* The Vulnerable Observer: Anthropology That Breaks Your Heart, An Island Called Home: Returning to Jewish Cuba, *and* Traveling Heavy: A Memoir In Between Journeys. *Her poetry appears in* Everything I Kept/Todo lo que guardé. *Behar won the Pura Belpré Award for her debut middle-grade novel,* Lucky Broken Girl, *and her second novel,* Letters from Cuba, *was a Sydney Taylor Notable Children's Book. Behar was the first Latina to receive a MacArthur Fellowship and was named a "Great Immigrant" by the Carnegie Corporation. She holds a Distinguished University Professorship at the University of Michigan, Ann Arbor.*

Don't Be a Woman Who Drowns in a Glass of Water

I was lucky to know all four of my grandparents. On my paternal side, Abuelo and Abuela were Sephardic Jews from Silivri, a Turkish town near Istanbul, whose ancestry went back hundreds of years to medieval Spain. On my maternal Ashkenazi side, my grandfather, Zeide, was from Russia and my grandmother, Baba, was from Poland. On the eve of the Holocaust, they all found their way to Cuba and made a home for themselves on the island. Like many Jews in Cuba, they had no wish to go north to the United States. Together with their children and grandchildren, they expected to remain on the island for generations. They poured their hopes and dreams into mom-and-pop shops and street peddling. After the 1959 revolution, these livelihoods were abolished, and so they left Cuba, feeling devastated, the memory of the island scratching at their hearts.

It was Baba, my mother's mother, who lived the longest. She made it to the age of ninety-two, dying in the year 2000, the start of the new century. We had settled in New York after leaving Cuba, where Baba and Zeide worked at a fabric store in Jamaica, Queens, under the rattle of the elevated train. When they retired in the late 1970s, they moved to Miami Beach.

After Zeide died in 1987, I would often visit Baba at her small condominium on West Avenue. At first, the sixteen blocks to the ocean didn't seem so far, but as she grew older, the walk became impossibly long and the sun felt too bright, so she stopped going to the beach. There was a Cuban restaurant on Lincoln Road where we'd go for dinner. Frijoles negros gave Baba indigestion; she'd just eat the caldito with white rice and savor it.

In Baba, I saw my closest mirror, for she was a thinker and an independent woman. Nothing was more pathetic to her than a woman so weak que se ahoga en un vaso de agua—"Who drowns in a glass of water." Baba tried hard to be tough. But I slept over enough times at her house to know that she suffered from terrible nightmares; she was always being chased into dark alleys from which there was no escape.

I never learned Yiddish, Baba's native tongue. Fortunately, Baba loved speaking Spanish as much as I did. That was the language we spoke to each other. We should have spoken of profound things—of life and death, of loss and grief, of laughter and longing—but I was in a rush. Miami was usually a stopover for me on my way to Cuba. In 1991, I began to return regularly, trying to reconnect with my lost home and the Jewish community that was then experiencing a dramatic revitalization. But Baba didn't like it that I was going to Cuba so much. She wanted me to stay with her, not leave her alone.

Baba would shake her head, watching me schlep the huge suitcases I took to Cuba filled with gifts for friends. As I went out the door, she warned, "You're going to get a kileh!" That was Yiddish for hernia. She was weighed down by memories, and I was going to Cuba in search of more memories.

For decades I have traveled back and forth to Cuba. Wanting to be strong for Baba's sake, I never told her how there's a part of me that's always scared about going to Cuba. What if a catastrophe befalls me there, will I be able to flee, as we did when I was a child? But I never wanted her to think I was one of those women who can "drown in a glass of water." I never shared those fears with her that I wrote about in my poems and essays.

These days I may not be as afraid as I was once, but I know Baba is my guardian angel, making sure that every time I go to Cuba I come back with my heart in one piece.

Audre Lorde

Audre Lorde *(1934–1992) was a self-described "Black, lesbian, mother, warrior, poet," but also an essayist and a professor. She was born in Harlem, New York, to Caribbean immigrants from Barbados and Carriacou, and in 1954, she studied for a year at the Universidad Nacional Autónoma de Mexico, a period she described as a formative time in her life as a poet and a lesbian. She also cofounded Kitchen Table: Women of Color Press, the first publishing house devoted exclusively to publishing women of color. Among her works are* Sister Outsider: Essays and Speeches, The Black Unicorn, Uses of the Erotic: The Erotic as Power, The First Cities, Zami: A New Spelling of My Name, *and* The Cancer Journals. *The following journal entry is from* A Burst of Light: and Other Essays.

St. Croix, Virgin Islands

April 2, 1986

This is the year I spent spring beachcombing in St. Croix, awash with the trade winds and coconuts, sand, and the sea. West Indian voices in the supermarket and Chase Bank, and the Caribbean flavors that have always meant home. Healing within a network of Black women who supplied everything from a steady stream of tender coconuts to spicy gossip to sunshine to fresh parrotfish to advice on how to cool out from academic burnout to a place where I can remember how the earth feels at 6:30 in the morning under a tropical crescent moon working in the still-cool garden—a loving context within which I fit and thrive.

I have been invited to take part in a conference on Caribbean women, "The Ties That Bind." At first I didn't think I'd have the energy to do it, but the whole experience has been a powerful and nourishing reminder of how good it feels to be doing my work where I'm convinced it matters the most, among the women—my sisters—who I most want to reach. It feels like I'm talking to Helen, my sister, and Carmen, my cousin, with all the attendant frustrations and joys rolled up together. It's always like this when you're trying to get people you love mightily to hear and use the ways in which you all are totally different, knowing they are the most difficult to reach. But it is the ways in which you are the same that make it possible to communicate at all.

The conference was organized by Gloria and the other three Sojourner Sisters, and it's an incredible accomplishment for four Black women with full-time jobs elsewhere to have pulled together such an ambitious enterprise. They orchestrated the entire event, bringing together presenters from ten different countries, feeding and housing us royally, as well as organizing four days of historical, cultural, and political presentations and workshops that were enjoyable and provocative for the more than two hundred women who attended.

Johnnetta Cole's moving presentation of the Cuban Revolution and its meaning in the lives of Caribbean women; Merle Hodges's incisive analysis of the sexism in calypsos; Dessima Williams, former ambassador from Grenada to the Organization of American States, proud and beautiful, recalling Maurice Bishop and Grenadian liberation with tears in her eyes.

In addition to being a tremendous high, these days are such a thrilling example to me of the real power of a small group of Black women of the Diaspora in action. Four community women, meeting after work for almost a year, dreamed, planned, financed, and executed this conference without institutional assistance. It has been an outstanding success, so much information and affirmation for those of us who participated as well as for those of us who attended.

It was a very centering experience for me, an ideal place for me to step out again, and I was so proud to be a part of it, and to speak and read my work as a Caribbean woman.

Tilsa Otta

Tilsa Otta *(b. 1982) is a writer and audiovisual artist born in Lima, Peru. She is the author of four poetry collections, a children's poetry book, a comic book, and a collection of short stories translated into the English language, titled* The Purity of Air. *Her alternative sexual-awakening novela* Lxs niñxs de oro de la alquimia sexual *was published in 2020. She is the coauthor, with her father, Vicente Otta, of the biography* Pepe Villalobos: El rey del festejo. *"Body of Thought" was translated from the Spanish by Anna Rosenwong and María José Giménez.*

Body of Thought

I appear before the people and take the floor,
before the bewildered worthies I remove my muzzle
and lick as much as I can of myself, sucking my fingers.
I point at you. I pinch your pearly lips,
I take your measure and inflame the masses
with the sanctuary promised in your silhouette
shadowing my face.
I unplug my breasts from the color-saturated screen,
and pierce you with a kiss like a portal into nothingness,
brush off the moths drawn to your eyes.
I caress a body of thought.
The interior is crucial,
the column that sustains discourse
and the river's course pumped by the heart.
On your trunk I carve our names,

they only hurt at the beginning.
Then they stop being our names.
I tell you that poetry is the placenta
that connects us to the world,
that we must enter,
because the world
needs more nutrients and we
need a little more of the world.

If we strip down together tonight
Dance hand in hand and cast spells
Will we be burned by someone other than ourselves?
Will anyone dare compete with the fire we are?

Credits

Gloria E. Anzaldúa (1942–2004), born in Harlingen, Texas, was a Chicana, Queer poet, essayist, children's book author, and feminist theorist. She coedited, with Cherríe Moraga, the trailblazing anthology *This Bridge Called My Back*. Her other notable works include *Making Face, Making Soul/ Haciendo Caras: Creative and Critical Perspectives by Women of Color*, and *Borderlands/La Frontera: The New Mestiza*, a semi-autobiographical book that explores borders between language, country, class, gender, and the self.

"A Writer's Prayer" by Gloria E. Anzaldúa. Published with permission from The Gloria E. Anzaldúa Literary Trust.

"La respuesta a Sor Filotea de la Cruz" by sor Juana Inés de la Cruz (1691) was first published posthumously in 1701 in *Fama y obras posthumas: tomo tercero del fénix de México, Sor Juana Inés de la Cruz, religiosa, en el convento de San Gerónimo; recogidas y dadas a luz por Juan Ignacio de Castorena y Ursua*. (Lisboa, Miguel Deslandes).

"Clepsydra" by Cecilia Vicuña was first published in *El zen surado* (1966). Copyright © 1966 by Cecilia Vicuña. Rosa Alcala's translation to the English first appears in *New and Selected Poems of Cecilia Vicuña* (Kelsey Street Press, 2018). Permission to publish by Cecilia Vicuña and Rosa Alcalá.

"Os pés do donçarino" (The Dancer's Feet) by Conceição Evaristo was originally published in Portuguese in *Histórias de leves enganos e parecenças* (Rio de Janeiro, 2016) 41–44. Permission granted by Conceicao Evaristo. Translation by Elton Uliana. Permission granted by Elton Uliana.

Excerpt from "The Life (Chapter 14)" in *Selections: María Sabina*, by Álvaro Estrada, edited by Jerome Rothenberg (Berkeley: Univ. of California Press, 2003), 45–49. First published in *María Sabina: Her Life and Chants* by Álvaro Estrada, translated by Henry Munn (Santa Barbara, CA: Ross-Erikson,

Chapter 1 fragment from *Wonderful Adventures of Mrs. Seacole in Many Lands* by Mary Seacole was first published in 1857 in London by Thomas Harrild, Printer, 11 Salisbury Sq. Fleet Street.

"Hombre pequeñito" (Little Man) by Alfonsina Storni, from the poetry collection *Irremediablemente*, was first published in 1919.

"Nemesis" from *Land of Smoke* by Sara Gallardo. Copyright © 2018 by The Heirs of Sara Gallardo, English translation Copyright © 2018 by Jessica Sequeira. Published with permission from Pushkin Press.

"Reorientation" by Naima Coster was originally published in *Cosmonauts Avenue* (2017) and *SohoNYC* (2020). Published with permission from Naima Coster.

"My Sister's Restaurant" by Julia Alvarez. Copyright © 2023 by Julia Alvarez. With permission of Stuart Bernstein Representation for Artists. All rights reserved.

"Translation" by Nicole Cecilia Delgado was first published in *Guernica* magazine (2021). Published with permission from Nicole Cecilia Delgado.

"Necrología" (Obituary) by Dolores Veintimilla was first published in a flyer on April 27, 1857, Cuenca, Ecuador. "A mis enemigos" (To My Enemies) was published posthumously.

"On This Night, in This World" by Alejandra Pizarnik was originally published posthumously in *Revista arbol de fuego* (1971).

"A Woman is Alone" by Aída Cartagena Portalatín was first published in Spanish in *Una mujer está sola* (1955). Published with permission from the heirs of Aída Cartagena Portalatín.

"Cesen dardos!" (Cease the Darts) by Lolita Lebrón. Published with permission from Casa Lolita Lebrón Inc. Lcdo. Carlos Mondríguez.

"Ele" (He) by Alê Motta was originally published in Portuguese in *Revista Vício Velho*, 19. "Vidas" (Lives) by Alê Motta was originally published in Portuguese in *Revista Vício Velho*, 22. Permission to publish granted by Alê Motta. Translation by Elton Uliana.

"Mujer negra" (Black Woman) by Nancy Morejón first appeared in Casa de las Américas magazine in 1975, International Year of the Woman. "Mujeres nuevas" (New Woman) first appeared in With Eyes and Soul / Images of

Cuba (Con buenos ojos/ Imágenes de Cuba) bilingual edition. Poems by Nancy Morejón. Translated by Pamela Carmell and David Frye. Foreword by Sonia Sánchez Buffalo, New York, ed. White Pine Press, 2004, 115 pages. Reprinted with permission by Nancy Morejón and Agencia Literaria Latinoamericana.

"Favela" by Carolina María de Jesús was first published in *Onde estaes felicidade?*, edited by Raffaella Fernandez and Dinha. Translated from the Portuguese by Elton Uliana with the support of University College London. Published with permission from the Estate of Carolina María de Jesús.

"Ya no" (Not Now) by Idea Vilariño was translated by Jesse Lee Kercheval and were first published in *Poemas de amor/Love Poems* (2002). Permission granted by Jesse Lee Kercheval, the Estate of Idea Vilariño.

"The Afternoon" by Danielle Legros Georges was first published in *Ibbeston Street* (2021). Published with permission from Danielle Legros Georges.

"I Look in the Mirror" and "They Inseminated our Sisters" by Daniela Catrileo were first published in Spanish in *Guerra Florida/rayulechi Malon* (Del Aire Editores, 2018). Published with permission from Daniela Catrileo.

"Nacer hombre" (To be Born a Man) by Adela Zamudio was first published in *Ráfagas* in 1914 (París; Librería P. Ollendorff).

Expert from *Ifigenia* by Teresa de la Parra was first published in France in 1924.

"If God had been born here" by Mary Grueso Romero was originally published in *El mar y tú*. Copyright © 2003 by Mary Grueso Romero. Published with permission from Mary Grueso Romero.

"Epitah," "Pueblo," "Extraordinary," and "In the Past," by Amada Libertad were published in *Larga trenza de amor* and *Burlas de la vida*. Published with permission from Argelia Marxelly.

"Mi corazón" (My Heart) by Virginia Brindis de Salas was first published in Spanish in *Cien cárceles de amor* (1949). Published with permission from the estate of Virginia Brindis de Salas.

"The Ineffable" by Delmira Agustini is from originally published in Montevideo, Orsini Bertani, 1910.

Fragment of *A Ballad of Love and Glory* by Reyna Grande was first published in 2022 (Atria Books). Copyright © 2022 by Reyna Grande. Permission to publish granted by Reyna Grande.

Acknowledgments

An anthology of this breadth and scope is a powerful literary community endeavor. So many forces came together to make this work possible. The ancestor writers who are here, the contemporary voices who said yes, and all the hands, minds, and hearts who shared their time, effort, and wisdom. My deepest gratitude to all the contributors and the heirs. It is an honor to be trusted with your work. Many writers, when invited to submit, enthusiastically pointed to other women who did not get their due credit in leading literary movements, writers who were/are marginalized or erased from history altogether. Latine scholars, educators, and book lovers also pointed to amazing roads. I was thrown into a delightful and productive journey, and I loved every word of it. One of the exciting features of this anthology is that half of the writers included were translated into the English, some for the first time. As I wrote in the opening essay, most of the texts of the First Nation scribes traversed a trinity of linguistic realms—from their mother tongues to Spanish and English. It is no small matter that many of them still write and speak in ancient mother tongues. They are fighting for existence and defy the horrific statistic—every twelve days an indigenous tongue dies around the world. Including their texts in their languages was important, and a tangible experience that they survive both an ethnocide and linguicide. Thus, the work of the more than fifty literary translators was fundamental in the creation of this book as I mentioned in my introduction, they are creative artists in their own right who gifted us the glory of understanding new worlds and ways of seeing the world. I am so grateful for their passion, their work, their talent, and for helping to usher in the many writers who are making their debut in English. While I served as the anthologist, this is a book that was created within the tribe of Latine women—artists, word lovers, and wordsmiths who champion the talent of the Daughters of Latin America.

✦ ✦ ✦

I am deeply grateful to the extraordinary editor Tracy Sherrod, a champion of this book, whose absolute trust and faith in my vision and talent fortified me through the days. Tracy envisioned the anthology and me as its editor before I did. She gave me editorial freedom to soar. I am so thankful to my editorial assistant, Mariana Gonzalez, whose impeccable literary taste, enthusiasm, and research prowess was invaluable. I am also deeply grateful to agent Leticia Gomez, who was inspired to want a Latine version of the exquisite *New Daughters of Africa: An International Anthology of Writing by Women of African Descent*, a sister anthology edited by Margaret Busby that served as an ancestor anthology and one of my inspirations. Editor Jennifer Baker was a steady hand in tumult. I am deeply grateful to Gabriella Page-Fort for her ferocious enthusiasm and support during a liminal time. So very grateful to Edward Benitez and Viviana Castiblanco for their unwavering support and joy and for ushering a Spanish-language edition of this book. The wonderful team at Amistad and HarperCollins, so many to thank: Emily Strode, Nancy Singer, Stephen Brayda, and Francesca Walker. And to the artist Camila Rosa, whose art blesses the cover. My beloved husband, the brilliant Willie Perdomo, my rock and my heart, served as both an inspiration and a cheerleader, and he let me pick his beautiful brain and encouraged me as I journeyed through long hours of the curation. I am thankful for the sage and beloved literary agent extraordinaire Marie Brown, who generously shared her heart, wisdom, humor, and literary savvy. And I'm so grateful for my beloved sons, mis amores, my hearts, Bobby Román and Neruda Perdomo, who shower me with unconditional love. My brothers and sisters, Wanda Ivelisse, Lydia Maritza, Miguel, and Alexander and nieces and nephews—my large clan whose love and humor keeps me grounded. Que las Diosas y los Dioses los bendigan siempre. Thank you to my agent Frank Weimann for the encouragement and support. To my literary north star, Toni Morrison, who accompanied me on the journey. To my bestie Rossana Rosado for her loving friendship through all of it. And to my Lipster hermanas— thirty years strong! I am grateful to the ancestors who connected me to each and every one who wanted to gather with us in this most blessed project. And I am expecially thankful to wise woman, literary star, memoirist, and novelist Esmeralda Santiago, who served as this book's hada madrina. Esmeralda was all love, humor, and everything I needed. She listened, encouraged, and opened doors, all the time reminding me that this anthology was necessary and urgently needed. And finally all my love and gratitude to my ancestors who are by my side protecting, guiding and blessing me. Most especially, my beloved mother, Lydia González Santos Román, Chagarita, Careya—brave rootwoman and matriarch whose blessings and dream visits from the ancestor plane nourish and inform. Te amo. Bendición.

Index

About the Editor

Sandra Guzmán is a writer, editor, Emmy Award–winning producer, and documentary filmmaker. Her work explores identity, land, memory, race, sexuality, culture, and gender. She was a producer of *Toni Morrison: The Pieces I Am*, the critically acclaimed film about the art and life of her literary mentor. She was the last journalist to interview the legendary Nobel laureate before her passing in 2019. Sandra is the author of the nonfiction book *The Latina's Bible* and was editor of *Latina* and *Heart & Soul* magazines. Her essays have appeared in *Audubon* magazine and in the anthologies *So We Can Know*, edited by Aracelis Girmay, and *Some of My Best Friends*, edited by Emily Bernard. Her documentary work in *The Latino List, Volumes I and II* aired on HBO, and *The Women's List* and *The Boomer List* on PBS for *American Masters*. Her journalism has appeared in *USA Today* and *El Diario La Prensa*, and on NBC News, CNN, Univision, and Telemundo, among other media outlets. She is an Afro-Indigenous daughter of Borikén where she was born.